Winter's Prison

The Winter Murders, Book 3

E.L. Johnson

ARE YOU SIGNED UP FOR DRAGONBLADE'S BLOG?

You'll get the latest news and information on exclusive giveaways, exclusive excerpts, coming releases, sales, free books, cover reveals and more.

Check out our complete list of authors, too!

No spam, no junk. That's a promise!

Sign Up Here

www.dragonbladepublishing.com

Dearest Reader;

Thank you for your support of a small press. At Dragonblade Publishing, we strive to bring you the highest quality Historical Romance from some of the best authors in the business. Without your support, there is no 'us', so we sincerely hope you adore these stories and find some new favorite authors along the way.

Happy Reading!

CEO, Dragonblade Publishing

Additional Dragonblade books by Author E.L. Johnson

The Perfect Poison Murders
Winter's Poison (Book 1)
Winter's Crown (Book 2)
Winter's Prison (Book 3)

The Perfect Poison Murders
The Strangled Servant (Book 1)
The Poisoned Clergyman (Book 2)
The Mistress Murders (Book 3)
The Deadly Debutante (Book 4)
The Betrayed Bride (Book 5)

The Lyon's Den Series
The Lyon and the Bluestocking
A Lyon to Die For
In Service to a Lyon
Love, Lies, and the Lyon

Chapter One

In the Year of Our Lord Eleven Hundred and Forty-One, July, on the road to Winchester

A FLY LAZILY buzzed around Bronwyn Blakenhale's head. She swatted at it and shifted irritably, rubbing at her sore backside. She'd been riding for hours and no matter how warm the summer's day was, how sweetly the birds sang in the trees, she felt itchy, sweaty, and sore. She squirmed in the stiff leather saddle.

Bronwyn gave her armpit a subtle sniff and wrinkled her nose at the scents of horse and sweat. She wanted to jump in the nearest river, which was nowhere to be found. A quick peek to her left made her dizzy, and she leaned back in the saddle. The ground looked too far away from up high for her liking, and she gripped the reins tightly. The horse flicked its tail as if to say it wasn't happy about having *her* around, either.

She hadn't learned how to ride until very recently and was still learning. All those knights and noblemen who made it look easy were wrong, in her opinion. She could spend a lifetime riding and still fail at guiding a horse with her knees or her feet.

She tugged gently on the reins and once the mare had stopped, she slowly slipped off the saddle, preferring to walk. She groaned and rubbed the backs of her legs, taking the horse's lead in her hand. To say her legs and rump were sore would have been an understatement. The ride had finally driven her mad, and whilst she knew her feet would not thank her later, anything was better than the monotony of the slow march along the road to Winchester.

She waited patiently as a fellow servant took hold of the reins, planted one foot in the stirrup, and climbed up easily. The gaunt servant looked relieved to be off his feet and handled the reins with an easy confidence as he patted the horse's neck. Bronwyn wanted to roll her eyes and glared at the horse. The mare seemed much happier with her new rider.

Bronwyn joined the party and resumed walking. Ever since the fiasco that was Empress Maud's attempt at a coronation in London, Bronwyn had been one of the party that had fled the city, running from a London mob. She remembered the dire, tension-filled moments when in the warm, stifling Westminster Abbey. There had been an attempt on the empress's life, the people had revolted, and hell had broken loose.

She and the closest thing she had to a friend, Lady Alice Duncombe, had gripped each other's hands so as not to lose each other and had fled in the empress's wake with her trusted men. Bronwyn's heart had been in her throat. With each step, her ears had buzzed with the shouts and curses of angry Londoners and her chest had tightened at the fear and panic that threatened to grip her, as she knew that if caught, she might have been trampled by the mob that had demanded the empress's blood.

Empress Maud and her party had escaped, just, by the grace of God. Bronwyn wasn't a particularly devout young woman, nor did she much care for the politics of this country, but she knew that that day had been extraordinary, and she wouldn't forget it in a while. Not just for escaping with her life from a London mob, but also due to her saying farewell to a particularly charming and chivalrous young man: Theobold Durville.

A squire to the head military commander in Empress Maud's court, Sir Robert of Gloucester, Theobold was tall and fair with dark curls, hawk-like eyes that pierced her soul, and a slight arrogance that at times both annoyed and thrilled her. A quiet but proud soul, he seemed to prefer the close-knit friendships and loyalty of a small group of people over a wide acquaintance. Even if he had first been instructed to get close to her by the empress, his interest and their relationship had developed into something more. He pursued her with a flirtatious delight and now she didn't know what they were, now that he had ridden off on an errand for the empress, in search of his cousin Lady Morwenna, who had tried to poison Empress Maud. As he'd ridden away, Bronwyn didn't know if she would ever see him again. She did know that she felt extremely conflicted and stuck in her feelings for two men. For there up ahead, rode another squire who had stolen her heart: Rupert Bothwell.

If Theobold was the moon, then Rupert was the sun. Rupert was full of life, laughter, and warmth. The popular young man had a friendly smile for everyone, and he'd looked out for Bronwyn when no one else would, which had raised no small number of eyebrows amongst the ladies-in-waiting and servants in Gloucester castle. With a strong chin and thick, wavy, reddish-blond hair that shone in the sun, he reminded Bronwyn of a lion. If only he weren't basically affianced to her friend, Lady Alice.

Rupert and Alice were sweethearts, and it rankled Bronwyn to the core. He and Bronwyn were friends and while he looked out for her, she couldn't deny her attraction to him. His sunny smile, his kind way of escorting her around, especially if it was after dark. Even his light teasing warmed her heart. But his lightheartedness made it hard to be around him when he and Alice were together.

Despite him being a squire and Alice coming from a noble household, Alice had taken a shine to Rupert almost instantly and spent all her time with him. She had a dark look for any young woman who got too close, and that included Bronwyn.

But Bronwyn needed more to be happy than a girl who was sometimes a friend, and a young man to occasionally flirt with who wasn't even hers. Her plan was to be a baker and run her own bakery someday in a city like her hometown of Lincoln, and maybe raise a family, if she was so lucky. Currently, she lived under Empress Maud's employ and traveled with her as needed or worked in the castle kitchens. But Bronwyn wanted more from life than working in the kitchens and sharing the occasional smile with a handsome young man, only for it to lead nowhere. Life had to be more than constant turmoil and disruption and not knowing where she would sleep at night. She craved some sort of stability, and yet it didn't matter if she slept beneath the stars or by a castle fire, she did not feel safe or secure.

Her life wasn't working out the way she'd thought it would. She had grown up to the ripe, old age of eighteen in Lincoln, only to have her life turned upside down in the space of an evening. What had started with her family's bakery selling expensive bread rolls to a nobleman had led to a man being poisoned, with her father accused of the murder and landing in prison, and Bronwyn given just a few weeks to find the real culprit.

I succeeded, but it almost doesn't matter now, Bronwyn thought bitterly as she walked on, holding a hand up to shade her eyes from the sun. Since then, she had rescued her father and made the acquaintance of Rupert and Lady Alice. But the trio had barely escaped with their lives as the city of Lincoln had come under attack, and they'd joined Empress Maud's camp, only to stumble across a plot to steal the royal crown and prevent her coronation.

The plot to ruin Empress Maud's coronation almost didn't matter now, as the ceremony had been ruined by an angry mob that had chased the empress and her servants out of London. Now on the road to Winchester, Bronwyn walked with the other members of the camp that the empress had requested to join her.

A year ago, Bronwyn would have pictured her immediate future very differently. She'd imagined spending her days in her family's bakery in Lincoln, which was now no more than a hovel that squatters had taken over. Nothing remained of her family, and she didn't know if they were alive or dead. It pained her just to think about it.

As the sun beat down on her blonde hair, Bronwyn squinted to see ahead. She traveled with a long line of cooks, servants, maids, and men-at-arms in the empress's entourage.

Since leaving London, the empress had moved with urgency. Men rode on horses, armed, casting glances around, as if they expected an attack at any moment. When they stopped in towns and nearby villages to buy food to feed the army and entourage, what they couldn't buy, the soldiers simply took.

Bronwyn was horrified by this. It wasn't right. She didn't like it at all. The empress didn't hear about it, and when people did protest, the men told the empress it had all simply been donations, given in support of the army and her just cause. It had taken a few weeks before Bronwyn had realized that not even an empress learned all the information.

But rumors filled the air that King Stephen's wife, Queen Matilda of Boulogne, was raising an army of her own while her husband sat in Bristol Prison. Bronwyn had served her before, when Empress Maud's cousin King Stephen had ruled over the land, and had been struck by the firmness of her character and strength of will. The former queen possessed an intelligence that many men overlooked. She wondered at the might and power of the petite and steadfast queen, and whether the rumors were true. Would Queen Matilda succeed in raising an army? Bronwyn didn't know. But it wouldn't have surprised her. The woman was capable of anything, the empress liked to say. She didn't know just how true that was.

Days later, Bishop Henry of Blois's forces had attacked Winchester Castle. The empress had been furious. She had sent messengers, scouts, ambassadors, and men, singly and in groups, to speak with Henry and convince him to stay with her. But like so many others, the man was fickle. Each messenger who'd returned bore the same message: No. He'd changed his mind, his colors, his allegiance, and had gone back to Stephen's side. Now he had fled to Farnham, and word was that the queen was coming with mercenaries and an army over a thousand strong.

The empress had been furious. She had counted on his support, and this had been a failure in her eyes. She blamed everyone for everything. People had walked on their toes around her, figuratively. Bronwyn had heard that her rages had been legendary, and no crockery had been safe.

Bronwyn marched behind the large army, led by the empress's half-brother, Sir Robert, the Earl of Gloucester, and master of Theobold. The days were warm and with a large army to feed, Bronwyn and the other cooks made quick work of the provisions, preparing what they could in makeshift tents, largely open to the elements. The empress and her close advisors were fed first, from the best birds, fish, and game caught that day. The rest of the people simply had to wait.

Bronwyn was gutting a river fish when one of the scouts came in for a bite to eat. He stood by, watching her work, and stole a day-old roll for himself, biting into it. "Word's come in."

Some of the cooks looked up. Seeing he was the center of attention, the sweaty, pimply scout bit into his roll and chewed, letting more people stop and to pay attention. He swallowed and said, "Don't know if you've heard, but the rumors are true. Matilda of Boulogne has raised an army for her husband and marched south. She convinced that traitor, Henry of Blois, to switch sides and throw in his cap for Stephen once and for all."

Bronwyn looked at the other cooks' expressions and tried to make sense of this. Judging from their grim and sour looks, this was bad news. Part of the empress's claim to being a legitimate ruler came from having the bishop's support, especially when it came to being crowned in London. But considering how well that had turned out, perhaps this move of Henry's was not so surprising after all. He seemed like an opportunist, in that regard, Bronwyn thought.

"How does that affect us?" she asked.

The scout looked at her, his eyes flicking to her face and bosom, and ate more of his roll. "Henry moves to join Matilda's camp, so their numbers will be greater. Our move may not be fast enough. We've seen their army on the move as well, to Winchester."

"You've told the empress?" one cook asked.

"Aye. She knows. We leave at first light." He nodded and left.

Bronwyn looked at the other cooks, her hands dripping with fish guts. The smell of raw fish sailed to her nostrils, but she didn't care. What mattered was what was to become of them all. They had been marching for weeks, ever since she and the others had fled to Oxford and regrouped with the empress's forces, then begun a march to Winchester.

A messenger came through a few minutes later; the empress wanted a delivery of bread rolls. Bronwyn looked up. The page looked around the kitchen. "Is there a Mistress Bronwyn here?"

Bronwyn raised her hand, still covered with muck.

The page's mouth twisted as he came over, and he sniffed. "The empress wants you to deliver some rolls to her. I can do it, but she wanted you to come in person. I don't know why."

Probably to make sure they aren't poisoned, Bronwyn thought. She shrugged. "Don't know. There're some that we made an hour ago. I can bring those."

She washed her hands in a bucket and dried them, then put a few of the fresh bread rolls on a wooden platter.

The page watched hungrily and licked his lips. She took an extra one and passed it to him. He nodded his thanks, and it disappeared in moments as he turned and led the way out of the kitchen.

Being on the road again, they had no building under which to take cover if attacked. They worked beneath tents, largely to prevent the food from getting rained on. Bronwyn was grateful for the fine summer weather, as it meant she could sleep beneath the stars at night and not get too cold.

She followed the page, and he led her through the makeshift camp to a series of tents. She recognized the empress's right away, for it was the largest and the grandest. Upon entering, she noted the empress sat at the head of a long table, and around her was Sir Robert, the Earl of Gloucester; Sir Miles Fitzwalter, her cousin and close confidant; and some other knights and squires, including Rupert and Theobold.

Her heart skipped a beat. Theobold was back.

The conversation stopped as a pair of guards let them enter the tent, and Bronwyn felt many pairs of eyes on her as she strode forward with the platter of bread rolls. The page said, "Your Grace, here are the rolls you asked for. From Mistress Bronwyn."

"Yes, I can see that. Go on." The empress waved a hand for him to depart.

The page bowed and left. Bronwyn curtsied and slowly raised her eyes to the empress.

Empress Maud stood tall, with her dark hair plaited in two long braids, with a headdress topped with a golden circlet. She wore a form-fitting navy dress embroidered with shining thread, as well as a gold necklace and woven belt at her waist. The empress had the knowing eyes of a bird of prey and missed nothing. Well into her forties, Empress Maud pursed her lips as she appraised Bronwyn.

A part of Bronwyn enjoyed the attention, especially as she was being watched, she was sure of it, by two young men whom she fancied. But there was also danger in that tent, and one wrong word could leave her without her head.

The empress held her gaze, her eyes steady. She did not speak and instead was quiet.

Bronwyn held her tongue. In another world, another life, she might have questioned this. But she was standing before an empress, and she knew well the danger that might befall her if she were to speak first.

"Good evening, Mistress Bronwyn," said the empress. "How good to see you again. You have rolls for me?"

"Yes, Empress."

"Good." She motioned for her to approach, and Bronwyn began bringing them around the table, offering them to the empress first, then the men. She waited until everyone had taken one and paused for the empress to bite first.

Empress Maud nibbled at her roll, and the men partook,

devouring their bread rolls within seconds. The empress ate hers and dusted crumbs off her hands.

Bronwyn bowed her head. "If that will be all, Your Grace…"

"No. That is not all. Mistress Blakenhale, what do you know of messages?" the empress asked.

"This is a bad idea, Empress," Sir Robert said. "You should not involve her."

Empress Maud held up a hand. "I will speak to whomever I please and involve whomever I wish. If you have no stomach for it, Robert, you may leave."

Sir Robert stayed but held his tongue. His eyes were frosty as he surveyed Bronwyn.

"Your Grace?" she started.

"Do you know much of messages?" the empress asked.

"I'm not sure what you mean," Bronwyn said, holding the platter by her side.

"Can you read and write?"

Bronwyn felt a bit of shame come over her and lowered her eyes. She dearly wished to learn to read and write and make something more of herself. Perhaps a bit of reading might do that. But she didn't know how, and she didn't feel comfortable asking anyone who might show her. "No, Empress."

The empress said, "I find this conversation tedious. Sir Miles, you tell the girl." She drank out of a fine goblet.

Sir Miles, a tall, thin gentleman with a shock of short, dark hair and pale skin that had recently seen the sun and so bore a slightly pinkish tan, peered at Bronwyn with his brown eyes. "It has come to our attention that someone has been sending messages to Her Grace."

"'Messages'? You mean like what a scribe would write?" Bronwyn asked.

"This is a waste of time," Sir Robert said.

"Hush, Sir Robert. Sir Miles, continue," the empress said.

Sir Miles cleared his throat. "No, not those sorts of messages. Scribbles. Writs. Someone has been writing and leaving the empress little messages. Notes and sketches."

"Oh." So why did they wish to tell *her*? Bronwyn had already had to admit she couldn't read or write.

"These messages are... Threatening. Rude. Callous. They make japes and threaten Her Grace's life," Sir Miles said.

Bronwyn's eyebrows rose. She glanced at the empress, who looked at her steadily, toying with her wine. "And what is this to do with me, Sir Miles?"

His upper lip curled. "We wish for you to tell us if any of the servants have voiced... discontentment or anger towards the empress."

"No, sir. Why would they?"

The empress smiled, but Sir Miles's look suggested she was being naive. He said, "Who knows? Any foul person will come up with reasons to hate a ruler. They might all be flights of fancy, but in any case, we wish you to keep your eyes and ears open. Let us know if anyone voices such thoughts. Do many of the kitchen servants read and write?"

Bronwyn shook her head. "Not that I know of. Maybe the head cook, perhaps. But I couldn't say."

"Well, in any case, you will let us know. We expect a fight when we reach Winchester, and it will be an opportune time for someone to attack Her Grace."

Bronwyn glanced at Empress Maud.

"Someone here wants me dead," the empress said. "Aside from my cousin and that witch wife of his. But someone in my court is sending me notes, and I want to know who. I want them found."

"What if it's just a jest, Your Grace?" Bronwyn asked.

Empress Maud's mouth withered. "This is no jest. Show her the notes."

Sir Miles pulled a scrap of parchment from a pouch at his waist. The trusted advisor being so tall and thin, his belt was cinched tightly around his hips, with no weapon to speak of. Bronwyn thought it odd, as most of the fighters and men at camp were armed. But an idle thought struck her: maybe he didn't need a sword to fight his battles, but words instead.

He laid the scrap on the table. Bronwyn peered at it. The note, hardly more than a few finger-spans wide, bore a crude sketch of a woman wearing a crown lying on the ground, with blood beneath her. It sent a chill through Bronwyn's veins.

She leaned back. "That's horrible."

"It's not the only one. We received this and more, once our forces aligned with Sir Robert's," Sir Miles said.

"Are you insinuating that one of my men had the gall to do this?" Sir Robert asked.

"Only that it is a strange coincidence. Tristan, bring forth the others."

A young man stepped out of the shadows of the tent. Bronwyn jumped. She hadn't even noticed he was there.

He stood tall and thin, with broad shoulders and light-blond hair, cropped short. He was young, in his twenties, perhaps, with a slight, blond mustache and fuzz at his chin. His mouth quivered with a sneer. Then he ignored her and opened the pouch at his waist, removing more scraps of parchment. He laid them on the table before them all.

Each bore either a crude drawing or worse, words she could not read.

"What do they say?" Bronwyn asked.

"Threats. They threaten the empress's life," Tristan said, his voice low. A baritone. He looked at Sir Miles. "Master, why am I showing these to a servant? Who is she?"

Bronwyn bristled, her mouth hanging open. *So rude.*

"She is useful to me and has a sharper mind than most girls her age. She is not so silly as some of the ladies I know," the empress said. "And do not question your master, boy."

Tristan bowed his head.

Bronwyn tried not to smile. A compliment from the empress was a good day, indeed. She turned to the empress. "What would you have me do, Empress?"

The empress's smile was like a cat luxuriating before stretching its way over. "The last note I found was beneath my trencher of food at dinner, but the pages knew nothing about it. And I found another beneath my cup at the midday meal. It is odd."

"Even your taster didn't see anything," Sir Miles said.

"Your Grace has a taster?" Bronwyn asked. She'd heard about tasters before and thought, *If only King Stephen and the queen had employed one, then the person might have judged for themselves the mushrooms were poisoned and my father might never have landed in prison for a crime he didn't commit.*

"Ever since there have been attacks on my life, I take no chances. I have hired a taster to try my food first," Empress Maud told her.

Bronwyn's eyebrows rose higher, then she nodded. Life at court was not easy.

"You will no doubt soon meet my taster, Mistress Agatha Carre," Empress Maud said. "She will make herself known to you. Make sure she tries everything that is to be served to me at mealtimes. I want nothing to go untested. I take no chances."

And yet, the empress had just eaten bread in front of her, with no taster present, after demanding she bring it to her herself. Perhaps it was a test, to see if she had poisoned the rolls, or as a part of her dared hope, the empress actually trusted her?

Bronwyn nodded. "I understand, Your Grace."

"Good. Now go. If you see anyone acting suspiciously or slandering my good name, I want them reported immediately. You may tell the squires; they will let me know. Off with you." The empress made a shooing motion with her hand.

Bronwyn curtsied and left, holding the empty, wooden platter by her side. As she exited the tent, she heard Sir Robert mutter, "I still don't understand what you see in that girl."

"She reminds me of me at her age," the empress replied. "She's young but hungry. I can tell."

"We're on the road. *Everyone* is hungry, Empress."

"That is not what I mean, Sir Robert. She is smart. I could

make something of her someday, if she lives that long."

Bronwyn walked on, wanting to get away. Part of her wanted to dally and try to hear more, especially as they were talking about her, but there were two guards in front of the tent, and besides, she felt a chill run through her.

It was now July, but she gave a slight shiver. These knights and rulers talked so commonly about people's lives, as if they were disposable. Perhaps they were. Maybe she was too. And yet, a part of her felt... something akin to pride. The empress trusted her. She had complimented her mind, which was rare. Bronwyn straightened her shoulders and felt a smile come over her face. Perhaps the empress's camp was an all right place to be, for now.

She returned to the cooking tents. She'd felt Rupert's and Theobold's eyes on her whilst with the empress but had dared not address either. She had not even wanted to look at them. She hadn't known what she'd say. They were like the sun and the moon, and she found herself caring for both.

Back at the cooking tents, Bronwyn was arms deep in gutting fish, when a familiar, low voice said behind her. "Hullo, Mistress Baker."

She turned her head, a warm blush coming over her cheeks. It was Theobold. She couldn't help but grin as she held out a fish head, its spine still attached. "Hullo, Theobold. Fish?"

His handsome face twisted and he turned his head at the smell. "No, thanks. I came to see you."

She looked at him. He didn't seem to mind that her hands were covered in foul-smelling fish guts. For some reason, that made her smile more.

"I just got back. Can we talk? Somewhere that doesn't smell like fish?" he asked, eyeing her hands.

"Sure." She waved against the buzzing flies, then washed her hands again, stepping aside for another servant to take over, and dried her hands with an apron before leaving the tent.

The warm July air circulated around them, and she breathed in, happy to be away from the fish for a time.

Theobold walked beside her. "How many of those fish do you have to clean?"

"As many as were caught today. What we don't cook, we'll preserve and take with us. Why?"

"No reason. Will you really do as the empress asks and report on the other servants?" he asked.

She glanced away for a moment. "I don't know," she admitted. "It wouldn't feel right. But then again, it is the empress, and a royal order. I feel like I'm bound to obey."

Theobold nodded unhappily.

"How was your errand?" she asked. He'd been gone for well over a month, on a mission for the empress. But there was more to it than that, for he'd gone chasing after a lady-in-waiting, Lady Morwenna, who, as his cousin, was closely linked to him and his family, but who had betrayed the empress. He'd gone searching for her and now was back.

His face clouded. "I can't say much."

"Did you find Lady Morwenna?" Much as Bronwyn disliked the former lady-in-waiting, she disliked more seeing Theobold unhappy.

"I did. She has returned to her family. In disgrace, as you might imagine. I—" He paused.

She got the sense he wanted to say more but could not. People walked around them; there was no privacy to be had. There never was at a camp.

Theobold took her hand and squeezed it. "Bronwyn, I want you to promise me something. That no matter what happens the next few days, you'll look after yourself."

She cocked her head. "What do you mean? What's happening in the next few days?"

"You know we move to Winchester, but our scouts anticipate there will be fighting with Bishop Henry of Blois's men and Matilda's." He paused. "Empress Maud may not show it, but she's afraid."

Bronwyn tensed. As the squire to the empress's right-hand

man, Sir Robert of Gloucester, he wouldn't be saying this lightly. She asked quietly, "Theobold? What is happening?"

He rubbed the side of his face. "The empress has tasked us all with finding out who is behind the notes, but with a battle coming, I wanted you to be on your guard. Just take care, Bronwyn." He touched his arm, where tied to it, was her kerchief, her favor, that he'd asked for and that she'd willingly given, before he went riding off on his last errand. "This kept me safe." He raised her hand to his lips and then walked away.

She watched him go. A part of her wanted to ask him to wait, to tell her more. But he was already off, a tall, armed figure that soon disappeared into the camp full of people.

The next morning, dawn's early light hit Bronwyn in the face, a white hue amongst the black trees. She was wrapped in a cloak and lay on the ground with other women servants; they banded together for protection. Some people did have romantic liaisons while at camp, but Bronwyn was not interested in that. She'd heard stories of young women sharing a man's bed, only for him to be killed or never return, and for her to be with child. She did not want to be one of them and so kept to herself. What few smiles she did get from men, she kept a polite distance from them, preferring to be seen as a servant and not a camp wench to be bedded and discarded.

She rose early, went into the woods to relieve herself, and wiped her hands on the grass, still wet with the morning dew. She wore a long, purple dress with laces across her bosom. She made sure these were tied tightly and with her thin cloak around her shoulders, went to the makeshift tent used for cooking and began to help.

The orders came from on high; only the fighters were to be fed first. It was a matter of priority; the men were on the march and needed their bellies full for the fighting ahead. The rest of the servants and non-combatants would follow once it was safe.

Bronwyn worked and did not see Rupert, Theobold, or anyone else she recognized leave, but she knew the knights would take their squires with them. No man worth his salt would want to miss a battle. Especially when they fought for "the Lady of the English," as Empress Maud called herself.

The empress may have missed being crowned queen at Westminster last month, but she had still received confirmation from Henry of Blois that the church would support her claim to the crown. That was of course, before he'd changed sides.

Bronwyn was washing purple carrots and chopping them up fine for potage, when the sound came. The noise of men, calling, roaring, fighting. The clash and ting of swords and weapons, the strike of blades and shields, the whir of arrows, and the rush and roaring sound of the fight reached their ears. It sent birds flying out of the trees in sudden masses of wings and cries, as the morning's blue sky shone down on what would otherwise be a fine summer day. Bronwyn tensed and peeked out of the tent but saw nothing out of the ordinary, aside from fewer men present. She rubbed her hands down her skirts and wished for a blade. Would she need a weapon to protect herself? She looked around. There were butchering knives and sticks. Not quite what she'd want in a fight.

Another cook, an older one, came up to stand beside her as they looked out the tent flaps. "The fighting isn't here. It's not far off. We'll need to feed those we can and pack up quickly."

Once the people were fed, Bronwyn hurried to pack up. A scout came riding into the camp, the horse's hooves loud and thundering against the earth and grass. "Henry of Blois has besieged Winchester Castle."

Bronwyn exchanged worried looks with the other cooks. She felt stuck, as if she'd stepped in wet mud and it threatened to pull off her shoes. What did it mean? What were they supposed to do?

Her heart thudding in her chest, she brought the scout a drink. He accepted it and drank thirstily, as she asked, "What happens now? Where is the fighting? Who's winning?"

The scout, a slim young man in his twenties, glanced at her. "The fighting is happening at Winchester Castle. It's by the southwest corner of the city walls. Bishop Henry's put up a good fight, but Sir Robert of Gloucester will overpower his forces for sure." He returned the cup and rode off.

There was a cheer, and within the hour, another scout rode in and told the servants, "He's done it. Sir Robert of Gloucester has defeated Bishop Henry and won for the empress."

A cheer went up amongst the servants' ranks, and people clapped and whistled. Bronwyn let out a sigh of relief. They were all right. She hadn't realized until that moment just how much her personal safety and fate depended on the forces of Empress Maud. She relied on the men to win battles, or else she might have to run for her life and hide. Soldiers might take political prisoners, but cooks? Unlikely. A quick death might be a mercy.

The scout rode on to the empress's tent. Bronwyn's feet took her to follow him, and she wove and dodged around people and more tents. She walked around the back of the tent, where no one was, and listened closely.

The scout said loudly, "Your Grace, Bishop Henry of Blois is on the run. He's fled, and his men are holed up in Wolvesey Castle, at the southeast corner of the city walls."

Empress Maud said, "Excellent. Go and return to Sir Robert and tell him we will join him presently."

The scout left. Sir Miles said, "What is your will, Empress?"

"We leave as soon as possible and siege Wolvesey Castle. While they are fighting, we will take up residence at Winchester Castle. I will leave Sir Robert to decide the details of the battle."

Sir Miles said, "At once, Your Grace."

Bronwyn turned to go when a hand gripped her arm and spun her around. "What are you doing here? Snooping?"

It was Tristan, Sir Miles's sneering, self-confident squire.

Chapter Two

BRONWYN WINCED AT the pain. "Let go of me."

Tristan's grip on her left arm was like iron. His upper lip curled. "I ought to turn you in."

"I—"

"I don't trust you. You're that kitchen maid from the other day. What are you doing, lurking around the empress's tent? Wait till I tell my master about this. He'll be sure to throw you out." Tristan's smile was sly.

"Bronwyn, there you are. I've been looking everywhere for you." Lady Alice's voice cut through their exchange. She came up to them and said, "Oh, hello." She curtsied prettily and let her eyes rake up Tristan's tall body to rest on his face, lingering on his muscular arms and chest. "Who might you be?"

Tristan released Bronwyn's arm and bowed. "Tristan Langforde, my lady. At your service." His eyes rested on Lady Alice's bosom, flicking upwards to glance at her face.

Bronwyn thought Lady Alice looked especially pretty that day. The sun shone on her fair skin, with a light dusting of freckles on her nose. Her jet-black hair was combed and hung in soft waves around her shoulders, and she gave Tristan a sweet smile. She wore a long, green dress with a thin, leather belt around her waist and a bodice with strings that only showed off her bosom. She was a fetching young woman at age nineteen and knew it—from the way she walked to the slightly flirtatious stance and hand resting on her right hip.

Nineteen. Yes, she was a year older now. She had missed doing anything special on the day of her birth, a day in early June, which her family had sometimes chosen to celebrate with a nice meal, if times had been good and they could afford it. The realization she'd missed that day made her ache with homesickness all the more.

"Bronwyn, if I'd known you were talking with a knight, I'd have gone myself." Lady Alice batted her eyelashes at Tristan.

Tristan turned pink and tugged at his shirt collar. "I'm no knight. Not yet. I'm a squire to Sir Miles Fitzwalter." His chest puffed up ever so slightly and he ran a hand through his short, blond hair.

Bronwyn tried not to roll her eyes as Lady Alice smiled prettily and ducked her head. "My mistake. I should have known. But then, you look so strong, I instantly assumed you were a knight. Anyway." She thrust a finger beneath Bronwyn's nose. "You went running off, when I'd told you I wanted breakfast. You were looking for that young man of yours, weren't you?"

"I..." Bronwyn stopped, turning pink. Lady Alice was giving her an alibi. "He's not my young man."

"Oh, ho, this is good. Who is he?" Tristan asked.

"No one." Bronwyn looked away.

"I'll tell you, as it's no great secret," Lady Alice said. "She fancies Theobold Durville, the squire to Sir Robert."

Tristan whistled. "Him? What do you like *him* for?"

Bronwyn glared at Lady Alice, her cheeks flaming. "I don't. I mean..."

They laughed and Bronwyn turned her head. She knew it was all in jest, but she had never liked teasing.

"Go and prepare my breakfast, Bronwyn. I'll be waiting." Lady Alice made a shooing motion with her hands. "Go on now."

Bronwyn flushed. She wasn't some stray dog to shoo away. She was a person.

"And I'll tell Theobold you were looking for him," Tristan

said with a grin.

Bronwyn ducked her head in a small nod and turned and dashed away, slipping into the crowds of people. She held a hand to her cheeks. She hadn't thought she'd blush so easily.

True to her word, she brought Lady Alice a bowl of potage and a roll, right before the tents were being packed up. Lady Alice accepted the bowl gratefully. "Thank you. I can't believe you were caught snooping. If I hadn't helped you, you could have landed in real trouble." She took a wooden spoon, blew on the steaming potage and tasted it.

Bronwyn relayed what she'd heard.

"That's a relief. I mean, I had no doubt that the empress's forces would overwhelm Henry of Blois's men, but now we will be in haste to take residence." Lady Alice quickly finished her bowl and pushed the empty bowl, and spoon into Bronwyn's hands. "That was tolerable at best. I will never get used to living life on the road." She gave a little sigh. "I cannot wait until we are in a castle again. Real civilization. None of this *sleeping on the ground* nonsense."

Bronwyn looked around the tent that Lady Alice shared with one or two other ladies-in-waiting. They had pallets and blankets and even chests of clothing with them. She wisely held her tongue and said, "I'd better go."

"Wait."

Bronwyn paused.

"Aren't you going to thank me? I did save your skin earlier," Lady Alice pointed out.

"Thank you."

"What were you really doing there? It was risky, hanging around the empress's tent."

"I wanted to know more about the fighting. The scout who'd ridden into camp had said some, but not a lot," Bronwyn said.

"It's not your business, Bronwyn. You should stop nosing around. They'll tell us when it's time for us to know."

Bronwyn cocked her head at Lady Alice. Sometimes they

were friends, and other times, they were rivals, it seemed. "I'll go."

"Bronwyn—wait a minute. That's not what I wanted to talk to you about."

"What is it?"

"Rupert."

Bronwyn swallowed. She'd only thought about him twice today already. "What about him?"

"He's been… distant lately," Lady Alice said. "Like his mind is elsewhere. He says nothing is wrong, but I don't believe him. Can you talk to him? I know he views you as a friend, or like a sister."

There was a lump in Bronwyn's throat. Talk to Rupert about his romantic relationship with Lady Alice? She'd rather fall into a deep hole. "Um…"

"Thank you. I wouldn't ask this of you, it's just… I don't have anyone else to turn to. No one I can trust."

"What about the other ladies-in-waiting?"

"Lady Susanna? No."

"Wait. Lady Susanna is back?"

"Yes. She pleaded and begged for the empress to take her back and said that her locking Rupert and Theobold in the room was a prank, for she didn't trust them ahead of her coronation. The empress agreed and believed every word she said. I think it's because she has such a naturally innocent face, and she's always so kind and sweet."

Bronwyn's body stilled. The day was warm, but she felt a chill run through her. Lady Susanna was a young woman with a sweet expression, an expert at convincing others of her innocence. She absolutely could not be trusted. The noblewoman was a liar and had locked Rupert and Theobold away at precisely the wrong moment, when they would have been present to help the empress at her coronation. Thank goodness they had broken free.

Lady Alice let out a noise of frustration. "And now we've got that horrid taster woman sharing our tent as well."

"Lady Agatha Carre?"

"She's no lady," Lady Alice said. "I can tell you that. *Mistress* Carre. She's a snoop, and she's got a nasty habit of digging through other people's things. I found her in here the other day going through my clothes."

Bronwyn's eyebrows rose.

"I know. Inexcusable behavior. I demanded to know what she was doing and she said, 'Just looking.' Can you imagine? In what world would someone like her have the right to go rummaging about in someone else's things?"

"It is odd," Bronwyn agreed. She hadn't even met the woman and yet already suspected her of being up to mischief. It wasn't a good sign. And being a servant, one did not dare rummage through a noble person's clothes unless directed to do so. Otherwise, it was just inviting trouble. "I should get back. They're packing up the kitchen."

"Oh, yes, of course. You will talk to Rupert for me and come back and tell me what he says, won't you?"

Bronwyn bit her lip. She didn't like all these requests to spy and talk about other people behind their backs.

"Please, Bronwyn. As a friend."

"I don't know. It feels wrong. Can't *you* just ask him?"

"I have, but he won't say. He just says everything is fine and then trains and sharpens his sword." Lady Alice pouted prettily.

Bronwyn thought on this. He was probably nervous about the battle ahead. In a way, the ladies and servants had it easy because they missed all the fighting and stayed out of the battlefields until it was over. But if their side lost, they would all suffer for it.

"I'll talk to him." If there was something bothering Rupert, she wanted to know. Friend or no friend, even if that was all Bronwyn would ever be to him. She still cared. And even though Bronwyn wouldn't admit it aloud, Lady Alice's request gave her an excuse to talk to him. A part of her warmed at that thought. But did she tell him that Lady Alice had sent her? To whom did she stay loyal? The squire she fancied, or the young woman who was sometimes a friend?

Bronwyn joined the ranks of the servants and helped wash and pack up everything. In an hour, they were on the move, walking on foot toward the Winchester city gates. Bronwyn looked up high, as the stone gates were formidable, and the road was clear of travelers, as many stayed back to avoid the fighting. The sounds of the fighters could be heard, with great cries and shouts, and many thunderous poundings of horse hooves that drummed the dirt roads.

Bronwyn looked around. She moved at a slow walk with the other servants but still felt wary. The stone walls of the city were strong, but would they protect people from a siege? She would hate to be with Henry of Blois's forces at that moment.

With the empress and her retinue leading the way, their party entered through Winchester's city gates and past homes, great buildings, churches, and even a nunnery to the royal castle. Unlike other times when rulers would be lauded and praised, the people of Winchester stayed indoors and did not come out to welcome the empress and her forces. They hid behind their wooden shutters and closed doors, and it wasn't quiet, but there were no crowds of cheering people to welcome them.

Bronwyn wondered how the empress would react to this, then decided that all must be taken as it happened in war. For that was what this was. She released a nervous exhale, not realizing she'd been holding her breath, as if expecting an attack at any moment. Even as she breathed again, she still felt her shoulders raised, as if she expected arrows to fly or a fighter to call out to duck and hide. She didn't feel safe, even within the city walls.

An eerie silence hung in the air as Empress Maud's retinue walked, their shoes and boots making a steady echoing yet monotonous, repetitive thud as they reached farther into the city. Winchester was a grand city, Bronwyn could tell. Its buildings were a mix of small and large but overall charming, and the dirt roads were wide. Winchester itself was not so big, but she got the sense that without an invading army passing through, the streets would have been teeming with people.

They eventually climbed the hill and reached the gates of Winchester Castle and were welcomed by armed guards, who lowered the gates. Bronwyn joined the other crowds of servants who followed in the empress's wake, passing into a decent-sized castle courtyard. Horses were seen to, groomsmen, stableboys, and men in livery, all of whom had a bustling, busy chaotic energy, but it was comforting in a way. This was chaos she knew and recognized. When she reached the kitchen, she imagined she would relax further still.

Perhaps it's part of being a city person, Bronwyn thought. Give her merchants and hot bread, a great big oven, and herbs, and she would be happy. No being out in the open, waiting for an attack.

Bronwyn was about to head down to the kitchens when she heard a lady call out, "Branwine? Bronwin Baker? Browinna?"

Most of the servants ignored her. But her name was not especially common, so she came forward and nodded. "Yes? I am Bronwyn. Bronwyn Blakenhale."

"You are Bronwyn the baker?"

"I am."

The older woman surveyed her from head to toe. She herself looked about fifty, with an angular face and short, brown hair interwoven with silver, pinned back beneath a veil. She wore a dress of grey wool that looked dirty from the journey, and her skin was tanned and weatherworn. Her eyes were sharp.

"I am Agatha Carre. You are the kitchen maid the empress has told me about." Her lower lip jutted out, and her nose twitched, as if she smelled something obnoxious. She eyed Bronwyn from head to toe, taking in her dull, purple woolen dress, the plain kerchief around her long, blonde hair, and the rough-spun apron at her waist, which draped down to the thin shoes she wore.

Bronwyn had been assessed by people of higher rank than Agatha before and was used to their looks and the intention behind them. The look was no doubt meant to put her ill at ease, to make her feel *less than*. But she refused to let them make her feel this way, so she raised her chin higher, meeting Agatha's eyes. "Yes, Mistress Carre."

The woman harrumphed. "Well, you have manners, at least. Fetch some food and wine for the empress."

Bronwyn said, "I'll send a page for it, mistress."

Agatha's gaze sharpened. "I told *you* to do it and do it you shall. Or you'll feel the worse for it." Her right hand clenched and Bronwyn got the impression the woman was not above slapping servants to get her way.

"Yes, mistress." Bronwyn did not bow or curtsy and simply turned her back on her. There was a loud, indignant sniff at her back, but she did not care. The woman had airs, and Bronwyn had yet to see how she deserved them.

Bronwyn found her way to the castle kitchens, which were of a good size, and reported to the cooks in charge. The head cook, Master Hugh Hoyle, a big, swarthy fellow with black hair and brawny arms as thick as hams, fixed her with a solid stare. "You've just gotten here and you're already giving me orders? No."

"Master Hoyle, it *was* ordered. If the empress ordered it and doesn't get what she wants…"

"Oh, yes, I know. And we can't displease the empress, now, can we?" he muttered as he wandered a few steps, then said, "All right." He pointed to where the servants prepared fresh bread, the cooking spits, the worktables, and where she might find flour and grain. "Some loaves have just baked, so take some of those and go see the brewer. Tell him Master Hoyle sent you and don't go sampling the wine yourself, girl. Off with you."

Bronwyn first ventured to the brewery, which was a few rooms away, belowground. She did not mind wandering about the castle, for it was a new place to explore. Her feet felt tired and sore, but it was all kind of exciting. A new place, a new castle. She wondered how long they would be staying and followed her nose to the smell of fermenting beer and ale.

Bronwyn walked down, disliking the lonesome echo of her shoes hitting the stone steps. The air was moist, the area dark but for a few torches. She called out, "Hallo?" and stepped down into the brewery. Squinting into the dark area, Bronwyn breathed in the strong scents of hops, barley, wheat, and beer. The cavernous space was dimly lit and filled with hundreds of wooden casks.

The sound of scratching hit her ears. In the center of the space stood a tall, middle-aged man with a narrow face, working atop an overturned barrel, writing with a quill and ink on a roll of parchment. His eyes flicked to her. "You there. You lost?"

"No, I've got an errand."

"And you are?"

"Bronwyn Blakenhale."

"Well, Bronwyn Blakenhale. I'm Peter Fforde, the master brewer here. You said you had an errand?"

She nodded. Master Peter seemed like a kind enough fellow. Upon closer inspection, she noticed he had thinning, short-brown hair, a rather pointed nose and angular chin, with red cheeks and with a few burst veins. His dark eyes were merry as he pushed up the sleeves of his blue shirt and picked up a stray, wooden cup and filled it from the cask. "Taste this."

Bronwyn backed away. "Why?"

"Tell me what you think. Go on. It won't harm you."

She took the cup and tasted the liquid. It had a funny odor that made her wrinkle her nose. "Um… It smells like wine. But it's a little… sour?"

"Rancid. I knew it. If bottled too long, wine can turn to vinegar. Can't serve that. But there will always be some who are ready to drink it. We'll save it and give it to the servants for later. What was it you wanted?"

She returned the cup. "Just a bit of wine for the empress."

"So she's here. Brilliant. We'll have someone to test the wine. And she's French. I bet she'll be a real expert on fine wine." He rubbed his long hands together and crossed the room to fill a wine bottle from a cask, then corked it.

As he worked, she cast her eyes down at what he was writing. She couldn't read or write, of course, but she could make out that he was drawing some funny pictures and doodles on what looked to be a ledger or list.

He approached, a wine bottle in hand. "This is better. Take this and let me know what she thinks. Don't forget."

"All right." Bronwyn thanked him and returned to the kitchen, where she explained her errand, taking some fresh bread on a wooden trencher. But once she exited the kitchen, Bronwyn realized she didn't know where to go. She stopped a servant. "Um… I have these for the empress. Do you know where she is?"

"I'll take you," Tristan said, from behind her. "This way."

She followed him, trencher and bottle in hand, conscious he did not offer to help her carry anything. This lack of concern was made especially clear as they walked up a circular staircase and she had to be careful not to drop anything. She was shown the way by Tristan and delivered the tray of bread rolls and the bottle of wine, along with a small stack of cups tucked under her left arm.

The empress was absent, and the ladies-in-waiting largely ignored her, aside from Mistress Agatha, who clapped her hands. "Finally. It took you long enough."

"I didn't know you ordered food and drink," Lady Alice said, looking up from her sewing.

"I was hungry and thought you all might want some."

"I thought these were for the empress."

Lady Alice glanced at the taster. "You told her these were for Empress Maud? You lied?"

"No, of course not. I mean, they are, in a way…"

The room had gotten quiet, then all the ladies started talking as Mistress Agatha grew red in the face.

Bronwyn quickly set up the cups, wine and bread, bowed and quit the room, where Tristan was waiting for her. "Who are you?" he asked.

"What do you mean?"

"Are you someone's daughter? A high-born niece? Some half-royal bastard twice removed?"

She blinked at him. "What makes you say that?" *I'm nobody,* she thought.

"The empress called for you by name. You're trusted. Otherwise, they wouldn't have asked you about the messages the empress got. And you're a servant, but not just any ordinary servant. Otherwise, they wouldn't have asked you to spy on the others. And the other squires couldn't take their eyes off you earlier. Who are you?"

She hoped her warm cheeks didn't betray her. She didn't want to blush and reveal to him that she cared. Rupert and Theobold had been watching her? If only that were true. She wished, nay hoped, that their curiosity meant something more. That she meant something more to them than just a young woman worth some idle curiosity.

She looked up into Tristan's eyes. They were blue and wary, unfriendly. He wore a short sword and scabbard at his waist, with a coin pouch, and rested his hands easily, one on the wall barring her exit. He didn't look apprehensive at all about disturbing her; in fact, he seemed completely relaxed about it all.

Attractive as he was, Bronwyn didn't know him, and that meant she couldn't trust him. "I'm nobody. Nobody important, anyway. And no one's bastard niece, twice removed. Just a servant. I work in the kitchens. I come from Lincoln and—"

"Enough. You're no one, I understand. I don't need your life story." Tristan turned on his heels and left her standing there.

Rude, Bronwyn thought. But perhaps that was the world as Tristan had come to know it. People served a purpose, and if they weren't someone important, they were useless and beneath his notice. Maybe *he* was the bastard.

Bronwyn returned to the kitchen and joined the staff in preparing geese and ducks for the nobles' dinner. She didn't serve at the high table but listened eagerly as the pages returned with empty platters and trenchers to the kitchen and regaled them with news. One page, a scrawny youth of about age ten, said, "Sir Robert is leaving."

Master Hugh stopped. "What do you mean?"

The page said, "I heard them talking. He's planning to take his men to Wolvesey Castle in the city and defend there, and the empress and her men will stay here. They're planning to fight," he squeaked.

Bronwyn breathed in and out through her nose. If the rumors were true, then Henry of Blois truly had turned his back on the empress and was allying with Stephen's wife, Matilda, or as the empress called her, "the Witch of Boulogne."

Master Hugh made space for the pages at the table, where they ate a quick dinner. As everyone tucked in, he rubbed the back of his neck and waited. Once Hugh had everyone's attention, he said, "Right. I don't know the empress's plans for the castle and what we know now might not be true tomorrow. But there are a lot of new faces here, and I know that we might not all agree on politics. Don't matter if you like the new empress or not. It concerns all of us, so listen up."

Bronwyn tensed, then realized he was right. The empress had taken over Winchester Castle, but just a day earlier, the castle and its servants had been under the rule of Henry of Blois. Now that the bishop had thrown his lot in with Stephen, what did that mean for the remaining servants? Where did their loyalties lie? Bronwyn swallowed. How much could she say about her own situation? And she had an ever-plaguing thought: to which ruler was she loyal? She didn't entirely know. She would never forgive the king for imprisoning her father when he'd been innocent; the time in prison had not been good for his health or mind, not to mention his spirit. But the queen had been kind to her, and the empress was complimentary, even if she was demanding most of the time. Mostly, Bronwyn felt tired of being pulled into one scheme after another. Not for the first time, she wished she could go home. But she had no home, not any longer. Since the battle of Lincoln, she didn't even know if her family members were still alive.

Theobold had been kind enough to take her back to visit their old bakery a few months back, but it had been empty, except for squatters. So now she stayed with the empress's camp. At least here, she felt safe enough, and she had work and food. Here at least, she felt useful.

Master Hugh continued. "But this is the situation we're in, so let's make the best of it. Work together and survive the day. Everyone who's not had a bite to eat yet already, eat. Then it's clean up and off to bed, you sorry lot."

Bronwyn finished a hot meal of potage on a stale bread trencher she shared with another cook and cleared away dishes, washing and stacking bowls and trenchers and wiping down tables. She worked until there wasn't much left to do, and even the pot washers and spit turners had gone to bed. A voice at her side said, "Oi. New girl."

Bronwyn looked. A kitchen maid stood there. She stood small, thin, with wispy, blonde hair. "I'm Mary. Do you know where you're sleeping tonight?"

"No." Bronwyn hadn't thought much about it and wiped sweat off her brow. No matter the season, the kitchen was hot.

"Right. There're a few spaces left on the floor of the great hall, or there's space in the loft, the towers, or the cellar. What do you fancy?"

"Where do the women sleep?"

"Anywhere."

"Show me the cellar?" Bronwyn asked. "It'll be cool in there."

"Sure. Come on, you can sleep by me."

Bronwyn nodded and followed Mary through the series of corridors and back stairs and down floors. Mary wasn't much of a talker, and Bronwyn quickly lost her way. "Where are we?"

"This way. Not much farther."

To Bronwyn's surprise, they weren't in the brewery, but a small, chilled dairy slightly below ground. The air changed and was slightly cooler, and she loved it. After walking in the hot sun and then working for hours, it was as though her body started to relax, and her legs and thigh muscles ached. Her feet began to drag and soon tiredness came over her.

Mary whispered to her for quiet and motioned for Bronwyn to follow. Down in the dairy, it was cool and dark, and Mary carried a candle with her, its small flame flickering, casting shadows on the still-lying forms of servants already sleeping like the dead. But then when there was such work to be done, it was no great surprise that the people slept heavily. Mary showed her a spot next to a wall and gave her a spare blanket. Almost as soon as she'd laid her head on the ground, Bronwyn fell asleep.

The next day, Bronwyn woke before dawn. As she stretched, tiptoed out of the cellar's darkness so as not to wake the other servants, found the privy and went to the kitchen to start on cooking for the day, she peeked outside one of the castle windows.

Birds chattered and tittered amongst themselves overhead, huddling on trees and parapets adorning the castle walls. The air was deliciously cool and even though the city was full of houses and buildings, the sky had a pink, hazy hue, which soon became interspersed with swatches of golden clouds. When the sun appeared, it was an aggressive, angry ball of orange and red, blinding anyone who dared look.

Bronwyn quickly looked away and went in search of some food. Once she had eaten a bit of bread, she started preparations for baking. Sometimes days were chaotic, but some things stayed the same, and the demand for bread was constant. She started to prep the dough and roll it out, finding the work relaxing. With her blonde hair tied back in a plain kerchief and the apron at her waist, she whistled a little tune, however off-key.

The brewer she'd met the previous day, Peter Fforde, had entered the kitchen in search of food. He had a bottle of wine to taste and was just about to pour a cup when a maid came down, looking shaken. Bronwyn turned to her. "You all right?"

The maid shook her head.

"What's wrong?"

"The empress. She… She's had a fright," the maid uttered.

Bronwyn and Peter looked at each other. "Give me the bottle," Bronwyn said.

Peter thrust it at her. She took it and the cup and bid the maid to lead her to the empress.

The maid, evidently relieved at having something to do, started to get a hold of her wits and led the way, through corridors and up circular, stone stairwells, to a high series of rooms. They heard shouting and cursing, and armed men tromped through the corridor.

Bronwyn followed the maid to a closed door, which was barred by two guards. The guards held pikes in front of them. "Clear off," one said.

"I've got wine for the empress," Bronwyn explained.

One of the guards raised an eyebrow. "Doubt she'll be wanting wine at this hour."

"Who knows, Alfred, she might do," the other said.

"Who's there? What's all that racket?" a female voice called out from within.

"That's it." The second guard opened the door. "A maid for you, Your Grace."

"Send her in," a voice called.

The guards stood aside. The maid was going no further, so Bronwyn lifted her head high and strode in.

The empress had taken residence of a large, grand bedroom, Bronwyn realized. A solar, as it was known, where the master of the castle slept. It looked very fine and held tables, chairs, traveling chests, a raised bed with fine furs, and beside it, stood a very frustrated-looking empress, whose light-brown hair was long and disheveled, her expression pinched, and her lips pursed in displeasure as she clutched her robe about her. Beside her stood the lean form of Sir Miles, who looked none too happy at the interruption.

"What do you want?" Sir Miles asked.

"I heard…" Bronwyn started. "A maid said the empress might

like some wine."

The empress's hard gaze flickered at Bronwyn. "Yes, I would. Pour me some."

Bronwyn stepped forward, the cup and bottle in hand, keenly aware of eyes on her. Her nose wrinkled at an odd, pungent smell in the room. She opened the bottle when Sir Miles said, "Stop. Don't pour it in that. That sort of cup is for servants. Pour it in this." He pointed to a metal goblet.

Bronwyn nodded and set the cup aside, pouring the wine instead into the goblet.

"W-What if it's poisoned?" the empress asked. "Where is Agatha? My taster?"

"I do not know, empress," Bronwyn said.

"*You* taste it, then."

Bronwyn looked down at the goblet she held. She knew at once that the empress would not care to drink from a goblet that had touched her own lips, so she poured some of the wine into the original plain cup and tasted some. The rich, red wine made her blink. "It's good."

"Fine. You may leave," Sir Miles said.

"No, wait. Stay a moment, Bronwyn," the empress said.

Bronwyn waited.

"What do you see?" The empress gestured toward the bed.

The bed was very fine, decorated with lavish coverlets and furs. Except for an odd smell. It smelled like... feces. Urine.

She looked closer. The sheets and covers were smeared with both, as if someone had emptied a chamber pot over the empress's bed.

Bronwyn tensed at the sight. "What happened?"

"What does it look like? Someone came in here and dumped that filth on my bed. I was at prayer in the chapel and wasn't here at the time, thank goodness. But whoever did it left that mess for me to see." Empress Maud shuddered.

"Who would have done this?" Bronwyn asked.

"Someone wishes to scare her. I think it is the same person as the one who has drawn all those nasty pictures, empress," Sir Miles said. "There is a traitor in our midst." He looked sourly at Bronwyn.

"It's clear to me," the empress began, "that there is a killer here. No doubt planted here by Stephen and his witch of a wife. I'm sure they hired some poor fool to do their bidding. But who? Who would dare?"

Silence was her only answer.

"Bronwyn," the empress started, "you were good at finding out Sir Bors's treachery, and Lady Morwenna's... mistakes. Look into this for me. Tell no one. The only people who know about this are in this room. And the maid outside. Understand?"

Bronwyn met Sir Miles's eyes, and the empress's. A part of her wanted to refuse. Her place was in the kitchens, baking bread. Preparing meals, not hunting down foul tricksters at a royal court. But... another part of her wanted to help. It wasn't right, this person, messing about with the empress. And if she were being true to herself, she liked the thrill of the chase, asking questions and learning information, to solve a crime. She'd been useful, more so than just by delivering a platter of bread and jug of wine, or making a nice meal. She felt valued for her mind, and that filled her with pride and she dared think, ambition.

"Yes, Empress," Bronwyn said. There, she'd said it. There was no turning back now.

"Good. I want this traitor found."

Sir Miles escorted Bronwyn outside the room. "Girl. Bronwyn. Whilst the servants clean away the mess, I will pen a message for Sir Robert of Gloucester, and I want you to take it to him. He's at St. Swithun's, on the northeast side of the city. It is a church, built over the gate. He should be there. If not, he'll be at the cathedral."

Bronwyn blinked. "Why not send a page, or a pigeon?"

He cocked his head. "Because the empress trusts you, and I wish to test your mettle. What I have is of utmost importance and besides, servants go everywhere. No one will notice another one walking around."

She swallowed. "Is it safe?" Then she realized, did she have a choice? If she walked away now, she could kiss any hope of being useful, necessary, and important goodbye. She would become and have proven herself to be exactly how she had described herself to Tristan earlier: a nobody. But this was a chance. This might just be her chance, to prove her worth to people who made decisions. She could make her mark on history; she could—

"It will be less safe the longer you dally. Now, will you take my message or not?" Sir Miles asked.

She nodded. "I will."

"Good. Follow me." He led the way down the corridor, to a smaller set of rooms. He entered and sat at a small writing desk, dipped his quill in an inkwell, and set to work, his goose-feather quill scratching on a bit of parchment. He blew on the ink to dry it quickly and once satisfied, folded and sealed it. He gave it to Bronwyn. "Deliver this by hand to Sir Robert, and him only. No one else. And you can't read, can you?"

She shook her head.

"Good." He motioned for her to leave.

She dashed down to the kitchen and told Master Hugh where she was going. He frowned but waved a hand. "Be off with you, but come right back. The city's not safe right now, day or night."

Bronwyn left the castle and trudged down the grassy hill, the folded-up bit of parchment tucked away in her sleeve. She walked through the city, losing her way several times. The few people she passed were in a hurry and looked nervous. Few were willing to stop and give directions, mostly just pointing. Eventually, Bronwyn found St. Swithun's church and was let in, once she said she had a message for Sir Robert of Gloucester.

The guards at the gate looked down their noses at her, when horns blazed, and the sound of hundreds of marching feet sounded in the distance. Bronwyn froze. "What's happening?"

One guard said, "The fighting's starting. Go home." The guards shuffled her aside as fighters hurried past. Bronwyn passed armed men, fighters, hurrying by in armor, swords and shields in their hands. She did not see Robert anywhere, and everyone was too busy to ask. Racing up and down corridors, Bronwyn finally went up to the turrets and parapets, where she found him. Breathless, hot and sweaty from climbing stone stairwells, she spotted Sir Robert standing at the top of the walkways, a hand over his eyes.

"Sir Robert," she said, approaching him.

He turned, surrounded by a handful of men, Theobold among them.

Her heart beat faster at the sight of Theobold in his element. He was dressed for fighting, his expression serious. His eyes widened at seeing her, but he made no comment.

Sir Robert's bushy eyebrows furrowed. "You? What do you want?"

"Sir Miles asked me to deliver a message for you." She plucked the folded-up bit of parchment from her sleeve and held it up.

Men stared at her, their unfriendly eyes raking her from head to toe. Bronwyn ignored them.

"Sir Miles sent you? Fine, give it here." Sir Robert snatched it and read its contents, his frown growing at every written word. He crumpled the paper and tossed it aside. "I don't have time to waste with Miles's messages. The empress will have to hold out where she is. You should return whilst you can."

"I'll see her out," Theobold said.

"No, Theobold, I need you." Sir Robert rattled off orders and sent Theobold on his way.

As Theobold passed her, he touched her hand and whispered, "Stay safe."

Bronwyn tensed. The sound of men marching grew louder. From atop the parapet, she had an excellent view, and it made her breath catch.

It was her first time seeing an army up close. Rows and columns of men marched in formation, up to the city gates, stretched as far as she could see. Cavalry moved in formation. Men armed with spears, pikes, swords, and bows and arrows. They were far too close. Hundreds upon hundreds of men stretched back as far as she could see.

And there, marching at the head of the column, sat aside a white horse, was Matilda, the Countess of Bourlogne. Her long hair flowed over her shoulders like streamers, waving in the wind, and she wore a breastplate of armor over her dress. Bronwyn blinked at the sight. Matilda was beautiful, but somehow even more so in her simplicity, for she rode alone at the head of a column of hundreds of men.

"My god, is that...?" a man said.

"It's Matilda. Stephen's wife," Sir Robert said darkly. "She's got balls, I'll give her that."

Bronwyn watched as the queen entered the city gates and approached.

Matilda, resplendent in a cloak, helmet, and sword, pulled her white horse up short and called out, demanding the release of her husband. She entreated their surrender and her husband's safe return. Her beauty was unmistakable and her gaze fierce, even from far away. She looked up at the parapets, where Sir Robert stood. Her hair shone in the sun, and the rows of hundreds of fighters behind her stood solemnly, awaiting her command. They stood in formation, ready to fight.

Sir Robert pulled up his belt and called out, "End this foolish tirade, woman. Your husband failed and now rots in a Bristol prison. Do not come crying to me because he was foolish enough to get caught."

Matilda's cheeks turned rosy. "Where is your mistress, Sir Robert? Or is she too afraid to show herself? I could well understand, considering the people's reception of her in London."

The men laughed at this behind her, all smiles. It was no great secret that the empress had fled London pursued by an angry mob.

They traded insults a while longer before Sir Robert motioned to the archers to be ready. The archers along the parapet raised their bows, and the queen paused. "I ask you one more time, Sir Robert. Tell your mistress to end her foolish crusade. Enough men have died. This country belongs to my husband, the true King of England."

There was a roar and a cheer as the men behind her clapped and voiced their agreement. Matilda waited for this to quiet down and held a hand for silence.

Sir Robert bellowed, "Fine words for a woman. Shame your husband isn't here to defend himself. But then, it's hard to from prison, eh? Has he sent you to lead his army?" He jeered, and the men laughed with him.

Bronwyn's mouth set firmly. Why couldn't a woman lead an army? She felt annoyed on behalf of the queen. To be put down because of her sex would be rude and embarrassing, but then, that was Sir Robert's tactic, she realized. He was being petty on purpose.

"I'll not be answering to you. This country belongs to Englishmen. Not French bits of pastry."

Matilda shook her head, her long hair swaying prettily. "That is unfortunate, Sir Robert, for now, the city of Winchester will suffer for your mistress's selfishness. She has already lost, and it is a poor loser who refuses to give up when the game is over. I do not wish to kill you, but if you do die today, know that it was in service to a lost cause."

Queen Matilda rode back to the front of the line, her cloak billowing, her long hair streaming behind her like a wave. She raised a sword and called out, a sharp cry that the men took up. What began as a cry rose into a bellow, and then a roar, with the thunderous sound of crashing fists against helmets and shields, the thumping of pikes and spears against the ground, and the yell of men, ready to fight. Any chance of a parley was over.

The battle began. The men started to march.

Sir Robert raised his hand, and the archers raised their bows and shot. Suddenly, the air filled with arrows, almost darkening the morning sky. They whistled and fell, peppering against hundreds of helmets and shields.

Bronwyn gasped. The cries of men who fell, their bodies pierced by deadly arrows assaulted her ears. She never wanted to hear that again.

Sir Robert narrowed his eyes at her. "Get back and stay out of the way," he told her. "Hold the line!" he shouted to his fighters.

Bronwyn looked around. "Where's Squire Rupert?"

Silence and stony expressions met her. She didn't understand. The archers ignored her and kept shooting. Theobold approached her with gritted teeth.

"Your friend Rupert is a filthy traitor, a bloody coward. He turned tail and left when he saw the army coming." Theobold shook his head. "I should've known. Did you know?"

Her jaw dropped. *Rupert, a coward? No. It can't be.*

Seeing her shocked expression, he said, "I guess not. Well, he's fooled both of us. That's what we get for trusting one of Stephen's men."

Bronwyn's right hand darted to her mouth. Her hands trembled as she touched the stone wall for comfort. She wanted to hold on to something stable and solid. She had thought he was allied with the empress now, especially as his master sat in prison with the king in Bristol. But perhaps he'd stayed loyal to his master. Still, his desertion surprised her.

Theobold said, "You should head back. It's not safe for you here. Do you know the way?"

"I'll find it." Her eyebrows knit together.

"Go now." He gave her left hand a squeeze. "Go with God, Bronwyn."

She squeezed his hand in return. "You stay safe too."

Their eyes met, and he winked. "Always do. You worried about me?"

She opened her mouth to speak, Sir Robert ordered, "Archers, fire!"

Bronwyn ran. She moved faster than she thought her feet

could carry her, down the parapet and the stone stairwells to the main west hall, where she fled out through a servants' back passage that took her out a side entrance into the street, near the latrine block, judging from the noxious smell.

She dodged around people and into empty streets. People had fled and were hiding. The birds no longer sang, and all was quiet but for the steady sound of marching, men's booted feet and horses approaching. She dimly heard Sir Robert roar, "Fall back! Fall back to the cathedral!"

Bronwyn got lost on the way, becoming confused while trying to avoid the men filling the streets. At a loss, and what felt like hours but must have been just minutes, she found her way back to Winchester Castle and climbed the hill, her legs groaning from the sudden exercise as she climbed up and clawed at tufts of grass and earth. Panting and out of breath, her face streaming with tears, she begged the guards to be let in.

The guards at the gate paused at first. "Who are you? Why aren't you hiding?"

"Please."

They took one look at her bedraggled state and let her in, not stopping to hear her babbling, and she ran in without a moment's thought, running for her life. She was breathless, lurching as if she were drunk. She had to move to escape the sound—the stamping of hundreds of men's boots, the thundering of war horses' hooves striking the ground, the cries of men dying—it terrified her.

The noise grew louder, and Bronwyn ran up to the towers, the parapets, to see. The space was full of archers, but she crept near the entrance and saw. The attacking fighters had not only entered the city, but they were also marching through the streets. Hundreds of fighting men beat their hands and weapons against shields and armor, raising an almighty clang, their voices rising in a dreadful cheer.

A light rain began to fall. The streets soon muddied, the hard-packed earth becoming wet and slick with churned-up muck from horse hooves. The men didn't care and kept coming. The voices of the attackers hooted and whooped, and in the hundreds, it sounded like waves and crashes of thunder.

She saw from afar, the men retreated, and Queen Matilda's forced had gained ground, stopping just short of entering the castle. But it was close.

Fires raged and buildings burned, but they were safe, for the moment. Bronwyn leaned against the stone wall and panted, catching her breath. She was glad to be alive. She didn't know it was to be the start of six weeks of stalemate.

Chapter Three

FOR THE NEXT few weeks, Bronwyn learned the ins and outs of Winchester Castle. The inner hall was grand, with great stained-glass windows, bearing portraits and names of saints. She spent hours with the other kitchen servants toiling in the expansive garden, tilling the soil and pulling up weeds.

It was hot, sweaty work in the September warmth, but she appreciated the change of routine. It beat working inside the underground kitchens, where she never saw the light of day usually.

But all was not well. She was safe, and for that, she was grateful. But there was trouble afoot. More than once, she found Master Hugh giving the other servants dirty and suspicious looks. One morning, Bronwyn had opened the grain stores and storage cupboard to find an entire loaf of bread gone, but when she'd asked the other servants, no one had known where it had disappeared to.

Worse, she spied Lady Alice walking around the gardens at times with the other ladies of Empress Maud's, but there seemed a distance between them. One morning, Lady Alice approached Bronwyn in the garden and asked, "Might I have a word?"

Bronwyn glanced at the other servant facing her and straightened from her weeding. She nodded and motioned for Lady Alice to precede her whilst wiping her hands clean on her apron. "Yes?"

Lady Alice walked quickly, not wanting the other servants to hear. "I dislike this. Your hair is piled up around your head like a washerwoman or a kitchen maid, and your dress and apron are dirty."

Bronwyn arched an eyebrow. "I *am* a kitchen maid?"

"Yes, well… You're more than that and you know it. Anyway, I wish you would dress better. I dislike having to walk about with someone so unkempt. What would people think?" Lady Alice's face was pale and pinched, her lips pursed tightly. Her eyes squinted from the midday sun, and her jet-black hair rippled behind her shoulders. She was anxious, Bronwyn realized. She wondered if Lady Alice knew Rupert had quit the empress's army.

"What's wrong?" Bronwyn asked.

"Nothing. I am perfectly fine." Lady Alice kept walking. "It's just… Everything is wrong. And I have no one else to talk to but you. You can be sure, I wouldn't do this if I had someone else, of my own station and rank."

Bronwyn realized that Lady Alice was definitely unhappy, bordering on upset. The young noblewoman was sometimes fair, sometimes foul, but more often than not, she was a friend. Lady Alice only pointed out the differences in their situations and was particularly cutting when she was upset.

"You have the other ladies-in-waiting," Bronwyn pointed out.

"Ha. What a joke. You should train with the fool; he'd find you funny too." She paused and, finding a bench nearby, sat on its cool, stone seat.

Bronwyn sat beside her. "What's wrong?"

"I… Rupert is gone."

Bronwyn tensed.

Lady Alice sighed. "He's stuck at that blasted St. Swithun's with Sir Robert and the men, and I haven't heard from him since the battle began. He's not sent me any messages to tell me of his affection for me, and I don't know if he's all right or not. He could be wounded or…What if he's *dead?*"

Lady Alice will lead herself into a fit if she isn't careful, Bronwyn thought. But her words struck a chord within her, and Bronwyn rested her hands on her knees. What if Lady Alice was right, and Rupert was injured? There was no way to know. And what about Theobold? Was he safe and well?

Bronwyn looked away, at a small row of herbs that were growing nearby. So Lady Alice didn't know. Was Bronwyn the right person to tell her? And if so, was this the right moment? She bit the inside of her left cheek.

Lady Alice said, "I can see from the way your brow wrinkles that you're thinking about this too. You're worried about Theobold, aren't you?"

Bronwyn blushed and instantly felt guilty. "I worry for them both."

"As well you should. Theobold has practically fallen at your feet and Rupert thinks of you like his own sister. I know because he told me. So, you see? We are stuck like this together, waiting."

"We'll hear about them, for certain. I know they're all right."

"How can you say that when you don't know? They could be lying in a ditch somewhere," Lady Alice said.

"I just know." Bronwyn felt they were all connected, somehow. If Rupert or Theobold were dead, she felt she would know it, the moment it happened. She brushed at a piece of nonexistent lint on her skirt and said, "There's something you should know."

"What? Do you know something?" Lady Alice's gaze was hopeful.

Bronwyn swallowed. "Rupert defected."

"What?" Lady Alice froze.

"He went back to Stephen and Matilda's army."

Lady Alice gave her a flat stare. "No. It can't be. You're wrong."

"I'm not." Bronwyn winced. "I wish I were. I was sent to deliver a message from Sir Miles to Sir Robert at St. Swithun's. Theobold was there, but Rupert wasn't. There was no sign of him."

"He might have gotten lost in the fighting. It was chaos, for sure." Lady Alice tugged on her skirts. Her voice was too high-pitched and hopeful-sounding.

"It was chaotic," Bronwyn admitted. "But Theobold told me he'd defected. He said Rupert had rejoined Matilda's ranks as soon as the fighting had broken out."

"No. No, he wouldn't do that. He wouldn't be so dishonorable." Her voice rose. Lady Alice gripped the edge of the stone bench with her hands. "He wouldn't leave me."

Bronwyn sat by her. "I'm sorry."

"I don't believe you. He wouldn't. Not without telling me." Lady Alice was quiet.

"I'm surprised too."

They sat quietly together. *Sometimes*, Bronwyn thought, *you don't need to say words in order to support someone.*

"How long have you known?"

"A little while." Weeks, but she had busied herself with life at the castle under siege and hadn't given Lady Alice a second thought. But that wasn't true. She had thought about Rupert, and how Lady Alice would react to the news of his defection had crept into their thoughts each day. Would all be over between them? Her very thoughts sounded traitorous to herself. What kind of a friend was she? She bowed her head.

"You should have told me straight away. A friend would have done that, as soon as she heard." Lady Alice's shoulders drooped. "You didn't say anything, did you? You didn't encourage Rupert to go back to their side?"

"No." Bronwyn let a firmness enter her tone. "No, I didn't. I wasn't able to talk to him after you asked me to."

"Watch your tone with me, Bronwyn. We may be friends, but I am still a lady, and you are a commoner. Don't forget that."

Bronwyn cocked her head at her. "You seem to choose when we are friends and when we aren't."

"And just what is that supposed to mean?"

"Sometimes we are friends; sometimes we aren't. But you always seem to decide when we are and when we aren't, and it makes me dizzy at times." Bronwyn stood.

"What?" Lady Alice stood as well. "Don't tell me you're offended."

"I am, a little."

The young women faced each other.

"I bet you did. I bet you did say something to him. Tried to convince him to come back and leave me. Well, I won't have it, you understand? I won't. I always get what I want, and I want him. And no one is going to stand in my way." Lady Alice's eyes flashed in anger. "You're a baker. Go bake me a cake or something."

Bronwyn snorted and began to walk away, when Lady Alice said, "Wait. Um… What do you know about Mistress Agatha Carre?"

Bronwyn's interest was piqued. "The empress's taster? Only what you've told me, and her being rude and imperious toward the servants. Why?"

"No real lady of quality would treat others so. I think she's a nobody. I think she's common as dirt," Lady Alice said maliciously, in a rush.

Bronwyn blinked. Lady Alice spoke with venom, as if she'd been holding these thoughts in her mind for some time, and now it was a relief to get them off her tongue.

"What makes you think that?" Bronwyn asked.

"Just the way she acts and talks. She wears fine dresses and eats at our table like she's one of us ladies, but her manners are coarse, and she doesn't have the manners for a fine table like the empress's. She barely washes her hands, hoards the best bits of meat, and I think I even saw her slipping some into her sleeve for later. Can you imagine?"

Bronwyn nodded. She well could, for since they were being besieged, food was becoming scarce, and the grain stores and preserved dairy were getting lower by the day.

"But that's not the worst of it. She… I think she's vicious." Lady Alice flicked her hair over her shoulder and glanced around, as if to see whether they might be overheard.

"What do you mean?"

"Well, I was walking with Lady Susanna the other day and she saw Agatha in the same dress she'd worn the day before, with grease stains around the bodice and sleeves. Lady Susanna asked an innocent question and asked Agatha whether her maid had seen the state her dress was in. Lady Susanna is sweet and kind but not always thinking before she talks." Lady Alice huffed.

"Well, Agatha thought she was poking fun at her and was offended. She walked away and we thought nothing of it, until that evening, when Lady Susanna sat on the bench at dinner. We always sit in the same places usually, and she got up with a start. She'd sat on a bit of grease and ruined the seat of her dress."

Bronwyn's eyebrows rose. "Really."

"Yes. The servants were asked, of course, but no one had dared spill grease on the bench. So Lady Susanna had to leave immediately and change, and by the time she returned, most of the food was gone. You know how these people are. Hardly anything left for her."

Bronwyn nodded. Lady Alice didn't know that what leftovers the nobles didn't finish, the servants ate. For days there had stopped being leftovers, and the servants were getting leaner. "And you think Agatha did it? That she put grease in Lady Susanna's spot?"

"Who else could have? No one would think to, and the servants are always clean and take care when bringing out the food. Besides, when Lady Susanna stood and raised a cry, Agatha was the only one who smiled, as if she'd won an argument. She didn't notice, but I saw."

"Did she say anything?" Bronwyn asked.

"Only a remark that her maid will have her work cut out for her. She said Lady Susanna should be more careful. But Agatha spoke with such a snide smile, I knew she was behind it. Lady Susanna looked as if she were about to cry and left."

Bronwyn nodded. That confirmed what she already suspected—that the empress's taster was not very nice at all. "Did Lady Susanna figure out she did it?"

"No. But she was upset. She didn't like looking like a fool, and she liked her dress. It took her maid ages to get the grease stains out."

"Have you told anyone else about Agatha?"

"No, just you. I thought with all these strange occurrences happening, you would want to know."

"Why not tell the empress?" Bronwyn asked.

"And be asked to prove something I cannot? Don't be daft. You know as well as I do that the empress is growing more frightened every day. The last thing she needs is to suspect those closest to her."

"But what if they're the problem?"

Lady Alice shook her head. "Bah, now you're jumping to wild fanciful ideas. You'd have us all suspect each other soon. Agatha is vengeful and a snoop, but that's it. Lord, I can already see your mind jumping to conclusions. I simply wonder if she is behind the empress's accidents, that's all. Knowing your mind, you probably already wonder if she's a killer. Lord, Bronwyn. With you, it's always murder on your mind. No wonder people keep dying around you."

"Oi, that's not true." Bronwyn's mouth pulled into a half-frown.

"Isn't it?" Lady Alice tossed her hair behind her shoulder and walked off.

Bronwyn returned to her work. But as she toiled with the other servants amongst the rows of finely tilled cared-for plants, pulling up weeds and wiping the sweat from her brow, her thoughts drifted to Rupert and Theobold. A part of her cared for them both, deeply, with a passion that surprised her. She hadn't expected to care for these two young men so much. They were so different, and she'd only known them both a short time. Was it love, or a misplaced affection for friends? She wasn't sure. She smiled at the brewer, Peter, who stood across the field, walking away, having finished a conversation with another servant. She raised a hand in greeting, but he walked past her, his face as dark as a storm cloud.

That evening, Bronwyn decided to pay a visit and brought a spare roll she'd made that day. It was one of the mistakes, meaning one that the head cook, Hugh, had deemed too rough and not good enough to serve to the aristocrats and empress's men at the high tables. She pocketed the roll, a simple, round bread roll dusted with too much flour, and walked down to the castle brewery, relishing the heady scent of hops, barley, oats, and alcohol.

She enjoyed the rich smells and found Peter working busily as in the cavernous underground space, he surveyed wide vats of liquid that gave off an unpleasant smell. She pinched her nose and wrinkled her eyes as she waved.

"Hello there, Bronwyn." He put aside the quill, ink, and parchment he was working with.

"What are you working on?" she asked.

"A bit of tallying figures." He moved the parchment aside, but not before she saw a humorous doodle on the outside of his tallying list.

"Sorry to disturb you. I brought you this." She gave him the roll.

He took the roll with black ink-stained fingers and ate it in about two seconds. "Delicious, although not as good as your other ones." He wiped the crumbs from his shirt and looked out over the vat.

"What is that?" she asked.

"Malting." He grinned. "I'm brewing grain. We steep this in water, and when it's warm enough, this will sprout. When that happens, it releases noxious vapors in the air and the malting mix of grain will change into a sort of sugar within the grain."

Bronwyn scratched her head. "Is it safe?"

"You wouldn't want to drink it yet or eat it. But once the process is finished, it can be a light or dark beer, depending on whether I roast the grain." He raised a bushy black eyebrow. "What can I do for you? I presume you didn't come all this way to learn about brewing."

"No reason. I saw you earlier in the castle gardens and waved, but you didn't see me and looked angry. I wanted to make sure you were all right."

His expression softened. "I'm fine. Just a difference of opinion."

"Oh?"

He cocked his head. "None of your business, girl. Or shall I start calling you 'Bronwyn the Busybody'?"

She smiled thinly. "Just asking." She turned to go.

"Wait a minute. Stay." He breathed in and said, "I don't know how much you know about what goes on here, since you're new and all. But… Not everyone is happy here. There were some who agreed with Henry of Blois's decision to leave the empress, and who would have gone with him."

"Who?"

He tapped his nose. "Like I'm going to start wagging my tongue like a common fishwife. No, girl. Just be wary of who you talk to. Not everyone believes in the empress's claim to the crown, and they won't like a young woman going around asking questions."

"Do *you* believe in her claim?" she asked.

"Of course. I always have. I'm the empress's man, through and through." He smiled, showing too many yellow teeth.

Bronwyn nodded and left, feeling Peter's eyes on her back, like an itch between her shoulder blades. She'd gone to check on him and left feeling rather wary. Perhaps he wasn't as honest as he seemed, or maybe she had just offended him slightly. Either way, she felt uneasy as she left the brewery.

That evening after dinner, Bronwyn was walking through the castle corridors, away from the kitchen, when she heard a voice call out, "Mistress Bronwyn?"

She turned. At the top of a stairwell stood Lady Susanna. Her face was pale.

Bronwyn stared at her. The last time she'd seen the lady-in-waiting, she had been acting suspiciously ahead of the empress's attempted coronation last June. Seeing her in the flesh now, Bronwyn wanted to turn and run. Anything to stay far away from this troublesome young woman. Instead, she asked, "What's wrong?"

"Come. Please," Lady Susanna beckoned. Still plump, with dark-auburn hair and rosy cheeks, with freckles, the young woman looked as pretty and innocent as ever, but Bronwyn knew better.

Bronwyn followed her up the winding stone staircase and up into the hallway that led to the ladies' rooms, including that of the empress. Lady Susanna swallowed. "Um… How good are you at cleaning up messes?"

"Good enough, why?"

"Good. In here." Lady Susanna led the way down to the empress's bedroom and motioned for the guards to move aside. "It's me, let us in. She needs to clean the mess."

"What mess?"

"In here." Lady Susanna motioned for Bronwyn to follow her in, where there, on the empress's fine four-poster bed, was a mess. One of her pillows had been sliced and torn to pieces, and feathers had littered the bed like snow, covering the fine coverlets and the floor. A stark, angry-looking knife with a wicked blade pinned the pillowcase to the bed, a warning.

Lady Susanna babbled, "The empress bid me fetch her a shawl from her room, and when I came in, I saw some of the tapestries move, as if a spirit were walking around. I nearly fainted when I saw the mess. Do you think it was a spirit sent by God to warn her?"

Bronwyn walked over to the bed, surveying the mess, picked up the knife, and hefted the handle. The knife had some weight to it. This was no slim, delicate knife, like what a person would use for eating, or that a more discerning woman might use for defense. From its wickedly curved blade and the slight discoloration on it, it was evident it had been used before. This was a killing weapon, pure and simple. Even to Bronwyn's unpracticed eye, she knew this weapon was made for murderous intent. The fact it was found plunged into the empress's pillow sent a chill through her. She pinned the blade's handle to her side and picked up the ruined pillowcase, her fingers going through one of the cuts. "No, Lady Susanna. Somehow, I doubt spirits carry knives."

Chapter Four

BRONWYN CLEARED THE mess of feathers as best she could, using a sack she'd purloined from the kitchens. She sneezed and blew stray feathers away from her ticklish nose. "Why didn't you call for the servants who usually clean the empress's chamber?"

"I did, then thought better of it. We ladies decided amongst ourselves that we don't want to disturb the empress with these little incidents. She's already nervous. This would just bother her more, when she's already got so much to worry her. Can you help me?"

Bronwyn looked at her. So far, Lady Susanna had done nothing to help clean up the mess aside from stand there. "Yes, all right. Help me put the feathers into this sack."

Together, they picked up every feather, sneezing from time to time. Lady Susanna looked forlornly at the empress's deflated pillow on the bed. "This is terrifying. If the empress knew about this, she'd be so scared."

"Who could have done this?"

"I don't know. That's what's so frightening. The guards won't let just anyone in. They wouldn't have let you pass if I hadn't brought you."

Bronwyn left Lady Susanna a moment and went over to the pair of guards manning the entrance to the empress's solar. She cleared her throat, and one of the guards looked over his shoulder. She asked, "Did you let anyone in here before Lady Susanna?"

The guard's expression turned grumpy. "I don't take orders from you."

"Please," Lady Susanna said from behind her. "We need to find out who did this. Someone came in here, without *you* knowing. The empress won't like it if you refuse to help. She might even blame you."

The guard's jaw hardened, and his eyes narrowed. "We didn't let anyone in besides yourself a short while ago." He peered at the feathers scattered around the bed. "What a mess."

"You didn't hear anything?" Bronwyn asked.

"No. But… I only took up my post half an hour ago. Didn't see or hear anyone but yourselves."

"Who was guarding here before you?"

"Thomas and Edwin. This time of night, they'll be in the stables."

"Why the stables?"

He looked around. "They like to play dice in the evening with the grooms."

A haughty gasp came from inside the room. Bronwyn and the guard looked at Lady Susanna, who put her hands on her hips. "Playing dice is a form of gambling, and that's sinful."

Bronwyn coughed to hide her snort. Considering Lady Susanna was rumored to have been having a secret love affair with a man a few months ago, it seemed rather hypocritical of her to be condemning others for being sinful.

The guard rolled his eyes. "You want to speak with them, that's where you'll find them. Best you don't bring her along."

"I heard that."

He smiled and turned back to his post.

Bronwyn finished clearing up the feathers with Lady Susanna. She wasn't sure what to do with it all, but it was obvious they couldn't remain in the room. She tied the bag tightly to ensure no feathers escaped and peered over at the ruined pillowcase.

The knife fit awkwardly in her hand. It wasn't made for a woman's hands, but a fighter's. The wooden pommel was heavy and uncomfortable to hold. The handle, which bore ornate whirls, had been carved well. She didn't dare touch the blade; it looked incredibly sharp. Bronwyn held it up. "Have you ever seen this before?"

"Hmm, I'm not sure. Maybe." Lady Susanna peered at it. "What an ugly thing. I don't recognize it, but it could belong to anyone."

Bronwyn shook her head. "A blade like this wouldn't belong to just anyone. You wouldn't use this at dinner, either."

Lady Susanna *hmmm*ed again. "You're right. But how could someone have gotten in here without anyone seeing? Could the spirit have helped them?"

Bronwyn grinned, then tried to hide her amusement at Lady Susanna's serious expression. "I don't think a spirit was involved here. But you should go back. The empress will be wanting her shawl."

"Oh. I can't believe I forgot. She'll be furious at me for dallying so." Lady Susanna crossed the room to the empress's wide, wooden chest at the foot of her bed and began to rifle through until she found a soft, woolen shawl. "I'll be going. You shouldn't stay, either."

Bronwyn nodded and followed her out, hefting the bag of feathers over her shoulder. She slipped the knife up her sleeve. Whomever it belonged to, she meant to examine it more closely. "Lady Susanna?"

"Yes?"

"Who do you think would have done this?"

"I couldn't say. If not a spirit, then… someone who didn't like the empress. Or her pillows."

Bronwyn laughed.

"I'm serious. A bad pillow is horrid for your neck and back, so they might have been trying to do her a favor."

Bronwyn cocked her head.

"No, that can't be right, after all. A knife in her pillow is a horrid sight. Someone wanted to scare her, I think." Lady Susanna shivered. "May I see it again?"

Bronwyn showed her the knife.

"Hmm. This is different from the swords that the men carry, isn't it? They always like big swords and daggers and things. I wonder if it's meant for someone smaller like—"

"What a woman would carry," Bronwyn finished.

"Yes, exactly. Good luck. I always thought you were smart, so I know you'll figure this out. I knew you were the right person to ask for help." She beamed.

They parted ways. Bronwyn brought the sack of feathers down to a storeroom, where she knew they'd go to good use. The empress might notice one of her pillows missing, but perhaps she'd take that over a knife and a mess. It was clear to her it was a warning, and yet who would have done it? If Lady Susanna was right, then the weapon belonged to or had been stolen by a woman.

Keeping the knife close to her side, she walked out to the stables, hunching her shoulders against the night's chill. Even though it was August, the day's warmth had given over to an evening breeze. Bronwyn walked hurriedly to the stables, where a light and welcome warmth beckoned.

She opened the stable door and closed it behind her. The gentle nicker and whinny of horses greeted her, watching. The smell of hay, horse, and dung met her nose, and she headed toward the sound of men talking and laughing, teasing each other.

At the sound of her approach, one of the men glanced over. He froze at the sight of the weapon. "Who are you? And what are you doing with that?"

Bronwyn held up a hand. "I'm nobody. Just wanted to talk with Thomas and Edwin."

Two men glanced up from the dicing. Both were of a similar age, in their twenties, if she had to guess. Instantly, they looked at her hair, bound up in a kerchief, her face, her bosom.

Bronwyn blinked and suddenly realized her decision to come to the stables alone at night might've been unwise. One, with a head of short, cropped, dark-brown hair and leering eyes, said, "That's us. What you want?"

"To ask you about the empress's room. Spare a minute?"

His mouth curled in a smile. "I'll give you more than that." He rose.

"Ease up, Thomas, she's protected. She's a pet of the empress," Sir Miles's squire, Tristan, said, not looking up from his dice. "Flirt all you like, but you touch a hair on her head and you're a dead man."

Thomas glanced at Tristan, who calmly looked at him. His hand rested on his knee as he sat on an overturned bucket, and he didn't look away. The other men had frozen, and none said a word. But the sight of Tristan's short sword hanging from his scabbard at his hip didn't go unnoticed.

There was a quiet moment, then Thomas looked away. He marched over to Bronwyn. "What's your question?"

"Tonight, did you let anyone into the empress's room when you were guarding it?"

"No. Just the empress herself."

"Did anyone try to come in, or ask you to let them in?"

"No. It was dull. And I didn't hear anything, either."

"That's not true," the other man who'd looked up from before said. He was tall and tanned, with towheaded blond hair. "You remember, Thomas, the noises we heard from inside her room. It sounded like someone was moving around in there, but when we looked, there was nothing amiss. Figured it must've been mice."

Bronwyn nodded. So whoever had knifed the empress's pillow had done it after the room had been checked. That didn't leave much time for the person to go in and out of the empress's room before possibly being discovered.

She held up the knife from her sleeve. "Either of you ever

seen this before?"

The pair looked at the blade, eyeing its keen edge, which looked needle sharp, and its ornate, wooden-carved handle. Edwin said, "No. But there's lots of people who might carry a knife like that. It looks foreign. Some men might carry one if they'd been to the Holy Lands."

"You hear or see anything that was strange? Anyone come talk to you during your time guarding her room?" Bronwyn asked.

The men shook their heads. "Why all the questions? Did someone—"

"No, nothing like that. I was cleaning her room earlier and found this, that's all."

The men nodded. "What's your name?" Thomas asked.

"Bronwyn. I work in the kitchens."

"Why'd they have you clean the empress's room?"

"One of the ladies called me to clean. The other servants had gone to bed."

"Exactly where you should be. Come, Bronwyn, I'll walk see you back. I've taken enough of these lads' coins, anyway." Tristan grinned and rose, dusting off his clothes. That led to a chorus of calls and jeers from the others, and Tristan motioned for Bronwyn to precede him.

Together, they walked out of the stables and into the cold. As they closed the stable door behind them, Bronwyn said, "Thank you. I didn't think—"

"You never do, do you?" He shook his head and ran a hand through his ruffled, blond hair. "God, Theobold was right. I thought he was joking when he asked me to look after you, but you really do need protection. I didn't think it'd be from your own stupidity."

"Oi, that's rude. And I wasn't being stupid, I—"

"Was going along with the subtlety of an ox, barging into a dice game without a care. I was building a relationship with the men, and you interrupted it. Ever think I might've been trying to get information too?" Tristan asked.

"You were? About what?"

He couldn't have known about the latest act of vandalism.

"None of your business. Now, what's all this about cleaning the empress's room? We all heard you. You need lessons in how to question someone. And whose knife is that?"

Bronwyn handed it to him, and he looked at it in the moonlight. "It's hard to tell, but the lads are right. It's different. Looks decorative. It's practically a quill. Only a lady would carry that."

"What would she use it for?"

"Something like that? It's too fine for eating with, but she could do. Why ask? You could have figured that out yourself."

"I don't carry knives."

"Maybe you should. But not that many ladies carry knives." He escorted her back to the castle. In the main courtyard, he paused at the entrance to the kitchen and said, "You shouldn't go walking outside alone. It's not safe." He turned again to go.

"Wait."

He looked at her, waiting. His face could have been carved from rock.

"Did Theobold really ask you to watch over me?"

"He wanted me to keep you out of trouble. I was hoping it wouldn't be a full-time job. I do have my own master to look after. But yeah. He did. So don't make life difficult for me, yeah?"

She nodded. "Did he say anything else? Give a message for me?"

"No." He grinned. "You ladies and your messages. Always wanting to get little tokens and gifts and things. Nothing's ever good enough for you, is it?"

She narrowed her eyes. "Don't know what you mean."

"Never mind. I'm off. Don't go wandering around the stables at night again. I can't always be there to watch your back."

Bronwyn nodded. So she had a protector now, of a sort. That was new. The knowledge sent a warm feeling through her chest. Theobold cared enough to ask Tristan to look after her. That was sweet. She wondered idly if Rupert had done the same for Lady Alice.

The next day at dinner, Bronwyn was sitting down to an evening meal with the other servants, about to dine on the cheaper cuts of fat and meat prepared for the nobles that were considered too burnt or not good enough to serve. Those cuts, with a bit of fresh bread and potage, were a welcome sight after a day of working in the castle gardens under the hot sun and then hours of cooking and preparing meals.

They had just said a prayer over the food and were passing a bowl of water around to wash their hands, when a scream rent the air.

Bronwyn stopped, her hands in the bowl of water. She wiped them quickly. "What was that?"

"I think it came from—" one servant started.

Voices rose in an uproar. Shouts and protests came from the main hall, where the nobles and aristocrats were dining. Shouts and raised voices filled the air, and Bronwyn exchanged worried looks with the other cooks. People began to rise from the benches, and she was one of the first to leave the kitchen to investigate.

She hurried down the corridor to where pages began running to and from the hall. Bronwyn stopped one. "What happened?"

"Mistress Agatha, she's sick."

"Agatha Carre, the empress's taster?"

"Yeah, uh-huh." The page ran.

Bronwyn stopped and considered this. If the taster was ill, that meant only one thing. Someone had tried to poison the empress, and whoever it was had managed to slip past her notice. *Heads might roll this evening,* she thought, as she entered the dining hall.

Chapter Five

A CACOPHONY OF voices, shouts, and protests heralded Bronwyn's entrance as she entered the main hall. Men and women stood, some shouting and wringing their hands, pointing and pulling each other back from the table.

Drinks had been knocked over, food flung about. The table still bore the platters of meat, bread, sauces, and fish, but wine had been spilled, lords and ladies stood around the benches whilst one man tried to help Agatha, who was coughing in fits on the floor.

In a moment, Agatha coughed again and sat up, staring at a piece of meat on the floor. Her voice weak, she uttered, "The chicken. It's poisoned."

Bronwyn tensed. She dashed over and said, "What happened?"

The empress's face was pale. Her eyes had dark shadows beneath them and her expression was pinched. "Bring the head cook here immediately." Empress Maud's voice was icy.

Bronwyn sent one of the pages to fetch Master Hugh.

Lady Alice turned to her. "Oh, Bronwyn, it's horrible. We sat down to dine and—"

"I'll tell her, Alice. It was me being sick, after all," Agatha said, leaning heavily on a knight's arm to stand. Once brought to her feet, Agatha wavered slightly. She wiped her mouth and said, "I tasted the empress's food as normal, but as soon as I smelled the chicken, I thought something might be wrong. It didn't smell right. I wondered if the seasoning was off. I don't like hot food, or any food with too much seasoning or salt." She looked at Bronwyn accusingly. "Then when I bit into it, I began to cough and choke. It felt like my throat was going to close up and steal my breath away. Can someone bring me a drink please?"

A cup of wine was pushed into her hands. Agatha drank deeply and exhaled, affecting a weariness at the people watching her. "It was the chicken. Don't touch it."

Bronwyn looked at the wooden trenchers that bore the chicken carcasses. There weren't many chickens left, thanks to the siege. The chicken coop they kept on site had dozens, but without new supplies, their food stores were dwindling. The cooks simply could not afford to take any risks with the food at this time, not when there were so many mouths to feed and limited supply. Bronwyn's heart felt heavy as she looked at the platters of barely touched chicken decorating the tables. Her shoulders slumped as she looked around and saw people looking at her for direction.

A stray thought occurred to her. What if the chicken wasn't actually poisoned, but perhaps underseasoned or even undercooked? Not that Master Hugh would allow such a thing in his kitchen, but still. Mistakes could happen. Could Mistress Agatha simply have been unlucky?

Seeing as dozens of pairs of eyes were on her, Bronwyn said to the pages, "Remove the chicken. Bring it back to the kitchen and we'll dispose of it. All of it." She looked at Agatha. "Was the rest of the food all right?"

"Yes, the rest was safe." Agatha's voice carried, and she allowed the knight to help her sit back at the table, at the left hand of the empress.

Word of the poisoned chicken spread through the room like wildfire, as Bronwyn helped clear the platters, directing pages to bring them back and out of the room. She was just leaving as Master Hugh entered the room, drying his hands on his apron.

He was a big man, with red cheeks and a sweaty brow, his dark-black curls glistening in the candlelight. He marched over to the empress like a criminal awaiting judgment. "Empress, I—"

"I am shocked at you, Master Hugh," the empress snapped. "Shocked. You let soiled food leave your kitchen. It could have poisoned me. It already made Mistress Agatha ill. If she dies, I will blame you for this."

Hugh's face turned a shade paler. "Please, Empress. I don't know what happened. This has never happened before."

"Well, it has now, and I want answers. Find out which one of your servants is a traitor and bring them to me. I want to know who would dare." The empress's voice was cutting.

"Yes, Empress." Hugh bowed low and backed away.

Bronwyn curtsied and began to leave, when the empress beckoned her forward. In her ear, she whispered, "Mistress Blakenhale. Find out who did this. You have some experience with these matters, but my patience is not endless. You have not informed me of who upturned their chamber pot on my bed from days ago and now this. I cannot have this sort of incident happen under my roof. Find out now, or I'll find someone who can." Despite her voice being low, the empress's French accent came out strong.

"Yes, Your Grace."

Bronwyn curtsied again and finished supervising the removal of the chicken. People whispered and talked behind their hands in low voices as she walked out, her shoes shuffling against the wooden floorboards. She held her head high and yet couldn't miss the guests' suspicious glances and darting looks, as if she were the one in trouble.

Bronwyn met any gaze that looked her way, and once outside the hall, let out a large sigh of relief. Once the last servant had borne the questionable chicken away, she stood outside the entrance.

Agatha said, "Oh, I must go. I'm going to be sick." she burped and rushed past, pushing by Bronwyn and darting toward the privy.

Bronwyn watched her go and then excused herself. Back in the kitchen, Hugh surveyed the platters of chicken left on a worktable. The room was quiet as he scratched his head. "I can't figure it out. We sent it out and there was nothing wrong with it. How could it have been disturbed?"

A few of the cooks had suggestions, but in the end, no one had any useful ideas. Bronwyn said, "It could have been done by a page, when they were serving it to the empress."

"But Agatha takes her portion from the trenchers like everyone else. Whoever toyed with the chicken would have had to risk everyone she shared a serving platter with getting sick. It's a big risk to take."

But not so great for a person who wanted the empress dead, Bronwyn thought. Her mind went back to a time a few months ago, when she had first entered a castle's kitchen, and a nobleman had died from poisoned mushrooms. The poisoner had meant for the king and queen to be harmed, but the nobleman had gotten in the way. Could someone be trying to kill the empress?

"Mind if I take a look?"

"Be my guest. No one here has any good ideas," Hugh said.

Bronwyn sniffed the chicken on each platter and asked one of the pages standing by, "Do you know which one was served to the empress?"

"I think it was that one." The boy pointed.

Bronwyn looked at the disturbed chicken carcass on the wooden platter. The smells of rich chicken made her mouth water. It looked fine, if messy. She sniffed it but couldn't discern any strange smell.

"Well?" Hugh asked.

"I can't tell yet." Bronwyn looked over the chicken closely, searching for any suspicious toppings or herbs that might have been added. But there was nothing. The chicken on that platter and all the others looked perfectly fine. They all looked delicious. And it was odd. What were the chances that someone would have managed to poison exactly the right platter of chicken the empress would dine on?

It would have to be someone close to the empress, who either knew her and could add something to the chicken quickly, or a servant. But who? It seemed unlikely one of the ladies-in-waiting would have done such a thing; the risk would be too great and they would be found out immediately. That left one of the servants. Or one of the ladies who'd sat by the empress, such as Agatha herself.

Bronwyn had a thought. *What if...*

She popped a piece of chicken into her mouth, just a small piece, and nibbled it.

"Bronwyn, what are you doing?" Hugh asked, his eyes wide. "Don't be foolish, girl. It's not worth it."

The other cooks stared as she chewed and swallowed. "It tastes fine."

"You say that now, but you'll be sick in no time, just like Agatha was. Boys, get her a bucket to spew her guts in."

The servants looked askance at each other, none wanting to get too close.

"I'm fine," Bronwyn said. She waited.

"What possessed you to do such a thing?" Hugh asked.

"I'm testing an idea." She tapped her foot. Her stomach felt fine.

"Are you mad? You could die. You'll be sick."

Bronwyn helped herself to another piece. The cooks were watching her now. One of the cooks' mouths had dropped open.

Master Hugh's expression grew angry. "If this is your idea of a prank to try to get out of work, you've got another think coming." He took her arm and pulled her away.

Once they stood away from the cooks, he said in a hushed whisper, "Just what do you think you are doing? You're frightening the others. Why on earth would you eat poisoned meat?"

"Because it's not poisoned."

"How do you know?" he asked.

"I don't. But I think it's a ruse. It's a ploy to take revenge and scare the empress, to make her fear for her life."

He put a hand over his eyes. "Lord save me from courtly schemes. What if you're wrong?"

"Then you won't have to worry about me for very long," Bronwyn quipped.

"That's a horrible thing to say, girl."

"I know. Sorry." She looked him in the eye. "Watch me for the next few minutes. If I get sick, we'll know I was wrong."

"And if not?"

"Then I want to know why Agatha was lying."

They watched and waited. The minutes rolled by. The servants kept an eye on her, but when she didn't get sick or fall over, they started to return to their tasks, until just Hugh watched her. He gave her a cup of beer and sat on one of the two benches that stood beneath the long table where they ate their meals and prepared food.

"I don't understand," Hugh said. "Why would Agatha fake getting ill? Could she just have had a sour stomach? Something she ate or drank earlier?"

"It's possible," Bronwyn said. "But I think she meant to do this. As a trick."

"If that's the case, it's a nasty joke. God." He ran a hand through his thick, black curls. "The trouble that's caused. Do you realize that if the empress hadn't been feeling so benevolent, she might have blamed me, and all of us, for this? She could have us imprisoned or…" He turned a shade pale.

"I know. That's why I wanted to test the theory."

"You could have fed the chicken to a dog."

Bronwyn shook her head. "No. I like dogs. I wouldn't want to do that. What if it got sick?"

Hugh looked at her. "So you'd risk your life instead?" He snorted. "I don't know whether to send you packing or hug you."

Bronwyn helped herself to another bite. "Put me back to work, I say."

The servants helped themselves to the leftover meals of

chicken, and no one got ill, although one greedy servant did suffer indigestion from eating too much, too quickly. Word got around that the chicken was fine, and Agatha had been mistaken, but only amongst themselves. Although knowing how easy it was for rumors to spread in the castle, Bronwyn knew the truth wouldn't stay quiet for long.

After dinner, Bronwyn entered the main dining hall and sought out Lady Alice. Her friend sat with the other ladies-in-waiting, who gathered near the empress. Some people talked, and others listened to a minstrel playing the lute.

"Bronwyn," Lady Alice said, "have you found out what was wrong with the chicken? Was it poison?"

"No. We think it might have been improperly cooked by one of our novice cooks, not paying attention." Bronwyn turned to Agatha and lowered her eyes. "I'm terribly sorry you felt ill, Mistress Agatha."

There. If the taster saw her making apologies, she might believe everything was fine, for the moment.

Agatha put a hand to her throat. "Well, I won't say it wasn't frightening, but I suppose there was no harm done. I was very ill."

Bronwyn lowered her gaze. "I hope you are feeling better."

Agatha sniffed. "A little. Fetch me a cup of wine, girl."

Lady Alice shot her a dirty look as Bronwyn filled up a cup, handing it to her.

Agatha drank and wiped her mouth. "You're just lucky I didn't report the cooking staff. I know we are in a siege, but that's no reason to allow sloppy cooking. That chicken could have killed me."

Bronwyn made her apologies again and disappeared. As she left the hall, Lady Alice cornered her. "What are you up to?"

"The chicken was fine. It wasn't poorly cooked at all. She was lying. She made it all up."

Alice's eyes widened. "She did? But why?"

"I think you're right about her. Did Agatha have an argument with any of the ladies-in-waiting today?"

"No, but… She did. Well." Lady Alice looked across the room and leaned against the doorframe for a moment, surveying the people. "You know the empress is a native French speaker and demands all us ladies speak it or learn it. Agatha had bragged that she had studied the language for six years and had a French aunt and uncle. When the empress spoke to her in the language, however, she could only make out every third word and couldn't remember the word for oysters."

"'Oysters'?"

"Yes. *Huîtres*, in case you were wondering. Anyway, the empress laughed at her and hinted that she needed to study with the rest of us, as Agatha clearly didn't remember very much. The other ladies were amused and had a laugh at her expense. Agatha bore it well, but her face was as red as a strawberry. She was furious. Do you think she might have faked it to get back at the empress?"

"It would fit the sort of behavior you've told me about," Bronwyn said.

"What will you do now?"

"I'm not sure. I'll check on her later and see what I can find out."

The young women parted ways. Later that evening, before bed, Bronwyn crept up the circular staircases to the rooms of the ladies-in-waiting walked down the corridor. It was relatively quiet, but she smelled something. It smelled like… chicken.

She followed her nose to the door of one of the bedrooms and spotted a man going in. Bronwyn crept forward. The door was slightly ajar, and she stood a little ways outside it when she heard a familiar voice. It was male. "I thought I'd find you here."

"What do you want?" Agatha's voice carried.

"You. Your little show tonight might have convinced the empress, but it didn't fool me. You're lucky you weren't found out."

"What are you talking about?"

"Don't deny it. That chicken was fine. You just put on a show to make the empress feel afraid that someone was trying to kill her. I'm surprised it worked," the man said.

A sniff. "Get out."

"Not until we have a little chat, you and me." The male body leaned against the door, closing it.

The voices were muffled, but Bronwyn crept closer and listened, although it was hard to make out.

"You're going to do a little job for me," the male voice said. His weight shifted and the door opened ever so slightly. He mumbled something.

Bronwyn inched closer to the door.

Agatha laughed. "And if I don't?"

"Then I'll tell the empress you were faking. That you played a cruel trick on her. You'll find yourself out on the street. I'm sure the empress won't have a use for a taster who lies."

"She won't believe you," Agatha snapped.

"Won't she? The kitchen staff already don't trust you. They know you lied. That busybody Bronwyn is on your tail, and the empress actually trusts *her*. Imagine what Empress Maud will think when I tell her about your little joke."

A sigh. "What do you want?"

Bronwyn heard a noise nearby. She crept away, back down the stairwell, before she could be seen. So someone was blackmailing Agatha, but who?

Guards were marching down the stairs, so she shuffled aside and went down, back to the great hall, where she curled up to go to sleep.

Over the next few days, Bronwyn worked in the kitchens day and night. Over time, she had come to help and keep an eye on the potboys, scullery boys aged seven, eight, and nine who washed the plates and scoured pots until they were dry.

Bronwyn helped wherever needed, from grinding grain between stones to make flour to kneading dough until it was fine enough to shape into a grainy, rustic bread. She was learning how to season and poach fish, as well as how to preserve meat, and she spent hours at the large roasting spit, turning the joints, be it lamb, chicken, or beef.

But all was not well. Aside from the ever-present threat of the siege, something was amiss. Hugh, the head cook, came into the kitchen, shaking his head.

Bronwyn came up to him. "What's wrong?"

He frowned at her. "Not your business."

Bronwyn returned to her task, which at that point was turning the spit. She felt his eyes on her and worked quietly, conscious of the hot, sweaty work.

An hour later, a page entered the room. He came up to her. "Lady Alice wants you."

Hugh stood nearby and growled, "Who does she think she is? You can't just pull one of my cooks away whenever you feel like it."

The page reddened. "Sorry, Master Hugh, it's just… She said it was important and to fetch Bronwyn as soon as I could. It can't wait."

Hugh glared at Bronwyn, as if she were personally responsible for this interruption. "Go. See what she wants. But you come right back here, understand? No dallying."

Bronwyn nodded, handed over her task to another cook, and followed the page from the kitchen. He led her upstairs to one of the rooms, where Lady Alice looked up from her prayer book and berated the page for not knocking.

Once they were alone, she said, "Bronwyn, something is wrong." She closed her book. "Ever since Lady Morwenna fled, the empress has wanted more companions, but I think maybe one of the ladies has a beau or male friend or something. A lover, maybe. Like Lady Susanna used to speak of months back. She won't talk of it now, but I don't want to think what else it could be."

"Lady Alice, what are you talking about?" Bronwyn asked. "Master Hugh didn't like you calling me away from the kitchen.

You said it was important."

"And it is, dash it all. And I don't care about your Master Hugh; he'll find someone else to bake bread. Listen, since the siege began, Empress Maud has been on edge. You know about the little accidents that have occurred?"

"Yes. She asked me to look into them. I've seen the drawings," Bronwyn said.

Lady Alice nodded. "That's not even half of it, we think. Lady Susanna thinks there is a spirit."

Bronwyn smirked. "Yes, she mentioned that theory to me, too."

"I don't believe it, either, but two nights ago, Empress Maud returned to her room from dinner and screamed. A rotting apple had been left on her pillow. With a worm in it."

Bronwyn recoiled. "The kitchen would never—"

"I know that. But she didn't. The empress was horrified. And remember, we've only been here a short while. Who's to say one of the kitchen servants didn't decide to send her a little message? But the strange thing about all this is that there were two guards posted outside her room and no one entered or left before she came in, so how did the apple get there? I was there when Empress Maud spoke to the guards. No one had been there. And the apple didn't just appear."

Bronwyn tapped her chin in thought. This action was similar to the upturned chamber pot and the knife in the empress's bed. Both incidents had occurred in the empress's room, and someone was slipping in and out of the chamber without the guards noticing. That meant either a serious lapse in security, or someone had another way into the chamber. Some method that was not commonly known.

"But that's not all," Alice continued. "Last night, a scrap of parchment was slipped under her door, and it had a horrible drawing of a woman wearing a crown, dying in a fire. I know it was meant to be the empress."

"Did she see it?"

"No. We picked it up before she could see. But the guards didn't know anything about it. No one had gotten past them, so how did it appear?"

"What about the servants? The maids who clean her chamber?" Bronwyn asked.

"From what I understand, they have already been questioned. But they didn't know anything, either. They seemed scared. But I think they were more afraid of the empress's wrath than the idea that someone might be delivering horrid things into her chamber. One of the poor wretches actually got on her knees and begged the empress's forgiveness."

"But she didn't admit to the crime?"

"No. The poor girl knew nothing about it. Strange, isn't it?" Lady Alice said.

"Yes. What do you think happened?" Bronwyn asked.

"I don't know. It's why I'm talking to you. But it's not right. Someone is tormenting the empress, and it's disturbing her mood. When she greets us in the morning, she is tired, and I see dark circles under her eyes. And… she has asked us ladies to take turns sleeping in her room. On the floor." Lady Alice spoke with distaste. "Like a servant. I mean, I would do anything the empress asked of me, but…" She squared her shoulders. "The things I do for the crown."

"If it makes the empress feel safer, I would do it," Bronwyn said.

"I will. But it's not a question of doing it or not; we don't have a choice once Her Grace asks. I just wonder if something else will happen whilst I'm there." Lady Alice shivered and gave herself a little shake. "I cannot look weak or untrustworthy to the empress."

Bronwyn nodded. "The empress asked me to look into the matter too."

"Then you know at least some of this already. What else have you heard?" Lady Alice asked.

Bronwyn related what she knew, which wasn't much. She felt

a blush of embarrassment cross her cheeks. She hadn't been investigating, not properly. She was a cook and had lost sight of the empress's commands on her time, especially when there had been dishes to prepare and most of her spare thoughts had dwelled on Theobold and Rupert.

Lady Alice pouted. "What I don't understand is why has Her Grace asked *you* to help when you're just a kitchen maid? She could have asked me. I am one of her ladies. All she does is give you undue distinction. Why is that?"

Bronwyn cocked her head. She hadn't left the kitchen at Lady Alice's request just to be insulted. "I can think of a few reasons."

"Like what?"

"I'm smart." Bronwyn looked Alice in the eye and ticked the reasons off on her fingers. "I've solved these sorts of problems for her before. And she might have thought this was beneath you."

Lady Alice raised an eyebrow. "You're developing a honeyed tongue for flattery. You really are smart."

Bronwyn looked at her sometimes friend, sometimes enemy. Lady Alice seemed pleased, but the way she'd said it, it was clear her words weren't a compliment.

"There is also another reason," Bronwyn said. "She may think you are a suspect."

Lady Alice pouted at that, but Bronwyn turned and left before her friend could respond.

Bronwyn returned to the kitchens, only to be pulled aside by Hugh. "What did Lady Alice want?"

Bronwyn gave a little shrug. "Not much. Why?"

"These nobles, always ordering us around. We serve the empress, not them." He snorted and said quietly, "Some food is missing from the stores. One of the leftover chicken carcasses from last night has been stripped clean, and some of the bread is gone."

Bronwyn raised an eyebrow. The bones would still have been good to use to make stock for a broth, but for someone to have helped themselves to such little meat was a bit surprising.

Master Hugh was good in that in his kitchen, he made sure none of the servants went hungry. Full bellies meant content servants, and he was a firm believer in that. So for someone to steal food wasn't just alarming; it was unnecessary. But with the siege having gone on for weeks, the portions had grown smaller, as he was having to closely ration the food for the number of people in the castle.

"When did you first notice this?" Bronwyn asked.

"Don't know. At least a day or so ago. But now I wonder if it's been longer."

"What do you want to do?"

"Not sure. No one usually steals. There's no need to. And no one here goes hungry, but…" He gave her a dark look. "We have had more servants join us since the empress took the castle."

"But just because there are more mouths to feed doesn't mean someone would steal." She raised her chin. "Like you say, no one here goes hungry." Her forehead wrinkled in thought. "I have an idea."

That night, Bronwyn waited until the kitchen closed. She didn't take up her usual spot against the wall in the great hall and instead waited with Hugh and took up places in the corners of the kitchen storeroom. He hid in the shadows of the kitchen itself, whilst she hid by the food stores, where they kept the leftovers from that day.

The spaces were full of shadows. The delicious smells of cheese, bread, and preserved meat hung in the air. Torches that had burned throughout the day had mostly died to mere embers, and only darkness remained. Bronwyn curled up behind a barrel and a few sacks of grain and flour and prepared to wait, her back against a wall. But after a long day of work, in no time at all, she fell asleep.

Bronwyn opened her eyes with a start. Something had moved in the dark. Not a regular noise like the scurrying scuttle of mice as they ate. This was different. It was a rustling, a slight shift and movement of cloth, a quiet step. Was it a rat?

Fully awake now, Bronwyn waited, holding her breath. Her butt was sore from sitting so long and her knees and feet tingled. She wiggled her toes to get rid of the sensation. She could dimly hear Hugh's snores from the kitchen. *Looks like he's fallen asleep too*, she thought with a smile.

And then she spotted it. A lone, slight figure, quiet as a mouse, gliding across the floor. It barely made a sound.

The tall intruder wore a distinctive long habit or dress, her face and head hidden by a veil. The person drifted toward the stores and went straight for the cupboard. The smell of fermented yeast, grain, and beer hit Bronwyn's nose. Was it Peter? No. The lithe form was definitely feminine.

The woman opened the cupboard and began to help herself. She stiffened at a sudden noise, or lack of one. Hugh had stopped snoring. The woman paused, then reached for more food with a quick, frenetic motion.

Bronwyn watched silently until the woman had a loaf of day-old bread in her hands, tearing a piece of bread free and putting it in her mouth. Rising from her place against the wall, Bronwyn opened her mouth to speak, when Hugh's voice cut through the silence. "What do you think you are doing, girl?"

The intruder started, dropping the loaf. One of her hands drifted to her veil, and she uttered a sharp cry.

Bronwyn came forward. "It's all right."

Seeing her, the woman fretted and crossed herself.

Bronwyn held up her hands. "It's all right. We're not going to hurt you."

Bronwyn's eyes had adjusted to the darkness, and she could see from the woman's movements that she was middle-aged. The smell of oats, hops, and unwashed body was stronger now.

The tall woman looked from her to Hugh's large bulk like a deer caught in a trap. She glanced at Hugh blocking the exit, her gaze flicked down at the fallen bread, and she uttered a sob.

Hugh's mouth dropped open. "Bronwyn..."

Bronwyn picked up the bread loaf and handed it to the woman. "Here. Take it."

The woman snatched the bread from her hungrily and clasped it to her chest, eyeing them as if either might try to take it.

"What's your name?" Bronwyn asked.

The woman tore off another piece of bread and stuffed it in her mouth, chewing furiously. Her eyes were wide as she swallowed a large mouthful. Her voice was like a low alto. "Sister Rebecca. I'm a sister with St. Mary's here in Winchester." She held the bread tighter as if for comfort. "Our nunnery fell in the fighting. The men in Matilda's army… They came in and didn't care what they broke, what they destroyed. I've never seen such violence. They didn't respect the sanctity of the church, or the chastity of my fellow sisters. They did not care for our vows. We are… We *were* a holy faction and now…" Her hands shook.

"It's all right," Bronwyn said.

Sister Rebecca looked at Hugh warily. "I'm sorry. I was just so hungry. Sister Joan and I…"

"There are more of you? Where?"

"We were fifty, but now… Only Sister Joan and I escaped."

"How?" Bronwyn asked.

"I grew up around here, just a few streets away. I've known these roads and all the good hiding places since I was a child. I just never thought I'd have reason to use them." Sister Rebecca blinked away tears. "Please don't throw me out. I'm sorry I took the bread. I'll give it back. Just please, don't cast me out. Not outside." She held out the bread warily.

"Keep it," Hugh said.

"No one is throwing you out," Bronwyn told the nun.

Hugh looked at her as if to say, *That's not your decision to make,* then said aloud, "Bronwyn is right. It's not safe. But you shouldn't have been stealing. There's no need to go hungry. You and your sister would be welcome. The empress wouldn't turn you away."

"Oh, thank you. Thank you," Sister Rebecca babbled. "Please, what's to become of us? You promise you won't throw us out?"

Hugh shook his head. "I won't." His voice was gruff.

Bronwyn wondered if perhaps behind his grizzly exterior, he had a warm heart.

Sister Rebecca closed her eyes and exhaled. "Thank goodness. When I heard that man talking, I grew so afraid, I knew we had to keep hiding. It wasn't safe for us."

"What man?" Bronwyn asked.

Hugh scratched his head. "Never mind that now. Come to the kitchen, Sister, and we'll get you a bite to eat."

"Please, can I fetch my sister? She's still hiding."

"Yes. Where is she?" Hugh asked.

Holding the bread loaf tightly as if loath to let it go, Sister Rebecca led them out of the kitchen stores and through the corridors, down to…

Bronwyn sniffed. Based on the nun's subtle odor, she had a strong suspicion she knew where the nun would be leading them.

"The brewery? You're hiding here?" Hugh asked.

"Yes. There is a back door that leads down the hill. It's hidden, but if you know it's there, you can get into the brewery from outside."

Bronwyn's eyebrows rose. A way in and out of the castle. That was valuable information.

The nun led them into the brewery, which was dark and full of shadows and sleeping forms. The air was filled with the even snores and subtle breaths of servants sleeping, tinged with the scent of sweat, the odor of unwashed bodies, and the heady smell of oats, hops, and beer.

Sister Rebecca moved silently through the shadows, drifting amongst the darkness as if she knew it well. After a few minutes, she walked around the rows of tiered casks and whispered, "Sister Joan."

Silence.

Sister Rebecca whispered, "Come out, Sister, it's all right. We're safe."

Sister Rebecca called again, when a small head with a pale

face and big, round eyes popped up behind a cask, giving Bronwyn a start.

"Heavens, girl. You'll make my heart stop. Warn a man before you jump out like that," Hugh said.

Bronwyn straightened and held up a finger to her lips for quiet. "Sister Joan, yes?"

"Yes," came the hushed reply. The young woman, maybe about twenty years of age, slipped out of the shadows to face them. Her very movements were tired and her eyes darted back and forth between Hugh and Bronwyn, as if they might attack.

"Are you hungry? We have food," Bronwyn said.

Sister Joan nodded and followed them and Sister Rebecca to the kitchen. Hugh stood by, fetching them more bread and drink, whilst Bronwyn sat with the women at the long table where the servants normally ate.

The nuns sat close together, as if afraid to be separated. Sister Joan tore into the bread loaf from Sister Rebecca, eating quickly, stuffing her cheeks. The women washed down huge mouthfuls with swallows of beer and one of the sisters coughed.

"Take your time. There's no hurry," Hugh said.

Bronwyn watched as the sisters ate and took in the sight of them. Sister Rebecca was tall, rail-thin, with fair, wispy, blonde hair that peeked out from beneath her veil. The beer put a bit of color back in her cheeks. She was aged perhaps in her late forties, but Bronwyn couldn't be sure.

Sister Joan was younger, short and petite, with stringy, brown hair and wide eyes that darted around, looking at everything. She ate furiously, as if afraid her current bite would be her last.

"When did you two come here?" Bronwyn asked.

"About a week ago. We fled when the army attacked and hid with some Good Samaritans, until we had to leave. It wasn't safe. Sister Rebecca knew the way and we hid in the brewery."

Hugh crossed his burly arms over his broad chest. "I think that's when I first noticed the food going missing. A few days ago, I'd been looking for some spare capons to make for dinner and could have sworn there were more of them. Now I know why."

So that's one crime solved, Bronwyn thought.

"We're sorry," Sister Joan said. "We had nowhere else to go and didn't have anyone we could trust."

"You're safe now," Hugh said.

Bronwyn sat with the young women quietly as Hugh rustled up some extra blankets from nearby. He stepped out of the brewery only briefly and returned with his arms full. He said, "Bronwyn, have them bed down with you. They'll be safe in the main hall for the night. We'll sort out the rest in the morning." He let out a massive yawn and put the blankets in their hands.

Bronwyn led the nuns to the main hall and stepped around the sleeping forms of the other servants. She made sure the women were safe and comfortable near her, backs against the wall, and whispered to Sister Rebecca, "You said there was a man you overheard. Where? What did he say?"

The nun paused. She looked around and said quietly, her voice so soft that Bronwyn strained to hear it. "In the brewery, from my hiding place, I heard him and another man talking. One said to *keep up the writs*? The drawings. And to write him more."

Bronwyn looked at her. "Go on."

"The other man seemed unhappy about it all. He refused, and the first man said that if he didn't do what he wanted, he'd tell the empress what he'd done and he'd lose his position. The man told him off. He used some very... un-Christian language."

Bronwyn thanked her and let the woman go to sleep. The nun soon was sleeping soundly.

But Bronwyn lay awake for some time, blinking in the darkness. Whom had the nun heard talking? First Agatha Carre was being blackmailed into doing something, and now a man was behind the scribbled drawings of the empress. The question was: who was behind it all?

Chapter Six

T HE NEXT DAY, Bronwyn rose to the sound of thundering rain, but then it stopped. She rose silently, throwing off the small, thin blanket she wore, getting used to the chill of the floor and the rushes on it, and sat up. The noise started again, a thundering patter against the walls.

She went to the courtyard entrance and gazed at the morning sky. The sun had barely risen and the sky was a dusky-blue hue of early twilight, fading into whitish grey. But it wasn't raining. Then she realized: the sound. It wasn't rain. It was rocks.

The invading army had decided to wake the entire household with a barrage of stones. She fled back inside, hiding as great shadows of rocks and stones struck the castle walls. There were a few worried faces, but being inside the safety of the castle, people soon got used to the noise and went about their errands. Following the example of other older servants, Bronwyn left the nuns in the capable hands of Hugh and went about her chores. The young women were introduced to the other servants and soon word spread about the young nuns in the castle. But as Bronwyn rolled out bread dough for the day's bread, she wondered, *Who was the man the sister had overheard?*

After an hour, she was summoned to the empress's solar. Escorted by a page and looked at closely by a pair of unfriendly guards manning the entrance to the chamber, she knocked and was admitted.

The empress sat at a small table in a round chair covered with furs. Her hair was long and she wore a simple circlet, as well as a dark-burgundy dress. She set down a cup of wine and said, "Ah, Mistress Blakenhale. Come here. You can leave now," she told the page and the guards. "I'll call if I need you."

Once they were alone, Bronwyn curtsied and approached the empress. "Good morrow, Empress."

"Good morrow. Or is it? I've just received word that all our messenger pigeons have been killed. We'll no doubt use them for food, but this is intolerable. Those were highly trained birds. Now we can't easily deliver messages to our allies." She frowned. "And if that's not enough, in the past day, my best pillow has gone missing, and someone tries to poison my dinner. It appears to me we have another poisoner in our midst. What have you to report?"

Bronwyn weighed her thoughts carefully. "I have my suspicions, Empress."

"Tell me," Empress Maud commanded. She leaned forward in her chair.

"But I have no proof. Only hearsay."

"I cannot hold someone accountable on hearsay. Why have you no proof?"

"I need to catch them in the act."

"Who is it you suspect?" the empress asked. She gripped the sides of her wooden chair.

"I—" Bronwyn started.

There was a noise. A rustle of cloth, a creak of a chair. Lady Alice leaned forward and said, "Oh, I dropped my needle. Pardon me. Do go on, Bronwyn. Just ignore me."

Her voice was carefree and light, but there was no mistaking Lady Alice's warning look. Beside her, chairs facing away from Bronwyn so she hadn't at first noticed them, sat Lady Susanna and Agatha. They all sat doing needlework but were as quiet as church mice, and no doubt listening to every word.

"I'd rather not say, Empress, until I know for sure," Bronwyn said.

"Very well. But be quick about it. I can't have another ruined meal like yesterday. Go." She waved Bronwyn away.

"Yes, Empress." Bronwyn curtsied and left. As she walked out and down the corridor, she was sure, more and more, of Agatha's guilt. But how to prove it?

Bronwyn worked in the kitchens that day. Even though the September sun was shining, the constant pelt of rocks and stones hit the roof and castle walls, and it wasn't safe to go out. All it took was one servant to be hit by a stray stone crossing the courtyard and that was enough. The castle steward decided it was too unsafe. They were in a siege, after all. No one was to go outside, not unless they were a fighter.

Upon orders from the fighters, Bronwyn helped mix up a vat of bubbling pitch, black liquid filth that stank to high heaven, which Hugh promptly refused to allow in the kitchen. She wasn't sorry to see it go. She baked bread, went to the pantry, and surveyed its contents. With the chicken being perfectly fine, the cooks had torn the carcasses to shreds and used it in pies, so the nobility would be less likely to notice where the meat had come from. Not that any nobleperson had outwardly said they would refuse to eat chicken after the little mishap with Mistress Agatha, but Bronwyn could well understand if anyone was hesitant. It would still taste good but would be masked by adding some beer and vegetables, like the thin, reedy purple carrots, onions, and leeks that grew from the castle garden.

The garden itself was large, but the stones from the attackers had already destroyed part of it. Bronwyn wondered idly how Theobold and Rupert were doing in their separate camps, and how dangerous it would be to send them messages or to slip out via the secret passage from the brewery. She was sure she could convince the nuns to show her. It was also somewhat of a safety risk. If they knew about it, what was to prevent other people from using it and the attackers getting into the castle?

She went to Hugh to tell him, when she bumped into Lady Susanna. "Oh, I'm sorry."

Lady Susanna wiped her eyes, streaking ink on her face. "Oh, no, it's my fault. I wasn't looking where I was going..." She paused, her face turning red.

"Lady Susanna?" Bronwyn cocked her head. "Are you all right?"

Lady Susanna's chin wobbled, and she nodded, her lips pressed tight. "I'm fine," she squeaked.

"Are you sure? You've got ink on your cheek." Bronwyn looked at her.

"Oh." Lady Susanna wiped her cheek, smearing more ink.

"No, the other one. Now they're both... Here. Let me." Bronwyn took part of her apron and wiped Lady Susanna's cheeks. The ink wasn't coming off so easily. "Here. Let's go to the kitchen and—"

"Oh, no, I couldn't go there. That's for kitchen servants. I'm not a servant. I'm a lady." Lady Susanna sniffed.

"I know. But you've got ink all over your face. No one will care if you use a bit of water to clean your face."

"Couldn't you bring me some?" Lady Susanna asked.

"Yes. Where shall I bring it? Where's your room?"

"Oh. Actually, never mind. I'll go with you." Lady Susanna made as if to follow Bronwyn, who led the lady-in-waiting down to the kitchen, where she bid her to take a seat at the wooden bench and brought over some water. Bronwyn dipped a rag in it and wet it, then handed it to Lady Susanna, who accepted it tearfully.

"What's wrong?" Bronwyn asked.

"You. You're just... No one has asked me how I am for a long time. And you apologizing for bumping into me, when I ran into you. It's the first polite word I've had all day." Lady Susanna's chin gave a treacherous tremble.

Bronwyn gave her a thoughtful look. She didn't trust Lady Susanna, but she also hadn't heard anything about the young woman's lover. Could it be that the romance had ended and Lady Susanna was a bit fragile as a result? "Why?"

"I... You see... The other ladies-in-waiting feel I'm letting them down. Agatha told me so. The empress expects the best from us. When she is with us, she means to have the best conversation, the best laughter, the jokes, the witty remarks, and for us to look beautiful at all times and better than the maidservants."

"That sounds like a lot to put on you," Bronwyn said.

"It is. And I... like to read. I thought I knew French well, especially what with Lady Alice's instruction and lessons, but... I forgot a lot of it. I don't think I know French very well at all anymore, and the others point this out all the time. Lady Alice tries to help me sometimes by practicing, but... I'm hopeless. I don't understand it and I'm terrible with languages. I was practicing writing when I got ink on me and then Mistress Agatha said I looked like a fool with all that ink on my face and laughed and I just had to leave. I'm sorry. I'll go."

"No, wait. Where are you going?" Bronwyn asked.

"I don't know," Lady Susanna admitted. "But I can't stay here. I'm in the way. I'm always in the way." She looked over at a servant who was rolling out dough near a large dish for another pie and licked her lips. "That smells delicious," Lady Susanna told the servant.

The man glanced at her and stared at her ink-splattered face, then winked.

Lady Susanna had missed the wink and raised the damp rag to wipe her cheeks. "You see? I'm of no use to anyone. I'm hopeless."

"I don't think you're hopeless." A hopeless woman wouldn't have the courage and daring to lock two squires in a room overnight, on the evening of a royal coronation. That spoke of deviousness, deception, and planning.

"What do you know? You're just a servant," Lady Susanna said. "I'm sorry. I didn't mean that. That was rude. It's just what the ladies would want me to say, and it popped into my head. They constantly tell me I have to be harder, and not so weepy or naive. When I left to wash my face, I overheard Mistress Agatha say, 'She's probably gone off to cry in a corner now.'" Her face reddened.

Bronwyn stiffened. The woman's rudeness had surprised her. Was this Lady Susanna's true nature showing itself? Was she actually a mean person inside, and her so-called politeness and sweet demeanor were just a mask?

Bronwyn took the rag from her and wiped Lady Susanna's cheeks clean. "There you go." She lowered the rag. "I don't think you're hopeless at all. I think learning French is hard."

"You think so? I only studied it for a few years, but I feel like such a novice. And then when the other ladies test me, the words go out of my head, and I can't remember anything."

"I think it's their way of teasing you, to put you on the spot. They don't sound very nice."

"Well, Lady Alice is all right, sometimes. When she's not going on about Rupert this, and Rupert that. He's her fellow."

Bronwyn nodded, feeling a lump in her throat. She thought about him at least once a day. She thought ruefully about Lady Susanna's past actions toward Rupert and reminded herself to be wary. What if the noblewoman was threatening the empress now? Perhaps it would be good to stay near. "I had a thought. What if you taught me French?" Bronwyn said.

"What?" Lady Susanna looked at her.

"Well, it's just that the empress occasionally wants me to say French words, and I have trouble understanding her accent at times. So, it would be useful to me to learn how to say a few things and to know what they mean." And it would help her observe the noblewoman more closely.

Bronwyn was talking to the table at that point, her eyes glued to the hard wooden surface. She expected a swift rebuke. But there was only silence. Her eyes flicked up to Lady Susanna's face.

"I'd love to." Lady Susanna clapped her hands together. "It's a wonderful idea."

"You think so?"

"Mm-hmm." Lady Susanna nodded.

"Oh, good. I mean, I don't have hours to spend learning, but I could learn a few words here and there, when I'm not working."

"Yes. We can do that. And I can test you." Lady Susanna's eyes lit up. "I mean, we can practice together. I'm not fluent by any means, but the empress is always telling us to get fresh air and take a brisk walk to strengthen our bodies. We could walk together and talk then."

"That would be nice," Bronwyn agreed.

The young women shook hands and Lady Susanna smiled, her shy demeanor and dimples practically lighting up the room. The first phrase she taught Bronwyn was '*à bientôt,*' or a friendly 'see you later.'

Bronwyn went back to her duties, a slight smile on her face. She liked learning new things. But now she also had a reason to be near Lady Susanna.

And maybe by learning French, she would become more useful. She could only see the benefit in learning a new language. No doubt Lady Alice would have something to say about it, but maybe Bronwyn and Lady Susanna didn't need to tell anyone. Perhaps it might remain secret for a while. Perhaps. A part of her liked having a secret, even though it wasn't really a secret at all, and it was completely harmless.

Just thinking about the phrase '*à bientôt*' and repeating it in her mind made her think of the nun overhearing the whispered conversation. Who would have access to the empress's room and reason to want to ruin the bed in the first place? Who had the empress hurt or made an enemy of? There were three ladies-in-waiting she knew of. Lady Susanna, Lady Alice, and Mistress Agatha, who in her mind, didn't really count. Lady Susanna was easily the sweet and innocent one of the bunch despite being highly suspicious, and Lady Alice she knew well as a trusted confidante. She also knew that Lady Alice relied on the empress's goodwill to advance and wanted to prove herself. Would she do something to damage that? No. Lady Alice would rather eat poisoned meat than ruin her relationship with Empress Maud. Lady Susanna, she didn't trust, but Agatha was even more suspicious.

But speak of the devil, Agatha walked into the kitchen like she owned the space, her hands on her hips. A silver curl peeked out from beneath her veil, and she said, "I want to inspect the food for tonight's dinner. I don't want any more surprises like a few nights ago." Her voice carried in the space.

Hugh came up to her. He opened his mouth wide to blast her, when Bronwyn said, "Apologies, Mistress Agatha. That won't happen again. I trust you are feeling better?"

Hugh shut his mouth and looked at her. A big, bushy eyebrow rose as if to say, *What are you up to?*

Agatha nodded and sniffed. "Yes. I am on the mend. But I spent hours in the privy that night and then with my chamber pot. It was not my choice way to spend an evening, I tell you."

Bronwyn bit her lip to keep from laughing. They knew she'd lied, but details of her outgoings made her want to smile. As it was, a few snickers and amused looks caught their attention. Agatha's face turned pink. "What are you preparing for tonight's dinner? I cannot have anything too spicy, or it will hurt my stomach."

Bronwyn nodded. "A warm broth, perhaps, for you."

"No, that won't do. I can't have any special treatment. It is kind of you to suggest, I suppose, but my concern is for the empress. I must have what she is having. I have to taste a bite of each of her dishes before she does to ensure her safety. It is a hard life, and as you saw, dangerous at times. But that is my calling."

Bronwyn turned away to hide her smile. *A hard life, indeed.*

The taster decided to come back later, once the empress's dishes were prepared and ready for serving.

THE AIR OUTSIDE whistled from arrows arcing through the air, like angry screeches. Bronwyn stayed clear of the windows, but she needed not worry, as each available space was taken up by archers at their posts. The parapets were covered with men crouched down, hiding and shooting arrows down at the attackers who were camped below. Winchester Castle stood perched upon a raised grassy knoll that stood easily more than thirty feet high.

It offered some of the best views in Winchester, for one could see for miles around, but it also made attacking the castle very difficult. Archers manned every post, and the grassy knoll was incredibly steep. Even if one were to scale it, one wrong step and a person could lose their footing and tumble down to the rocky ground below. They would be lucky not to break bones, and that was the least of it.

Bronwyn swallowed a mouthful of ale as she sat down to luncheon with the other servants. The nuns joined them, their faces gaunt, and after some grumbling, the other servants made space for them.

Sister Joan, the younger of the two, sidled in next to Bronwyn and shared her stale bread trencher. Dollops of potage were dropped onto their trencher, and fresh bread was passed around once everyone had taken a turn to wash their hands. Sister Joan tore off a hunk and helped herself, using the bread and a wooden spoon to mop up the hot, steaming potage. She ate like she hadn't eaten in weeks and hunched over the trencher, spooning the hot food into her mouth.

Bronwyn sat back and watched, giving her some space. She drank more of her ale and made eye contact with the other servants, who were openly watching Sister Joan.

Hugh said, "Slow down, girl. You'll choke if you're not careful."

Sister Joan turned pink and sat back. She opened her mouth and belched, making the others laugh. "Sorry. I've just been so hungry."

"Decorum, Sister," Sister Rebecca said, eating sedately from her trencher with her spoon.

Sister Joan shot Bronwyn a small smile and rolled her eyes. Bronwyn grinned, and using a bit of bread, used it to scoop some of the potage into her mouth. It was hot and filling and it burned her tongue.

"What will you do now, Sister?" Hugh asked.

The other servants watched as Sister Rebecca laid down her spoon beside the trencher she shared with another servant. "I do not know. The empress has been most gracious in allowing us to stay. I think we may provide spiritual guidance to those who need it. And we will stay close to the church and spend our days in prayer."

Sister Joan squirmed on the wooden bench beside Bronwyn. "And we will help wherever we are needed, too. In the kitchens, cleaning, anywhere." Sister Joan shot her fellow nun a look. "It is the charitable thing to do and a good and proper way to earn our keep."

"Yes. Quite." Sister Rebecca raised the spoon to her lips and blew on the steaming-hot potage. She swallowed some. "This is very… nutritious."

"It's wonderful. We were hiding for days and stealing bread to survive," Sister Joan said, helping herself to a cup of ale. She swallowed the cupful and burped again, earning a few smiles from the servants.

"Sister," Sister Rebecca started, frowning. Her eyebrows furrowed in disapproval. "Show some manners. Just because we are out of the nunnery does not mean we act like heathens."

"Sorry."

Sister Rebecca sniffed.

After the midday meal, Bronwyn took the nuns to a spare room that was often used for bathing and helped them heat up water to wash in. The large, round, wooden circular tub looked inviting, and she left the women to it. She was just closing the door when Sister Rebecca said, "Bronwyn, stay a moment."

Bronwyn turned around.

"Are we safe here? Everyone has been kind, but I cannot

ignore the imposition and strain we have added to the castle's people. You are under siege and cannot want more mouths to feed."

"It's not my decision, Sister. But I think if the empress has welcomed you, then she is true to her word."

"What do you do here?" Sister Rebecca asked. "You seem more than an average servant."

"You have a kind soul," Sister Joan said, pulling the veil off of her head to reveal a head of disheveled, brown hair. "I know we are safe."

"It's never wrong to be too careful," Sister Rebecca said. "You may leave us."

Bronwyn closed the door behind her. Sister Rebecca struck her as a bit formal, but she was civil enough, though with stiffer manners. She liked Sister Joan more, but the young woman seemed a touch wilder and more reckless.

After the evening meal, when the servants were cleaning up, washing pots, wiping down wooden trenchers, and serving platters, Bronwyn saw a few cooks talking together. One looked confused, another angry. A few darted little suspicious looks around.

Bronwyn wiped her hands on her apron and wandered over. "What's wrong?"

One of the cooks, an older man with strong features, a sloping chin, and dark hair that fell into his eyes, said, "Come quick. There's been a spot of bother out by the sheep's herd."

Bronwyn cocked her head and raised an eyebrow. "What is it?"

"Come." The cook beckoned, and Bronwyn followed him out, with a few others. Once outside, she could hear Hugh's bellowing voice from a fair distance away, and it soon quieted to angry mutters.

"Did something happen?" Bronwyn asked. She wondered, *What's wrong with the sheep herd?*

The cook didn't answer.

She took a path around the castle, to behind the stables, where a shepherd stood off to the side of a group of men. Bronwyn recognized the group as guards and cooks. She approached the shepherd first.

"Hullo," Bronwyn said.

The shepherd, a young man with short-cropped, blond hair and tanned skin, nodded to her. He leaned on a shepherd's crook and watched the herd mournfully.

Not very talkative, Bronwyn thought. She stepped around the group and shouldered her way in to see the mess. Hugh stood with a number of the cooks, guards, and men-at-arms.

She asked one of the cooks, "What happened?"

The cook pointed. Then she saw it. The carcass of a sheep, slaughtered. Blood was everywhere. But strangely enough, the head was missing. It was a bloody stump of gore, bone, and gristle. Bronwyn repressed a shudder and felt queasy. "Who would do such a thing?"

The cook cursed and shrugged.

She looked over and the shepherd, a towheaded young man perhaps a few years older than her, stood off to the side, leaning on his shepherd's crook. His young face was drawn and unhappy, and he said not a word to anyone.

Bronwyn approached him. "Are you all right?"

His eyes flicked to her. He gave a slight shake of his head.

"Can you tell me what happened?" she asked.

"What does it matter? A sheep is dead." He breathed in and out through his nose.

She swallowed and nodded. "Where were you when it happened?"

He glared at her. "Asleep. It's not safe to sleep outdoors." His gaze flicked to the tall, stone walls. "But now I'm not leaving. That's the last time I sleep away from the sheep. I knew when Spot started barking that something was wrong, but I didn't pay attention. And now one of them's dead." His shoulders slumped. "I should've listened to her."

"Who?"

"The dog, Spot. She knew something was wrong." He watched a small terrier circle around the sheep herd, barking.

"When was this?"

"Middle of the night. She just started barking and I took her outside so she could piss, and that's when she ran off toward the herd and I found her. Like that."

The ground was trampled over many times by sheep, the blood having stained their hooves and the bottom of their shaggy coats. Bronwyn felt slightly disgusted, knowing that the dead animal's fellow sheep had trampled on the scene. But that was animals, she realized. She ignored the group of men standing around talking and walked around the scene, examining the ground. The area was dirty, as one might expect, and the space was covered in bloody hoofprints and men's footprints. She peered at the ground when a male voice said, "What are you doing?"

She turned. It was Tristan.

"Looking for anything that might show who did this."

He laughed. "You're a strange one. You think you're going to find anything like that in the mud?"

She shrugged and felt her face warm. She didn't like being laughed at. "Maybe."

"Good luck. The whole area is covered with blood and dirt. Next, you'll be thinking one of the other sheep did it." He grinned.

She bit her lip. "I'm not thinking that. But…"

"What?"

"Well… Whoever did it didn't know what they were doing. It's messy." She peered at the neck of the butchered sheep. "Whoever did this didn't use a cleaver, or one of the big blades we have in the kitchen."

A few of the cooks were listening now. "How do you know that?" one asked.

Bronwyn stepped closer to the animal carcass and pointed at

the bloody stump of the neck. "Look at it. I don't know much about butchery, but that looks messy to me."

One of the cooks stepped over and inspected it. "She's right. Hugh, come take a look at this."

The men gathered around and looked down at the carcass. "You're right. Whoever did this isn't one of us."

Tristan said, "I'm playing the devil's advocate here, but how do you know that? How many of you know how to butcher a sheep?"

The men looked at him as a group. Their expressions were unfriendly. One growled, "We know our craft, lad."

Tristan backtracked. "I'm saying there's a skill to it, right? Not just anyone could do that. So why couldn't it be one of you?"

Bronwyn's eyes widened a fraction. Tristan was digging himself into a hole here, metaphorically speaking.

Some of the cooks looked confused and one scratched his head, another his beard.

"So wait, are you calling us unskilled?" one cook said.

"Or do you think we could've done it?" another asked.

Tristan held up his hands. "Neither. I just mean—"

"Why don't you go back to your business, lad, and leave this to us. Unless you have butchery skills we don't know about?" Hugh asked.

Tristan turned pink. "No, I just was saying that—"

"We've heard enough of your talk. Clear off." One cook jerked his thumb away.

Tristan stepped back. "All right, all right. I was just saying—"

"We know what you were saying," Hugh said. "Go on, lad."

"My name is Tristan Langforde. I'm the squire to Sir Miles Fitzwalter."

"Aye and when we want Sir Miles's opinion on a dead sheep, we'll know just who to ask," Hugh said, earning a few smiles from the cooks.

"Where is Sir Miles now?" Bronwyn asked.

"Here of course. He's helping the empress. She needs all the help she can get."

A few of the cooks exchanged looks at this. Bronwyn noted that Tristan seemed completely unaware.

"That's the empress you're talking about, son," Hugh said.

"Yes, well. My master is an important man. I'm looking after his affairs whilst he's busy sorting this siege." Tristan puffed his chest up slightly.

"Then mind you go back to your own business," Hugh said. "We'll handle this."

Tristan gave a loud sniff and walked away, swinging his arms with purpose. A few of the cooks snickered as he went, but Bronwyn was more interested in the scene.

Hugh approached her. "I've had about enough of him. What are you thinking, girl?"

Bronwyn tugged her blonde braid. "I think whoever did this doesn't work in the kitchen."

The men looked pleased to hear that. "Why is that?"

"Because the cuts around the neck are so messy. Butchery is a skill. Even in the dark, a man with butchery skills would fall into the practice he'd learned; he wouldn't make a hash of it. I think even if he were trying to make it look like someone else had done it, it would still show some of those skills here."

The cooks murmured their agreement and hauled the carcass away to the kitchen. The shepherd shooed his dog away, returning to the sheep. A few of the cooks gave Bronwyn approving looks and nods and one clapped her on the shoulder.

Bronwyn waited till they had left, then said to Hugh, "Let's assume that it wasn't one of the cooks who did it. This crime didn't happen too long ago. Wouldn't the culprit be covered in blood and smell?"

"Yes. They would," Hugh said.

"So then we need to find the dirty clothes, and whoever smells strongly like, well… blood."

"Ah, but that's easily worked around. They could've chucked the head away and then taken a bath."

"So let's check and see who bathed in the last few hours. And see if there's a trail. A blood trail, for when they carried the head away. It would have leaked."

"Saints alive, Bronwyn. Your mind is enough to make a man ill," Hugh said. "I don't think I'll be able to sleep tonight after all this talk."

"Sorry." She gave him a small smile. "Do you see any trails of blood on the ground?"

"No."

Together, they looked but saw nothing. "He must've hidden it well," Hugh said. "I can search the kitchen and look at the servants, but they'll likely be innocent. Unless someone's trying to pull a nasty trick on us. But we're in the middle of a siege. This isn't the time for pranks. And this is a pretty gruesome one, if you ask me."

Bronwyn agreed and looked around at the cooks, the servants, but found nothing. And the guards weren't keeping track of who bathed, so as there were hundreds of people in the castle, it could have been anyone. Feeling glum, Bronwyn went back to her chores. The cooks and she spent the next few hours butchering the carcass, preserving what parts they could, and serving the rest for the nobles' dinner. Everything went to use, even the hooves, which were boiled down to make soup and a jelly.

But that night, she was settling into her pallet and pulling a blanket over her head, wondering how Theobold was doing over in Wolvesey Castle when a scream rent the air.

Her mind woke up. Had she really heard it? It was late at night. She could have dreamed it. But what if she hadn't? She yawned beneath her warm blanket when a voice whispered, "Bronwyn." A woman's hand touched her arm.

Bronwyn's eyes flew open.

"It's me, Alice."

"What is it?"

"There's been some trouble in the empress's chamber," she whispered. "The guards are there. She needs you. Come on." She shivered. "Lord, it's cold down here. Why is there no fire?"

"We're conserving wood."

"Oh." Lady Alice motioned for her to follow.

Bronwyn rose quickly and walked after Lady Alice through the dark corridors. Small candles in tall iron candelabras lit the way, and their small flames wavered as they passed. She drifted upstairs, past the sleeping forms of archers and men-at-arms, following Lady Alice up the circular staircase and down the corridors, to the empress's chamber.

The guards at first glared at Bronwyn, then Lady Alice motioned them aside with a hand. "Move aside. Let us through."

The guards parted ways and opened the door. Lady Alice led the way inside.

Bronwyn went inside. The empress stood there, huddled in a thick, fur-trimmed robe, holding her arms to her body. Candles burned brightly and a small fire had burned out in a small hearth, largely down to its embers. It gave off an inviting warm glow. But the warm feelings of the room disappeared as she laid eyes on the empress again.

Empress Maud's face was pinched and pale, her eyes haunted. Lady Susanna and Agatha stood not far away, watching.

"Ah. Bronwyn, good, you're here," the empress said.

"What is it? I heard there was a commotion." Tristan entered the room, followed by the guards. "What happened here?" His voice was hard.

"L-Look. There." The empress pointed.

Bronwyn crossed the room to see. The bed looked harmless enough. But then, sitting on the bed beside the empress's pillow, was the missing sheep's head.

"Is that...?" she started.

"A sheep's head. Looks like we found it." Tristan picked it up and turned around, the head in his hands.

Lady Susanna fainted dead away.

Chapter Seven

B RONWYN TOOK A step back. The sheep's head had been found, and it was gory. The pink tongue stuck out of its mouth and the blank eyes stared at her. She shivered and felt sick, then spared a thought for Lady Susanna.

Tristan cursed. Lady Alice dashed to Lady Susanna's side, fanning her with a hand.

Bronwyn stiffened. "How did it get there?"

"Someone put it there, obviously. How else does a snake get into someone's bed?" Empress Maud said. "Get it out of here. Now."

The squire made to leave, when Bronwyn stepped in his path. "Wait," Bronwyn said. "Let me see it."

"It's a sheep's head. You want it for your dinner?" Tristan joked.

"This is not the time for jokes, Tristan," Lady Alice said.

He shot her a leering smile and straightened when he caught the empress's eye. "I agree. Why would you want to see it, Bronwyn? It's obvious. Someone left it here to frighten her."

"I want it gone," Empress Maud said. "Tristan, dispose of that thing."

Bronwyn said, "Empress, could you tell me what happened?"

The empress sat back in a chair and pulled her robe tighter around her. In the shadowy candlelight, she looked older, her features drawn. Her hair was long and hung in great waves down her back. She shivered and said, "I was asleep in bed when I shifted and felt something in the bed with me. I felt something wet on my hands—and sticky. A fly hit my face, and I woke up and saw it and screamed."

"We all did," Lady Alice admitted.

Bronwyn noticed the blood on the empress's hands. "You touched it?"

"Yes. I thought maybe I was having a dream, but then when I saw what it was…" Empress Maud shook her head. She looked at her hands dazedly, as if seeing them from far away. "I should wash these. Does someone have a basin?"

Lady Alice rose to her feet and ordered a quick instruction to the guards outside to fetch a basin of water. One of the guards left without a word.

"I am sorry for that, Empress." Bronwyn paused. "How did none of you see it before? Was it in the bed before you all went to sleep?"

"No. It wasn't," Lady Alice said. "That's the strange thing. Everything was fine."

"I did smell something odd," Lady Susanna said from the floor. She slowly sat up.

"You did? Why didn't you say anything?" Lady Alice asked.

"I thought it was nothing. And I didn't see why none of you could smell it, either, so I kept quiet. I thought maybe one of you had left food in here or something."

"You should have spoken up," Agatha said. "We would never leave food on the floor. It brings flies."

Bronwyn's eyebrows knit together. No one had mentioned the floor before this. As she peered at the floor, little white, wriggling lumps inched across the floor from the bed. She stepped back. Maggots. The decomposing sheep's head had attracted flies and maggots. It made her recoil. She looked carefully at the ladies-in-waiting. "When did you first notice the funny smell, Lady Susanna?"

"I don't know. Maybe this evening, as we were getting ready

to decide who would sleep in the empress's room."

"And who slept here tonight?"

"Mistress Agatha. We take turns," Lady Susanna said.

"Were any of you out of the room this evening?"

"Yes." Lady Susanna said as she and Lady Alice exchanged looks. "We all were. We go where the empress bids us."

"What are you trying to achieve with these questions, Bronwyn?" the empress asked.

"A timeline. We found a slaughtered sheep on the grounds earlier this morning but without its head."

The empress paled. Agatha looked as if she were going to be ill. Even Lady Alice looked away and fanned herself.

"We thought perhaps it was a prank. And we couldn't find the head," Bronwyn said.

"Until now," Tristan said sourly. "Can I get rid of this already?"

"Go." The empress waved him away.

The head was crawling with flies and maggots. The smell and wriggling larvae were enough to make Bronwyn retch.

"Why did no one report the slaughtered sheep to me?" Empress Maud asked.

"I suspect the men thought it was beneath your notice, Empress. The men thought it was a nasty prank."

Empress Maud sniffed. "Quite right. But still. For the head to go missing…" She shuddered. "It doesn't bear thinking about. And these little accidents keep happening. First the notes, and that filthy chamber pot, and now this."

"Not to mention the attempted poisoning on your life, Your Grace," Agatha added.

Bronwyn couldn't help but give the taster a hard look. She wanted to challenge her but held her tongue.

"Yes, I cannot forget that. Truly." Empress Maud nodded. "Very well. Figure this business out, Bronwyn, and fast. I want no more of this nonsense taking place under my roof. We are at war. Just because we are at siege outside the castle does not mean I should be facing trouble within the walls as well."

"Yes, Empress." Bronwyn was given the empress's bloody bedding, which bore horrid stains from the sheep's head and small maggots and flies. She bundled it up in her hands and took it out, but not before waking up another servant to visit the empress's chamber and refresh the bedding. She took the horrible bundle outside to the castle courtyard and shook out the sheets, flinging flies and maggots and spare offal into the night air.

As she peered into the night, feeling the cool air on her face, she wondered how Theobold was doing in Wolvesey Castle, and how Rupert was in the queen's army. It was strange that they could be just across the city and yet seem so far away. Were it not for an invading army at their doorstep and for Rupert's defection to the other side, she might see them. She sighed and turned to take the bundle inside to wash, when she stopped.

Facing her, quiet as a mouse, stood Agatha.

"Mistress Agatha," Bronwyn said. She wrinkled her nose. The woman smelled like beer.

"What are you doing with Tristan?" Mistress Agatha asked. "You're working with him, aren't you?"

Bronwyn cocked her head. How much should she reveal?

"You shouldn't work with him," Agatha said. "It's not right. It's cruel."

"I'm sorry?"

"He uses people. You're a smart girl, or so Lady Alice seems to think. I saw the way you two were exchanging looks, as if you both had a secret the rest of us didn't know. You should take care he doesn't use you for his own ends."

Bronwyn realized she meant romantically. "I promise you, I have no interest in him. We aren't—"

"You foolish girl. Ugh. Why do I bother?" Agatha gave a dramatic sigh. "Look. Just heed my warning. If you value yourself, do not trust him. He's not got anyone's best interests at heart but his own. Don't lose your way and fall in with him, all right? It's bad enough Lady Susanna is making eyes at him. Stay away from him."

Bronwyn blinked. If she was flirting with other men, did that mean Lady Susanna's romance with her man was over? "Mistress Agatha, did something happen?"

Agatha ran a hand through her brown, greying hair, which looked black in the darkness. "No. Everything is fine. Just a little advice. I would hate to see a young woman like you waste herself keeping company with a man who is like a rotten apple."

Bronwyn's eyebrows rose. *Maybe she wasn't speaking romantically, after all.*

Bronwyn washed the dirty bedding and hung it out to dry, then went straight to bed. The next day, she let the castle's laundress know it was for the empress. With that well in hand, she returned to her pallet on the floor for a few hours' sleep, then joined the cooks and kitchen servants for an early morning meal and set about her duties.

The siege resumed at first light, with the air full of arrows, whistling and screaming through the sky. Bronwyn sometimes brought food up to the archers and men on the ramparts; other times, she tended the wounded. But there was less food than before, as the weeks of siege were taking their toll. The empress's armies and noncombatants who relied on her couldn't last like this forever. And whilst the weather was still fine, the September sunshine would fade soon enough, and Bronwyn did not want to be stuck in a besieged castle for the winter with little food.

There had to be a way out. She instantly thought of the secret entrance that Sister Rebecca had talked about, but what would that achieve? She couldn't just slip out herself. Wandering around alone in a city under siege was a good way to get captured, or worse. But she needed to do something. Anything was better than walking around waiting for the invaders to break down the walls.

Bronwyn took her frustrations out on some bread dough she was preparing, and rolled it into a ball, then slapped it against the wooden worktable again. She thought about what Agatha had said the night before. Why did the woman care if she was working with Tristan, and why did she mean to warn her against him? How had they crossed paths in the past?

She paused for a moment. This must have been what Sister Rebecca had overheard. A man telling—no, *threatening* Agatha with what he'd seen. Like her, he too had noticed she was faking illness during her pretense at poisoning in front of the empress, and he'd called her on it, but to use her for his own nefarious ends. What if the man whom Sister Rebecca had overheard had actually been Tristan, and the sheep's head had been put there by Agatha? She would have smelled it but did not comment, as she would have been the one to put it there in the middle of the night. It would have been easy for her, especially if she was sleeping in the empress's chamber that night. But Bronwyn wasn't certain who the man who had blackmailed her into doing it was. Had it been Tristan, or someone else? The brewer, Peter Fforde, also came to mind. Something about him just made her add him to her list of suspects, but what it was, per se, she couldn't be sure.

At that moment, Bronwyn wished she had Rupert or Theobold around to talk to. She could relay her thoughts about the situation to one of them, and they would talk it over with her. No doubt they would annoy her and point out the flaws in her thinking, but they also might point out things she had missed. She also admitted to herself, she missed their handsome faces. She longed to look upon Theobold's kind but serious eyes and feel comforted by Rupert's easy smile.

Bronwyn thought to herself, *What would Theobold do? What would Rupert say?* Then she gave herself a little shake. They hadn't been tasked with solving these little crimes and finding out who had carried out these threatening acts; she had been. The empress had tasked her with them, and to work with Tristan. As much as she didn't care for him but couldn't put her finger on why, he might be able to help. Once she had finished preparing her dough and was letting it prove, Bronwyn wiped her hands clean and went off in search of Tristan.

She made her way out of the kitchen and realized she didn't know where to go. She asked around for where he was, but no one seemed to know. It was odd.

Her search having turned up nothing, Bronwyn returned to the kitchens and went about her work. Tonight's dinner was bread with steaming-hot potage along and preserved baked fish. After the meal, she went in search of Lady Susanna, whom she found in the small castle chapel sitting with the nuns.

Lady Susanna looked delighted to see her. "Bronwyn, hello. Were you looking to learn some French?"

"Yes and no. Happy to learn another French word, but I wanted to see how you all were."

The nuns looked at Lady Susanna. "We are well," Sister Rebecca said. "Now that we are out of that brewery, life is much better."

Sister Joan grinned. "She didn't like smelling of beer."

Bronwyn smiled. "I normally don't mind it, but I think I'd get tired of it too."

Sister Rebecca hmmmed and crossed her arms. "Sister, we should return to our prayers. You will excuse us." She went up to the floor before the small stone altar to pray.

After a moment, Sister Joan joined her, leaving Lady Susanna and Bronwyn alone.

"Did you want something? I can teach you more French," Lady Susanna said, "*Bonjour*. That means *hello*."

"*Bon-jore*," Bronwyn said.

"Keep practicing." Lady Susanna smiled.

"How are you feeling? You fainted last night."

"I'm all right now," Lady Susanna said. "The sight of that hideous sheep's head scared me. And it was so brave of the empress. She didn't faint at all. And to think, someone had put it there when she was asleep. I'd have screamed the castle down."

"Where were you when it happened?"

"In the next room. Lady Alice and I were asleep when I heard a scream, and I hurried to the empress's room. The guards let me in, although they looked half-asleep, and that was when we found the empress, pointing at the bed. The men-at-arms stabbed it when they realized what it was. Agatha screamed, I screamed, and Lady Alice ran out. Then you came, and you know the rest."

Bronwyn scratched her head. "Who do you think is doing this?"

"I don't know. But if I had to guess, I think Lady Alice."

Bronwyn's eyes widened. *Her friend?* "Why is that?"

"Well… she always thinks of herself as better than the rest of us. I mean, I understand why. She's from a good family, they are wealthy, and she's noble, whereas my family owns fewer lands and isn't as rich. And Lady Alice is so strong. Such an independent mind. It's not good to have in a woman. It's bound to get her in trouble. And she's so smart. But I think the empress might…" She paused. "You won't tell anyone what I'm saying?"

"No, I won't."

"Good." Lady Susanna nodded. "I think the empress doesn't value Lady Alice the way she should. I know you two are close, but I wonder if Lady Alice meant for this incident to hurt her and remind her of what's important."

"Her attitude aside, what makes you suspect Lady Alice?"

"She's always around, isn't she? I don't know. I just think she's unhappy. And not just because her young man is away."

Bronwyn cocked her head. She meant Rupert.

"Lord, she's always talking about him. But now she's stopped."

"Why is that?"

"Well, Lady Alice was talking the other day at dinner about how dashing and daring her Rupert is, and Mistress Agatha I think got a bit jealous. She said, 'If he's so dashing and brave, why hasn't he tried to find you?' And that made Lady Alice stop as if her mouth were full. She didn't say a word about him after that, at least not that I heard. I think she's pining for him. But it must bother her so, for her young man to do nothing."

Bronwyn snorted softly. "We are under siege. The streets aren't safe."

"I know, but—"

Bronwyn shook her head. "It's not fair to expect him to try to reach her when there's a war going on."

"I know, but—"

"And besides, why would he contact her, anyway? It's not like they have an understanding."

"Yes, they do. Lady Alice said so." Lady Susanna paused, her eyes widening. She clapped a hand to her mouth and giggled. "You're jealous."

"What? No, I'm not." Bronwyn's face warmed.

"Yes, you are. You're jealous of Lady Alice and her squire." Lady Susanna laughed. "It's nothing to be ashamed of. We all get jealous sometimes." She grinned and shot Bronwyn a knowing look.

Bronwyn shook her head. "I'm not. Really."

"'Course you're not. Don't worry, your secret is safe with me."

Bronwyn was ready to roll her eyes and thought better of it. "There's no secret. Rupert and I are simply friends."

"Sure, you are."

This was getting her nowhere, and she had a mystery to solve. Bronwyn decided to push back. "The rumors I heard last were that you had a secret lover, Lady Susanna."

The noblewoman froze for a second, then buffed her nails on her dress, examining them. "Don't know what you mean."

"I think you do. How about you start telling me the truth?"

"What are you talking about?"

Bronwyn had the noblewoman's full attention now. The teasing smile had disappeared from her face.

"Back in June, the night before the empress's coronation in London, you locked up Theobold and Rupert in the room with the jewels—"

"No, I didn't."

"It wasn't a question." Bronwyn's voice was hard. "What I want to know is why."

Lady Susanna's mouth dropped open. "I... First of all, even if I did do that, which I didn't, there's no way to prove such a thing. And it's in the past, anyway, so why would you care?" She put a hand on her hip.

"They were missed on the day. They could have helped. Lady Morwenna and Sir Bors attacked—"

She tittered. "It was just a little joke. They kept nosing around the empress's jewels, so I didn't trust them. Thought maybe a night with them might teach them not to go snooping around. But I don't see how that matters now." She raised her nose in the air.

"What about your lover? You've been quiet about it since you got here. Is it Tristan, the squire?"

"Ha. Why are you so concerned about my love life...? Oh, I see. You were worried about him. Theobold. Still fancying him, are you?" Lady Susanna snorted. "I thought you would have learned your lesson by now. You shouldn't be mixing with your betters. Fancy him all you want, but he'll be a knight someday, and you..." She looked her up and down. "Maybe you should set your sights lower, to someone more suited to your station in life. I'm sure there's a lonely cowherd or shepherd out there, looking for love." She laughed and walked away.

Bronwyn sighed and sat on one of the few stone benches toward the back of the chapel. She closed her eyes for a moment and clasped her hands in her lap, when a familiar voice asked, "Are you praying or are you asleep?"

Bronwyn's eyes opened. "I'm not asleep."

Sister Rebecca stood there.

"But I wasn't praying, either," Bronwyn admitted sheepishly.

The nun took a seat beside her. "What troubles you?"

"Nothing."

"Nonsense. I may not be a priest, but I can tell when something's not right. What is it? Are you fretting over the sheep's head in the empress's bedchamber?"

Bronwyn stared at her. "How do you—"

"Lady Susanna told us. She has a kind heart but is not good at holding her tongue."

"I think you are right." She inwardly winced at the stories Lady Susanna could be spreading at that moment about her, Lady Alice, and Rupert. What if Theobold heard?

"What troubles you so?"

"It's not the sheep's head. I mean, part of it is. But it's more than that. Sorry, I don't want to impose."

"Please. I'm happy to listen. It's much more interesting than my own prayers." Sister Rebecca smiled thinly.

"Well... all right. We don't know how the sheep's head got there. Whoever did it would have been covered in sheep's blood, but there's no sign of that anywhere."

"Could they have hidden their clothes?" Sister Rebecca asked.

"Yes. But they would smell after a while and would likely be found. Especially now, when the guards and servants are aware of it. They would need to clean them or bury them if they didn't want to be discovered." Bronwyn clapped a hand to her head.

"What?"

"The laundry. The blooming laundry. Excuse me." She bolted and ran from the chapel, not stopping until she reached the laundry. There, Bronwyn found the laundress, Mistress Gregoria, a large, tall woman with streaming, brown hair and ruddy cheeks, who nodded hello. "It's not more bloody bedding, is it?" She clucked her tongue. "Before you came with the empress's bedding last night, some fool dumped a set of clothes in one of the tubs. Pure stupidity if you ask me. They must've been walking around naked, practically. It stank to high heaven and was just floating there. Covered with blood."

Bronwyn started. "When did you notice this?"

"This morning. Why?"

Bronwyn clapped a hand to her head. Why hadn't she thought of this before? "Did anyone come by looking for the clothes?"

"No."

"Can I see them?"

"No. They disappeared later that day. I never saw who took them." Gregoria pointed and Bronwyn went to the clothes hanging on lines to dry. "I can tell you one thing: they were a man's clothes. Wool shirt and trousers. If that helps. Whoever's they were, they must've been walking around with just their shoes and small clothes. Unless they were noble and had another set of spare clothes to wear."

Bronwyn left and mentally cursed herself for not coming sooner. She returned to the kitchen, her mind buzzing with what she'd learned. A man had butchered the poor sheep and thrown his dirty clothes into the laundry. He'd known his way around the castle and likely had washed himself too. If he was noble, he might have had a few spare sets of clothes. If he wasn't, he might not have walked around naked for a while, as even some servants had a spare shirt and trousers or dress in the case of women. As it was, it seemed like the man had tried to wash the clothes himself and then jumped in the tub to remove any trace of the blood. But he hadn't done a good job, apparently.

Bronwyn worked in the kitchen that day and night, thinking over the facts. First, someone was causing little pranks of mischief to disturb the empress at the worst time, whilst she was experiencing a siege. Second, Agatha had faked her own poisoning to bother the empress, and someone else knew about it and had wanted her to do something to the empress's bed. It stood to reason that she was involved somehow. Maybe she was acting as an accomplice, or maybe she'd put it there herself. Third, a sheep had been slaughtered by a man, and its head left in the bed. She pondered this. She needed answers.

But before Bronwyn could do much, she was interrupted by Lady Alice, who pulled her into a small stone alcove and said, "What are you about, Bronwyn?"

"What do you mean?"

"Lady Susanna is telling everyone that you fancy Rupert, and that you wish you two were sweethearts, when he is *my* fellow."

Bronwyn gave her head a little shake. "I told her we are just friends."

"That's what I said, but she's a little gossip. She'll tell anything she thinks might be true, or even a half-truth." Lady Alice's dark-brown eyes darted to her face. "There is no truth to the matter, is there? You didn't give her any ideas?"

"No, Lady Alice. He's a friend." That's all he ever could be, even if it pained her to say it. "But I care about him, and I'm worried about them both."

"Both? Oh, you're thinking of Theobold." Lady Alice began to smile.

Bronwyn nodded.

"Good. As well you should. But you shouldn't worry. Lady Susanna will find another distraction soon enough." She whispered, "She's been making eyes at that squire, Tristan."

Bronwyn wrinkled her nose. "Why?"

"He's handsome enough, you silly. Just because you have eyes for Theobold doesn't mean you can't look at other men. I can appreciate male beauty, even if you refuse to."

Bronwyn smiled back. She eventually found Tristan on the parapets with the archers, surveying the city. She nodded to the men and stood by, shading her eyes against the sunlight.

Below the castle, the city of Winchester was enveloped in smoke, with small buildings on fire. These had resulted from the invading army, which meant to loot, plunder, and destroy the area. The idea behind the siege was simple enough, she supposed. Ruin everything to prevent the local population from being able to eat or defend themselves. They would either flock to the castles for protection or flee for their lives. If the former, it would drain the castle's resources more. If the latter, they would be hard-pressed to survive in the woods, especially as autumn was now in swing.

Bronwyn shielded her eyes from the sun and watched as the rows of archers lining the parapets raised their bows and as one, fired in waves. The air filled with the deadly lines the arrows made, like scratches against the sky. The silence filled with whistles as arrows screeched down to rain on the invading forces.

Bronwyn stiffened as the arrows shot and impaled men, who cried out and screamed in pain. Their cries were like an unholy cacophony, and she clamped her hands on her ears, then looked around. The men around her did not cover their ears, and so neither should she. She lowered her hands and hugged her arms to her chest, watching. This was war. There was no use hiding from it. It was literally on her doorstep, and men were dying before her eyes.

"Bronwyn? What are you doing up here?" Tristan approached her.

"I was looking for you."

"Why?"

"The empress tasked us both with finding out who is behind these little incidents," she said. "We need to do this." She cocked her head at him. How much could she trust him? And what if he was Lady Susanna's mysterious lover?

"I've already figured it out," he said confidently, running a hand along his smooth hair.

"Really?"

"I'm not going to tell you. Not yet. You'll have to wait along with everyone else," he said.

Bronwyn peered at him. A bruise had bloomed on his face, near his eye, and his sleeves were pushed up, revealing more bruises on his arms. She asked, "What happened to you?"

"Huh? What do you mean?"

"Why are you covered in bruises?"

His expression darkened and his eyes narrowed. He looked down and lowered his shirt sleeves. "I got into a fight. One of the grooms pushed me too far."

Bronwyn raised an eyebrow. "Who was it?"

"None of your business. Why do you care? Don't tell me you fancy me as well?" He buffed his nails on his shirt.

"What?"

"Oh, yeah, you're after Theobold." He smirked. "Just as well. I could handle more than one woman, but you're not my type."

She cocked her head at him.

"The Lady Susanna is… She keeps following me around and then when I try to tell her off, she giggles and walks away, then I see her following me again. She's always around and nearby when I'm trying to look after my master, and it's annoying. Can't you do something?"

"Like what? I'm just a servant." She scratched her head. Could he have been lying?

"I don't know. Give her a bad roll that makes her sick to her stomach and lying in bed for a week. Something. It's driving me mad. Now I know what a deer feels like when it's being hunted."

Bronwyn snorted. Maybe he wasn't Lady Susanna's lover, after all. Perhaps he was just tired of the noblewoman. "I'm not going to make a woman sick just so she stops following you. If you don't like her, tell her so."

He flinched. "Yeah, yeah, I will."

She looked at him. What if he actually was Lady Susanna's lover, but in secret? What if he actually enjoyed the attention and preferred to complain about it? "Unless there's someone else you fancy?"

"That's none of your business, baker. Go back to the kitchens." Tristan eyed her levelly.

"You still won't tell me who you think is behind all this?" she asked.

"No."

"Then I'll suppose you'll be telling the empress," Bronwyn said.

"Of course."

"I'll look forward to hearing it then."

"Bet you will."

They locked gazes, but this was more combative. Suddenly, she felt more than anything that he had been lying to her this entire time. About his relationship with Lady Susanna, about knowing the culprit behind the incidents plaguing the empress, and possibly more. Call it a hunch, a gut feeling. She just knew. "You don't actually have a suspect, do you?"

"Shut your mouth. Of course I do." Tristan straightened his shoulders and peered out at the invading army in the countryside again.

"So why haven't you told the empress yet?"

"I'm waiting for the right time. She's busy."

"That's rich, since she's been asking if I've found the culprit every time I see her."

"Maybe you should spend less time bowing and scraping and stick to the kitchen, where you belong. You're too dumb to find out real answers and instead you go bumbling about asking questions and sticking your nose where you shouldn't. If anyone's a suspect, it's you for making the empress think you can actually help. Stick to making bread rolls, Bronwyn. At least there you're useful," he told her.

His words fell on her ears like the rain. Annoying for a moment. She shrugged and left.

THAT DAY, BRONWYN was stirring a great big cauldron of soup, when Hugh approached her. "You're close to the empress, yes?"

She nodded. "Mm-hmm. I guess so."

"She's not going to blame us for the sheep's head, is she?"

"I don't know. I think she was more frightened than angry."

Hugh tugged at his shirt collar with a thick finger and swallowed.

Bronwyn looked at him. "What is it, Master Hugh? What concerns you?"

"Nothing, nothing. I just don't want her blaming the servants for these little mishaps, is all. Here, bring her some bread rolls. That'll keep her happy."

"I thought those were for the servants' dinner."

"You thought wrong. Go." He handed her a plate and shooed

her from the kitchen.

Bronwyn brought up the plate of fresh bread rolls for the empress and found her pacing the throne room. The room was lined by men-at-arms and guards, who watched her most carefully but said not a word. The empress beckoned her forward and took a bread roll, then hesitated.

Bronwyn met her gaze. "I brought them up from the kitchen myself, Empress." But she hesitated. She hadn't watched them being made, however, and knew very well that they could have been tampered with.

"Then you won't mind taking a little bite," Empress Maud said. "Go on."

Bronwyn took a crumb from the plate and swallowed it. "Perfectly fine."

The empress said, "Fine. Go about your business, then. No, wait."

Bronwyn handed the plate to a page standing nearby. "Empress?"

"This person, whoever it is who is a spy in our court, sent from Stephen and that witch wife of his. Have you found them?"

"No, Empress. But I think Tristan knows something. He seems confident in his abilities." *And perhaps that confidence might be his undoing*, she thought.

"Then bring him here at once. No, wait. On second thought, tell him I want him to reveal the person's name in front of us all at dinner. We are in need of some entertainment, and I want my court to see I deal with intruders swiftly. This search has gone on too long." The empress ate another bite of the roll and beckoned forward a servant who held a jug of wine. "I notice *you* do not put forward any suspects. Did I ask too much of you?"

Bronwyn gave a slight shake of her head. "Nay, Empress. I too have my suspicions."

"But…"

"I haven't the proof yet to back them up."

"Many nobles act without proof."

"But I am not a noble, Empress." Bronwyn felt her cheeks warm at this admission. She lowered her gaze, then slowly raised it to Empress Maud.

Empress Maud was in her forties or so, but was fierce, like a bird of prey. Her light-brown hair was pinned back beneath a veil, but her angular face was pale and lined from poor sleep and the strain of it all. Her eyes were sharp with intelligence, wit, and calculation. It was the last quality with which she looked upon Bronwyn now.

"Some think I am making a mistake in relying on you, a servant girl. They think I raise you up from nothing, you who are as poor as dirt. With nothing but your name and the clothes on your back. But I tell them they are wrong, and I value good counsel and sharp minds where I see them."

"I am grateful for your generosity." Bronwyn ducked her head.

The empress took a second bread roll and bit into it heartily. She swallowed the small bites and said, "Do not disappoint me, Mistress Blakenhale. I hate to be proven wrong."

Bronwyn nodded and curtsied. She turned to go when the empress said, "I want you in attendance at dinner tonight, too. Be on hand. *Tu comprends?* You understand?"

"Yes."

"Lady Susanna tells me she is to give you lessons in French. Is that true?"

"Yes."

"Good. I approve You will need a working knowledge of French to be useful to me. You should have asked me permission, of course, but it is a good occupation for her, and I approve of people trying to better themselves. Especially those born in poorer circumstances. Maybe these lessons will keep Lady Susanna out of trouble. She needs to atone for her little prank in London. Go." The empress motioned for Bronwyn to leave.

Bronwyn worked steadily in the kitchen that afternoon, after reporting to Hugh that the empress liked the bread rolls well enough. He was relieved until she told him the empress's request.

His expression clouded, his bushy, black eyebrows knitting together. "You serve at the table? Like a page? Why? Why you?"

Bronwyn shrugged. "She likes me? I, uh…" She paused and added quietly, "Tristan thinks he knows who is behind these little incidents with the empress. She wants to have him reveal it at dinner. She wants me there I think to support his claim."

"And who does he think is behind all this?"

She shook her head. She couldn't tell Hugh of her real suspicion, that Tristan might be behind this. "He wouldn't tell me."

Hugh frowned. "What do you think?"

"I… don't know. Not for sure. I have an idea, but I cannot prove it just yet."

"You need to hurry, girl. I don't know what I'd do."

She thought for a minute. Back to her days on the road, where they'd been scrounging for food and setting traps, or hunting. "I think I know."

"Go on."

"Tease the person out with bait, like you would an animal. See if they fall for it." *And with any luck*, she thought, *Tristan will reveal the flaw in accusing his so-called culprit, which may lead to proof of his own involvement in these crimes.*

Hugh scratched his chin. "That's not a bad idea…"

Bronwyn entered the small chapel within the castle grounds, craving some solitude. It wasn't a large building, as she might have imagined. She considered that being so close to the cathedral, the need for a chapel was small, and thus it was of a proportionate size. *A quiet place to think would be welcome right now,* she thought as she opened the stiff, wooden door. But as the door creaked open, she saw she wasn't alone.

Inside the church already knelt the empress before the altar, her head bowed in prayer.

Bronwyn hesitated, then decided that the church was open to all, and she needed a minute. As long as she didn't disturb the empress, her presence there might be tolerated. She looked at the guards who manned the door. Their faces were unfriendly.

"I've just come to pray," she said.

"Make it quick," one said in a gravelly voice. "The empress is at prayer."

Bronwyn walked forward, keeping a fair distance from the other parishioners. Inside the church stood the nuns Sisters Rebecca and Joan. Bronwyn nodded a greeting to them both and knelt on the stone floor, the cold of the flagstones biting into her bony knees. Even though they were in late summer, the siege made one day to the next feel like they were pieces moving in a prison. They weren't strictly behind bars or in cells, but life outside the castle walls and gates was not safe. The coldness of the stones reminded her that winter was never far away.

This will be quick, she thought. The floor was chilly. As she closed her eyes and began to pray silently, a gasp interrupted her. Her eyes flew open.

The empress staggered back, falling to her bottom as she dropped a book on the floor. In seconds, the nuns were at her side, along with two guards. "Empress?" Sister Rebecca asked.

"What's happened?" a guard asked, pulling the empress up by the arms.

"I'm fine. Let go of me," Empress Maud snapped.

Bronwyn got to her feet and stood by. The empress waved them all away and turned, her eyes alighting on Bronwyn. "You. Come here."

Bronwyn approached. "Are you all right, Empress?"

"No. No, I am not. For when I opened my Book of Hours, that letter came out." She pointed an imperious finger at a scrap of paper on the floor.

A guard picked it up and stiffened. He crumpled it in his fist. "I'll dispose of this, Your Grace."

"No. Hand it here." Empress Maud took it and handed it to Bronwyn, who smoothed it out.

It bore a black ink scribble, a sketch of a woman wearing a crown who lay on the ground, a knife in her back. There was no doubt it was a depiction of the empress.

"What does it mean?" the empress asked. "I have not looked at it properly and no time for such foul pranks."

Bronwyn pocketed the note in her sleeve. "It's a sketch of you. A nasty one."

"Yes, I know. Does that mean someone is going to stab me in the back?"

"It's certainly a threat." Bronwyn frowned.

One of the guards picked up the prayer book and handed it to the empress. She clasped it tightly and looked ready to leave, when Bronwyn asked, "Did anyone read your Book of Hours recently?"

The empress made as if to shake her head, then paused. "No. Not to read. But… there was a bit of fuss this morning."

"Oh?"

"I felt for the sisters and wished to loan them the use of my Book of Hours."

"Such a kindness," Sister Rebecca said, joining them.

"Yes. Well, this morning, Lady Susanna offered to fetch it, but Mistress Agatha said her hands were so dirty that she shouldn't touch it, so she offered to bring it instead. They argued and even tugged on it. It's precious to me, and so delicate. Its illustrations alone were costly to commission." She sighed. "I told them to quit fighting, and Lady Susanna ran off in tears. She's a sweet young woman but no temper in her at all. She needs more spirit." The empress *tsked*. "Mistress Agatha brought the Book of Hours down here to the nuns, and I came here later to use it. I had thought the church would be a quiet place." Her pointed expression said, *I thought wrong.*

"So out of your ladies, who touched the book?" Bronwyn asked.

"Lady Susanna. And Mistress Agatha was right; her fingers were dirty. Black, as if she'd been playing with soot. Mistress Agatha touched it too, and then the Sisters Rebecca and Joan, I suppose."

Sister Rebecca coughed. "Forgive me, Empress, but I must interject. We did not touch the book."

"I beg your pardon? When I came into the church, it was beside you."

"Yes." Sister Rebecca's cheeks colored faintly. "I mean to say, we accepted the little book with thanks but then had a disagreement."

"What about?" the empress asked.

Sister Rebecca shot her fellow nun a severe look. "I wished to use the book as it was intended, but Sister Joan disagreed. We decided it was a princely loan but felt it was too grand of us to use and so set it aside."

"Ugh." The empress looked up at the ceiling. "After all that, you didn't even use it." She shook her head.

Sister Rebecca bowed her head. "I'm sorry, Empress."

"Very well. Mistress Bronwyn? What have you deduced?"

Bronwyn peered at the scrap of paper and said, "I should like to see Lady Susanna's hands."

"No need. They were covered with soot. When Mistress Agatha asked what she had been doing, the young woman refused to answer. Mistress Agatha suspects Lady Susanna was trying to use a bit of ash to color her eyelids, to make them more attractive." Empress Maud rolled her eyes.

"Such wickedness," Sister Rebecca muttered.

Bronwyn ignored the nun. "Empress, who amongst your ladies have access to quill and ink?"

"Why, all of them, I suppose," replied the empress. "And they can all read and write, of course. But the paper doesn't have any words. So anyone could have done that horrid drawing. What do you think?"

Bronwyn gestured to the book. "What page did the paper fall out of?"

Empress Maud stiffened, and her lips pursed as if she'd eaten a lemon. "The Office of the Dead. I thought it odd that something was sticking out of the book, so I flipped to that section and the paper fell out."

Bronwyn shared a thoughtful look with the empress. "Whoever did this, all of this, is trying to frighten you."

"Ha. They're going to have to try harder than that. It takes more than a little drawing to scare me," the empress said loudly, her voice echoing in the chapel.

"Yes. May I see the page the paper fell out from?"

The empress opened the small book and delicately flipped to the pages, stopping on an ornately illustrated page. Bronwyn peeked at it and instantly understood what the empress had meant. The page was colored with gold and bore images of the saints, rich with colorful inks. It was a bit of art, and she marveled at its generous detail. She longed to trace her fingers over the page but dared not. Instead, she took the book and, holding it carefully, peered at the small page and its next folio.

"What are you looking for?" Sister Rebecca asked.

"Soot. Or ink. Any marks." Bronwyn handed the book back. "Thank you."

The empress looked at the pages. "There aren't any marks. What does that mean?"

"That Lady Susanna is innocent," Bronwyn said. "She didn't insert the drawing. The scrap of paper is free from stray ink or soot, and so are the pages in the book. So whoever added the page did not have dirty hands."

"My word. So the woman's dirty hands are a sign of her innocence," Sister Rebecca said.

"Yes. Exactly."

"Unless she inserted the drawing before she started playing with soot so she would be found innocent," Sister Joan pointed out.

The women looked at her.

"I doubt Lady Susanna is that calculating," the empress said. "She is much too innocent. Playful and teasing. She does like pranks, but... I do not believe she would do such a thing."

"I'm just saying, it's possible. Otherwise, that leaves Mistress

Agatha," Sister Joan added.

Bronwyn paused. "What if someone had already tampered with the book before this morning? Had anyone looked at it last night? When was the last time you read it, Empress?"

Empress Maud looked up, thinking. "I read it last night. But no one asked to look at it. I read it and said my prayers before going to bed. It was fine then."

"So, either someone must have touched the book whilst you slept, or it happened this morning," Bronwyn said.

"Well, Lady Alice was the one who slept in my room last night," the empress explained. "I wouldn't suspect her, except... She did have ink on her hands this morning. From writing a note, she said."

Bronwyn tensed. Could her friend be at fault?

"Could she have done it while you were sleeping?" Sister Joan asked.

"Sister, we shouldn't presume such things. It comes close to spreading false witness," Sister Rebecca said.

Sister Joan looked away.

Bronwyn said, "I will speak with her."

The empress looked mollified. "Good." She clasped the book close to her side and walked away, leaving the guards to follow.

Once they left, Sister Joan asked Bronwyn, "That was smart thinking. Do you really think one of the empress's ladies-in-waiting could be behind this?"

"It's possible."

"But why? Is she so terrible? Does she mistreat her ladies?" Sister Joan asked.

"Sister," Sister Rebecca admonished.

Sister Joan shot her an apologetic look, then glanced at Bronwyn.

Bronwyn shrugged. "I do not know. I don't think so. She is a ruler like any man. But for someone to do this at all is a great risk."

"Would they do this to a king?" Sister Joan asked.

"I don't know. But I rather doubt it."

"They wouldn't. It's because of her sex. They wish to disturb her mind with these senseless tricks," Sister Rebecca said. "Not to mention, the death of that poor sheep. I do not care for such beasts, but no creature deserves to be butchered like that."

Bronwyn pondered this. Of course the nuns would be aware of the sheep. Court gossip would be spreading that tale far and wide.

Bronwyn sniffed the scrap of paper.

"Why are you sniffing it?" Sister Joan asked.

"Because it smells."

"Can I see?"

Bronwyn handed it over. The young nun sniffed the paper and said, "Why, I've smelt that before. It smells familiar. Like food or drink. Almost like…"

Their eyes met. "Best not to say anything yet, until I can be sure." Bronwyn thanked the sisters and excused herself.

Bronwyn sought out Lady Alice, who was walking in the garden. Bronwyn noticed her hands had tinges of black ink upon them. "Lady Alice?"

Lady Alice turned around. "Bronwyn? What are you doing here? Did they release you from the kitchens?"

Bronwyn shook her head and relayed what had transpired in the church.

Lady Alice stiffened. "You don't think I had anything to do with that, do you?"

"No, but I have to ask. Why do you have ink on your hands?"

Lady Alice blinked and examined them. Her nails were long and the fingertips were stained black. She muttered, "I thought I'd washed them."

"What were you doing?"

"Writing. Not that it's any business of yours."

"Only writing?" Bronwyn asked.

"Yes."

"No drawing or sketching?"

"No."

Bronwyn surveyed her. "To whom were you writing?"

Lady Alice's look was mutinous. She huffed and tossed her black braid over her shoulder. "Rupert, of course. But I don't see how it's any business of yours."

"Lady Alice…" Bronwyn started. "No one knows where he is."

"So? I will write to him if I choose. And I will give this to him when I see him next. Bronwyn, I swear, you torment me like a flea. Why are you the empress's dog? You sniff around and hunt, and no one wants you in their affairs. Least of all me. I thought we were friends, Bronwyn."

"We are, Lady Alice." Bronwyn frowned.

"Then why do I feel like a suspect in your eyes? You look at me with such suspicion. What do I have to do to prove that I am innocent? You want to see the notes? I'll show you. Oh, wait, you can't read. It really doesn't matter, then, does it? You wouldn't be able to tell, anyway."

Bronwyn felt insulted.

"It is my privilege. It is something you would be lucky to learn." Lady Alice paused. "I heard Lady Susanna is teaching you French. What are you doing with her? Hoping to better yourself?"

Bronwyn stared at her. She disliked Lady Alice's tone. It was almost sneering. "Maybe. I thought it might help me to learn the empress's language."

"Ha. You may try all you like, Bronwyn, but in the end, you're just a baker's girl wearing a better dress. You'll never be noble."

Her words cut as cleanly as if with a knife, but deeper. So that was what Lady Alice thought of her. That she was trying to become noble, like her?

"I'm not."

"Aren't you? But who am I to say?" Lady Alice glared at her. Her eyes looked black, like pinpricks of anger against a night sky.

"Does Rupert read and write?" Bronwyn asked.

Alice's cheeks turned pink. "I'm sure he does. He is a squire, training to be a knight. I am sure he has learned. Knights don't just take *anyone* to be their squires."

"How are you going to reach him?"

"By messenger."

"How? It's not safe."

"One of the squires, Tristan, knows the area. He knows a safe way in and out of here without being seen. He'll be quick and will get my message over to him."

"And how would he find him? Rupert defected and rejoined Matilda's armies. And why would Tristan do that for you? What are you giving him in return?"

"Coin, obviously." Lady Alice pursed her lips. "The man chooses which court he will be loyal to, like I have. That doesn't mean we can't still be together. Now, are you done interrogating me? Did I pass your scrutiny?"

"Why are you so angry?"

"Isn't it obvious? Here I thought we were friends, but then I hear from Lady Susanna that you fancy Rupert. And then when I thought you had come to see me, you treat me like a common criminal, when you are no more than common yourself. It is rude. But perhaps I should have expected nothing less from you." Lady Alice huffed again and walked away.

That solved the mystery of Lady Alice's ink-stained hands at least, Bronwyn thought. Once again, Lady Alice and she were at odds. But the young, dark-haired noblewoman had a way of hurting her that others didn't. It surprised Bronwyn that Lady Alice was writing messages when they were at war, but when she thought about it, not so surprising after all.

Bronwyn went up to the ramparts to find Tristan and instead found him in the courtyard, chatting with Lady Susanna. They held hands. He whispered something in her ear and slapped her rump as she laughed and walked away, shooting a look back at him.

Bronwyn crossed her arms and leaned against a wall in the

shadows, watching. So they were definitely romantically linked. The question was: had they always been lovers, had they fought and separated and now were making up, or had Tristan been telling the truth, and they had only recently begun seeing each other?

Tristan grinned after Lady Susanna, but his expression grew stern when he looked at Bronwyn. "What do you want?"

"To tell you the empress wants you to share what you know about who is behind these accidents happening to her."

He scowled. "You've been talking."

"Someone put a nasty sketch of her in her prayer book. I was at church when she found it."

"Always in the right place at the right time, aren't you? You're just a little opportunist, eh? Always making yourself available, just in case she might need you. Bet she'll want her arse wiped too. Maybe you should go see." Tristan rested a hand on the pommel of his sword.

Bronwyn's face became heated. "She wants you to say what you've learned at dinner tonight. Be there." She turned on her heel to go.

He called, "Haven't you anything to say about my woman, Lady Susanna?"

Bronwyn said, "I'm very happy for you. Does she know you found her annoying at first, and wanted me to give her something to make her sick to her stomach?"

Suddenly, he gripped her braid and pulled hard, making her fall back. He said in her left ear, "Shut your mouth if you know what's good for you. Don't go spreading tales or it will be the worse for you. One of these days, you might wake up without your pretty braid."

That comment shot fire through her veins. "And what does Lady Susanna think of your attention to me?" Bronwyn jerked and he gripped her braid tighter. She gritted her teeth.

"She's a smart woman. She likes me fine. All ladies like me. And a man has needs." He shoved her away and she stumbled.

He laughed, and she walked on, her cheeks flaming.

That night's dinner should not have been different from any other, except that Bronwyn's stomach churned with unease. She felt nervous and queasy. It was likely nerves, or it could have been the day-old fish mixed with potage she and the servants had dined on for luncheon. She worked steadily and when the time came for dinner, she exchanged a look with Hugh.

He said, "Go on, girl. Don't keep them waiting."

Bronwyn unbound her dirty-blonde hair from her kerchief and pinned it back so it was long but out of her face. She wore a plain, purple dress and removed her floury work apron, wiping her face and hands on it so she might look presentable. She swallowed a quick sip of wine and as the pages came in to collect platters of food for the main dining hall, she picked one up and joined them. Hefting a platter of preserved salt pork, she brought the platter out in the queue of servers and entered the dining hall.

The room was large, and the long tables were set up in a horseshoe arrangement, with the empress dining at the head of the tables, surrounded by those loyal men and women. Bronwyn set down the platter on the nearest available space on the crowded tables and stood back, taking a place behind Lady Alice, Mistress Agatha, and the nuns.

Lady Alice glanced back and shot her a look as if to say, *What are you doing here?*

Bronwyn sent her a tight smile and looked straight ahead.

The empress began the meal, with the taster taking little bites of her food. It was normal enough, and the empress kept up a good and regular conversation with the men-at-arms and nobles in attendance. Then after a short time, she banged the table for silence. Once satisfied she had their attention, she said, "It has come to my attention that someone here has been playing little tricks."

Men and women glanced at each other.

"Someone has left little drawings of me around for me to find. And I have heard of other... disturbing incidents." She swallowed.

Bronwyn realized she must have been thinking of the sheep's head. She moved aside so that Lady Susanna could sit with the other women present. Lady Alice hissed, "Where were you? You're late."

"I was using the privy," Lady Susanna whispered back as she sat.

The empress muttered under her breath then said, "As I was saying. I find that someone is behind these little tricks, and I have tasked just the man to find out who."

Bronwyn's eyebrows knit together. *The man?* But the empress had tasked her too. Or had she forgotten?

The empress said, "I call upon the squire of my dear Sir Miles of Gloucester, the First Earl of Hereford, Tristan Langforde, to tell us all what he has found. For I have learned this very day that he has figured out the true culprit."

Heads looked around.

"Tristan?" the empress said.

There was silence. The empress waited a moment, then said, "Guards. Find Tristan."

Bronwyn couldn't ignore the empress's unspoken command: to bring him here. Now.

As people began to whisper, the empress said, "Mistress Bronwyn. Whilst Tristan makes his way here, tell us what you have learned so far."

Bronwyn gulped. Her? Talk in front of all these people? Even as Lady Alice turned and motioned for her to step forward, Bronwyn felt a stab of fear in her stomach. To speak in front of so many, whilst they all watched and stared at her... What if she made a fool of herself? What if she slipped or forgot something? What if—

"I am waiting, Mistress Bronwyn," the empress said.

Bronwyn swallowed. She had to act. What she wouldn't have given to run and hide. But she couldn't. Not now. She stepped forward, to a section at the corner of where the tables met, where there was a gap. People continued to eat and drink, but quietly. All eyes were upon her.

She opened her mouth and took a breath.

"Speak up, girl," a voice called out.

Bronwyn turned to the empress. "Your Grace asked Tristan and me to look into the matter of these incidents and to find out who was behind them. The first was—"

"A drawing. A rude sketch of me," the empress interrupted.

"Yes."

"I have been receiving such horrid notes since my arrival in this city. It stands to reason that someone here at court does not like my being here. I wonder who?" The empress's voice was clear as she gazed around the room. "Tell them of the note in my prayer book."

Eyes went to Bronwyn, who said, "Her Grace found a rude sketch in her Book of Hours when she went to pray. We believe it was put there by someone who had access to her prayer book, and who tampered with it that morning. We know of only two people who could have done this." She paused. "Lady Susanna and Mistress Agatha, who argued over it that morning."

Lady Susanna gasped. "I would never."

"Nor I," Agatha said. "You are mistaken, girl. Do not insult your betters. You deserve the switch."

Bronwyn swallowed. "The sketch was written with black ink, and I could tell that whoever did it had clean hands, for there was no ink or soot on the book's pages, or the sketch itself."

"Then I'm innocent, for I hadn't washed my hands this morning," Lady Susanna said, rising to her feet.

"Yes. That's right. But I also noticed that the sketch had a peculiar smell. Almost like… hops. Or oats. Or beer."

"Call the brewer here at once," came the imperial order.

Within minutes, a page had brought the brewer into the main dining room. Peter stood stiffly, his face a shade pale. He wiped his forehead with his sleeve.

"Master Brewer, a nasty note was found of me, and it smelled like beer. What do you know of this?" the empress asked.

"I had nothing to do with that. I don't know what you're talking about."

Bronwyn turned to him. "Master Peter, when we met a few weeks ago, I found you writing away with a quill and ink. The ink was all over your fingers. They were black with it."

He scoffed. "Many people use quill and ink. Or do you suspect everyone who can write?"

A few nobles chuckled at this.

The brewer took confidence at their reaction and added, "Do not insult me, girl, just because I can read and write, and you cannot."

"Then can you explain why the sketch we found in the empress's prayer book smelled like your brewery?"

His smile fell. "I cannot. Maybe someone visited the brewery or was stealing beer and later wrote the note. I don't know. I only declare I am loyal to the empress, and that you are at fault."

Bronwyn cocked her head at him.

"You go around, pointing fingers and sticking your nose everywhere when you are nothing but a kitchen maid. You don't deserve the raised status she gives you. Your goodwill toward this charity case is misplaced, I fear, Your Grace." The brewer addressed the empress directly.

Empress Maud's nostrils flared. "Answer the question, Master Brewer."

Peter frowned. He swallowed and hastily took a sip of wine. "I... I..."

"What about the knife in the pillow?" Lady Susanna asked. "Or the—" She stopped.

"There was a knife in my pillow?" the empress snapped. "Why did you not tell me of this before? Speak up, Lady Susanna."

"I'm sorry. I didn't want to frighten you. But... What of the sheep's head, found in your bedchamber, Your Grace?"

The empress frowned at her, and Lady Susanna's cheeks

turned pink. She sat down.

"A sheep was killed the other day. Beheaded," Bronwyn said.

This was not new information, but a few men showed distaste on their faces and tutted in disgust, while some of the noblewomen present clapped their hands to their mouths and looked mildly scandalized. They already knew, but a reaction was merited.

"Forgive me, I do not mean to shock you all. But it was a cruel act, for the poor animal was slaughtered." She didn't mention that they were eating the leftovers from the crime. She added, "The man who did it left his clothes in the laundry to be washed."

Master Peter snorted. "Next you'll be saying it was me, when everyone knows I spend my time in the brewery. I never went near any sheep."

"I did not say it was you," Bronwyn said.

"But the sheep's head was found in Her Grace's bedchamber. We didn't notice it until that night after we were asleep," Lady Susanna said.

"Yes. Whoever did it had a means and a knowledge of the castle and knows it well. They know how to move about some of the rooms, even without the guards noticing."

"Who?" the empress asked.

Bronwyn turned toward the head table, where the ladies-in-waiting sat beside the empress. She asked, "Mistress Agatha, being a taster for the empress requires a lot of experience, does it not?"

Agatha sat up straight. "It does. I have an excellent tongue. I must be able to detect any foreign tastes that could be harmful to the empress, or whomever I serve."

"Have you served many nobles before?"

That earned Bronwyn a sharp look. "Some."

"And you must have a very fine nose," Bronwyn said.

Agatha looked at her askance.

"I mean," Bronwyn said hastily, "you must be able to smell if a food isn't right, pretty much straight away."

"Ah. Yes, I can. I have an excellent nose and a strong sense of smell," Agatha said.

Bronwyn said thoughtfully, "Then why did you not notice the sheep's head in the room?"

Agatha's mouth dropped open. "I…"

"You said it yourself, you have an excellent nose. Surely, you would have noticed something smelled odd?"

"Well, I didn't. I mean—"

"And you mentioned the floor. Why would anyone have left food on the floor? Like you said, there's the danger it would attract animals. Mice and rats are common enough, but in the empress's bedchamber, I doubt anyone would leave food out."

Agatha leaned back. "I don't… That is…"

"I think you *did* smell something. You have a fine nose, don't you? So how could you not have smelled a rotting sheep's head from a few feet away?" Bronwyn asked.

"I…" Agatha gave a triumphant grin. "I didn't sleep there that night."

"She's lying," Lady Susanna said. "She did. And it was odd too. I'd slept there two nights ago, so it was my turn, but she said she'd do it, to be closer to the empress. I remember."

Heads turned to Agatha.

"She's confused. Such a sweet lady. She doesn't know what she's saying."

"You're wrong. I remember." Lady Susanna's face turned pink.

Lady Alice spoke up. "So do I. I was there too, if you recall. Agatha did volunteer to sleep in the empress's chamber for a second night, which I thought was odd. How strange it was that the sheep's head was put there and you never noticed a thing."

The empress added, "I too, know Mistress Agatha was there that night. I awoke to her snores more than once."

More heads turned toward Agatha, who paled. "I was asleep. Why would I notice something like when I was asleep?"

"That is exactly why I wished to have my ladies near me at all times," the empress said. "So you would wake and catch someone if they were acting against me. Why did you not notice?"

"Especially when you said it yourself, you have such an excellent nose?" Bronwyn said.

"I… I… may have been mistaken, "Agatha started.

"Out with it," Lady Alice snapped. "You killed that sheep, didn't you? You stole the head and put it in the empress's bed."

"No. No, I didn't! I swear," Agatha said.

Bronwyn shook her head at Lady Alice.

"She didn't?"

"No," Bronwyn said.

"Then who?" Empress Maud asked.

"The same person who, like me, discovered Mistress Agatha was faking being sick that night with the so-called 'poisoned' chicken. But he demanded you help him, didn't he?"

"No. You're wrong. I was sick. It was poisoned. You all saw it. I was very ill," Agatha said, her voice rising.

Bronwyn rounded on her. "You're lying. The chicken was fine. I tasted it and didn't get sick. I didn't die. I'm still here."

The empress glared at her taster. "Mistress Agatha? Is what she says true? You lied about being poisoned?"

"No. No, I didn't. I didn't," Agatha pleaded. "I…"

"She decided to give you a scare," Bronwyn said. "But it wasn't her idea to put the sheep's head in your bed. She was a pawn. It was on the order of someone else."

"Who?" Empress Maud asked.

"It was—" Agatha said, just as a servant ran into the room.

It was a boy, his face pale. He cried, "We found the squire, Your Grace. He's dead!"

Chapter Eight

B RONWYN TENSED. *TRISTAN, dead?*

Heads turned toward the servant.

Empress Maud said, "You. Boy. What do you mean, he is dead?"

"Tell us what happened," Bronwyn said, earning a sharp look from the empress.

The boy looked over his shoulder at a guard behind him, who said, "We went to his room to find him and conducted a search, Your Grace. His things were gone, his room was empty, and we couldn't find hide nor hair of him. That's when we looked down in the stables, and…found him."

"No," Lady Susanna said, her voice rising. "No. It cannot be."

Alice took her hand. Lady Susanna looked at the boy and the guard, her chin trembling.

"The young man was beaten to death, Your Grace. He was attacked and I think one of the horses had taken fright. He's been trampled in the stalls. One of the horses was out of its stall and scared. We had to calm it down."

Lady Susanna emitted a small cry and hid her face in her hands.

Bronwyn said, "Let me see the body."

That earned her some dirty looks. The guard looked at her, then at the empress, who waved her hand. "Show her. I want this matter cleared up immediately." She sighed. "We will eat. We are at war and cannot forget that. There is an army outside these walls fighting to get in. We cannot allow ourselves to tear each other apart with filthy words and accusations."

Bronwyn left, following the guard and the boy out of the main dining hall and through the corridors, out through the castle courtyard and into the stables.

The boy stood by the entrance and shifted his feet. "I don't want to go in."

"It's all right, lad," the guard said and turned to Bronwyn. "You're a bit peculiar, aren't you? A woman wanting to see a dead body? It's strange. Not right. Boy, you can stay out here, but be near."

The boy stood shyly by the door as Bronwyn and the guard went inside. A pair of grooms were there, and one asked, "You've come to see?"

"Show us where he is," the guard said.

The first groom motioned for them to follow.

The stables were poorly lit, and the groom held a torch aloft, leading the way. Together, they walked until they found the body. The grooms stood back. "We were heading to dinner and didn't think anything of it until we heard the cry. The boy found us and we went to go see, then sent him to find you." He swallowed. "He's there."

Bronwyn and the guard peered down. A body lay face-down on the straw and muddied ground, outside the door to one of the narrow stalls.

She gasped. "Tristan?"

She didn't expect him to answer. At the same time, she hadn't expected this. Maybe he hadn't been at fault, after all. But then what had he been doing here at this hour, when he'd known the empress had wanted him to report? Whom had he met, and where had they gone?

A dark-brown horse watched them, the torchlight shining in its jet-black eyes.

Bronwyn blinked. "Did you move him?"

"Yes. The horse was all disturbed, kicking and raising a fuss. He didn't like it at all."

"Quite right." The guard shot an affectionate look toward the horse.

Bronwyn scratched her head. "Was the body lying like that when you found him?"

"Yes. He was in the stall with Sorel here." The groom took a step back. The torchlight flickered in the musty space, playing shadows on his features. The man's eyes were wide. "What do you think happened to him? Was it an accident?"

Bronwyn knelt close to the body. The groom grunted in distaste, and the guard said, "What are you doing there? Get up."

"I'm looking to see what killed him."

"The horse did," the guard said. "It was an accident. He probably slipped in muck and hit his head, and that was it."

Bronwyn motioned for the groom to bring the torch closer, and he handed it to her. She pointed at the body. "If that's true, then why is there no blood on his head? Or muck?"

"He probably got hit somewhere else," the man said.

Bronwyn didn't like that explanation and shook her head.

"It was an accident, girl. Don't go gossiping and creating rumors out of nothing. Don't know why you're here at all."

"I work for the empress." She touched Tristan's neck. "He's still warm. This must have just happened."

The groom shivered.

The body was covered in blood. It didn't make sense. Bronwyn stared down at it.

"Was he cut? Did someone stab him?" the groom asked.

"I'm not sure," Bronwyn said.

"Oh, I'm telling you, girl, it was likely an accident. He probably had too much to drink, slipped, and fell. It happens all the time."

Bronwyn handed the torch back to the groom. She stood on her tiptoes and peeked over the stall door. "Can you shine the light here?"

"All right." The groom came closer. "What are you looking for?"

"Blood. If he did hit his head, there should be a sign of it." She peered over the edge. The horse, Sorel, watched her and backed up, stomping and stepping on the straw.

"Get back, girl. He's liable to kick soon," the groom warned.

Bronwyn stood back, just as the horse aimed a kick. She stepped back a few paces. The groom handed the torch to the guard and went to calm Sorel down, making soothing noises. He said over his shoulder, "There's no blood in the stall. Just a bit on the straw where we found him."

"Then he must have gotten injured somewhere else, and fell in the stables." She looked around. "I wonder what he was doing."

"Probably taking a horse out," the guard said.

"Now? At this time of night? When there's a siege on? It's not safe. He'd be shot quickly, wouldn't he?"

The guard grunted. "Maybe he got injured and fell in here. That's what I think happened."

"I think he was going somewhere. Look, there's his saddle-bag. He was leaving." The groom pointed.

Sure enough, a small bundle lay inside the corner of the stall. The groom fished it out and handed it to Bronwyn. "Doesn't feel like anything here but a spare set of clothes and a bedroll."

"No food or coin?"

The groom opened the bag. "No."

Bronwyn tapped her chin. This was interesting. "I wonder where he was going at this time of night. He knew he was expected at dinner."

"Maybe he had an urgent message to relay, on behalf of the empress," the guard said. "Maybe she ordered him to deliver it at once."

"No," said Bronwyn. "She had ordered him to report at dinner, in front of everyone."

"Maybe she forgot." The guard shrugged as both Bronwyn

and the groom looked at him. "I'm just guessing. I don't know. Anyway, we should be getting back."

"But what about the body? What do we do with it?"

"Got a cart?" the guard asked.

"Yes. We use it to shovel the horse dung," the groom said.

Bronwyn's mouth began to curl into a smile, but she maintained a serious expression. "We'll need to borrow it."

Minutes later, she helped drag Tristan's body into the cart. Aside from the bruises she'd noted earlier, there was no new bruising on him that she could tell. She gingerly felt his hair and did notice a hard lump on his forehead. That was strange. So someone had apparently hit him from the front. He'd faced his attacker, whoever it had been. She didn't think the horse had done it because the animal was so big and powerful, there would have been blood.

The guard wrinkled his nose at the smell. The cart had a singular purpose and it showed. Bronwyn asked, "Where is the cold storage?"

"I'll take him there. You tell the empress."

"What about his things?"

"Give them here. He can be buried with them." The groom tossed the saddlebag into the cart.

Bronwyn turned back to the groom. "You didn't hear anything? A fight, maybe?"

"No. Nothing. I heard the horse whinnying and making a noise, and I went to go see, along with the page. That's when we found him." He rubbed the side of his face. "What's going to happen? They won't hurt Sorel, will they?"

"I don't think so." Bronwyn returned to the dining hall. She glanced at the row of faces from the ladies, watching her. Lady Susanna's face was impassive, but she sat stock-still in her place on the bench. Her gaze never left Bronwyn.

At the sight of her, the empress motioned her forward. Bronwyn went to her side and spoke softly in her ear. "Tristan is dead. We found him in the stables. I'm not sure how he died. We think it might have been an accident. But he had a saddlebag with him. It looked like he was leaving. Did you task him with delivering a message, Your Grace?"

The empress hissed, "See me in the throne room immediately." She looked back at the nobles dining around her and replaced her expression with a pleasant smile.

Bronwyn curtsied and excused herself and made her way to the empress's throne room.

A few minutes later, she was joined by the empress, who paced the room as Sir Miles stood by. The empress wore a simple gold circlet on her head. She said, "I would not ask this of you, Bronwyn, but there are few whom I can trust. There is a spy at court, as you well know, and Tristan's death has complicated matters."

She shot a glance at Sir Miles, who gave a stiff nod.

"We are planning a tactical retreat, and we need to let Sir Robert know so he can cover our rear. I had not tasked Tristan with delivering such a valuable message, but now that he is gone, we need to move quickly and—"

"I would not tell the girl too much, Empress, in case she is captured and put to the rack. She cannot reveal what she does not know," Sir Miles said.

Bronwyn's eyes widened. "'The rack'?"

"That won't happen to you, I'm sure," the empress said. She stood back as Sir Miles wrote a quick note on some parchment and dripped some burning wax on the folded-up section. "Use my ring, Sir Miles. Then Sir Robert will know it's from me."

She gave it to him and he pressed it into the wax. "There." He handed Bronwyn the letter. "Take this to Sir Robert and guard it with your life."

Bronwyn balked. She was supposed to go out in the middle of a battlefield? If she were lucky, she would be shot by a stray arrow. If she were unlucky, she might be captured and tortured for information—or worse.

The empress crossed her arms beneath her chest. "We will

move soon, but that's not for just anyone to know. This siege has gone on long enough, and I did not take Winchester just to see my loyal subjects waste away under that woman's attack."

"Why me, Your Grace?" Bronwyn asked. "Surely, there are scouts or pages who could go."

"Because with Tristan dead, I need someone I can trust. Someone who will act, someone who is—"

"Unremarkable. Easily overlooked. You fit the bill," Sir Miles said brusquely. "We need a messenger who can pass unseen, and you're just a kitchen maid. No one will suspect you. They'll think you're running an errand or looking for roots or something." He looked down at her. He had a wiry look about him, and a pale face with a pointed nose and short, brown hair cropped short to his head, almost like a priest. "Do this, girl. Do not fail."

She looked at the man. He showed little concern or care for the fact that his squire had been found dead. Was he so uncaring, or was he too busy for such matters? Or did he show his emotion in private?

"But how am I to get out of the castle unseen? There are guards and the invading army…" Bronwyn started.

Sir Miles gave her a sour look. "I'm sure you'll think of something. Travel at night and stick to the shadows so no one will see you, if you want my advice. Go on foot. Do not take a horse."

"We'll be eating them soon at this rate," the empress muttered. She sat down in a chair and rested her elbows on the table that bore a great map of the city. "Good luck. And, Bronwyn…"

Bronwyn slipped the note up her sleeve and met the empress's hard gaze.

"Don't disappoint me. I don't think I need to explain just how serious this is, or how imperative it is that you don't get caught. I would hate to think what might happen if you were."

Bronwyn swallowed. Death—or worse. She didn't want to think about it.

"When shall I go, Empress?"

"Immediately. It will be dark soon, so you'll have a better

chance of not being seen. Tell no one we asked this of you. The fewer people who know, the better."

"If there were anyone else, we wouldn't ask," Sir Miles muttered.

Bronwyn breathed out through her nose. She took that to mean if there was anyone else less important who wouldn't be missed. She was expendable; that was the message. "I understand."

"Good. I knew I could rely on you."

Sir Miles waved her away with a hand.

As she exited the room, she overheard him ask, "Was that wise?"

"What choice do we have? Everyone else is too important. Like you said, we need someone who will be overlooked. As a servant, she'll just be another part of the scenery. I just hope she survives."

Bronwyn swallowed and went on her way. Being summertime still, the nights were still quite light out, and it didn't get dark until extremely late, well past the time she went to sleep. Instead, she made a decision. If she was to be part of the scenery, then she'd need to blend in. She bound her hair back in a kerchief and took a basket from the kitchen, as well as a few old, musty apples that were soft and squidgy, past ripe. Avoiding others, she snuck out of the castle, tiptoeing through the brewery and slipping out through the entrance that Sister Joan had shown her.

She breathed in the scent of fresh air and trod down the hill, taking care not to trip and fall as her shoes found purchase in the tall grass. The footing was treacherous and she had to carefully manage her feet so she didn't trip and fall. Bronwyn eventually made her way down and kept to the alleys, staying out of sight as best she could whilst men marched nearby. She vaguely remembered the way back to St. Swithun's and was most of the way there when a familiar voice said at her shoulder, "Mind telling me what you're doing?"

Bronwyn whirled around, her eyes wide. "Rupert."

Warmth filled her chest at the sight of him. She could see him in the encroaching darkness and his familiar smile sent a thrill right down to her toes. It had been weeks, and she'd missed him.

"In the flesh. What are you doing out here, Bronwyn? It's not safe." His voice held a note of concern.

"What are *you* doing here?" she asked. "How did you find me?"

"I've been watching since you left the castle. I thought I recognized that kerchief you wear."

She tensed. Had he noticed the secret passage? Bronwyn wanted to trust him. They had become close over the past few months and she'd come to rely on him as a trusted friend, a confidante. But he was allied to the queen, and Bronwyn was on a mission for the empress. She could not fail.

She touched a hand to her head and looked at him. "I was sent out to find food. They're starving in there."

He looked her up and down. "That doesn't surprise me. You're looking thin." He peeked in her basket. "And so you found some old apples."

"It's better than nothing. I thought maybe I could barter or trade…" She avoided his eyes.

"That's all you're doing?" he asked.

"What else? Like you say, it's not safe out here. I wouldn't go unless I had to." She looked over her shoulder. Bronwyn couldn't shake the sneaking suspicion that crept down her spine. If Rupert had seen her, who else had?

"But you're a cook. A baker. Why you?"

"I'm nobody. They figure I'm easily… I'm expendable. I have no family, so it doesn't matter." She swallowed the sudden lump in her throat.

He reached for her and touched her arm. "You're not nobody. And you have friends. You have me. And Alice. And Theobold." His mouth twisted at the name. "What I mean is, you're not alone."

Their eyes met, and a moment passed, then two. A part of

her relished the feel of his warm hand on her, even if it was just a friendly pat on the arm.

"I heard you… rejoined the queen's army," she said.

He dropped his hand. He shifted his weight and nodded. "It was the right thing to do."

"But what about Lady Alice?"

He looked away and rested a hand on his belt. "I always was the queen's man, Bronwyn. Alice seemed to forget that. For what it's worth, I never meant to hurt her."

"What do you want me to tell her?"

He shrugged. "I don't know." He eyed her. "You're quite close to St. Swithun's, where some of the empress's forces are."

She dug a hole in the dirt with the toe of her shoe. "I was hoping to see Theobold."

Rupert's mouth curved into a half-smile. "Of course you were. Come on, I'll escort you. It's not safe for you to be out here alone."

They walked together. The city of Winchester was lit with torches in some places, and men marched through the streets, but smoke lingered in the air, and all the regular smells and sounds that Bronwyn associated with a city were missing. There were no dogs barking or wives talking over hanging laundry. Men didn't stop in the street to chat or drink, and children didn't run and play in the muddy roads, chasing each other. The laughter was gone. The smells of horse dung, privies, and cesspits were still pungent, but there were far fewer people out. The night air grew a touch cooler, and Bronwyn got the sense that many people were hiding indoors.

As they approached the entrance to the grounds of St. Swithun's, Rupert stopped. "I can't go any farther, but you can. If you're not back within ten minutes, I'm coming in after you."

"Do that and you'll be slain. You're the queen's man, re-member?" she said with a smile.

He smirked. "Glad someone remembers it. But I mean what I said. Ten minutes, Bronwyn. Go."

Bronwyn darted into the grounds and hurried. Most of the guards overlooked her, especially as she either smiled or nodded and made as if she belonged there. A few guards helped themselves to the apples she carried, until she had none left. They were hungry too, she could tell. The men were all thin and some watched her warily, their clothes hanging on their skinny forms, some with a hungry look in their eyes. She entered the main hall and spotted Sir Robert, looking over a map of the area, surrounded by his men.

Theobold started at seeing her. He made to move, then stopped himself. He quickly said something to Sir Robert, who looked up. The men watched as she approached. When a pair of guards stopped her, Sir Robert said, "Let her through."

The guards raised their spears and she approached. "Sir Robert, I carry a message."

His eyes were sharper than a hawk's. "From whom?"

"Sir Miles and the empress."

"Bring it here." He motioned her forward.

She set down the basket, slipped the note from her sleeve, and handed it to him.

"Why have we received no pigeons? Why send a slip of a girl like you?" Sir Robert asked.

Bronwyn said, "Someone killed all the pigeons."

There were a few curses, mutters, and angry looks around the room.

"So it's true, then. As we feared. There's a traitor still in her castle." Sir Robert breathed out noisily, a grim expression on his face. "You didn't read this?" he asked, turning it over. He examined the unbroken seal.

"No." She shook her head. "I can't read." She felt embarrassed at having to admit it.

Sir Robert grunted and broke open the seal. He turned, reading it, then glanced sharply at Bronwyn. "Do Sir Miles and the empress wish for a response?"

Bronwyn stopped. "They didn't say."

"Very well. Tell her we will follow this plan. Go. Theobold, show her out."

Bronwyn waited for Theobold to come to her, then turned, picked up her basket, and began to walk. They walked quietly side by side until they passed around a corner and he pulled her into the shadows. She squeaked.

He tilted her face up to meet his. "You foolhardy, brave woman. I don't know whether to shake you or kiss you."

Bronwyn knew at that moment which she would prefer. Her breath hitched, and she felt her blood start to pulse in her veins. His hands on her arms sent warm tingles down her spine.

"Have you any idea how dangerous that was? Coming here alone with a message from the empress? Extremely, in case you're wondering." His dark eyes bore into hers, the black irises widening.

"I'm not alone. I ran into Rupert and he escorted me here."

That was the worst thing she could have said. At the mention of Rupert's name, Theobold's hands dropped. "Of course he did. How lucky you ran into the traitor on your way here. No doubt he was watching you."

She looked up at him. "Why are you so suspicious?"

"'Cause he's a traitor, that's why. The moment we were under attack, he broke ranks and ran. You remember Sir Ranulf, the knight of Maud's he was told to serve? He's royally angry with Rupert for leaving his service. Luckily for Rupert, the knight is fighting right now; otherwise, there'd be hell to pay."

She frowned at him. "Rupert's my friend."

"You choose strange company to be friends with. You may want to rethink your loyalties." Theobold glared at her and cursed. "I'm glad to see you alive and well. I..." He ran a hand through his dark curls. "I don't want to talk about him. I'd rather—"

"Theobold," a voice called.

"I'd better go." He met her eyes. "Promise me you'll be careful in getting back?"

She nodded. "I will."

"I assume Rupert's going to see you back there."

"I reckon so."

The voice called for Theobold again.

"Very well. I don't like it, though." He leaned down and kissed her slowly, on the lips.

The moment Theobold's lips met hers, her eyes closed, and a warm thrill fluttered through her. He cupped her chin in his hands, and she dropped her basket, letting it fall to the ground, forgotten. She kissed him back, liking the subtle roughness of his lips against hers. She felt the press of his body, all rough-hewn hard muscle but warm, as she was pinned against the stone wall. Her hands tangled in his dark curls as he pulled her against him, trailing soft kisses down her neck. They tickled. She gasped, and her eyes opened.

"Theobold," she hissed, trying to ignore the touch of his lips and facial hair on his chin against her neck.

"I'm sorry." He released her. "I should never have pushed you into that. It was wrong of me." He looked away.

"No, it's not that. I mean that's true, but I... We're not alone," she whispered.

He whirled around, covering her with his body.

Protecting her, she realized.

It was a page. "Sir Robert wants you, Theobold. Right now." The page nodded and left.

Theobold cursed and turned back to her, his eyes black. Then a slow smile crept up his face.

She knew it well, for it matched her own. He'd kissed her, and she'd liked it. She felt her cheeks; they were warm.

He laughed, and she blushed. Theobold winked at her, and she looked away, earning another laugh from him. He took her hand. "I'll see you to the entrance. For your protection."

She knelt to pick up her basket, but he was faster and picked it up for her. Holding it in his left hand, he entwined her left arm in his right, as if he were escorting a grand lady through the corridors. She smiled at the thought.

All too soon, they were at the entrance to the grounds. He returned the basket to her. "Will you be all right getting back? Even with *him* nearby, I…"

"Worried about me?" she teased.

The smile left his face. He gave a quick nod. "I would go with you if I could." He looked at his shoes. "People know me as Sir Robert's squire. If I were captured, they would torture me for information or ransom me. I'm not worth paying a ransom for, so I need to stay by his side."

She nodded. "I understand."

"Be careful, Bronwyn." He raised her left hand to his lips. "I mean it."

She exited the grounds, where Rupert met her a short distance away. He stepped out of the shadows and said, "You're acting different. What happened?"

"Nothing." She blushed, thinking of Theobold's kiss.

Rupert snorted. "Uh-huh. Sure. Then why are you walking with a twist to your hips and why are your cheeks so pink? You look like you've been…"

"I'm fine. I met Theobold."

"'Course you did." Rupert's expression darkened. "As long as he didn't force you into doing anything."

"No. Nothing like that."

He saw her blushing smile and laughed.

Once they were at a safe distance and were back at the castle, Rupert bid her good evening. "Tell Alice I said *hello*."

Bronwyn nodded and waited for him to disappear into the shadows before she took the precaution to make a circle around the castle first, then dart up the hill, using the secret passage through the brewery to get back inside.

She hurried as quick as she could to the throne room and begged an audience with the empress, on a matter of urgency. The guards frowned. "What's a maid like you want with the empress?"

"Please. She sent me to deliver a message."

"A maid? Don't you know there's a war on? Likely story. Look, not just anyone can see the empress, all right? Now get back to where you belong or I'll take my boot to yer backside." The guard looked interested in this possibility.

"Leave it, Edwin, I've seen her around before. Works in the kitchens." To Bronwyn, he said, "Wait here," and disappeared inside the room.

A minute or so later, he came out again and opened the door. "You're to go in. But keep it short."

The other guard, Edwin, was wide-eyed. "Her? What's the empress want her for?"

"Maybe she wants to place an order for food. I don't know, and I didn't ask. Go on in, girl."

Bronwyn took a deep breath and walked in, feeling her palms sweat as the guards shut the doors behind her with a loud *thud*. She rubbed her palms on her skirts to dry them.

She strode to the front of the room, where the empress sat on her wooden throne, with guards and Sir Miles by her side. At the sight of Bronwyn, he stared. "You're alive."

Bronwyn curtsied.

"Rise. I am glad to see you, Mistress Blakenhale. Tell me how you made it out there. You did not get accosted or give away all our secrets?"

"No, Your Grace. I delivered the message, as you bid me."

"And?"

"Sir Robert said they will follow your plan."

"No other message?"

"No, Your Grace."

"Very good. You may go." The empress waved her away.

As she curtsied and backed away, Bronwyn heard her say, "Well, wonders never cease. She made it back. I wonder how she did it."

Sir Miles said, "No doubt the soldiers didn't bother with killing a maidservant. She's too unimportant to be of use. They're only interested in warriors." A moment later, he said, "We'll have to use her again."

Once she'd returned to the kitchen, Bronwyn helped clean up the pots and pans, then scrubbed the cooking cauldrons from dinner. She needed busy work to help her mind consider what was happening. Who would want to kill Tristan, and why? He was the squire to Sir Miles, an earl, and one of the empress's trusted military commanders. Was his death a message to his master? Was there a spy or an enemy in the empress's court?

Or was the answer closer to home, in a way? As she scrubbed the inside of a pot with water and a scouring brush, she thought about how Tristan had said he'd figured who was behind the little accidents. Maybe he'd gotten too close, and whomever he'd suspected had overheard their conversation about how Tristan had needed to reveal all at dinner that evening and so the real culprit had killed him before he could escape. Maybe they had paid him off to leave. Or perhaps they had met to discuss something with him, and he'd fled out of fear, when they'd found him in the stables and killed him, making his death look like an accident.

She thought back to the scene of his death. There was no apparent murder weapon. So how had he gotten so much blood on him? It just didn't make sense.

She found a spot on the floor in the great hall near the other servants that night and slept. The floor was cold, but now being September, the summer heat was fleeting, and she was glad to be inside. There was a fire in the hearth, and it crackled. Its embers were warm and inviting.

A hand woke her up in the dead of night. Lady Alice stared down at her. "Bronwyn," she said, her eyes wide. "It's the empress. She's gone."

Chapter Nine

BRONWYN RUBBED SLEEP from her eyes. Had she heard that right? The empress was gone? It must have been the note she had delivered to Sir Robert earlier. It had involved plans for a retreat. Of course. She just hadn't through it would happen so soon.

She stared at Lady Alice, whose face was tight with worry. "Get up. I need you."

"What is it? I must've been dreaming. I thought you said—"

"The empress is gone," Lady Alice repeated.

Bronwyn jerked and shot to her feet. She'd been so tired after all the busyness and stress that she'd fallen asleep in her clothes and had been dead to the world.

"What do we do?" Lady Alice asked. "And I say, why aren't you surprised? Did you know of this plan?"

"I…"

Lady Alice tsked. "We are going to have a talk about sharing information between friends, but now is not the time. The empress has fled. Gone in the night. Lady Susanna was sleeping in her chamber when she came into ours in the middle of the night and said Empress Maud had never come to bed that evening and instead had been going to the chapel to say her prayers. Then Lady Susanna fell asleep and when she woke up, the empress was gone. Her bed wasn't slept in."

Lamps were being lit. Whispers filled the space. Servants

were being shaken awake. Torches around the room were being set alight and the word spread like wildfire. The empress had left, stealing away in the dead of night.

"I went out to the chapel myself. It was empty," Lady Alice said. "And now I've heard whispers that the city is burning. Matilda isn't just here; she's brought an army of a thousand men or more, and they're burning the city to the ground. It's not safe here. We need to leave."

"But go where?" Bronwyn looked around. The great hall was busy. She muttered a curse and stretched. Servants hurried past, their feet hitting the wooden floorboards with urgency, like unruly patters of rainfall.

Then she heard it. The sound of marching. Men's boots striking the road. The sound of cavalry, of knights, and horses neighing. Bronwyn went to the nearest window and looked out. The sky was already turning light as she saw hundreds of armored men approaching the castle, coming up the hill.

"Where do we go? They're practically on our doorstep. What do we do?" Alice asked. "Do we run?"

"I don't know," Bronwyn said. "But let's go."

They ran together. "Wait," Lady Alice panted. "We have to collect Lady Susanna. She won't survive on her own. She may be a prankster at times, but she means well. And she's utterly distraught at the death of Tristan. I think they were lovers, you know. We have to get her."

Bronwyn frowned, but this was no time to argue. "And the nuns, I'll not abandon them."

Lady Alice cursed. "We'll never get out at this rate. All right. Where do I meet you?"

"In the brewery. Meet me there."

The girls parted ways, and Bronwyn went in search of the nuns. But there was speed and urgency, and more servants began to run. Some stayed, happy to welcome the incoming army. Others took up weapons and tried to run. Some had already fled.

Bronwyn entered the chapel, running in the early-morning

blue-hued light, and threw open the chapel door. Sisters Joan and Rebecca knelt before the altar, praying.

"Sisters," Bronwyn said. "We have to go. The army is almost here," she said, panting.

The nuns exchanged a look. "We will come with you."

"But where do we go?" Sister Joan asked. "The city isn't safe. I heard it was burning and men were looting."

"There may be chaos and confusion with the army coming in. Now may be our only chance," Sister Rebecca said, looking at Bronwyn. "Let's go to the brewery. We'll make use of our little escape hatch."

The trio exited the chapel and went back inside the castle, just as the soldiers invading drew nearer. Rocks and arrows flew through the air.

They slipped inside the castle. Bronwyn looked around. Against the wall in the great hall, men were running. She stopped and picked up a sword. It was heavy, but it felt good to hold a weapon again. She felt safer and stronger for it.

"Bronwyn, what are you doing?" Sister Rebecca asked. "I hope you are not thinking of violence."

"I am thinking of defending us if there is a need for it."

"The Lord does not condone violence."

Bronwyn's mouth quirked in a smile. That was a bit rich, considering she'd heard of men going on religious crusades to the Holy Lands in the name of God. "I think he would want us to defend ourselves."

"Let us go. We cannot waste time talking," Sister Joan said.

"Indeed. You have said enough." Sister Rebecca glared at her fellow nun.

Bronwyn glanced at her, but Joan did not say more. She followed the women down to the brewery. Lady Susanna was there, but there was no sign of Lady Alice. "If you're looking for Lady Alice, she's gone to fetch Mistress Agatha," Lady Susanna said, her eyes red. Dark circles hung beneath them, as if she'd had little sleep. "There's no time." She looked at Bronwyn. "Lady Alice told me your plan. If you're looking to escape, I'm coming with you. She said I should come."

"I have to find her. I can't leave her here," Bronwyn said.

"But we have to leave. She'll be along, I'm sure. But we have to hurry now. It's not safe—"

"You go on. I'll follow." Bronwyn dropped the sword and hurried. The blade was heavy and she could run faster without it. She moved fast, running up the stone stairwells to the empress's rooms. They were unguarded. That came as no surprise to her, but she needed to find Lady Alice. Even if they were sometimes at odds, she still considered her a friend, and as she had thrown in her lot with the empress, it wouldn't be safe for her once the army arrived. She went inside the rooms, but they were empty. "Lady Alice?" she called. "Mistress Agatha?"

For the first time, she had a proper look inside the empress's room. She wanted to know just how the person had managed to enter the room and leave such things like the knife in the pillow, the sheep's head, and the note in the prayer book, all without being seen. How? There must have been a secret opening in the floor, a hidden stairwell, something. Unless of course, it had been one of the ladies inside the empress's chamber all along. Someone who was trusted.

But then she heard a woman cry out, and turned. There was no weapon inside the room. Indeed, the empress's chest of clothes was gone, as was her prayer book. There was no sign she'd ever been there.

Bronwyn ran from the room and into the corridor. Guards ran, men-at-arms marched past, and soldiers shouted. "Lady Alice!" she called.

She ran up to the parapets and stopped. The morning air was fresh and at that height, cold and windy. The wind picked up her hair and sent it flying around her face. She tugged at her kerchief wound around her neck before it could fly away and stared. Far beyond the castle walls, Winchester was in flames. The city was burning.

Bronwyn tensed and gripped the stone wall for support. Small fires had broken out around the city and whilst some of it seemed concentrated in certain parts, great plumes of black smoke sailed into the air, and large, orange fires, burning bright, caught her eye. She coughed and felt sick for all the people down there. They'd survived a siege and now this was on their doorstep. A worry plagued her. Theobold and Rupert—were they all right? Were they *alive*? She muttered a quick prayer for their safety.

She heard a yell, and it worsened. The chaos. *The hell.*

The air became littered with the screams of the fearful and fighting, the terrified and dying. Arrows screamed and flew through the air, landing against walls of houses and stuck in thatch, striking shutters and men like pincushions.

Men were cleaved through their helmets, boys trampled by cavalry, their small corpses thrown and trampled upon like ragdolls. Buildings burned as fighters and mercenaries stormed through the houses and buildings located with the city walls. The wooden structures were no match for the marching fighting men, who battered in the shuttered windows, kicked in doors to loot and pillage, and set fire to the thatched rooves.

Bronwyn trembled as more arrows filled the air, great shafts of death that rained down in slivers and whooshes.

Horsemen's steeds' hooves struck the ground with the sounds of thunder, riding forward, their shields at their sides. Horses whinnied, and men in armor with spears, pikes, and shields marched forward, whilst the defensive forces met them in the city streets.

Swords clanged and rang, punctuated with men's shouts, screams and horses' whinnies. The air was filled with the scents of smoke, fire, horse, steel, mud, and blood.

Men were cut down with swords, pikes, lances, and axes, and the screams of men and horses dying made the day worse as they cried out. The scents of smoke, blood, and iron sailed through the air, making her eyes water and cough.

Horses tumbled, terrified from the battle, and fell on their sides. Men were sheared through, their limbs cut off in the fight. Men were trampled, as others danced like puppets as their bodies were riddled with arrows. Soldiers with fire at the end of pokers stabbed and burned their foes, whilst men with sharp blades fought, their booted feet slipping in the mud. Some stabbed with short swords, and others hammered with axes, maces, and pikes.

Arrows pierced the stone and struck the walls. Soldiers hacked spare trees and then Bronwyn realized that Sir Robert's forces were retreating.

She took cover by dashing inside the entrance of the parapet, but so did five archers, and she was quickly stuck to the side as they crushed together against the wall. She fled, darting across the stone parapets as fast she could, and down the spiral stairs.

Time seemed to pass slowly as she ran. She was swift and ran quickly, darting around men and fighters, moving as fast as she dared, stumbling and losing her footing along the way. She heard, rather than saw, commanders' calls for the men to push forward.

The guards warned her away. "You shouldn't be here, girl. It's not safe. The archers are busy," one said.

"Are there any ladies up here? Any ladies-in-waiting?" Bronwyn coughed.

"No. No women. They're all gone to the kitchen to hide."

Of course. Agatha might have gone to gather food in the kitchen, or she might have left with the empress, especially if she'd been in the same room as her.

Bronwyn dashed down the stone steps to the kitchen, where the servants had mostly fled, others hiding, and things were in disarray.

Hugh saw her. "What are you doing here? Don't you know we're under attack? You should run and hide."

"I'm looking for Lady Alice, or Agatha, the empress's taster. Have you seen them?"

"No, I just got here. Roused from my sleep by someone saying the city was on fire. I've no time for this. Go hide, if you value your skin," he told her. "By the grace of God, we might meet again." He clapped her on the shoulder and ran.

Bronwyn looked around the kitchen. No sign of the women. She went to the pantry, where Agatha stood with Lady Alice, filling a small saddlebag with bread.

"I thought I might find you here. Come, we have to go," Bronwyn said.

"I know. That's why I'm preparing. Take a bag," Agatha ordered.

Bronwyn shook her head. "There's no more time. We have to leave."

"I'm not going till I know I have enough food to survive."

Bronwyn looked to her friend. "Lady Alice, we have to go. We need to leave—now."

Lady Alice nodded. "Mistress Agatha, we must depart. You have enough."

"I'm not going to share. This food is mine," Agatha said, hefting the bag to her side.

Bronwyn shook her head in disgust. But as much as she disliked the taster, the woman had a point. She took a spare burlap sack from nearby and popped in a loaf of bread, handing it to Lady Alice. "What you're taking should be for all of us."

The taster scoffed and kept filling an already full bag. "I don't take orders from kitchen maids."

Bronwyn huffed. "I'm leaving. Lady Alice?"

"Let us go, Mistress Agatha."

"Fine." Agatha's expression was mutinous, but she stopped filling the bag.

Bronwyn turned and led the way down to the brewery. Where once her steps would have echoed on the steps down to the brewery, now they were drowned out by the noise of men and women running. The sounds of men and horses outside grew louder, and on their way, Bronwyn couldn't help but peek out of one of the narrow window slits cut into the stone walls.

The hundreds of fighters were closer. Trumpets blared as the marching sounded. It was so loud, so monotonous, so quick.

Lady Alice pushed her aside. "Oh, my God. They're here. Matilda's men are here." Her hand drifted to her throat. "They're breaking down the doors."

Fear wormed into Bronwyn's chest. A chill ran through her as if she'd been doused in cold water.

Men-at-arms and guards ran past. One said, "Help us if you can. They're attacking the doors."

Bronwyn moved to join them when Lady Alice grabbed her arm. "What do you think you're doing? You can't help them. We have to escape."

"But—"

"Let her go. If she wants to die, let her," Agatha said.

Bronwyn shook her head. "Let's go."

The women moved toward the brewery. Together, they ran down the steps, where other servants had taken shelter and were hiding.

Bronwyn picked up the sword on the floor. Luckily, it lay in the same place where she'd dropped it. She and the others joined the group in the back of the brewery. They clustered around a back corner. Sister Joan and Sister Rebecca beckoned them over. "Ready?" Sister Joan asked.

"Where is Lady Susanna?" Bronwyn asked.

"Where are you going?" Peter Fforde's voice rang out.

Bronwyn froze. She locked eyes with Sister Joan and motioned for her to go.

"Stop right there," the brewer said.

Bronwyn slowly turned, sword at the ready. It was heavy and weighty in her palms. The pommel's rough leather binding rubbed irritably against her hands.

Peter sneered. "You look like you can barely hold up that thing." He stood, backed by two armed guards. His eyebrows knit together, his mouth turned downwards. The brewer stroked his beard with ink-tipped fingers and pointed a drooping feather quill at her. "Planning to escape, eh? You're not going anywhere."

Bronwyn glared at him. "There was a traitor in the empress's court. I knew it was you."

He flashed her a cold, cruel smile.

"The scribbles. The rude sketches. You were behind it."

"Of course. Who else had the ability? Most of the people here can't read or write." He snorted.

She shifted her weight and gripped the pommel of the sword at her side.

The men caught her movement. "Don't even try to escape. I know about the nuns' little secret entrance. Who do you think kept it open all this time?" The brewer winked at Sister Joan, whose mouth dropped open.

"You knew?" she asked.

"Of course. I knew the night you broke in."

"He was the one who threatened me. It's all his fault. He made me do terrible things," Agatha said, gripping her stuffed bag tightly. "The notes, the sheep's head—he made me put them in the empress's chamber where she'd find them. It was all his doing."

"W-What are you going to do with us?" Sister Joan squeaked.

"That depends." The brewer's smile showed far too many jagged teeth.

One of the guards behind him said, "Master Fforde, these women aren't dangerous."

"Yes, they are. Look, she's got a sword. And that other one with the black hair, she's a lady-in-waiting to the empress." The brewer pointed at Bronwyn and Lady Alice in succession.

"I am too," Agatha said.

"All right. Put down your weapons. You're coming with us," the guard said.

Sister Rebecca chose that moment to launch a spare bottle of alcohol at the guard with a mighty throw. It hit him in the face and he went down in a shatter of glass and liquid. He groaned.

"Run, girls," she urged.

The women hurried after Sister Joan toward the hidden exit as Bronwyn stood by.

"Go, Bronwyn. Go," Sister Rebecca said.

Bronwyn shook her head. As much as she wanted to flee, she wanted to make sure the others got out safely first. She aimed the sword at the brewer, who stiffened.

"You wouldn't dare," he said. "You're just a woman. You don't know how to use that thing."

Bronwyn's mouth curved in a half-smile. It was true, she didn't. But he didn't know that. And it shamed her to admit that she had killed before, by accident, when she'd been fighting for her life back at the battle of Lincoln, and when she had saved the empress from a sneak attack.

The other guard aimed a spear at them. "Don't move a muscle. You lot are coming with us."

"Make us." Sister Rebecca launched another bottle and the men ducked as it crashed to the floor behind them.

"Stop that!" Peter said. "You're wasting valuable wine."

"Let us go, or I'll do more than that," Sister Rebecca said. She eyed the nearest torch. "I'll set the whole place alight. Just see if I don't."

Peter's eyes widened. "You'd try to kill us all? But you're a nun."

Bronwyn was shocked too. "Go, Sister."

Sister Rebecca glared at the men and swiftly moved behind one of the rows of casks and bottles. "Come, Bronwyn. We must hurry."

Bronwyn turned to follow when a bottle struck her arm, sending her crashing to the floor. She dropped the sword as a shock rang up her right arm. It was sure to leave a bruise. The bottle began to roll away as she snatched at it, missed, and tried to picked up the sword instead when a boot stepped on her hand. She bit back a cry and looked up. The brewer shot her a nasty smile as they surrounded her, one of the guards holding a spear aimed at her throat.

"Stop causing trouble, girl. You're coming with us," a guard said. He spared her a glance as his fellow guard began to stand, brushing glass off of him. He shot Bronwyn a dirty look.

"But the others—" Peter began.

"Leave it. We've got more men stationed outside waiting." He nudged Peter aside and pulled Bronwyn up, gripping her hurt arm painfully.

Bronwyn winced as she was hauled to her feet. The brewer slapped her in the face, hard enough to her turn her head. It stung. She licked her lips with her tongue and tasted blood. Bronwyn glared at Peter.

He raised his hand again when one of the guards pulled him back. "Stop. Have some respect. We don't go hitting unarmed women."

"But she—"

"We don't. She's unarmed." The guard glared at him.

Peter muttered under his breath, but he backed off and stood aside.

Bronwyn met the eyes of the guard but said nothing. She had no wish to cause more trouble.

"Find the nun," the guard holding her arm said to his fellow. "I'll watch her." He stood back, spear in hand, and watched Bronwyn closely.

She stood, stiff as a poker. He was in his mid-twenties, with short hair cropped close to his head, and a light-blue, clear-eyed gaze. His expression was solemn. She wanted to thank him for pulling away Peter, who had proven to be no gentleman at all, but did not speak.

The guard looked at the brewer. "Where would the others have gone?"

Peter said, "Five rows back, there's a false partition in the wall, behind some stone that can easily be moved aside. It's large enough for a person to fit through."

"Go with him. Show him where." The guard's face was un-friendly.

"But I—" Peter stopped short and walked away quickly, mut-tering.

The guard relaxed once the brewer had disappeared. His grip on her arm loosened slightly. "Who are you?" he asked Bronwyn.

"Nobody."

"You're brave, I'll give you that." He looked at her mouth. "You all right?"

Bronwyn nodded. She could feel her cheek stinging.

There was a commotion. Voices raised. She looked back as the guard, Peter, and Sister Rebecca marched back at spearpoint.

"There were more. Where are they?" the guard asked.

"Meeting the others outside. They'll be rounded up in no time," the other guard said.

"You rat. You crossed us," Sister Rebecca said. She looked ready to lunge at Peter but stopped short at the sight of the other guard's spear. "Why?"

"I know where my loyalties lie. You chose the wrong side." Peter turned to the guards. "Lock them up in jail. The queen will know how best to deal with them."

Bronwyn gritted her teeth and looked longingly at the sword on the ground.

"Don't get any wise ideas," Peter said.

"Come on." The guards took them through a corridor and down, belowground to where the air was dank and dark, and the trickle of water could be heard. They were hustled out into the streets and marched through at spearpoint, where Bronwyn quickly looked around for Sister Joan, Lady Alice, and Mistress Agatha, but she didn't see them. Maybe they'd gotten away. That gave her hope as she and Sister Rebecca were pushed along. She glanced from left to right. Was there any way she could escape and try to rescue the others later?

"Oi. Don't get any wise ideas," one of the guards said, prodding her in the back with a spear.

Bronwyn kept her head down but still looked for possible escape routes. There was so much chaos around them, surely one could slip away in all the fighting…

Sister Rebecca clutched at Bronwyn, grasping at her arms and holding her fists tightly. "I'm frightened. But we must be strong. Together, we will survive this."

"Yes, we will, Sister." All thoughts of escape left Bronwyn's head.

Soon, she recognized the way. "Wolvesey Castle?"

"It's where the queen is. She'll want to see her prisoners." The brewer sneered.

The women were marched through an impressive gate, past dozens of men who were either tired, injured, taking prisoners, or fighting. Once inside the walls of the castle, they were led through a large courtyard.

Bronwyn looked around for any sign of Rupert but didn't see any. Any thoughts she had were drowned out by the clatter of horse hooves striking the ground as groups of knights rode by, and small contingents of armed men with pikes and spears marched after them.

Bronwyn looked up, and saw rows of archers stood on the parapets, arrows trained on them, some watching, some not. There was no quiet to be had, as men in the courtyard either marched to barked orders, called out, or ignored the cries of the wounded and dying. The sounds of the dying men threatened to tear her heart out, and she blinked back tears. This war was a grisly business, at the cost of human lives. The air was filled with smoke that made her throat close up and her eyes water, and she pulled her left hand away from Sister Rebecca's to cough. They were near groups of men, lying wounded, while others staggered to rest and some simply died where they lay, as far as she could tell. These men needed medicine, doctors, nursing. She could help. But that wasn't to be. Past the chapel, they went, and into a building, down a series of stone steps that led to a prison.

Bronwyn breathed in a large gulp of air as they entered an area that was instantly cooler and free from the smoke outside. Stepping inside the jail, Bronwyn found the area dark and moist. The scents of mildew, water rats, and rancid straw mingled, assailing her nose.

The guards kept the women up at spearpoint. Above them

were the sounds of men fighting, the screams and cries of people dying. Bronwyn knew that sound would haunt her dreams. She was shoved into a cell along with Sister Rebecca, and the door locked behind them.

Outside the cells, she heard Peter the brewer say, "Oi, what are you doing? I'm not with them. I'm innocent. Hey!"

There was a short scuffle and then the sound of a man's body hitting the floor. Sounds echoed down in the cells. With the iron creak of a cell door shutting, Peter banged on the bars and called out, "You're making a big mistake. I'm innocent! I was simply escorting the prisoners, same as you. Let me out."

Bronwyn snorted. At least Peter wasn't walking around free, either. That made her feel relief in her belly. Then she heard a gasp and looked closer into her cell.

Lady Alice stood huddled in the corner, shivering.

"Bronwyn," Lady Alice said, quickly enveloping her in a tight hug. "I didn't know if I'd see you again—or anyone else, for that matter. I thought you might be dead. What on earth possessed you to pick up a sword, anyway? You're no fighter."

I am. You just don't know it, Bronwyn thought.

Bronwyn clasped Lady Alice back and then stepped away. "I'm glad you're alive." And in that moment she realized, she really did mean it. Despite their often petty squabbles, she really did view Lady Alice as a friend, even if she was a noblewoman and Bronwyn was not.

Bronwyn gripped the iron bars of the cell and looked up at the ceiling, where the floors shook from the shuddering stamps of many hundreds of footfalls of booted warriors. She looked over at the next cell but couldn't see past the bars. They were separated by a stone wall. There was no light. Only torches lit outside it. "Hello?"

Sister Joan whispered back. "Yes? I'm here with Mistress Agatha." The young nun reached out a hand through the bars, and Bronwyn had just enough space to grasp it. They held hands, and Bronwyn bowed her head and closed her eyes, as the nuns began to pray.

Chapter Ten

HOURS PASSED. BRONWYN paced inside the cell.

"Stop that, would you? You're making me nervous," Lady Alice said.

"It's better than doing nothing at all."

"There is nothing to do," Lady Alice said grumpily.

Since they had been locked up, Bronwyn had taken note of their surroundings. The jail in the depths of Wolvesey Castle was large and held several cells. These ranged from being quite small and narrow to stretching to a space of about ten feet wide. The cell Bronwyn shared with Lady Alice and Sister Rebecca was one of the latter, for she'd walked its width and length countless times over the past few hours.

"Will we be here long, do you think?" Lady Alice asked.

Bronwyn looked at her askance. "I couldn't say." But inwardly, she shook her head at the naivety of her cellmate. They lived in a world now where siege was commonplace, and personal freedoms could be lost within minutes. This wasn't just a minor inconvenience. This could be their lives now, for weeks, or months. They might not see daylight again, or fresh air, for quite some time. Bronwyn swallowed at the thought.

"I'm hungry," Lady Alice said.

Bronwyn shrugged. There was nothing she could do. The soldiers had taken Agatha's bag of provisions she'd pilfered from the pantry stores, and there was nothing in their cell but straw on the floor and a chamber pot. Bronwyn dreaded this.

They didn't have to wait overly long, for more prisoners were brought into the jail and locked in the cells.

"Who is that they've brought in?" Lady Alice asked, coming up to stand at the iron bars beside Bronwyn.

"I don't know. I can't make it out." Bronwyn gripped the bars and looked out, but aside from a series of men talking, she couldn't tell and it was too dark to see.

A cacophony of voices sounded near them.

"What's going on?" Lady Alice asked.

"Don't know. More prisoners, it sounds like."

A woman's voice demanded, "Who else is here?"

Bronwyn leaned forward. She knew that voice. It belonged to not just any noblewoman, but a ruler.

"Just a handful of women, Your Grace," a voice said.

"Women? Why have you imprisoned women? They are harmless."

There came some quiet discussion, and the woman commanded, "Show me."

The sound of footsteps drew closer. Bronwyn stepped back from the iron bars. A familiar face appeared before them.

"You?"

Bronwyn curtsied. "Your Grace."

It was Queen Matilda. The empress's mortal enemy in this war, the director of the siege they had faced for the past six weeks, harrying Empress Maud's defenses. It was also the woman whose husband had months earlier had imprisoned Bronwyn's father for a crime he had not committed, and who herself had challenged Bronwyn to prove his innocence before imprisoning her as well. For all intents and purposes, Bronwyn should have reviled the very sight of her. And yet, a part of her was glad to see her former mistress.

The queen was beautiful, but in a demure, feminine way. Whereas the empress was all fire and might, Queen Matilda was quiet, her expression calm, her movements graceful. One might even call her wise. She looked at Bronwyn and Lady Alice with some emotion, but whether it was sympathy or pity, Bronwyn couldn't tell.

"Mistress Bronwyn. What are you doing here?" the queen asked.

"I was captured, Your Grace."

"*We* were captured, Your Grace. And rudely imprisoned, I should add," Lady Alice said.

Queen Matilda blinked. "Lady Alice. I am surprised to see you here, although perhaps I should not be." The queen turned to the guards by her side. "What crime did these women commit?"

The men looked sheepish and exchanged a few looks and mutters, avoiding the queen's eyes. *They don't know*, Bronwyn realized.

The brewer's voice called out, "They were with the empress's people and were trying to escape, Your Grace."

Queen Matilda sniffed and approached another cell. "Who are you?"

"My name is Peter Fforde. I'm a brewer at Winchester Castle."

"I see. And you are a prisoner here too?"

"By mistake, Your Grace. There was some confusion during the fighting and the guards thought I was leading them to safety rather than to your forces. It was I who led to these women's capture."

Bronwyn imagined that at that moment, he was puffing himself up like a toad, so proud he seemed of his treachery.

"Thank you for your confession." Queen Matilda turned to the inhabitants of another cell. "And you are?"

"Lady Agatha Carre, Your Grace. I am the empress's formal taster. I too have been imprisoned unjustly. That man, the brewer, forced me to do horrid things, things no woman should ever have to do. I am loyal to your cause, Your Grace. I too helped escort these prisoners to the cells."

Lady Alice sniffed and muttered, "She most certainly is not a lady."

Not hearing Lady Alice, the queen asked, "You did nothing to warrant your capture?"

"Only trying to escape with my life, Your Grace," Agatha said.

"And are you a good taster?"

"None of the rulers I have worked with died from poison." Agatha added, "I am a useful person to keep around."

The queen did not respond to this and looked past her. "You there. Who are you?"

"Sister Joan, Your Grace," Sister Joan's sweet voice said. "That is my Sister Rebecca in the next cell. We are sisters of St. Mary's nunnery in Winchester."

"What are you doing here?"

"We sought refuge from the fighting and hid in the castle of the empress, then when more fighting broke out, we tried to flee but were captured and brought here. We desire nothing but a peaceful life, Your Grace. We would care for the men and pray for their souls, if you would but release us."

"Don't listen to them," Peter called from his cell. "They're probably not even real nuns, but traitors, masquerading to deceive you and take advantage of your kindness, Your Grace."

The queen ignored him and moved on to the next cell.

AND SO IT went on. In each cell, the queen asked why the inhabitants were there, and who they were. She asked intelligent questions and wanted to know their circumstances. Eventually, she turned to the guards. "Release the women."

"What?" Peter protested. "Your Grace, you are mistaken. There's been a mistake. These women are treacherous. They're foul. They're—"

The queen held up a hand. "From what I have heard, these women were trying to escape from the fighting. That is no great surprise, considering what may have awaited them on the streets. I have seen no evidence that any of these women bear me any ill will."

"But, Your Grace—"

She silenced him. Or rather, he grew silent. She repeated her command, "Guards. Release them."

The guards fumbled with the keys and soon let out Agatha and Sister Joan. But when they approached Bronwyn's cell, the queen said, "Wait."

The guard paused, his hand raised with the key in the lock.

Bronwyn tensed, as she knew the next few moments could either spell out their release or continued activity. She swallowed as the queen approached the iron door.

"Mistress Bronwyn," the queen said, "and Lady Alice. I had not expected to see either of you here. I am inclined to release you. Bronwyn may work in the kitchens, as I am fond of those sweet white rolls you make. Lady Alice…" She paused. "You were once part of my retinue. Whilst I am glad to see you are alive, I did see you were one of *that woman*'s ladies-in-waiting. You were in London, I believe."

Lady Alice inclined her head. "Yes, Your Grace. I was at her coronation." She raised her head and met the queen's firm gaze.

Bronwyn liked Alice more for it. She was unafraid to meet her fate, whatever it was.

Queen Matilda's nose wrinkled at Lady Alice's mention of Empress Maud's failed coronation. "You were not a prisoner, then. You were there of your own free will."

"I was, Your Grace."

"And are you still loyal to that woman now?"

Lady Alice ducked her head. "I am, Your Grace," she said meekly.

"*Lady Alice*," Bronwyn hissed.

"I am, Your Grace," Lady Alice's voice grew louder. "I am loyal to a fault, but I *am* loyal. I believe in what the empress stands for."

"And what is that?" the queen asked.

"That the Crown of England is hers by right, and does not belong to your husband, or any man who decides to take it. As

Henry I's daughter, it is her birthright. Had William Adelin not died at sea, it would have been his, and no one would have contested it. This is all because she is a woman, and it is not right." Lady Alice spoke with passion.

Queen Matilda looked at her thoughtfully. "I disagree. But you are entitled to your opinion. What shall I do with you, Lady Alice? By all rights, I should keep you here in jail."

Lady Alice raised her chin, defiant.

A moment later, the queen said, "But I will not. You are a lady, and even if you are from a rival court, I would not treat a noblewoman thus. You may sit with my ladies and me and converse." She paused. "But do not expect preferential treatment, or for them to trust you."

Lady Alice nodded. "Thank you, Your Grace."

Queen Matilda motioned to the guard. "Open it. Let them out."

Bronwyn breathed a sigh of relief as the iron door was unlocked and they were set free.

The queen looked them both up and down. "You are both thin. Mistress Bronwyn, report to the kitchens. You will work there. Lady Alice, with me."

"What will become of us, Your Grace?" Sister Rebecca asked.

The queen surveyed the nuns. "It is not safe for women outside, alone, without protection. You may stay here in my court for the time being."

The nuns expressed their thanks. Queen Matilda began to lead the way out, when the brewer called, "Your Grace, what about me?"

The queen stopped. She turned and approached his cell. "Master Peter, I thank you for the confession you made."

Not far behind the queen, he nodded. "So, you'll let me out now."

"No."

"What?" He stared and gripped the iron bars.

"You knowingly deceived these young women and led them

to be captured, by your own admission. You are a traitor and didn't have their safety at heart at all. That I cannot forgive, and despite having your loyalty, I find I do not want it." Queen Matilda spoke simply, quietly, but with an undercurrent of anger. She glanced back at the nuns, at Agatha and Lady Alice, her gaze finally resting on Bronwyn. "Do not expect Christian charity from me, Peter, when you deserve none. From what I understand, you are a blackmailer and a traitor, and you therefore cannot be trusted. Not a single person here has spoken well of you. That alone tells me it is more valuable to have you stay here, than to let you wander around my court, causing mischief. You may stay here and think about your actions. Maybe in time, I will find it in my good humor to see you again." She swept away, and the ladies followed. The queen led the way out of the jail, holding her skirts up as she walked.

Bronwyn followed, when a voice caught her attention. "Bronwyn? Is that you?"

She turned toward the cell to her left, nearest the door. It was dark, but a torch outside the cell lit up its space slightly. A young man came up to the bars. His hair and face were dirty and streaked with blood, but her heart began to pound at the familiar sight of curled, black hair, what would normally have been fair skin, and eyes that sought her whole body.

"Theobold," she breathed. "You're alive."

※

Chapter Eleven

Bronwyn's mouth dropped open. It was him. The man whose pale skin and flirtatious smile had filled her dreams, with dark eyes that glittered like the night sky. She hurried to his cell and touched the bars. "What are you doing here?"

Seeing her, his eyes lit up. He moved to touch her hands and stopped himself. "I could ask you the same thing."

"Are you all right? Are you hurt?" she asked.

"No. Just a few cuts and bruises. My lord fared well enough." He shot a smile over his shoulder. "We gave them hell."

"What is going on here?" Queen Matilda's voice sounded behind them.

Bronwyn turned around and dropped her gaze. "I know him, Your Grace."

"Who is he?"

"My squire." A gravelly voice came from within the cell.

Bronwyn watched as a familiar middle-aged man stepped forward. He wore chainmail and armor and bore no weapon as he moved with a stiff, heavy gait. His eyes missed nothing. "Robert of Gloucester, Your Grace." He paid the queen a short bow. It was respectful—just.

The queen's eyes widened. "You. Well, well. We do have impressive prisoners, indeed. I didn't believe my men when they told me." Her smile filled Bronwyn with dread. "My dear Sir Robert, your mistress has left you. She has quit her castle, and this city, and abandoned you all."

Sir Robert's face could have been carved from stone.

"She is now on the road to Gloucester. She does not care about you. She makes no move to rescue you. And why should she? You have done a passable job of keeping my armies at bay, but no longer. She is lost without you, and I suspect, will not be able to drum up a force to fight back."

"She will, Your Grace. The empress always does," Robert said.

The queen's eyes narrowed. "Perhaps. Perhaps not. We will see. I do hope you find your surroundings comfortable, Sir Robert. You will be our guest for some time." She walked out.

Bronwyn hung back and waited for the ladies and the guards to pass. She turned to Sir Robert and Theobold. "What will happen?"

Sir Robert glanced at her. "You again. You're always around. I'm surprised you survived this long."

Bronwyn didn't dignify that with an answer and instead looked at Theobold, who was watching her. He said, "They'll try to ransom Sir Robert. See if the empress will pay for his safe return."

"And if not? What if what she says is true, and the empress left?"

"She did leave the city," Sir Robert said. "That was our plan. We were watching her rearguard when William of Ypres's men broke our line. Took us by Stockbridge, at the River Test." He settled back on a bed of straw in his cell. "She has done nothing we did not plan for."

Bronwyn met Theobold's eyes. "How are you?"

"I am well. Better now." He smiled, and it filled her with warmth.

"Stop flirting, Theobold," said his master. "Leave the servant girls alone."

Theobold stepped back. His smile faltered just a little. "I am glad you are well."

"So am I. I mean, I'm glad that you are well. I…" Bronwyn started.

"I thought I'd find you down here," a familiar voice said.

Bronwyn turned. "Rupert."

He strode over and clapped her on the arm. "Good to see you again, Bronwyn."

She tried to ignore the pleasurable tingle his touch sent through her skin. "You're not a prisoner. You're walking around free."

"He's a bloody traitor is what he is," Theobold said.

Rupert shot Theobold an unfriendly look and glanced back at Bronwyn. "I am free. My master is in Bristol Prison with His Grace the King. I served the other side for a short time, but when the battle came, I left and rejoined the queen's forces."

"He's a deserter," Theobold said.

"I returned to my liege," Rupert said hotly.

"Your liege is in prison. It's a bit rich to find you walking around like you own the place," Theobold said.

Rupert squared up to the bars, and Theobold faced him. If there weren't iron bars between them, Bronwyn would guess they were about to fight. Rupert sneered. "And yet you're stuck in there, while I'm out here. Hope the straw and the rats are to your liking."

Theobold glared at him. "At least I'm not a traitor."

Rupert's hands curled into fists. He turned and put a hand on Bronwyn's arm. "Come on, Bronwyn. Let's go. There's a lot we need to talk about."

Bronwyn nodded and let him guide her away, conscious that his hand drifted to her lower back. She looked over her shoulder at Theobold, who watched, his expression unreadable. But he watched, and that was enough. He was well; he was alive.

Once outside the jail and back up the stone steps, Bronwyn took a few deep breaths of fresh air and felt relieved. It was oppressive, dark, and dank down there.

"I'm glad you're well." Rupert removed his hand from her

lower back. Bronwyn felt its loss.

"What happened?" she asked.

"Nothing to worry about. Come, I'll walk you to the kitchens."

She frowned. Why was it that when a person said there was nothing to worry about, that was exactly what she did?

Rupert ran a hand through his dirty, unwashed, blond hair. It hung in unruly waves past his shoulders. She noticed his broad, bony shoulders and briefly imagined him working on a farm, with a team of oxen or horses pulling a plough. She smiled at the thought and then remembered where they were. *What* they were. They were friends, and he was in a romantic relationship with Lady Alice, even if they were on opposite sides of this war.

Rupert walked up the stone steps and waited until they'd passed by a few servants. "Did you tell the queen any secrets from your time with the empress?" Bronwyn asked.

"Nothing that she found useful. She's displeased with me. Wants me to continue allying myself with the other men and report back to her."

"Like a spy."

He raised his eyes and met hers. "Is that what you think?"

Bronwyn said, "I think she's playing you. Like a chess piece."

He bristled. "And what do you know of chess?"

"I know enough to see when I'm being used. Like you are. Aren't you tired of it?"

"I'm not being used. I serve my queen," Rupert said, crossing his arms.

"And what about Lady Alice? She's been worried sick about you."

"Ah. That…" He rubbed the side of his face. "I don't know. She knows we have different loyalties. We'll make it work somehow."

Bronwyn cocked her head at his good nature and sunny disposition. He seemed so sure it would all work out in the end. But unlike her, he hadn't suffered a loss. He hadn't lost his entire family from this war. He traded his service and risked his life for two rulers to play with, like children with a toy. Would he throw his life away for a principle, or if his queen asked him to?

"I should go," he said. "Glad you're all right."

"Point out where the kitchens are," Bronwyn said.

"Oh, yeah. This way."

They began walking.

"Rupert," Lady Alice's voice called from down the corridor.

Rupert looked. "Alice."

Bronwyn bit her lip as Lady Alice ran toward them as fast as she could. She stopped in front of them, a wide smile on her face. "You're alive. I was so worried."

Rupert reached out awkwardly and patted her arm, then ran a hand along the right side of his face. "I'm all right."

"Your hair is longer. I don't like it. You should cut it. You look like a ruffian. I hardly recognized you."

Rupert laughed, his gaze darting to hers. "You're looking well, Lady Alice."

"Tolerably well, considering. What are you two doing here?"

"I came across Bronwyn in the jail and thought I'd show her the way to kitchens."

"You didn't know I was here?" Lady Alice asked.

He shook his head.

That earned Bronwyn a hard look from Lady Alice. "You should have told him I was here, Bronwyn. It's the least you could have done. It's what a friend would have done." She sniffed.

"Sorry, I was talking to Theobold when he came in."

"Ah, yes. I suppose I can forgive that." Alice crossed her arms beneath her chest, earning an appreciative look from Rupert. "Well, I'm here now. But I hardly know where anything is. You will escort me."

"The queen knows you're here?" he asked.

"It was she who let us out of the dungeon. And quite rightly, too. Ladies shouldn't be in jail cells." Lady Alice raised her chin.

"Or cooks, it seems." He grinned at Bronwyn, then said to Lady Alice, "Let me show Bronwyn to the kitchen and then I'll show you around. Isn't the queen expecting you?"

"I dare say she is, but this place is like a rabbit warren. I have no idea where she might be. We got separated when she went to use the privy."

Bronwyn smiled. She doubted Lady Alice knew much about rabbits, and even less about how they lived. "You two should go. I'm sure I'll find my way."

Lady Alice nodded in approval.

"If you're sure," Rupert said.

"Yes, do hurry. I'm sure they need more cooks, now that there's more of us here," Lady Alice said. "Rupert, the queen is expecting me. I need your help."

Rupert nodded. "All right. Bronwyn?"

She turned.

"I'm here if you need anything."

Bronwyn nodded to them both and walked away, just as Lady Alice wrapped her arm around Rupert's. Bronwyn eventually found the kitchens, but it did take her a while. Lady Alice was right; the place was confusing, and in the end, she'd had to follow her nose.

The kitchen was led by a Master Christopher Langley, a tall, thin man with a pointed nose, angular features, and wiry arms. He moved with an awkward, frenetic energy and looked down his nose at Bronwyn. "So, the empress sends us her cast-offs, eh? Just what I need, another mouth to feed. But we always want more hands scrubbing pots." His grin showed missing and yellowed teeth.

Bronwyn's shoulders slumped. Once again, she would have to prove herself, starting with the scullery boys. Her fingers would ache and feel soggy and raw from scouring dirty pots and pans, but it would be worth it. Taking on the kitchen's lowest jobs was better than rotting in a cell.

She nodded and followed Master Christopher to where a pair

of youths was scrubbing pots. She introduced herself and got stuck in.

Hours later a page entered the kitchen and approached the head cook. Christopher shot Bronwyn a dirty look and muttered something to the boy, who left. He called over to Bronwyn, "What's this I hear about you making white rolls with honey?"

Bronwyn looked up. So the queen hadn't forgotten. She wiped her hands on her apron and approached the head cook. "They're something I used to make for the queen, back at Lincoln."

"I don't need your life story. Do you know how to make these rolls she's talking about?"

"Yes."

"Then do it. Be quick about it. I won't have any timewasters in my kitchen." Christopher said, eyeing her.

Bronwyn asked around to find the pantry and where the flour was kept and got to work. It wasn't very well stocked at all, and in truth, it was a mess. Flour sat in bags, open and discarded. Flour was precious. She peeked into a bag. Small weevils were there, making her wince and wrinkle her nose in disgust. She removed a small bag of the expensive white bread flour and carefully took just enough, tossing out any weevils she found. Finding a small, clear workspace to use, she made twelve small white bread rolls with a bit of honey, which was just as well, for Christopher took one once they were finished. "Not bad. Could be better," he said, chewing. "They're passable. I'll call for a page."

A page came and took the platter with the bread rolls.

"Bronwyn, go with him and see if the queen has any complaints. Wouldn't surprise me if she did. But if I hear you've been flapping your lips and talking about me, it'll be the worse for you." Christopher pointed at her.

She swallowed and followed the page out of the kitchen. What she had done to incur Christopher's anger and dislike, she didn't know. But that was the thing about some castle kitchens;

they were often full of prideful cooks, and she needed to get along with people to do well. She wandered through the corridors and up a circular stairwell, glad to have the page lead the way. The castle was organized in a similar formation to others she had worked at, but it was still a bit of a maze.

When the page finally paused in front of a door that was guarded by two armed men, Bronwyn stood up straight.

"We're here to bring rolls to the queen," the page squeaked. He couldn't have been more than ten years old.

"Go in," the left-hand guard said, opening the door.

Bronwyn went inside. Not so dissimilar to the empress's bedchamber, this was a sort of sitting room, where the queen sat on a wooden chair with a low back, surrounded by a handful of women, including the two nuns, Alice, Mistress Agatha, and another she didn't recognize. Her eyes widened to see Lady Susanna there, looking well and unharmed.

The queen clapped her hands and beckoned her forward. "Ah. Mistress Baker. Ladies, have you met my good baker, Mistress Bronwyn Blakenhale?"

Bronwyn curtsied and rose slowly. Judging from the ladies' watchful looks and amused smiles, her curtseying had improved over time, but not by much. Her rustic peasant ways stood out, and Lady Alice's hurtful words from before replayed in her mind. She would never be like them, so why even try? She hadn't thought there was any harm in trying to better herself by learning French, but...

Bronwyn stood by, hands clasped behind her as the page offered the platter of sweet white bread rolls to the ladies present. She looked on, half-expecting Mistress Agatha to intervene or at least comment on the need for her services, but aside from the woman looking slightly pink in the cheeks, Agatha said nothing.

Once each woman had taken one and the queen had taken a bite, the others nibbled politely at their rolls.

"Very good, Bronwyn, as usual. But that comes as no surprise."

"I am glad they are to your liking, Your Grace."

"And such a honeyed tongue. She always did have a way with words. But then I find most cooks do," Lady Alice said, setting her bread roll aside.

Bronwyn blinked.

"And do you converse with many cooks, Lady Alice?" Agatha asked, licking her fingers of crumbs.

Lady Alice turned pink. "No, not so often. But I imagine you do, as part of your work. Aren't you often in the kitchens, looking into the dishes to be served that day? I hear you're especially fond of chicken." Lady Alice's words held a sharp retort.

Agatha froze, and her cheeks turned red. "I think we are all partial to that."

"I agree," the queen said, nibbling her roll. She dismissed the page and said, "You may go, Bronwyn, but don't go wandering around. Stay in the kitchens unless I send for you. We have just ended our siege, and the men will be wanting a good meal tonight to celebrate. There is much to do." She rose from her chair, as did her ladies-in-waiting. "I must speak with my advisors. Do converse amongst yourselves." She swept from the room.

Bronwyn stood aside, mid-curtsy, as the queen left. Once the door had closed, she rose and turned to go, when the ladies began talking.

"Well. Who are you again? Some baker she's taken a fancy to?" the unknown lady-in-waiting asked. She stood of an average height, with a narrow face and a veil camped tightly over her hair that matched her dark-blue dress. She looked a trifle severe for Bronwyn's liking, but that could also be down to the woman's set jaw and angular features.

Bronwyn inclined her head. "Bronwyn Blakenhale. I'll just be going."

"Wait a moment."

Bronwyn bit her lip. Every moment she was away from the kitchen was a moment longer in which Christopher had a chance to get annoyed at her for being absent.

"So you are all from the empress's court." The lady-in-waiting shuddered. "I know the queen did you all a kindness in bringing you up from the jail cells, but honestly, I wouldn't be surprised if one of you tried to murder me in my bed."

Lady Alice sniffed. Agatha looked at the woman with thinly disguised distaste. "Lady Muriel, just because we were in the empress's court, does not make us murderers."

Bronwyn thought, *But you are a liar and a thief,* while Lady Susanna gave a little laugh. Her eyes were still red. Could it be from crying over Tristan? "Ha, that won't happen. We're just happy to be alive."

"Was it really so terrible, being at siege in that castle?"

Lady Susanna nodded. "Someone was playing nasty tricks on the empress."

"Lady Susanna," Lady Alice said.

"Sorry." Lady Susanna lowered her eyes.

Bronwyn quit the room. As she closed the door, she heard the lady-in-waiting say, "I don't see what's so special about her. She's just a cook."

"Yes, Lady Muriel, but she's the queen's little pet. The empress liked her too. Why, I don't know," Lady Alice said offhandedly. "She has an annoying habit of trying to ingratiate herself with her betters."

The women laughed, and Bronwyn left, dragging her feet down the stone stairwells to the kitchens. She should have been used to Lady Alice's insults, but her so-called friend's carefree dismissal of her sent a chill through her. Bronwyn spent the next few hours cleaning and scrubbing pots and joined the other servants at their dinner.

Master Christopher ran a decent kitchen, but he had a manner that was naturally suspicious and made offhand remarks that bordered on insulting. He often muttered under his breath when dealing with nobles, and in the days that passed, Bronwyn noticed that his mutters were not so quiet. He disliked it when the nobles talked over him or ignored him, yet he was expected to fawn over them due to their elevated rank. She could see how it might feel unjust, but that was simply the way of things.

She took it upon herself to bring food down to the prisoners. The kitchen did send down food and drink each day, but usually one meal a day, and it was more often than not stale bread and a bit of ale left over from the previous day. With hundreds of mouths to feed, the castle prisoners were often the last on the cooks' minds.

But to Bronwyn's surprise, she ran into the nuns in the jail. The women were often speaking with the prisoners and praying with them. Bronwyn supposed that was no harm done, and it was a kindness. She took moments to speak with Theobold, but Sir Robert of Gloucester called him away more often than not. He didn't trust Bronwyn; that was clear.

Until one day, when Bronwyn brought a trencher of table scraps and bread down to the prison to feed the prisoners. The rank smell of old straw and urine in the air hit her nostrils, and she wrinkled her nose but said nothing as she brought the platters into the dark space.

The brewer accepted his food and said nothing. As Bronwyn deposited platters of food down beneath the bars of the cells, she spotted Sister Joan kneeling outside one of the cells.

"Hello, Sister," she said.

"Good morrow, Bronwyn. I am here to pray with the prisoners so that they might find some comfort during their imprisonment." Sister Joan looked at the cell facing them. She rose and walked with Bronwyn back through the corridor. "They do not have much hope these days. It comes as no surprise, but still. I do what I can."

"That's kind of you."

"It is part of my calling. It is a good thing to do," Sister Joan said. "But, Bronwyn, something is wrong. The men, they speak of ghosts. Of spirits, of shades. They see a man who walks these corridors. They say he was one of them, but now he is dead."

"We're all dead. We're all dead men," Peter shouted.

Bronwyn stiffened.

"Don't mind him," Sister Joan said. "He misses the sun and is going mad from being stuck in a cell. That can play havoc with a man's mind, I think."

"I'm glad you and Sister Rebecca are all right," Bronwyn said.

"We are. My sister spends much of her time in the chapel at prayer, with the priests and the archbishop. She is happier in their company."

"Have you heard anything about your fellow sisters? Did any others escape?"

The nun shook her head. "There is little information on that. But from what I gather, no one else made it out alive." She crossed herself. "We will have to rebuild or seek to join another order. Once the fighting stops."

Bronwyn left the sister to her mission and went to visit Theobold. He stood by the bars, waiting for her. "Bronwyn, my master is sick. He needs tending."

"What's wrong?" She peered through the bars past his shoulder, but it was too dark to see.

"He got cut during the fighting. A gash on his side. When we were taken prisoner, he never saw a surgeon or got to clean his wounds. I worry they'll fester."

Bronwyn's forehead wrinkled. "I'll see if I can get a physician."

"Be quick. He's not eaten anything since yesterday." He looked over his shoulder, his dark eyebrows furrowed. "You're all right? You didn't get hurt?"

"No. I'm fine. You?"

"Same. Just a few cuts and bruises, but nothing serious."

He clasped her hand and squeezed it. She ran.

Bronwyn darted out of the jail and up the stone stairs until she reached the ground floor of the castle. She didn't know where there was an infirmary, or any physicians or nurses to be found. She stopped a servant and asked but got lost, and after asking a few more servants for directions, she found the castle infirmary.

The room wasn't a big space, but it had some beds for the wounded and sick, and a few monks or priests walked around.

Bronwyn went in and approached the first person who looked at her. It was an older man in ordinary clothes, not a monk or priest. "Excuse me, but there's a prisoner who's injured, and he needs help."

"Not interested in prisoners." He motioned with his hand for her to leave.

"But please, it's—" she started.

"Not interested. Clear off," he said.

She frowned. "But it's—"

"Are you hard of hearing? Clear off, I said. Go on, now, or I'll take a switch to you." The older man made a shooing motion with his hands.

Bronwyn gritted her teeth and backed up. Her face turned pink with embarrassment as the other men in the room began to watch and smile at the exchange. She turned and went to quit the room, when she was just a few feet out of the room and a young man said, "Oi."

She turned around, her blonde braids flying over her shoulder. "What?" It was rude, but she didn't care. She felt humiliated.

"What's wrong with the prisoner?"

"Why do you care?"

He looked affronted for a moment. "I'm a physician. I can help. Who is he?"

"You are?"

The young man looked about age twelve. He was one of those people gifted with youth, which Bronwyn supposed wouldn't work so well in his favor when trying to be taken seriously. He was comely enough, in a linen shirt and trousers, but no weapon at his belt, just a bag. "Do you want help or not?"

"Yes."

"Then let's go." He started walking. "I know the way."

They walked together in silence, which Bronwyn couldn't bear. "I'm sorry," she began. "I didn't mean to judge. You look so young."

"Yeah, I get that a lot. So who is the patient?"

"Sir Robert of Gloucester."

The young man whistled. "Right. Take me to him."

Together, they went down to the jail cells. The youth approached the guards at the entrance and said, "One of the prisoners is ill. I'm a physician. I need you to unlock his cell."

"On whose authority?" one of the guards asked.

"It'll be the queen's if you let him die. Show me to Sir Robert of Gloucester's cell," the youth demanded.

The other guard looked at Bronwyn, who nodded. They'd seen her often enough. The guards took a set of iron keys and went inside the corridor, unlocking the door. Before he opened it, he said, "Here, now, look. You, up against the wall." It was an order.

Theobold met his eyes and backed up against the wall.

The guard opened the cell and, in an instant, had a spear pointed at Theobold's throat. "You make one move and it'll be the last thing you do. Understand?"

"Mm-hmm," Theobold said.

The other guard stood back and guarded the open cell door. "Go on."

The youth entered the cell. "Girl, bring us a torch. It's too dark for me to see."

Bronwyn fetched a torch hanging from one of the small sconces in the stone wall and entered the cell. It wasn't very big, and with four men inside it already, the space was fairly cramped. She held the torch and approached the youth.

"Here, bring it here. Stand above me so I can see what I'm doing," the youth said.

"You're a doctor?" Theobold asked.

"Yes." The youth examined the form of Sir Robert of Gloucester, who lay motionless on the straw floor. Mice scampered and danced around their feet, squeaking. "What happened?"

"He was injured in battle, then taken prisoner," Theobold said. "We thought little of it, but he never got a chance to look after his wounds, and now I think one is festering. It's on his leg."

The youth rolled up the knight's right trouser leg, which bore a dark, sodden patch. He moved quickly, touching a hand to Sir Robert's forehead. "He's got a fever. He's burning up."

"What do we do?" Bronwyn asked.

"We have to move him. He can't stay here. It's too filthy." The youth turned to the guard manning the door. "I need you to bring some men. We need to bring him to the infirmary, and he can't walk in this state."

The guard shook his head. "I can't leave the jail until another comes to relieve me."

The youth's mouth set in a frown.

"I'll carry him. He's my master," Theobold said.

"And see you run away? Not on my watch," the guard pinning Theobold back said.

"We can't leave him here. He'll likely die. And he's too valuable." The youth let out a noisy breath of exasperation, rose, and said, "Stay here, all of you. I'll be back."

Bronwyn took the torch and followed him out of the cell. The guards locked the cell door.

The light from the torch played golden shadows on Theobold's face, flickering in the darkness. He looked thinner. Paler. It disturbed her.

Theobold said, "I have to go with him. He's my lord. I have to look after him. No one else will."

Bronwyn shook her head. "He'll be better off in the infirmary."

Theobold bit his lips, licking away a drop of blood. He crossed his arms and waited as the youth returned with two men and a stretcher, which was a strong sheet of linen tied between two poles. It proved to be hard work, but they managed to lift Sir Robert onto the stretcher and carried him out of the cell. The youth said, "Girl, come with me."

Theobold stood, mutely watching as Bronwyn replaced the torch in the wall sconce. She went to Theobold and said quietly, "I'll watch over him as best I can."

Bronwyn followed the man back to the infirmary. They lifted Sir Robert from the stretcher to one of the beds, in a far corner of the room. The older man from before looked on in disapproval, and the monks in the space watched. There was no noise as all observed the arrival of a most interesting patient.

Once he was situated, the older man who had initially shooed Bronwyn away now approached. "What do we have here?"

"Sir Robert of Gloucester, Master Reynold," the younger physician said. "He is important. We need him alive. But he's sick with a fever. One of his wounds is infected."

"That explains the smell. Let's see." The older physician motioned the men back and rolled up the trouser leg to examine the wound. It smelled. "Strip him. We need to see what other wounds he has."

Bronwyn moved away.

"Girl, help us. We'll need to wash him."

"I… I'm a cook. I work in the kitchens," she said. She did not want to spend her hours bathing a man. She blushed at the thought. And besides, Master Christopher would have her head if she was gone too long.

"Fine. Bring up some food for the patients shortly. Warm broth and stale ale, nothing else. You hear?" The older man narrowed his eyes.

"Yes." She turned and left.

Back in the kitchens, she relayed the order to Master Christopher, who threw his arms in the air and ordered her to make the broth. "They're sick and probably going to die, anyway, so there's no point in feeding them well," he said. "Use whatever scraps you like. Nothing expensive. They'll have what we can spare, which isn't much. Whatever's left can go to the prisoners."

Bronwyn raised an eyebrow. He was in a foul mood, and she saw little point in arguing with him.

A few hours later, she'd managed to scrounge up some vegetables for a plain broth and was stirring it when there was a polite cough at her shoulder. She glanced over to look, and it was the young physician from before.

"Hello," he said, "is that broth for the patients?"

"Yes." She dipped a wooden spoon into the pot and held it out for him to taste.

He leaned forward and sipped, then touched his lips. "It's hot."

She smiled. "It's supposed to be."

"Yes, well." He coughed and tugged at his collar. "I'm John Tynsdale. Junior physician to Master Reynold. And you are?"

"Bronwyn Blakenhale."

"What do you do?"

"I cook, I clean, and I bake," she said simply, returning to the broth. There was of course, more to her than that, but it was all she was willing to tell him at the moment. "I'm sorry I didn't believe you were a doctor."

"It's easily done. I look half my age. Would you believe I'm two and twenty?"

They shared a smile.

"How is Sir Robert doing?" she asked.

"He's got some wounds, but nothing so serious as the cut on his leg. We've cleaned him and made him comfortable, but the fever has him. It will be touch and go for the next few hours," Stephen said. "It was smart of you to tell us. We've cleaned his wound as best we can and are using maggots and leeches to eat the dying flesh. But it will be down to God's grace as to whether or not he will live." He shrugged. "Anyway. The queen needs to be informed."

"Why not send a page?"

"Not many pages come to the infirmary, except to bid Master Reynolds to dinner. I mean to go there now and thought I'd come by and say *hello* first."

"Nice to properly meet you."

Bronwyn nodded her head farewell to him when Christopher approached and held out a platter of rolls. "There's been a request for sweet bread rolls. I'm too busy to do it and I can't find any pages anywhere. Take these to the queen." He looked her up and down. "And wipe your face. You've got something on your chin."

Bronwyn took the platter and hastily wiped her chin with her sleeve.

John said, "Shall we walk together, then?"

"Good idea."

Bronwyn asked one of the other cooks to mind her broth for a few minutes and set off. She vaguely remembered the way to the queen's chambers and walked confidently through the corridor until they reached her door. Before the guards, the young man swallowed.

"What is it?" Bronwyn asked.

"I've never spoken with a queen before," he said. "What do I say?"

She started to smile and then saw his serious expression. "Wait until she addresses you. She will lead the conversation."

He nodded. To the guards, he said, "We need to speak with the queen." His voice was higher pitched, which earned him a smirk from the guards.

"She ordered bread from the kitchen. And he is a physician," Bronwyn said. "May we pass?"

The guards looked at her, him, then the platter she held. Without a word, they lowered their swords. Bronwyn opened the door and stepped inside.

The queen was there with Mistress Agatha, Lady Susanna, and Lady Muriel, although Lady Alice was not present. Queen Matilda said, "Ah, Bronwyn. Thank you for bringing the rolls. I have a fondness for them. And who is this?" She eyed the youth. "A brother of yours?"

Bronwyn shook her head. "Nay, Your Grace. This is John Tynsdale, a physician."

The ladies smiled and tittered behind their hands. Agatha

said, "He looks like a child."

"I work in the infirmary," John said, turning red. "Your Grace, we have a prisoner there."

"What do I care of prisoners? They are casualties of war." She tapped her hand impatiently on the wooden arm rest of her chair.

"This is Sir Robert of Gloucester, Your Grace."

Queen Matilda froze. She rose from her seat, wearing a fine blue dress, and said, "Take me to him. Right now."

The rolls forgotten, Bronwyn stepped aside as she set down the platter with the bread and followed them out.

Where the queen went, the guards went, and so it was a small little retinue of the queen, John, guards, and herself that all filed downstairs and to the infirmary. Upon entry, the room quieted as the men stared at her.

The queen wore a simple circlet of gold on her hair and veil, marking her status. She waited until all eyes were upon her, and all tongues had fallen silent. "Leave us. I want no one here but the doctors." She turned. "And you, Bronwyn. You are one of his camp. Perhaps you can be of use to me."

Bronwyn stiffened but inclined her head.

The queen walked forward and approached the cot where Sir Robert lay. Bronwyn moved aside as the men filtered out of the room, whispering amongst themselves. Once the room was quiet and empty but for their small circle and the invalids, Bronwyn kept a respectful distance as the queen stood by Sir Robert's side.

Queen Matilda looked at his resting form. "What happened to him?"

The older physician came to her side. "An injury sustained in battle, Your Grace. He has a fever from infection."

The queen raised a hand to her nose. "Is it spreading?"

"No, my queen. It remains with him."

She lowered her hand and motioned Bronwyn forward.

Bronwyn went to her side as the doctors stepped back a few paces.

"Have you a knife?" the queen asked.

Bronwyn blinked. "Yes, for eating."

"Give it to me," came the command.

She swallowed. The queen was asking for her knife, whilst standing at the bedside of the great military commander of her enemy. What she was planning was only too clear. Did she help?

Bronwyn breathed in, her hand on her belt. To help the queen kill Sir Robert would possibly end the war, but it would betray Theobold and break her promise to him to keep his master safe. But the queen stood before her and had demanded her obeisance. What to do?

Bronwyn removed the small blade from her belt, where it lurked beneath her apron. With a shaking hand, she removed it from its small scabbard and handed it, pommel first, to the queen.

The queen accepted it without a word and looked at it in her hands. She held it in one dainty hand, pale and unused to killing. "It would be so easy to snuff out his life like a candle. Would you have me do it?"

"Your Grace?" Bronwyn uttered, her voice unnaturally high.

"You were forced out of your home when Maud's armies came, led by him. He is one of her leaders, a great man. She would be lost without him and her plans would fall apart within weeks. You have been on the run for months and forced to go along with what that woman had planned. I do not hold it against you. You are merely a pawn to her. So, with one small blade, you could end so much suffering. I leave it to you, Mistress Bronwyn. Would you end this war?" Queen Matilda held out the blade. Her voice was soft, almost gentle.

Bronwyn met her brown-eyed gaze. The queen's expression was clear. There was no judgment. She could take the blade and as the queen said, end it all.

Or not.

She felt indebted to Theobold. He'd helped her out of scrapes before, and had taken pains to protect her, back when they'd been on the road in the empress's camp. He'd even taken her to visit her family's old bakery, when it had been exceedingly dangerous to do so for them both. Time and again, he'd worked to give her blankets and coats, and he'd been there for her when she'd needed someone. But it was more than a friendship. There were times when she actively disliked him—his arrogance and willful haughtiness, for starters—but she also admired his steadfast loyalty to his master and the cause he felt was right. And despite her better judgment, she had fallen for him. She often dreamed of his pale face and black curls, his arrogant smile that both annoyed and thrilled her. Could she betray his trust like this?

She paused. The queen closed her hand around the knife and lowered her palm. "You hesitate, Mistress Baker."

Bronwyn nodded.

"I would too." She handed the blade back. "It is not a decision made lightly, to take the life of a man." Louder, she said, "Good. I am glad to know you have mercy in your heart. It is Christian of you. Even after what he has done."

"What do you mean?"

"But of course, you wouldn't know. Our army was willing to make peace and settle with Maud, we were ready to strike a deal to avoid any additional bloodshed, but Sir Robert wouldn't hear of it. Once he'd captured my husband, he wanted to show the good people of Lincoln how he felt about their following us."

Bronwyn breathed in, her heart thumping loudly.

"It was he who gave the order for the shops and homes of the people of Lincoln to be razed." The queen watched her curiously. "I am surprised you survived the battle but pleased. But you are so young. Did you ever see your family again?"

"No." Bronwyn's voice was dull. "No, I did not."

"A pity. No girl should be without her family."

A lump rose in Bronwyn's throat, seemingly out of thin air. She had not expected this. She had gone back to her family's shop, months ago, but it had been abandoned and taken over by squatters and refugees. Her family had been nowhere to be seen. She'd followed in Empress Maud's camp, but now?

She felt stuck between two rocks, neither giving way. And

now, to learn that Sir Robert had given the order to let the empress's mercenaries raze and destroy the city. How could she ally herself with such a man? It might be all his fault that she had never seen her family since that fateful day. But then, the king had imprisoned her father and would have killed him and her both to pay for a crime. She might have been dead now if not for the invading army of the empress. There was no clear side to take.

"And now we have this important prisoner in our hands," the queen said. "Having him changes things. But you know that, don't you?"

"Yes." Bronwyn could see that.

"I thought you would. You're smart. Not so flighty like some of my women. It's why I like you. Go. You may return to your duties."

Bronwyn slipped the blade back inside the scabbard on her belt. She curtsied and walked toward the door.

Queen Matilda said to the physicians, "I want to be kept abreast of how he fares. If he wakes, I want to know. If he talks, send a messenger. I want to know." She looked at the doctors in turn. "Whatever you do, keep him alive. I don't care if you have to spend your days and nights at his side. Keep him alive. You understand?"

Both physicians nodded. "Yes, Your Grace."

Bronwyn marveled inwardly at the subtle change in the queen's demeanor. She gave off the appearance of a kind, almost shy, demure woman. And yet she commanded a certain presence that marked her as someone not to be taken lightly. That was her choice, Bronwyn supposed. In contrast to Empress Maud's loud shouts and often demanding behavior, Queen Matilda was quiet, but just as formidable, she realized. She too had overlooked the queen's character due to her overly feminine ways and appearance, and she knew in that moment that would be a serious mistake.

Bronwyn followed her feet. She didn't know which way to

turn. Her mind was full of dark thoughts. Before she knew it, she stood in front of Theobold's jail cell.

"Bronwyn," he started, approaching the bars. He wrapped his hands around the iron and looked at her. His face was dirty. "What's wrong?"

"Did you know?" Her voice faltered. "Were you there when Sir Robert gave the order?"

"For what?" he asked. "What are you talking about?"

"The day of the Battle of Lincoln. The queen said they were willing to make a truce, and have peace, but that once Stephen was captured, it was Sir Robert who called for the city to be razed and the shops looted and destroyed. My family's bakery. You took me there. Did you know it was on his orders?"

"Bronwyn…" Theobold's voice was gentle.

"Just tell me the truth. Were you there with him when he gave the order?"

He met her eyes and watched as a tear leaked from her right eye and coursed down her cheek. "Don't cry," he said.

She wiped the tear away angrily. "Tell me."

"I cannot tell you what I don't know."

"But you were there," she said.

"I'd gotten separated from him during the battle. It was chaos. In the fighting, it was messy, and—"

"Did no one spare a thought for the people of Lincoln?" she asked.

He cocked his head. "It is the way of things. We are at war, Bronwyn. I was not there for such an order. But it does not surprise me if that is true. And… I would not have tried to stop it, even if I had been present."

Her jaw set and her nostrils flared. "How could you?"

"How is it you are accusing me, as if I were at fault? That's not fair and you know it. I told you, Bronwyn, we are at war. Both sides make choices that are ugly. There is no right choice, only hard ones."

She glared at him, more tears leaking from her eyes. "How

can you be allied with such a man?"

"He is my lord and master. If he asks me to do something, I do it. I cannot deny him anything," he said simply. "Is it not the same with you and the empress?"

Bronwyn stared at him mutely.

"Whose side are you on? I thought you and I followed the same leader, but now I am unsure. How can you take the side of a couple who imprisoned your father when he was innocent and would likely have killed him when the real murderer was not found? I know the story. You accuse me of having cruel allies, but look in a mirror, Bronwyn. You are not so sterling yourself."

She looked away.

"Aha. So you are unsure as well. Well, that is something, at least." Theobold removed his hands from the iron bars and shivered. "Find out for yourself whom you are allied with, before you start pointing fingers at me. And I would not believe everything that the queen tells you. No doubt she has a plan of her own for you; otherwise, why would she involve you in her schemes?"

"She likes me. She likes my bread rolls." The words sounded dull to her.

"She wouldn't need to know your name. She could easily send a page to fetch some bread rolls." Theobold sighed. "You don't even see it. She wraps you around her little finger, and you like the attention. But, Bronwyn, you have to remember: you are not like them. You are a servant. A cook. A kitchen maid. You scrub pots and gut fish."

She raised her head. The tears were now cold on her cheeks. "You seek to put me down."

"What? No. I'm only trying to put you on your guard, to spell out for you—"

"You mean to remind me of what I am. That I am a peasant, and no more."

"That's not what I mean." he said. "Try to understand."

"I understand you perfectly." She wiped her cheeks clean

with her sleeve and turned her back.

He called after her, "Bronwyn."

She turned.

"Does Sir Robert live?"

Her back stiffened a little. She was such a fool to think he was calling her back to apologize, or that he cared for her at all. He only cared for his master.

"He does. For now." She tossed her blonde braid over her shoulder and returned to the kitchen.

Chapter Twelve

Bronwyn wiped her nose on her sleeve. She wasn't sure just what to do. It wasn't fair for her to blame Theobold for what had been his master's order, but he was convenient, he was there and easy for her to point fingers at. But he'd made her uncomfortable. He'd asked questions that demanded she take a look at herself and ask where her loyalties lay.

But she didn't know. It had originally been King Stephen and Queen Matilda, who had, less than a year ago, blamed her and her father for poisoning people in their court. They'd imprisoned her father for weeks as she'd worked to find the real culprit. But the danger of his impending death had loomed over her thoughts, and it had been by lucky circumstance that the Battle of Lincoln had happened, allowing them to escape. She shouldn't have been angry for that; she should have been grateful. So why was a part of her glad to see the queen again?

She stirred the broth. It was hot enough to serve, so she looked around for a page and gave him a bowl and cup of wine to take to Sir Robert, with instructions to return to the kitchen and bring some food back for the others. The patients in the infirmary and the jail got decent food, but she was not of a mind to serve them herself. Meanwhile, Master Christopher had the cooks working well into the evening, finally sitting down to eat a small dinner once the meal had been served already to the fine folks and guests at court.

That evening, she shared a stale bread trencher with a pot boy, taking a space on the bench beside him, noting Christopher's nasty smile. If there was a sort of pecking order to the seating arrangements at the table, it was always the same pattern, she noticed. And just as easy to see who was close to him and who was in disfavor.

For instance, he always sat at the head of the table, with two of his close mates on either side of him. Beside them were other senior cooks, who specialized in things like roasting meat and poaching fish, and then there were cooks and kitchenhands who were less skilled, who could be trusted to bake breads and pastries, or pluck birds, but more complicated cooking was left to the others.

Below them sat the pot boys and scullery maids, who scrubbed, cleaned, wiped, and scraped the wooden butcher's blocks clean for use. With them sat herself, as a guest of dishonor, or a new person to the kitchen, whose status was as yet undetermined. It also meant that whatever meats and bread made their way down the table, she usually got the last choice, which wasn't a lot. But she knew better to complain.

"How fare the prisoners, Bronwyn?" Christopher asked from the head of the table. "I expected to hear you scream. There are rats down there."

Bronwyn looked up and sipped her cup of ale. She was relieved he didn't know she had already spent time behind bars herself. That would surely give him one more thing to complain about.

"Well enough, Master Christopher. They're alive." She went back to her food. She didn't need to see his face. He liked being called by his title, as the head cook. He made sure everyone used his title. Status was important, especially in a kitchen, she found.

She sat back and let the pot boy sharing her trencher break off part of it to scoop up some of the hot, steaming potage. He was aged about ten and looked hungry, so she let him help himself.

"They don't matter. They're only prisoners. They only get

fed once a day. God's luck be with them," one of the male cooks said. "Hope they all rot in the cells. They're the scum of the earth."

"There's one important one," Bronwyn said. "Sir Robert of Gloucester. He took sick and had to be moved to the infirmary."

Heads turned. Bronwyn blinked. She hadn't meant to become the center of attention.

"Sir Robert?" one cook repeated.

"The military commander and half-brother of Maud?" another said.

Bronwyn swallowed a mouthful of potage and gave a swift nod. "Y-Yes. He was captured in the battle and was in jail when he got sick and had to be taken to the infirmary."

"Why didn't you tell me that earlier?" Master Christopher asked.

"I was making the broth, and you were busy."

He snapped, "That's no excuse. Political prisoners need to be on special diets and kept alive, for Their Graces' pleasure. If they die under our care, it's our heads. Stupid girl, can't you see that?"

"I'm not stupid." Her jaw set.

"Could've fooled me." Christopher snorted and knocked back some of his wine, dropping down his chin.

Bronwyn gritted her teeth. She had a very uncharitable thought about him but wisely kept it to herself. Instead, she took a bread roll and bit down on it savagely, tearing into the soft, risen roll.

Christopher laughed. "At least you know better than to argue with me. Most women talk too much for my liking. Eh, David?" He nudged one of the men at his side with his elbow. The man, a lean, dark-haired fellow with acne, grinned and nodded, drinking more.

Christopher smirked and said, "I'll be looking after Sir Robert from now on. Trust you to be trying to hog all the high-ranking prisoners to yourself. I'm not surprised at all, considering where you came from."

"What does that mean?" Bronwyn asked, her voice passing easily down the table. She looked up and saw that the other cooks were watching but not engaging. This was spoiling to be a fight, and she'd walked right into it. *Blast*, she thought. *Like a dove into a trap.*

"Well, you did come from that woman's court, didn't you? Bet you know a bit of French and have certain opinions about yourself. Bet you think you're better than us, eh?"

"No."

"I don't believe you. You come here and then start looking after those prisoners, almost secretive-like, not saying a word to anyone when you should be up here cleaning with the maids. And instead, what do we find? That you've come across a plum prisoner like Sir Robert and weren't going to say anything."

Christopher rose from his seat and stalked around the table. He stood behind her and said, "Bet you were gonna try to make it out to the queen like you're special, weren't you?"

Bronwyn's hand took a life of its own and curled around the handle of the pottery jug of wine on the table. She squeezed it tight.

All eyes were on her and Christopher as he whispered in her ear, "Bet you tried to give yourself to him and he wouldn't have you, eh? Am I right? You dirty, little—"

She rose and swung the jug at him. It connected with his head, and cracked, spilling wine. He crashed back to the floor. There was an uproar as the cooks shot up from the bench and all began arguing and shouting.

Bronwyn tossed aside the now broken handle, stepped over the bench and said, "I would never. You have insulted me, and you're nothing but a pig. I hope you rot."

Christopher lay on the ground and spat blood. He got up from the floor, a dark look glittering in his eye. "Take her, boys."

Bronwyn's arms were gripped by two of the elder cooks, who squeezed her arms with their thick fingers, tough and firm from cooking. She could smell their breath, soured with cheap wine.

Christopher leaned forward. "You know what we do to stupid little cooks like you?"

Bronwyn glared at him, tensing.

He raised a hand to strike when a voice demanded, "What is going on here?"

Rupert stood there, alongside two pages and another squire. Bronwyn felt hope rise in her chest.

Christopher lowered his hand. "She's mouthing off and hit me with a jug of wine. Can't allow that in my kitchen."

Rupert came forward and casually rested a hand on the pommel of the short sword at his belt. "Looks to me like you were about to hit her. A girl."

"She's more than that," one cook said.

Christopher nodded. "Thinks she's a French hussy, trying to throw herself at the prisoners."

Rupert laughed. "Her? You're joking."

The color drained from Bronwyn's face. She felt the cooks' stares, judging her. She looked at Rupert, who ignored her. She'd thought he'd been coming here to rescue her from being hit, and now… Humiliation and hurt wormed into her heart, like a maggot inside a dead cow's hoof.

"She's no hussy. But if you go hitting her, the queen will find out and want to know why you've been beating one of her favorite servants," Rupert told the cooks coldly. "Let her go."

Christopher's cooks released her arms. Her pinched arm muscles fell painfully by her sides, but she restrained herself from rubbing them. Her face felt warm.

"What do you want?" Christopher asked. "And who are you?" His small, beadlike eyes danced around, eyeing Rupert and his company of men.

"I'm squire to Sir Baldwin of Clare. The people are finished at dinner and wanted to know why there were no cooks or servants around to bring the empty platters away. They sent me to see what was causing the delay." He cocked his head ever so slightly, his blond hair shining golden in the flickering torchlight.

Christopher sniffed. "Just having some dinner."

"And drink, from the looks of it," the other squire said.

Christopher glared at him. "We're not finished here."

"I think you need to understand something, mate." Rupert motioned for Christopher to join him.

Bronwyn watched as Christopher, still dripping with the red wine, walked away with Rupert. He stood off a little ways as they chatted in private, and then Rupert and the others quit the room. Rupert spared a passing glance at her before he left but said nothing.

I'll need to fight this battle alone, she realized. This wasn't his domain, and his status as a squire would only go so far with these servants. She swallowed and smoothed down her apron, when one of the cooks said, "Girl. Bronwyn. Clean this up. You wasted good wine."

"He shouldn't have been about to hit me."

"He insulted you; he didn't touch you. Besides, you're lucky that's all he was doing," the cook snapped.

"What do you mean?"

The cook glanced at her, his eyes flinty. "Let's just say that you don't want to get on the wrong side of Christopher. But you 'ave, and that's your own fault. Tread lightly, girl. If he wants you out of his kitchen, he'll make it happen. Either this day or the next, you'll be emptying chamber pots rather than baking bread if you're not careful."

Bronwyn nodded and went to fetch a dishcloth. She returned a moment later and began to sop up the mess of red wine on the floor.

No one helped her. The other cooks simply resumed their places at the long table and continued eating their dinner, with a handful having gotten up to help the pages clear away the remaining trenchers from the main hall.

She was picking up pottery shards when a pair of wine-stained shoes appeared in her line of sight. Christopher stepped on a shard near her hand and said, "Seems you're the queen's little favorite, eh, Bronwyn? Lucky you. Don't know what you've done to earn her favor. It's not like you deserve it."

Bronwyn paused. A part of her suspected he was relishing this moment, seeing her on her knees, cleaning at his feet like some sort of base scullery maid. Which she supposed she was.

"That squire told me that she likes you," he continued. "Trusts you. And if anything were to happen to you, it would be my head. Can't let anything happen to her precious favorite, can we?"

Silence reigned. He stepped over to the table and there was a clink of some pottery, as he said, "But you are messy, girl. So dirty. Whoops."

Then she felt it. A soft pat of something sludgy and liquid hit her hair, sliding down her blonde braid and dribbling on her back and shoulders. She looked up to see his smiling face, which grinned at her with yellow and black teeth.

She raised a hand, touched the substance, and looked at her palm. Gravy. He'd taken one of the small gravy jugs and dumped it on her head.

"You really ought to clean that up," he said. "You're such a mess. Don't know how anyone could like someone so dirty."

"You never know, Master Christopher. Might improve her looks," one cook said, one of the bullies he'd befriended.

"Aye, you're right, David. At least she'll smell better." To Bronwyn, he said loudly, "Clear that mess up, and don't come back till you're clean again. I won't have any foul-smelling cooks in my kitchen."

With that, one of the cooks let out a loud fart, and Christopher laughed raucously. "Except you, Thom. You're all right." He laughed and walked away.

Bronwyn set her shoulders and made no complaint as she wiped the gravy from her hair and face as best she could and finished cleaning the shards from the floor. She felt the cooks' eyes on her and stood, walking away. Her cheeks burned with shame. Their words about her looks and her smell didn't overly bother her, but Rupert's laughter and comment about her being a hussy disturbed her. Why had he insinuated she was… undesirable? Was she?

The shards disposed of, she'd gone immediately to where there were large, wooden tubs and filled one with water. It wasn't warm or particularly nice, but at least it would clean the mess off of her. And to think, she'd never liked bathing much before. Now she positively craved it. By the time her bath was ready, the sludge had partially dried and gotten thick and stiffened in her hair. It was a mess. She'd have to clean her clothes as well, and she only had one other dress to wear.

Christopher's words rankled at Bronwyn as she sat in one of the wooden bathing tubs, holding her knees to her chest. The water wasn't completely cold, but it wasn't warm, and after the day she'd had, she was relieved at having a moment to herself.

She slapped the water, sending miniature waves to slop against the sides of the tub. Christopher's jeering burned in her mind. His suggestion that she was a hussy, and maybe even had tried to throw herself at Sir Robert, was cruel, not to mention laughable. She took herself seriously. And she believed in the church's teachings, even if she did not attend services as often as she should. But what truly hurt was Rupert's laugh at the very thought of it.

She furiously cupped water and poured it over her hair, trying to free some of the cracked and dried gravy from it. Was she truly so unattractive? For that was how she'd understood the meaning behind Rupert's laugh, and whilst it had put the men off from treating her like a wanton woman, not to be seen as desirable at all somehow hurt more. To think that Rupert wouldn't see her as pretty made her eyes well up with tears.

Bronwyn reached for the small bit of white soap that sat on a dish nearby. It was made of ash, quicklime, animal fat, and other materials, and it smelled. But it also had a bit of soapwort in it that made bubbles, and she used it to wash herself thoroughly.

To be accused of being dirty bothered her. One couldn't be

dirty and work in a bakery or kitchen. *It would only end in disaster,* she thought grimly as she submerged herself in the water and shut her eyes, briefly shutting out the world. She didn't like the world she lived in and felt like there was no one she could trust.

She sat up, pushing wet hair out of her face, and wiped her eyes. She felt mad, furious, even, and slapped the water with her fist, sending it slopping over the sides of the wooden tub. She didn't think she was ugly, but then she'd rarely been complimented about her appearance, either, aside from by her father on feast days or holidays, or her stepmother, Margaret, who'd always told her to wash her face. When men had leered at her, she had always dismissed them as being lecherous old men to avoid. She'd never thought younger men might not find her attractive.

She refused to believe that she was so unattractive as to be laughable to the men, and she rose from the tub, dripping. Bits of dirt, dried flour, and gravy had come off and were floating in the water, which she'd have to empty. But it was worth it, as the task gave her something to do whilst her mind wandered.

She wrung out her wet, blonde hair. The waves were a little matted and stuck together, and she tried her best to comb them with her fingers, but it was no use. Instead, she plaited them as best she could, knotting the ends. She looked at her messy, purple work dress that lay in a sad bundle outside the tub. She'd need to launder it, but the water she'd bathed in now was dirty. She wondered if the laundresses in the castle would allow her to use their tubs.

It was time to try out her new-yet-old red dress. On a whim a few weeks back, Lady Alice had gifted her with a stained, torn, old red dress of hers that she had deemed beyond repair. In her spare time, Bronwyn had taken to mending it and had now cleaned and altered it to fit her. Thankfully, she and Lady Alice were of a similar height, so it did not drag at her feet or hang above her ankles. She put on the red dress and decided it was fine, then retied her apron.

Once mostly dry, she dumped out the dirty water from the

tub and set aside the remaining soap. Then, taking the stained, purple dress in her hands, she went to find the laundry. The laundress present told her she could wash her dress herself and pointed her in the direction of a spare tub that brimmed with soap, suds, and clothes that were soaked. As no one was attending it, Bronwyn took a wooden pole and stirred the mix, thinking it was not unlike stirring soup, and once satisfied her dress was clean, she hung it up to dry.

A quiet but busy hour passed as she hung up sheets and other items of clothing as a way to return the favor, for letting her use the tubs and water, and was told she was welcome back anytime.

Bronwyn raised an eyebrow at this. Then looked and saw that the laundress and her helpers worked solidly, steadily, their hands rough and cracked from constant washing, but it was a friendly, chattering group that reminded her of a flock of geese. Still, they seemed nice enough, and she thanked them and went on her way. She had no real space of her own, or any possessions aside from the clothes she wore, so she tucked the purple dress away in a corner, away from sight, and took a path that would lead to the kitchen.

Then she stopped. That evening, Christopher had made it clear he didn't like her, so why should she rush back to work with him? Perhaps she didn't need to.

She turned around and instead went in search of Rupert but realized she had no idea where he spent his time. She peeked in the dining room, but he wasn't there. She spotted one of the servants who had been with him when he'd intervened in the kitchen and asked where he might be. The servant shrugged and said, "Think he was heading toward the stables."

She headed that way, twisting the end of her long braid around her fingers. She didn't know what to say. All she knew was she wanted to thank him for stopping Christopher from hitting her, but she was angry too. She wanted to face him, eye to eye, and demand to know if he thought she was that ugly. As a young woman of nineteen years, she wanted to know.

The stables were well-lit, the regular smells of horse, dung, and straw hitting her nose. But as she walked on, she could hear some odd noises. She walked farther, closer to the sound, and stopped short. One of the stalls was open. She went toward it and froze.

Rupert was there, pinning a young woman up against the wall of the stall, his hands in her jet-black hair, kissing her neck. She murmured.

Bronwyn tensed. She'd recognize that golden, shining hair anywhere. It was him. The person making the noise was none other than Lady Alice, who started at Bronwyn, then, after making eye contact with her, ran her hand down Rupert's back and said, "Oh, Rupert…" Her face began to curl up in a smile and she gave Bronwyn a knowing look. Lady Alice giggled. "Why, Rupert, that tickles."

Bronwyn stepped on a piece of straw and bumped into a crate of horse feed, making a loud noise.

Rupert's head whipped around. "Bronwyn?"

Heat flooded her face. "I-I'm sorry." Bronwyn turned and ran.

"Wait," Rupert called.

She ran faster, her blonde braid flying behind her in the chilly evening air. She was glad of the darkness, for it provided welcome cover. She felt shame to have witnessed such an intimate moment and to have been so non-thinking as to wonder why he might have been in the stables at such an hour. She wanted someone to talk to. Someone to share her humiliation with, as if tonight hadn't seen enough of that.

Bronwyn stormed out of the stables, shivering. She hadn't meant to see them together, but she had, and it hurt. She didn't want to think of Lady Alice's knowing smile.

"Bronwyn," Rupert called.

She kept walking.

"Bronwyn, wait," Rupert said, running after her.

She picked up speed and started to run, when he clapped a hand on her shoulder and whirled her around. "Bronwyn," he said, panting. "Wait. Stop."

She gritted her teeth. "What?"

"Why did you come looking for me? Why did you run away?"

"You were busy."

He shrugged. "You caught us at a bad time. What is it? What do you need?"

"Nothing. I don't need anything from you."

"Then why did you run out like that? You were looking for someone. Otherwise, you wouldn't have been in the stables this late at night." His hand still rested on her shoulder. "What is it?"

She glared at him. "You don't know what you're doing. You're making a mistake."

"What do you mean?"

"Being with her. You're..."

He snorted and dropped his hand. Rupert stood close, close enough that she could smell the sweat on him, the scent of hay and musk.

Part of her wanted to touch him, feel the press of his chest against her hands. But she didn't. Instead, she stepped back. "You are toying with her. She is a lady."

"And I am squire to a knight. What of it?"

"You aren't the same."

His handsome face clouded. She could see it by the light of the moon. His mouth turned downward, and his eyes pierced her, keen as a knife's edge. "What do you care? Alice and I are both consenting adults. It's no business of yours, anyway."

"You're right, it's not. I just don't want to see you get hurt is all."

"I won't." He laughed. "Is that really what you are afraid of? Thanks for your concern, but... I'm fine, Bronwyn. You don't need to care for me. I'm my own man."

She turned her back. She didn't want to see his amusement.

"You think she will break my heart, don't you?"

"Maybe."

"Maybe she will. But, Bronwyn, it's my heart to break. I'll risk it with whomever I choose."

"I know." But it would pain her to see him hurting, and she could see no other future for them, and their relationship. "But you're a squire. She is a lady-in-waiting to an empress."

"A queen now," he said, reminding her of their changed circumstances. "And things can change," he added, his voice even.

"Not this." She turned back around.

"That's what you're unhappy about. That you think it's wrong. You don't care if I get my heart broken at all. You think it's wrong we are together because she is higher than me." He snorted and ran a hand through his hair. "I didn't peg you for a snob, Bronwyn. I didn't think mere bakers had such opinions."

Her face flamed. "I'm not. I just—"

"I understand. You think that I'm not worthy of her. But let me tell you something. I will be a knight one day, and then I will be worthy of any gentlewoman," he said, so close to her face that their lips were inches apart. His glare was so close that she could feel the warmth from his face, almost feel the hairs of his blond beard. "And it is none of your business whom I kiss."

"You're right."

"Especially when you have your own man to care for."

She was quiet.

"You aren't together?"

She shook her head.

"Now that is a surprise. But maybe it isn't, come to think of it."

She looked at him. "What do you mean?"

"Your principles. You undoubtedly think that as a squire, Theobold is too high-ranking for you. Perhaps you wish to set your sights lower, like the other cooks. Maybe you think everyone should just be with other people of their own station."

She met his eyes. "Maybe they should."

"Well, that is a very small world you live in, Bronwyn. I

thought you were more open-minded than that. Now if you'll excuse me, I'll go back to my lady. She is waiting for me."

"Fine," she said.

"Fine."

They glared at each other.

"Ha." He turned, walking back to the stables.

Bronwyn went to the castle's main hall, where she took up a space against the wall near the other servants. She didn't see many people she knew but stayed near the women for safety.

She did not fall asleep right away but rather watched the dying crackling embers of the fire in the grand fireplace and remained quiet but for the sleeping forms of the servant women nearby.

She had no friends, no confidante. No one to talk to. And Rupert had made his preference for Alice known. And now since she'd walked in on them, she felt doubly embarrassed by going to see him in the first place. What had she been thinking? As her eyelids grew heavy, she fell into an uneasy slumber and welcomed the oblivion that sleep provided.

But it felt like only minutes before she was shaken awake. Her eyes snapped open, and she tensed. She said groggily in the darkness, "Sister Joan?"

"Come quick. It's Sir Robert. He's…"

"What's wrong?" Bronwyn sat up, fully awake.

"He's been attacked by an evil spirit."

Chapter Thirteen

Bronwyn rose. She followed Sister Joan quickly through the halls, their skirts whispering as they moved lightly, quickly, sliding through the shadows, their shoes hardly making a sound. It was the early hours of the morning, she guessed.

"What happened?" Bronwyn whispered.

The young nun stopped, her veil almost ghostly around her pale face. "I could not sleep. I walked the halls and decided to ask the physician monk if he might prepare me a sleeping draft. But when I came in, I couldn't see him. It was quiet but for the sounds of men sleeping. And then I saw it."

"Saw what?"

"A hooded figure, standing over where Sir Robert sleeps. I entered the infirmary fully and I said, 'Brother?' but it wasn't the monk, or his assistant. This man, he acted very strange, and he threw a candle at me, and I ducked, and he ran past. Thank goodness the candle went out; otherwise, I might've lit on fire."

"That is a relief. You're all right?"

"Yes. But I wanted you to come see. I called after him and the monks came; they woke up, but they just accused me of causing trouble. So I ran to get you."

Bronwyn scratched her head and followed Sister Joan to the infirmary. Torches flickered, playing dark shadows against their faces.

"What makes you think it was a ghost?"

"Because I recognized him, and he is not alive."

"Who?"

"The squire who died, Tristan."

Bronwyn's blood ran cold. "What?"

They hurried to the infirmary. Sir Robert still lay unconscious, and from her place at the door, it looked as though he hadn't been disturbed. Torches burned in their small sconces on the walls, casting a flickering warm light, whilst the air droned with the gentle sound of men's snores.

They were greeted by the senior physician and his young-looking assistant, Stephen. The men approached and the older physician whispered, "What are you doing here?"

Sister Joan said, "I saw a ghost. I brought her here."

The older physician's face clouded. "There is no such thing as ghosts."

Sister Joan pursed her lips in a frown. "I know what I saw."

"Which was?"

"A man. A dark shade, hovering over Sir Robert as he slept. I couldn't see past his hood. I thought it was you, but when I spoke, he looked up and ran past me. And he…" She shivered. "It's not right. I know what I saw."

"What were you doing here so late at night? You should be in bed, asleep."

The nun's frown disappeared. "I couldn't sleep. So I thought I would check on Sir Robert and the other sick here, perhaps pray by their sides."

The monk looked at her. "Very kind, but you shouldn't be wandering around the castle at night. It's not safe."

"Did he speak to you?"

"No. He ran and shoved me as he escaped." She bit her lip. "Are you going to go look for him?"

"No. I have no time for ghosts. How do you know he wasn't just a visitor?"

"At this hour? Besides, I recognized him. I know his face," Sister Joan said.

"But it's dark in here. How did you see him?" the older physician asked.

"From the candlelight. And when he pushed me. I saw his face. Then I went and got Bronwyn."

"Why her? Why not one of the guards?"

"I didn't think the guards would believe me. Just like you." Sister Joan looked down at her feet.

"We've been through trouble together before," Bronwyn added. "If she says she saw something, I believe her."

Sister Joan shot her a small smile.

"I just don't believe you," the monk physician said. "I didn't see anything. Did you, John?"

"No, Brother Reynolds. But I confess, we were both asleep. Anyone could have come in."

Sister Joan glared at him.

"Peace, Sister. I believe you saw something. But it could not have been a ghost. They do not exist."

"Then how do you account for the Holy Spirit?" she asked.

"I… That is the Holy Trinity you speak of, and you are not to question me or my faith. Go about your duties."

Sister Joan muttered darkly, "I know what I saw."

"I'm awake now," the monk said. "I will stay with the patients. John, relieve me in a few hours."

"Yes, Brother."

Bronwyn moved past them.

"What are you doing?" the monk asked.

"I want to see if the man disturbed Sir Robert at all."

"He didn't. The man sleeps soundly," Brother Reynolds said. "You should leave."

"I will. In just a moment." Bronwyn went to Sir Robert's bedside. She looked but did not see anything out of the ordinary. Whoever had been by his side earlier hadn't done anything. The monk was right; the man was sleeping.

But then she saw it.

Sir Robert's shirt was pulled open, and his blanket lay pulled down to his waist. But strangely, she leaned in and sniffed. There was a scent of something familiar. "He has an odd smell."

"His wound smelled when he first came here," John said. "It's likely that which you smell."

"No, this is different." She pointed at his shirt. "Look, there's something there."

John approached. "That's strange. It looks like a bit of straw or wheat." He picked it up. "I don't know what that is. Do you?"

"No, but I have an idea. Smell it."

He sniffed it. "I know this smell. It smells like…"

"Ale? Beer?"

"Yes, exactly."

"Whoever was here had a few drinks first?" John suggested.

Bronwyn took the bit of straw. "Mind if I take this?"

"No." John pulled the thin blanket back up over Sir Robert. "But it does suggest that someone was here. We've not given him anything to drink, and he's had no visitors. No one has attended him but myself and Brother Reynolds, and the nuns who pray."

"That means that someone was here. Sister Joan wasn't lying."

"I never thought she was. I only doubt she saw a ghost."

"I don't think ghosts shed wheat, or whatever this is," Bronwyn said.

They looked at each other. "Whoever it was here, they were real."

Bronwyn went back to the main hall with Sister Joan and tried to get an hour's sleep. But it was too short, and her mind kept spinning and she held the bit of straw in her hands. She got up with the earliest of the servants and as the nun slept made her way down to the cells. The guards recognized her by now, and if they were surprised by her early-morning visit, they asked no questions about it.

She went to face the brewer's cell, but it was dark and musty, and the straw moved around her feet. Mice, rats, vermin. She called to the brewer, but he did not answer.

"You won't get anything out of him. He hasn't talked for a day. He keeps ranting about ghosts and spirits. He's gone mad," Theobold said from his cell.

She ignored him. She was still angry with him. Instead, she peered at the brewer's cell, which smelled like a privy. She spoke his name again and said, "We came across this bit of straw up by Sir Robert in the sick room, and I wonder if you might tell me what it is. It is not straw; it is something else. And it smells like a brewery. Could you tell me what it is?"

"How did you come across it?" Theobold asked.

"Just as I said," she said over her shoulder. To the brewer's dark cell, she added, "Sister Joan found a man standing over him a few hours ago and startled him. She thinks it was a ghost, but we found this." Bronwyn held out the bit of straw. "This proves it wasn't a ghost. A spirit wouldn't drop things."

"I don't care about spirits. Was he hurt?"

Bronwyn stiffened. Of course, Theobold would only be interested in the welfare of his lord. That was where his true loyalty lay. She had been mistaken in thinking she placed higher in his regard. She turned her head. "What do you care about, Theobold?"

She walked to his cell. "What is it you care about most? Is it our Lord God? Your master? Yourself? What is it?"

"All of those things and more." He faced her, and she could smell his sour breath, his unwashed body. He needed a bath.

Theobold met her eyes. "What is it you want me to say, Bronwyn? That I love you? I don't. I hardly know you. You're just some woman I took a fancy to."

His words bit at her like frostbite against her fingers. She took a step back. Dark hollows sat beneath his eyes, a sure sign that the lack of sunlight and exercise as well as the dark, damp conditions were taking a toll.

There was a low chuckle from one of the cells. Bronwyn glanced over and turned back.

"I care about my lord because I must. That is my duty. I can't afford to waste time on girls when we are at war." He gave her a searching look. "Especially ones who aren't fixed in their mind as to which side they fight for."

Bronwyn turned her head. "I don't know why I keep coming here."

"Because you are lost."

She raised her eyes to look at him. It felt like a slap in the face. She would prove it to him. She wasn't lost. She would solve this mystery, once and for all. She would prove that she had worth. She was more than a spare set of hands to clean pots or bake bread rolls when the queen wanted them. She would solve this on her own. She had to. She had nothing else.

Bronwyn turned away, walking toward the brewer's cell and repeating herself softly. "We found this by the side of Sir Robert. I thought you might recognize it." She held it out through the iron bars.

No sound greeted her but silence. She stood there, feeling like a fool. She waited one minute, two. She turned around when—

Two cold, bony, ink-stained and dirty hands grabbed her, whisking the bit of straw out of her fingers.

She turned back and stiffened, but the hands refused to let go.

"Let her go," Theobold growled.

Bronwyn stared into the brewer's thin face. It was gaunt; he hadn't been eating. Peter's eyes were like black pinpricks against shadow. His breath was rank as he sniffed. "It's hops; what we would use to make beer." He rubbed it between his fingers and sniffed it again.

Her heart went out to him, a little. "Why did you scribble those nasty little notes against the empress?"

Black pinprick irises darted up to meet hers. His voice was dull. "Just having a little fun." He ran a hand through his oily, greasy hair.

"Then why? Why do it?"

"You don't understand."

"So tell me. Help me understand why."

He beckoned an index finger forward, urging her to come near.

She pressed against the iron bars, leaning in close. Her voice was soft. "Was someone making you do it? Did someone have something over you?" She looked for his eyes but saw only darkness.

He spoke not a word.

"Did someone make you do those drawings of the empress?" she asked. "Did they threaten you if you didn't?"

She waited. One moment, two. She sighed and shifted when a cold hand grabbed a hold of her fingers. The brewer's face was inches away from hers, as he screeched, "A ghost. A ghost walks among us," he spat, spittle hitting her cheeks. "It once was a man, but now it walks and visits me in the night. It promises to kill me if I get out, but I die if I stay here. Maybe *I* will become a ghost." He cackled.

"Let her go!" Theobold shouted. "Guards."

"Beware the ghost that walks among us," Peter warned. "He walks and threatens death to us all. Do not cross him or you will die." He cackled gleefully.

Bronwyn tugged at her hand, but the brewer refused to let go. "You're hurting me," she said as the air filled with the loud thumps and thuds of the pair of guards hurrying over, spears at the ready.

Seeing the guards aim their spears at him, Peter let go and flung himself back into his cell, giggling.

"He's mad," one guard said. "You all right, girl?"

"Yes, I'm fine." She pulled her hand back and wiped spittle from her face.

"Bronwyn," Theobold said.

"What?" She turned around.

"Are you all right?"

"Yes." She rubbed her hand. "Thank you," she said to the guards as she followed them out.

So what did this mean? Someone had been standing over Sir

Robert. That much was clear. But why, and why had he run away when Sister Joan had come in? If he had been innocent, then he wouldn't have run away. Unless he was scared. And what was that nonsense about a ghost? Sister Joan had mentioned seeing one, and now the brewer. But that didn't make sense. Tristan was dead. She'd seen his body herself. She'd felt him when he had still been warm to the touch. He *was* dead, wasn't he?

Back in the kitchen, she joined the pot boys, scrubbing. She earned a few looks and glances, but no one said anything. Bronwyn worked in the kitchen that day and hardly spoke a word to anyone. It was a relief, scrubbing pots, in a way. The day seemed to be passing peacefully, until one of the cooks said, "Bronwyn."

She looked over.

The cook, an older man, stood with a page. "That's her," he said.

A small shiver of alarm came over her. What did the page want?

The page, a youth aged about in his early teens with acne on his nose, approached her. "You are Bronwyn the cook?"

She nodded. His face wasn't friendly.

"You are summoned to William of Ypres. He wants to speak with you. Now."

She wiped her hands on her apron. "Lead the way."

He left and she followed, feeling the other cooks' eyes on her. There were a few murmurs and muted talk, but she held her head high and followed him.

The page led her through the corridor and into the great hall, where a group of men sat around a long table, drinking. Servants stood by and held pitchers and jugs of wine and were silent as the men talked. Heads turned as the page brought her farther into the room.

Bronwyn waited for the page to bring her to the men, but instead, the lad escorted her to where a middle-aged man in his fifties sat by the fire, drinking alone.

A large, burly man, with a head of thinning hair and a sword and scabbard hanging at his belt, he sat stiffly on the stool and spun a sword around, the pommel twisting in his hands as the point spun into the wooden floor.

"My lord, this is the cook." The lad bowed and left.

The man had a grizzled look about him; he needed a shave. A swarthy man, with a set frown on his face, he looked up and surveyed her. He did not speak for a moment, so she stood, her eyes on the floor. Then slowly, she raised them to meet his gaze. He rubbed at his eyes. "You are the cook? Brawnwinne?" he asked.

His accent was different from the English and French ones she'd heard in her nineteen years. "Bronwyn Blakenhale. From Lincoln," she said, with a slight lift of her chin.

Again, he was silent.

"Why do you not sit with the other men?" she asked.

From their watchful gazes, it was clear the knights were keeping an eye on them both. A few kept talking and drinking, but others were openly watching.

He grunted. "They do not like me."

She blinked. Oh. She'd always thought that the men fighting on both sides were friendly with one another, but perhaps working as a team didn't necessarily mean everyone was friends; they simply worked together for a common cause. She reflected on this. If Christopher's kitchen was any example, she felt rather similar to Sir William of Ypres in that moment. "The men in the kitchen do not like me, either."

"I overheard a few of the squires say that too. Why?"

"What?"

"Why do they not like you?" he asked.

She shifted her feet. "I don't know. I think it…" She paused. "You did not call me here to ask about me. What is it you want?"

His expression did not change, but he straightened on the stool. He wore a long-sleeved shirt despite the lingering summer warmth outside, despite it being September. "You are direct. I like that. I hear that you alerted the guards that Sir Robert was ill, and a little nun disturbed someone coming to see him at night."

"That is true."

"Why? Are you allied with Sir Robert?"

"No." She looked at the floor. She was not allied with Sir Robert, who had made no bones about the fact that he did not like or trust her, and if the queen was to be believed, may have ordered the attack that had uprooted her family and perhaps led to their deaths. And she was most definitely not allied with his squire, Theobold. "No, I am not."

"Are you allied with King Stephen?" he asked.

She hesitated, a moment too long. A smarter young woman would have said *yes*, instantly, just to save her own hide. "I don't know."

"Why not?"

"Because he and the queen imprisoned my father for a crime he hadn't committed, and I had to find out who had done it and prove his innocence. Even with my investigation, they would have killed us both that morning but for the Battle of Lincoln that happened. They didn't trust me and—"

"So why are you here?"

"I fell in with the empress after the battle and she liked my cooking. She treated me well enough, so I stayed, but then during the last battle, I was captured with some others. The queen freed me and sent me to work in the kitchens." It all came out in a great breath, as if she had been holding it in.

He looked at her thoughtfully. "You are acquainted with a man I know. Sir Nicholas."

Bronwyn's eyes widened. "The head of the guard for the king and queen. How is he?"

"Dead."

A flash of pain went through her. Sir Nicholas had been like a stern uncle or grandfather to her. He'd disliked her at first, but then they'd worked together to find the culprit behind the crimes her father had been imprisoned for. She felt his loss like a blow to her stomach. "How?"

"Died in battle at Lincoln. He fought well." Sir William of Ypres reached down and picked up a cup of wine, drinking.

"Why did you want to see me?" she asked.

"When I heard your name, I wanted to meet you. The day he died, Sir Nicholas had asked me for a favor."

She cocked her head. "What was that?"

He drank again and set the cup down. Sir William motioned for a page to bring a pitcher forward, but none came.

She watched carefully. It was not that they did not see him; they just avoided looking in his direction. And when some did boldly look at him and ignore his motioning for their attention, Bronwyn's eyes opened at the sleight. She understood the behavior well. If questioned, the servants could simply deny they had not seen his request, and no one would be the wiser. It would all be dismissed as an innocent mistake. But Sir William of Ypres would know. He grunted in displeasure.

"Excuse me." She marched up to a servant and said, "Pardon, I need to borrow this." She did not wait for an answer and instead took the pitcher of wine. Ignoring the pairs of eyes on her, she brought it to Sir William, filling up his cup. She set the pitcher down beside him.

He gave her a ghost of a smile. "That servant won't like you."

"I don't care. I'm not here to be liked." She'd proven that in the kitchens.

"The queen likes you. Well, as much as she likes anyone. Sir Nicholas liked you. He asked me to look out for you if you survived. He'd learned from Sir Baldwin's squire where you were. Said you were likely to be an orphan, and a pretty one. If you lived past the battle, I should seek to raise you up, like the king did me."

Bronwyn's heart warmed. Rupert had told Sir Nicholas about her. It made her feel like someone actually cared for her. That very thought would keep her warm on a cold night. "What do you mean?"

He scratched his chin. "What do you know of me, Bronwyn?"

She shrugged. "Only that you are the main commander of the king and queen's forces." She added after a beat, "And you are not from around here."

The right corner of his mouth curled into a smile. "That's true enough. I'm Flemish."

"Where's that?"

"Flanders. Far from here." He drank more and set down the cup. "I can see why Sir Nicholas liked you. All right, girl. Tell me what you know about this business. He said you attract trouble like fruit does flies. How fares the empress's half-brother?"

"He was sleeping when I last saw him."

"You tell me if he receives any more visitors, yes? I want to know if anyone bothers him, or if we need to move him back to the cells."

"But the wound on his leg is bad. The air down there in jail is poor. If you move him there, you might as well kill him."

He looked at her frankly. "We might have to, at that. But for now, we will make sure he lives. He is too valuable."

She raised an eyebrow. "You mean to ransom him?"

"Yes. It is what is normally done in these things." He burped.

"What will happen?"

"He will stay in the infirmary until he is well, then he will stay in the cells. He is too valuable; he cannot be allowed to walk free."

"And then?"

"Then we see how much the empress can pay."

"What about an exchange? Doesn't the queen want her husband back?"

He smirked. "Of course she does. He rots sitting in Bristol Prison. But we have the upper hand. When he was captured at Lincoln, that was a setback. But now we have something Maud wants, and now we are in control." He rubbed his hands together. "Well met, Bronwyn. You need help, you come to me. I'll do what I can." He looked at her. "I do not give my word lightly. You understand?"

She thought so. She nodded her thanks and returned to the kitchens, where she was greeted by one of the cooks, who said that she was to report to the infirmary, as the doctors were asking for her. She went immediately.

John greeted her at the entrance. "There you are. You made good time. He's awake."

Bronwyn looked past his shoulder and saw that Sir Robert was indeed awake, and sitting up. A young woman stood by his side.

"Lady Susanna?" she approached.

"Hullo, Bronwyn. I didn't think you would be out of the kitchens." Lady Susanna's smile faded. "I heard there was a very important patient here and wanted to see for myself."

"I wanted to check on Sir Robert," Bronwyn said.

The man in question raised an eyebrow. "Whatever for? You're just a maidservant."

Bronwyn said, "When you took sick down in the dungeons—"

"She's the one who told us and made sure you were moved up here to recover," John said." Without her, you might have died."

"And who are you?" Sir Robert asked.

"John Tynsdale, a physician."

"You look young to be a physician."

John's smile was strained. Bronwyn got the sense he was thinking something uncharitable but was wisely holding his tongue. "You should rest."

"I've rested enough. Where's my squire?" he demanded.

"Down in the cells. Where you'll be if you don't keep quiet."

"I don't need to keep quiet." He threw back the blanket and stopped. "What the?"

The ladies looked away. "Oh, my," Lady Susanna said.

"What have you bloody done to my trousers?" Sir Robert asked.

"We had to cut the leg off one of your trouser legs to get at your wound. It was festering."

Lady Susanna looked pale. Bronwyn tried to hide a smile. Of all the indecent things she'd seen in her lifetime, a man's legs weren't one of them.

"I need to get up and move." Sir Robert swung his legs over the side of the bed and tried to rise, then wobbled and fell back. He muttered a sharp curse.

John crossed his arms. "You're weak and your body needs to heal. You'll need to stay abed for at least a few more days."

"How many?"

"A week, I'd imagine," John said. "Don't know why you're so keen to get back to jail. It's miserable down there."

Sir Robert shot him a dirty look and pulled the blanket back over his legs. "You all can go now. I'll rest."

The group turned to leave, when Sir Robert said, "Maid. Girl. Come here."

Bronwyn turned. Sir Robert was beckoning to her. She approached and stood by him as he kept his mouth shut, watching Lady Susanna and John move away, quietly talking between themselves.

"What is it?" she asked.

"'What is it, *Sir Robert,*'" he corrected. "When you address me, use my proper title. I'm not some kitchen friend of yours."

Bronwyn's cheeks flamed. "What is it you need, Sir Robert?"

"Don't be cheeky." He warned. "I need you to give Theobold a message for me. Can you do that?"

She nodded and bit her tongue. She was still mad at Theobold, but she couldn't deny her attraction to him. She knew that if Sir Robert asked a favor of her, she would do it. For Theobold, if for no other reason. He would want her to help.

"First of all, does the empress live? Did she escape?"

"I don't know."

"Find out. We have to act. They'll want to hold me for ransom, but I need the empress not to cave. She needs to hold strong." He leaned forward and winced in pain. "I need you to listen in on their plans and find out what's happened. Can you do that?"

"I…"

"I need your help, girl. There aren't many I can trust." He looked at her. "Never mind. I can see it's too much I'm asking. But if you care at all about Theobold… Well. The Bronwyn he's not stopped talking about would do it."

She felt like he was making use of her emotions to his own advantage. Which she supposed was precisely his aim. "Theobold was talking about me?"

"The lad wouldn't stop. He's smitten, I'd say." Seeing he had her attention, his mouth curved into the ghost of a smile. "Never mind about the lad. Sir Miles will know what to do. Do you know if he survived?"

Bronwyn shook her head. "I've no idea. I was captured along with some of the other women and the queen freed me and put me to work in the kitchens."

He snorted. "She's very trusting; I'll say that for her. I'd be worried you'd poison me the first chance you got."

"I think that would be the obvious move, if I wanted my head chopped off."

He started as if insulted. "You don't shy away from sharing your opinion, do you, girl?"

"No, I don't. And my name is Bronwyn."

Their eyes met. Sir Robert was in his mid-fifties, she guessed, and looked weary from the strain of battle and his injuries.

"I'll help," Lady Susanna said, interrupting their conversation. She stood there. "I want to help."

"You're risking a lot, aren't you? By helping. Are you still loyal to the empress?"

Lady Susanna balked, as if Bronwyn had just asked her to stand on her head. "That is a very personal question. But yes, I am loyal. And I want to do my bit."

She didn't say to whom she was loyal, Bronwyn thought. But if Lady Susanna was in fact loyal to the empress, why then had she

locked the squires away the night before the empress's coronation? It spoke of trickery. Bronwyn just didn't understand why.

"You? But you're just a lady-in-waiting," Sir Robert said to the
noblewoman.

Bronwyn snorted. At least his underestimation wasn't just
restricted to her; it was his view toward all women, it seemed.
"She's a lady-in-waiting and can go almost anywhere."

"I sit with Matilda," Lady Susanna said.

"She could see things that other people might not, as can I,"
Bronwyn added.

"That's true. Servants are overlooked," Lady Susanna said
with a half-smile at Bronwyn.

"Sir Robert, what do you think the queen's forces will do
now?"

"If my half-sister escaped? She will regroup and likely send an
envoy to begin negotiations, or at least a messenger. If she didn't,
she would be here with us. So we have to assume she escaped,"
he said.

"Where would she go?" Lady Susanna asked.

He shrugged. "Gloucester. Oxford more likely. Not London."
He looked closely at them. "Keep your eyes and ears open and
report back to me with any information you overhear. Bronwyn,
tell Theobold I am well. Lady Susanna…"

"I shall report back too. I know where my loyalty lies." She
bobbed a curtsey and swept away.

Bronwyn followed and found Lady Susanna waiting for her
outside the infirmary.

"It's good to be working together. How exciting. I'm glad to
be able to help. Although… I'll be honest. I did mention to the
other ladies that you fancied Rupert. I know it's not true because
Lady Alice tells me so." She giggled. "But then… It's true, then,
that you and Theobold are together? I wouldn't blame you, you
know. He is quite popular at court. Many ladies find him
attractive."

Bronwyn looked at her. "What about you, Lady Susanna?"

"Me? No, I have my own man." She blushed.

"Tristan, you mean?"

Her blush deepened. "Fine. I'll admit it. I do, I mean, I *did* fancy him."

Bronwyn looked at her curiously, leaning in ever so slightly. Had the noblewoman just had a slip of the tongue? Or did she know more about Tristan's supposed death?

"I'm sorry about what happened to him."

Did she wipe away a tear? Bronwyn wasn't sure. She hadn't meant to disturb her. "I was thinking I would visit Winchester Castle and visit his body to pay my respects. Would you like to come with me? We could speak to the priests there about laying his body to rest. It would be a kindness." She thought uncharitably, *In this heat, his body was likely to smell.* "I want to confirm that Sister Joan was mistaken. She wasn't seeing ghosts, and she needs solid proof that she didn't see Tristan walking around."

Lady Susanna gasped. "No." She clapped a hand on Bronwyn's wrist. "You can't leave. Don't do that."

"What? Why not?"

"It's wrong. You shouldn't go disturbing his body when he is at rest. The priests and other folk there likely already buried him. You'll just bother everyone. Besides, you're a prisoner here. You can't just go walking around wherever you feel like it. Matilda won't let you leave. How would it look for her to just let random prisoners leave whenever they felt like it?"

Bronwyn blinked at her. She had become so used to being able to go anywhere in the castle as a servant, she'd lost sight of the fact she was a prisoner too. She would need to slip out somehow. "I only meant—"

"I know what you intend. You want to go digging around in his things and figure out where he was going the night he died. But it's wrong, and I've got half a mind to tell Matilda what you're planning. She won't think highly of any servant who's going about disturbing bodies."

Bronwyn's mouth dropped. "Lady Susanna…"

The noblewoman's grip hardened on her wrist. "I mean it. Leave it alone. He's dead. Why can't you just let him rest in peace?" She blinked back tears.

"I'm sorry, I—"

"Don't lie. I've heard enough about your scheming ways from Lady Alice. I didn't always pay her attention, but I do now. Don't bother his body. The kindest thing you can do is leave him be. He doesn't deserve your attentions." Lady Susanna released her wrist and sniffed, lifting her chin.

"I'm sorry. I'll leave you now."

"Where will you go?" Lady Susanna asked, one eyebrow raised.

"The brewery, I think. I want to know if that herb we found on Sir Robert's person came from there."

She curtsied to Lady Susanna and walked away, feeling the other woman's eyes on her retreating form. Why such a strong reaction from Lady Susanna? Had she really been that attached to Tristan? From what Bronwyn had seen, he didn't care for her at all. She had been a passing fancy to him.

Bronwyn entered the small castle brewery. The place was largely empty, and she walked amongst the barrels, smelling the air that was scented of hops, oats, and fermenting barley. She hadn't much of a taste for ale and preferred wine when she could have it. But as she walked, relishing the quiet, she couldn't help but wonder at the figure standing over Sir Robert, with the strand of hops. She walked along rows and rows of stacked barrels that led up to the ceiling. As Bronwyn walked along, the scent grew stronger, and she followed it, when there was a sound. A footfall.

She wasn't alone.

She whirled around. She wished she had a weapon. A knife, a broken bottle, anything.

"Hello?" she asked.

Maybe it was the local brewer. Another servant, or two, caught amidst a tryst.

There was silence.

She started to walk away and turned around a corner, when something hard struck the back of her head and everything went black.

— ❦ —

Chapter Fourteen

"B RONWYN?" A VOICE asked. "Bronwyn?"

Her eyes fluttered and she let out a groan. The back of her head hurt. She opened her eyes and saw Rupert and Lady Alice standing over her. "Huh? What happened?"

"I saw Lady Susanna and asked if she'd seen you," Lady Alice said. "She said *yes*, but then you parted ways, although you'd mentioned you were going to the brewery. Were you really that thirsty?"

"No, it wasn't that." Bronwyn started to sit up.

"Whoa, careful there. Slowly." Rupert helped her, putting a hand to her back.

Feeling groggy, Bronwyn looked around. The ground was cold where she lay, and the air was heavy with the scents of oak barrels, hops, beer, ale, and barley.

"What were you doing down here, anyway?" Rupert asked.

"Sister Joan found someone standing over Sir Robert in the infirmary, but she scared them away. Whoever it was left a bit of herb behind, and the brewer recognized it as one of the hops he'd use for making beer. So I came down here to have a look. We need to—" Bronwyn stopped.

Rupert and Alice knelt across from her, but they were on different sides. She swallowed. "I came down here to see if I could find where the reed came from when something hit me from behind."

She reached to the back of her head and felt something sticky. Her hand came away with a few drops of blood. They looked dark on her hand.

Lady Alice turned pale. "Oh, my. Could it have been an accident? Did you bump into something and hit your head?"

"I don't think so."

"I don't like this," Rupert said. "You shouldn't be wandering around here alone. What if you were attacked?"

Bronwyn shrugged. "I'm glad you two found me."

"Tell us more about the person standing over Sir Robert. What was he doing there?" Rupert asked.

"Or her," Lady Alice added.

"I don't know, as I wasn't there," Bronwyn said. "Sister Joan spotted them. I wondered if perhaps it was a person who worked down here, or maybe had escaped during the fighting and was hiding out here."

"So you went looking for them alone?" Rupert asked. "Never mind. I know the answer to that question." He rose to his feet and started walking.

"Where are you going?" Lady Alice asked.

"To see if anyone's here. If so, they've got a lot to answer for. You two stay there."

A few minutes later, he returned. "Nothing. If there was someone there, they're gone now. Let's get you out of here."

Bronwyn got to her feet and wavered a bit, but under the watchful eyes of Rupert and Lady Alice, made her way back up the steps. Rupert said, "You should go to the infirmary."

"I'll take her," Lady Alice said. "She shouldn't be alone."

"It's all right. I'm fine," Bronwyn said.

"Nonsense, your hair is all bloody. It's disgusting. Come along." Lady Alice brooked no argument and began walking ahead.

Bronwyn snorted softly. It was clear Lady Alice expected her to follow.

Rupert said, "You decide to do any more investigating, you

let me know. I don't want you to do this by yourself."

She smiled, too brightly. She didn't want Rupert to report her to the queen. She still wanted to find out who had been behind these incidents that plagued the empress. "I'm fine."

"And look what happened to you. I'd—"

Lady Alice interrupted. "She said, she's fine. Let the girl be. Bronwyn, come on. I'm waiting."

"Bye," Bronwyn told Rupert as she walked away.

Rupert shot her a frown and walked off. "I'm going to have the brewery searched. Don't come by here again alone," he called.

Bronwyn and Lady Alice walked together. "He's right, you know," Lady Alice said once they were out of earshot. "You shouldn't be doing this all alone. You should have help."

Bronwyn didn't want to say the obvious, that she had no one to help her. With friends and enemies on both sides, there was no one she could truly trust. Not really.

Lady Alice let out a little sigh. "I'm mad at you. I *was* mad at you."

"Why?"

"Because that night when you saw us in the stables, and he came running after you."

"I'm sorry. I didn't mean to see you two…" Bronwyn started.

Lady Alice shook her head. "That doesn't matter. I didn't care. I wanted people to see. To know that we were together. Even if it meant my reputation might be… blackened by it. I want him. But he cares for you, and I see it now."

Bronwyn glanced at her. "What do you mean?"

"Don't you see? He was with me, and I was in a state of undress, yet as soon as you showed any kind of unhappiness, he came running after you. I've never felt so insulted in all my life. He should have stayed with me. Any ordinary man would have. But not him. Not Rupert."

"Oh."

"I suppose that's why I care for him so much. He's extraordinary. But it cut me to the quick to see him running after you. Then I realized, he views you like a little sister. He wants to protect you, look out for you. *That's* why he went running."

Bronwyn had, for a moment, allowed herself to hope. She should have known she'd be wrong. "That must be it."

"I'm sure of it. Why else would he leave me like that? It makes no sense." Lady Alice tossed her black hair over her shoulder. "Now, what we are going to do about this mess? Clearly, someone doesn't want you snooping around. Normally, I'd agree with that thought, but this won't do. You could've been hurt."

"I was."

"You're lucky we found you," Rupert said. "You shouldn't be wandering around the castle alone like this. It's not safe.

"Well, never mind," Lady Alice said. "I will help you solve this and find out who is trying to kill Sir Robert. I have no doubt that whomever Sister Joan found standing over him meant him harm, and now you, too. We just need to figure out who that might be."

"And why would someone want to kill him?" Bronwyn wondered.

Lady Alice shot her an even look, as if the answer to that were obvious.

"Why *now*, I mean. He is captured and in ill health. He is going to be ransomed off soon. Why would anyone want to kill him? He's a prisoner here, and he's worth more alive than dead."

"Perhaps someone is afraid of what he knows. Maybe he's been privy to some secrets."

Bronwyn shrugged. "I don't doubt it. It still doesn't explain why someone would attack him now."

"I would think that one of Matilda's men would want him dead. Maybe out of revenge for all the lives he's taken."

"Maybe. But to do that would run a great risk, since both the queen and Sir William of Ypres want him kept alive."

"I can't help but think that someone must have a good reason for wanting him dead. Maybe one of his own men?"

"The only men of his here are in prison. They can't get out," Bronwyn said, thinking of Theobold.

"Then it must be someone else." Lady Alice stopped. "I know. I'll tell Matilda and suggest she assign a guard to watch him."

Bronwyn smiled. "I'm sure he'll enjoy that."

Lady Alice put her hands on her hips. "It doesn't matter if he appreciates it or not. We need to keep him alive. The empress depends on him."

"What about Sir Miles?"

"Empress Maud's cousin?" Lady Alice looked around, as if to see if they were at risk of being overheard. "I think he has not Sir Robert's war record, or way with the men. I see Sir Miles as more of an ambassador figure. It's such a shame his squire died. Lady Susanna was quite beside herself."

Bronwyn paused. "Lady Alice, what do you say to a little visit back to Winchester Castle?"

"I'd say you're wasting your time. Not to mention my going would attract attention. We're not supposed to be wandering around too much, you know. We are prisoners, remember. Why do you want to go?"

"There's someone I want to visit."

"Oh, no. You're getting that look on your face. I know that look. It only means one thing." Lady Alice shook her head.

"What?"

"That you're going to land us in trouble, and *me* somewhere disgusting I do not like. The last time you had that look on your face, we left a castle via the privy, if you recall?"

"I do."

"So do I, despite trying to forget. Forgive me if I don't wish to repeat the experience. I'll see what Rupert finds out from his search of the brewery instead." Lady Alice walked away.

Chapter Fifteen

BRONWYN DECIDED TO take matters into her own hands. The fighting between the armies had ended and there was a tentative peace in the city. People had begun to come out from their homes. The sun shone, offering a warm September heat. Bronwyn no longer felt any compunction about abandoning the kitchen. She had no friends there and there was no one to look out for her. With Theobold in jail and Rupert watching her, she needed to play up the fact she was a servant and sneak away, particularly from his prying eyes. Aside from Lady Alice's fair-weather friendship, she had no one she could rely on, and she didn't even know if her family was still alive, or if she would ever see them again. The very thought pained her, and she felt hollow inside, so empty.

As Bronwyn slipped outside the castle grounds, she bumped into Sister Rebecca. "Good morrow, Sister."

"Bronwyn." The older nun inclined her head. "Where are you off to?"

"Um, I thought I'd go visit Winchester Castle."

The sister's greying eyebrows knit together. "Whatever for?"

Bronwyn revealed her desire to see Tristan's body. Sister Rebecca's polite smile disappeared. "I'm not sure of your intentions. But I will go with you. It is fortuitous that we met."

"'Fortuiwhat'?"

"Lucky," Sister Rebecca said.

"Like fate?"

"I don't believe in fate. Only our Lord, Jesus Christ. Now come along. If you are determined to do this, you shan't do it alone."

Together, they walked through the city. They came to the smoking ruin that was the nunnery, and Sister Rebecca's eyes watered. "This was our nunnery."

"Oh."

They stood and looked at the building, which had fallen into disrepair. It had been largely destroyed by fire. Sister Rebecca walked through the wreckage, ignoring Bronwyn's warnings about safety. She came out, her face drawn. "I will come back here. We'll need to rebuild it."

"Where will you get the money?" Bronwyn asked.

Sister Rebecca's mouth twisted in distaste as if Bronwyn had said something vulgar. "I will ask the queen for it. Or I shall beg. The Lord will provide, one way or another."

They walked on. The weather was warm that morning and people were walking around, talking, huddled in small groups. Armed men patrolled the streets, and she climbed up the hill to Winchester Castle, out of breath by the time they had arrived at the castle courtyard. The hill had been steep, and it was no wonder the invading army had struggled to take it over. She wondered what would remain of the people who'd been working there.

Bronwyn entered the corridors and was easily overlooked as a servant, flanked by the nun. She made her way to the kitchens and ran into Hugh, who clapped his hands on her shoulders and pulled her into a hug. "Thanks to the Lord, Bronwyn. I thought you must've been taken prisoner or died. And, Sister, good to see you again. Are you all right? What are you doing here?"

Bronwyn blinked away tears, so happy she was to see a smiling face. And a person who actually liked her. Even Sister Rebecca's firm expression had softened. "Hullo, Hugh." Bronwyn returned the hug. "I'm on an errand. I'd... like to see the cold storage."

"What, where we keep the cheeses and preserved meats?"

She bit her lower lip. "Not exactly. You remember the squire who died before the empress left. Tristan?"

Hugh scratched his head. "Yes, I remember." He shot her a look. "You mean to view his body?"

She nodded.

"But why? That's morbid."

"I want to check something."

He frowned. "I don't like this. Especially when so many people have died. A lot of them were put in there to wait before they have proper burials. The room will have a lot of bodies, Bronwyn. You shouldn't go down there."

She swallowed. She'd seen bodies before, but not necessarily in these circumstances. "I've seen dead bodies before."

Hugh's face was serious. "For some reason, that doesn't surprise me. Trouble follows you around, girl. All right. You know where you're going?"

She shook her head.

"Fair enough. I'll show you. Don't like you being there alone, anyway. It's not right."

"I'll be with her. You need only show us the way," Sister Rebecca said. "Someone will need to speak with the priests around to arrange burials."

Hugh rubbed at his nose with his sleeve. "Good luck with that. There aren't many religious folk around here these days." He led them down a set of stairs, below the east wing of the castle, where the air grew colder. "You may want to cover your noses," he warned.

He wasn't wrong. The smell hit Bronwyn's nose immediately and she held her sleeve to her nose, trying to breathe in through her mouth. The space that was normally used for storing cold food items had been taken over and now served the dead.

They walked into a medium-sized storeroom, where bodies had been laid out on the floor and on the shelves. Meat carcasses hung and the air buzzed with flies. Where possible, the faces of the deceased had been covered, but flies were unstoppable, and more than one sheet moved with the telltale hint of flies and maggots burrowing into the soft decaying flesh beneath.

Sister Rebecca uttered a curse. "I'm going to be sick. Excuse me." She went back up the steps, coughing.

Hugh turned to Bronwyn. "This is a sorry place. Be quick about it, yeah?"

"I will." Bronwyn stepped around the rows of bodies, looking. The quiet of the room, the stillness, disturbed her. She pinched her nose and lifted up the cloth covering every face, hurriedly putting them back. The faces of the dead were gruesome, and the sight of more than one made her feel physically ill. This was not for the faint-hearted, she realized. She looked upon every shelf, and finally, turned to Hugh. "I'm done."

Together, they walked back up the steps. "What were you hoping to find?" Hugh asked.

"I wanted to examine Tristan's body and look through his things. He may have been carrying something that would give us a clue as to why he was killed."

"But you're empty-handed."

"Yes."

"So you didn't find him?"

"No. Have there been many burials for the past few days?" she asked.

"No. None at all. And Lord knows we need them. This place stinks." He gave her a sidelong glance. "So what does this mean?"

"His body is missing. I mean to find out why," she said.

Sister Rebecca had gone to find a priest, whilst Bronwyn waited for her to return. She returned to the kitchen with Hugh, who put her to work kneading dough.

"There's not been a lot of work since the empress left," he said, "but we have to make sure the kitchen is stocked and ready, should the king and queen wish to return and use this as their base of operations. Not many servants were killed in the fighting.

I'd say it was a quick fight. Didn't last long after that siege."

"Did you ever speak with Tristan before he died?"

"Me? Not really. Did wonder why he was wearing his best seat of clothes and where he was going to. He said his only other seat was dirty. Too much fighting with the other squires."

She clasped arms with Hugh and said goodbye, then joined Sister Rebecca to return to Wolvesey Castle. The sister had had no luck in finding a priest, so there was no development in arranging burials for the dead.

But once the ladies had returned to the castle, they parted ways. Bronwyn went to the kitchens, where Master Christopher pinched her by the elbow and steered her toward the worktables. "And just where have you been?"

"I—"

"Dodging your work, that's what. And it's bloody lazy of you when the rest of us are hard at it. We've had an order for manchets, and sweet white bread rolls with honey for the queen. But when we made it, they sent it back. Can you believe it? The bloody rudeness of it all." He glared at her as if she were at fault.

"I'm sorry?" She pulled her elbow away. It smarted, but she made no move to touch it.

"I bet you are. As well you should be. This is all your fault. If you hadn't been going around dallying with the ladies and talking about how bloody wonderful your white rolls are, the queen might never have asked for them. But now she has and surprise, surprise, she doesn't like them when someone else makes them. Now she blames us, when it's all your doing."

Bronwyn raised an eyebrow at him. She had a feeling he was about to bluster on about what he would say, when she rather suspected he was full of hot air. Her gaze was firm, and she put her hands on her hips. "Shall I make some rolls, then?"

"Yes, obviously. It's too late now; Her Grace is already angry. But see if you can cobble something together. She might not kill us in our beds." He walked off, cursing.

She snorted. So not only was he full of bluster, he was also on the dramatic side. She shook off her nerves, set her shoulders, and got to work.

SOMETIME LATER, STANDING over a worktable and kneading dough, Bronwyn gave a small sigh of pleasure. There was a beauty in her work, she decided. Working her fingers in the bread dough gave her time to think, and it was time away from scrubbing pots or turning the spit, which was nice.

She prepared the manchets and cut the dough into small loaves, working with a bit of honey. Once they were set to baking in the oven, she washed her hands clean in a bucket and wiped them dry on her work apron.

Some of the cooks were watching, but none spoke to her. She helped scrub pots and turned the spit, keeping an eye on her rolls. Once they were ready, she took them up to the queen.

Upon entering, Queen Matilda sat with Sir William of Ypres, drinking wine. The ladies-in-waiting stood some distance away, in a corner of the room, near the windows. All watched as Bronwyn brought forward the platter. She felt their eyes on her, but none made any movement to acknowledge her.

The queen took one and bit into it. "Delicious. I am glad you survived the battles, Bronwyn."

Bronwyn snorted softly. At least she had a purpose. She felt morbidly amused that the queen was glad she wasn't dead, in order to make the rolls she enjoyed. At least she seemed to trust her, despite all their past history with poisoning.

She nibbled delicately as Sir William took a roll as well. "And are we any closer to finding out who is behind the attacks on Sir Robert?"

"I've taken the matter in hand, Your Grace," Sir William said. "I've arrested the guilty party."

Bronwyn almost dropped the platter. "You have? Who?"

"That squire, Rupert, said you'd been hurt by someone in the brewery, but we didn't find anyone. I figured out who was behind the attacks on Sir Robert—easily too. Sometimes the simplest answer is the right one. It's that nun who's always skulking around, Sister Joan. She's been nosing around him again at odd hours, when she shouldn't be. Wouldn't leave him alone."

"But surely, she was just praying for his good recovery," Bronwyn said.

"Not likely. Besides, it was you who found her there before, wasn't it? When the so-called ghost first made an appearance?" he said.

"Yes, but—"

"What's to say she didn't make it all up?"

"You're accusing a nun of lying, Sir William," the queen pointed out. "Isn't that against her faith? The Commandments?"

Sir William shrugged. "That's as may be, but I warrant she's up to no good. Why else would she be constantly by his bedside? There are other men to pray for. No, I know a culprit when I see one."

Mistress Agatha nodded and rubbed her hands together. "I never trusted that woman. Always too secretive for her own good."

Bronwyn swallowed. She set the platter aside and excused herself, then fled down to the jail. She found Sister Joan, sitting quietly in a cell all alone. "Sister," she said. "What happened?"

"I was praying by his bedside when I got into a disagreement with the monk who manages the infirmary. He told me to leave and then called Sir William of Ypres to throw me out, saying I was acting strange and hysterical. He accused me of having inappropriate thoughts about the man, as if I would ever. Sir Robert is old enough to be my father." She sniffed.

"So they tossed you in here."

"Yes. I don't know what to do. Can you speak to Sir William or the queen and explain it was all a big misunderstanding?"

"I'll try." She felt that Sister Joan was innocent but could not ignore, however, the thought that whenever Sister Joan did wish to say more, the other nun seemed to always be in a position to interrupt and stop her. She wondered why. Were they hiding something? And if so, what could it be?

Bronwyn returned up to the queen's chamber just as Sir William was leaving. "What do you want, girl?" he asked.

"I've spoken with Sister Joan. It was just a misunderstanding," she said.

"Of course she would say that. The monk was certain she was planning something. It wasn't right, her not leaving his bedside like that." He scratched his head. "You don't think she's one of his bastards, do you?"

Bronwyn blinked. "I doubt it."

"Her special attention to him doesn't make sense, then. And I don't like it when things don't make sense. Don't like it at all." He set his shoulders. "She can spend the night in jail, then I'll talk to her. See if a night behind bars loosens her tongue."

"But she didn't do anything wrong."

"Maybe not, but I hear she was telling tales about a ghost. You know as well as I do that ghosts don't exist, so why is she lying? Either she's telling stories or she's actually seeing visions, which makes me worry about her mind. In any case, a night in the cells won't do her harm. Nothing can happen to her there."

Bronwyn relayed the news to Sister Joan, who gripped the bars and crossed herself. "What if… What if the ghost gets me? The brewer said the ghost walks these corridors, even down in the jail."

"Ghosts don't exist, Sister Joan."

"This one does, Bronwyn, I'm telling you, I saw it." Her eyes were wide.

Bronwyn looked at the sister and offered a slight smile. She hoped it was reassuring. But from what she had seen, or rather hadn't seen, it all pointed to the suggestion that Tristan was still alive, or that his body had been moved. Either way, he was not a ghost. But she couldn't trust the nun not to spread the word if Bronwyn did reveal that his body was missing. That would just make the nun worry more and perhaps even support her argument for the existence of ghosts.

"You probably saw someone who was hoping to rob him or maybe tell his friends he saw Sir Robert of Gloucester. He is well known."

Sister Joan's face contorted in anger. "You don't believe me. You don't think I saw a ghost at all, do you?" Her eyebrows knit together.

"I believe you saw someone. I just think it was a real person, not a ghost."

"Then what about the brewer? Why is he talking about ghosts as well?"

Bronwyn glanced over at the other cell. "I think his time down here has affected his brain."

Sister Joan let out a noise of frustration. "Fine. Mark my words, Bronwyn, but there is a ghost here. I know it, he knows it, and soon everyone else will too."

"I'm sorry I angered you. I didn't mean to."

"No, you mean well, as does everyone else. But none of you believe me. You think I'm hysterical. When I'm not. I'm telling the truth." Sister Joan wiped away a tear.

"I'm sorry, Sister."

"Go. Leave me. I'll see you in the morning." She turned her back on Bronwyn and waited for her to leave.

"All right. Good night, Sister." Bronwyn walked on. She paused outside of Theobold's cell, but he was silent. She couldn't tell if he was asleep or not, so she kept walking. She would tell him Sir Robert's message when he awoke.

The next morning, Bronwyn nipped to the kitchen and prepared platters of food to take to the prisoners.

Noting her arms full of food, the guards said, "More food? The prisoners will be getting fat at this rate."

Bronwyn paused. "What do you mean? They haven't been fed since yesterday, I thought."

"You're wrong. A fellow came through here with food for them last night. A gift, he said."

A creeping suspicion went down her spine. Bronwyn stopped

and set down the food. "I didn't hear about anyone getting extra food for the prisoners."

She went into the cells. The people were quiet. But as she passed by the brewer's cell, Peter grabbed her wrist and said, "The ghost, the spirit, he's back, he's back. He came and now he's gone and it's too late, too late to save her."

"What? Who?" She pulled her wrist back.

"Don't touch it. Don't touch it," he warned.

"Sister Joan," Bronwyn called. "Sister Joan." She hurried to the cell. "Sister?"

A small form lay on the floor.

"Sister?"

There was no sound.

She took a torch from its sconce in the wall and lowered it to the cell. Sister Joan's lifeless eyes looked up at her, a bread roll in her hand.

Chapter Sixteen

Bronwyn let out a cry and called for the guards. A shuddering sigh escaped her. Sister Joan, dead. Fear gripped her, making her chest feel tight. The woman was so young, not far off her own age. What had killed her?

"Theobold?" she croaked, her voice fraught with worry. "Theobold? Are you alive?" she called louder.

Silence.

"Theobold?" Her heart beat in her throat.

"I'm here," a male voice called back. "What is it?"

He was alive. He lived. Thank the Lord.

But she didn't have time to explain. Letting out a sigh of relief, she leaned close to Sister Joan's cell, blinking back tears.

She peered at the bread. It looked to be coated in some substance. She reached for it, then stopped. A mouse scurried past and she moved her hand away.

The guards came. One stiffened at the sight of Sister Joan's body and asked, "Is she dead?"

"Yes."

The other guard tutted. "Shame. She was a pretty one."

Bronwyn gritted her teeth. *Never mind Sister Joan's looks. The fact that she's lying there dead is slightly more important,* she thought grimly. Sister Joan was only supposed to have been there for one night, and she hadn't survived. If only Bronwyn had been able to convince Sir William to let her go. "Who was it who came down here before?" she asked.

"Don't know." The guards exchanged a look.

"What did he look like?"

"Tall. Looked like any other man."

"You need to report this, immediately," Bronwyn said.

One of the guards glared at her. "We don't take orders from you. You're not the mistress of us. You're just a maid."

She glared right back. "You're right. So *you* get to tell the queen why some poor girl died under your watch."

"She's just a prisoner. What does it matter? One less mouth to feed." The guard sneered at her. The other looked at her mutely.

Bronwyn wished in that moment that she had someone with more rank with her, to tell, cajole, coax, or bully them into action. Someone they would listen to. She felt powerless, hurt, and guilty over Sister Joan's death. She didn't need to feel ignored as well. "We need to see if anyone else died. Will you help me?" Bronwyn asked.

The guards did not speak but joined her as they made a sweep of the cells. "The nun is the only one who's dead," one of the guards reported.

"The man who brought the food, what did he say?" Bronwyn asked the guards.

"Just that he came with a gift from his mistress."

"How long did he stay?"

"No long."

"And he didn't say anything else to you?" she asked.

"No. He left."

Bronwyn's shoulders slumped, and she stepped away to a familiar cell. "Theobold? Are you there?"

He came up to the bars. "Hullo, Bronwyn." His voice was dull. He looked gaunt, with deep hollows beneath his eyes and in his cheeks. He still stood tall and handsome, but the curled black locks of his hair hung limp, and a dark beard covered his chin.

"Are you all right?"

His hand curled around hers. His fingers were big, and cold. "I'm fine."

"You didn't eat the bread?" Her words came out in a rush.

"No."

"Oh, thank goodness." She breathed a sigh of relief. "I'm so glad."

"What happened? I heard—"

The brewer called, "It was the ghost. The ghost, I tell you. He's come here before, walking the halls. He was there before, but now he's here, and he's coming for us all."

Bronwyn squeezed Theobold's hand. "I'll be back."

She went to Peter's cell. "This ghost. What did he look like?"

"You know him, and he knows you." The brewer cackled. "Don't eat it. Don't eat his gifts. He lies. They're not gifts at all. They're deadly." He grinned, showing yellow teeth.

"This ghost. He brought food for all of you?"

"Yes," he hissed. "He tossed rolls to me and the girl. The sweet nun. She stayed awake saying her prayers, but I told her, God is not watching over us. She thought it was Christian charity, but she was wrong. I told that pretty nun, but she didn't listen. She said God would protect her. But where is he now?" He looked at his shoes. "I fed my bread to the rats, to see." He stood back and pointed.

There in the back of his cell was a dead rat, the bread roll beside it.

"You see? Dead. Dead, like we all will be, if we stay here. Soon we will become like ghosts too."

She returned to Theobold's cell. "The bread was poisoned. Tell me, what did you see?"

"The man, whoever it was, came in during the night. I was sleeping, so I didn't see him. I only heard the brewer shouting about ghosts again. I thought it was nothing. It wasn't until this morning that he shouted to me not to eat it and said it was poison." He gestured to the partly-eaten bread roll on the floor of his cell. "By the time I'd woken up, rats had nibbled mine."

Two dead mice and a rat lay a few feet away. Bronwyn repressed a shiver.

"Bronwyn," said Theobold, "trying to make sense out of the brewer's nonsense will have you running in circles. The man's gone mad; there's no reasoning with him."

Bronwyn nodded. "Only eat the food I or the guards bring you." She turned away, then paused. "I'm glad you're still alive." She felt a treacherous flutter in her chest at the sight of him. She was supposed to be focusing on this crime, not thinking about the darkness of his curls, his pale skin that reminded her of the moonlight, or the way his fingers had enveloped hers.

He looked at her. "Me too. Bronwyn, there's something you should know." He glanced down the corridor. "The other prisoners were complaining they didn't get any food, whilst we from the empress's camp did. I think whoever did this and managed to poison the nun, well…"

The realization clicked in her brain. "They are only targeting people who were staying with Empress Maud's camp. But why?"

He shrugged. "Only the maid, myself, and the brewer got the dodgy bread rolls. Seems like someone doesn't want us alive. Stay safe, Bronwyn." He took her hand through the bars and kissed her fingers.

Another flutter went through her chest. She interlaced her fingers with this. Sometimes words didn't need to be spoken. Just the barest touch was enough. She cared for him. Truly, deeply.

She went and distributed the fresh food to the prisoners, then, sparing a dirty look for the guards, she went up to report the body.

Queen Matilda had not yet risen for the day, but when Bronwyn explained to the queen's guards about the dead nun, one of the maidservants went to wake her. Ten minutes later, Bronwyn was shown into a room where the queen and Sir William stood. The queen wore a long robe of soft, lilac silk, bound at the waist with a sash and embroidered with flowers. Sir William looked like he had just been roused from sleep and let out a huge yawn. He was dressed simply, wearing a stiff, burgundy-colored tunic over grey hose, belted at the waist. A small scabbard with a short blade hung at his belt. *Armed, even in the early hours*, Bronwyn thought.

"Tell me what happened," the queen said.

Bronwyn relayed what she'd discovered.

The queen's eyes blazed. "His mistress sent him with those rolls? But I did not order any such thing. Why would I want to kill a nun?"

"This makes no sense. She was only there for the night. I'd planned to question her today about her attendance on Sir Robert. Why would she be killed, and by poison? From your kitchen." He looked at Bronwyn pointedly.

She shook her head. "The only ones who are in there are the cooks and scullery maids, pot boys. Pages come in to deliver messages or take food out, but otherwise, no one would be allowed in. It's not a community bakery."

"Then how did he get in, this killer?" Sir William asked.

"Those guards should've been keeping a proper watch out for anything suspicious. And why am I hearing about this from a baker and not the guards themselves? Are they ill? I want them replaced. They let a murderer in to my jail." The queen's petite hands curled into fists.

"I'll see to it at once, Your Grace," Sir William said.

"And the kitchen. What a lapse of security. How did the man do it? That shouldn't have been possible. Where were all the cooks? What were they doing, so this man was able to just walk in and poison some bread, unnoticed?"

Bronwyn felt obliged to defend the kitchen where she worked. "Your Grace, someone might have brought the poisoned bread in from outside the castle."

Queen Matilda looked at Bronwyn pointedly. "May I remind you, this is the not the first time you have been at the scene of such a crime in my court."

Bronwyn swallowed. She understood the queen's suspicion. "Whoever it was must've done it in the night, when the kitchen was empty. Master Christopher wouldn't let anyone just walk in. The man must've taken rolls from yesterday and poisoned them."

"I'm curious about why he said it was a gift from his mistress," Sir William said, pacing around the small room.

"You think he means Maud?" the queen asked.

"It's possible. But why would she want to kill a nun? Besides, she wouldn't know anything about it. She's back on her way to Gloucester by now. She's at least a few days' ride away."

"So then either she'd given orders for the nun to be killed, or this was a random attack. But who would want to kill a nun?"

"It wasn't only the nun, Your Grace. Sir Robert's squire, Theobold, and the brewer were also given the rolls." Bronwyn thought on this. "I think it was someone who felt Sister Joan was getting too close, or who had seen him. Maybe she recognized him." She stopped. "The ghost. The one she kept talking about."

"Not you too. I thought you had some sense, girl. Ghosts don't exist."

"I know, but what if the man Sister Joan saw is supposed to be dead?"

"What do you mean? You're speaking in riddles."

Bronwyn said, "Your Grace, may I have two of the prisoners brought up for questioning?"

"If you think it would help. But I want to know, where did this poison come from, if not from the kitchen?" the queen asked.

"I will find out."

"See that you do," Queen Matilda said. "Sir William, have the prisoners brought to the throne room tonight, after dinner. And for God's sake, keep them alive."

Bronwyn returned to the cells. The surly guard said, "What do you want?"

"I want to see the nun's cell. I want to see the bread that poisoned her."

"Why? It's from the kitchen. Shouldn't you be looking there?"

"I will."

The guard looked down his nose at her. "You know, not

everyone likes young maids who stick their noses in other people's business."

Bronwyn gritted her teeth. *And not everyone likes guards who are useless at their jobs*, she thought. But something in his scowl and stance made her think he was aiming for a fight, and he outweighed her by at least fifty pounds, if not more. She smirked. In good time, this man would be fired from his post by Sir William and if there was any justice in the world, he'd be shoveling horse manure in the stables.

He squared up to her. His smile was nasty. "I'll give you something to smile about."

"Mate, if you touch her, you'll have the queen to answer to. She's the queen's favorite," Theobold drawled from his cell. He sounded bored.

The guard glanced over. "Her? She's just a kitchen maid."

"She's more than that," Theobold said. "The queen likes her. She's like a little pet, or a loyal dog. If she comes back sporting a black eye or can't walk, the queen will want to know whom to blame. You really want to take that chance?"

The guard glared down at Bronwyn again. "You're the queen's dog, eh? What a little pup you are."

Bronwyn's face felt hot. She met the guard's eyes, refusing to back down.

The other guard sighed and said, "I'll take her."

He led her down the cells. The guard nodded to Theobold and escorted Bronwyn to the nun's cell. It was empty. He unlocked it and opened the door. "You shouldn't provoke him."

"I didn't." *I held my tongue*, she thought. She bent down to the floor and reached for the mysterious bread roll.

"Wait a minute," the guard said.

"What?"

"If that's what killed her, maybe you shouldn't touch it. Look at what it did to the mice." He nodded toward the two dead mice lying by the bread.

Bronwyn took her apron and carefully picked up the bread

roll. "You're right. It looks sticky, like it's covered in something."

The roll was small. She held it in her apron, taking care not to touch it.

"Here," Theobold said, nudging up the bread roll in his cell with his boot. "You can have mine too."

Bronwyn picked it up and walked back to the jail entrance. At the entrance to the jail, she turned to the helpful guard. "Thank you." She met the surly guard's glare but said nothing and walked up the circular stone steps, carefully holding the bread rolls in her apron.

She first went to the infirmary, where she was met by John. "How is Sister Joan? Did she survive her night in the cells?" John asked, a smile on his face. He saw Bronwyn's dour expression and his smile fell. "What's happened?"

"She's dead. Someone brought them poisoned bread rolls. Apparently, they were a gift from his mistress, and Sister Joan ate one. She's dead," she repeated. Her voice sounded cold to her, but she blinked and looked down at her toes. She swallowed the lump in her throat. She'd liked the young nun.

John crossed himself. "I'm sorry."

She nodded. "I have some of the bread. We know they're poisoned because mice and rats ate them, and they died too." She held out her apron.

He looked down at the rolls. "They look sticky. Could they be coated in something?"

"That's what we wondered. Do you think they're safe to touch?"

"I don't know. Put them here." John led her to a small work-table and frowned. He put on a pair of gloves and picked up one of the dirty rolls, sniffing. "I know this smell."

The older physician came over. "What's this? What are you doing?"

John relayed what had befallen Sister Joan.

Master Reynolds crossed himself. "That poor woman."

The men surveyed the bread rolls. "This is monkshood.

What's it doing on the bread?"

"That's what I'm wondering," Master Reynolds said.

John cleared his throat. "It that doesn't surprise me. A few days ago, I found our medicine box open, with the lock on the ground. Someone had broken into it."

Bronwyn's eyebrows rose.

John nodded. "A vial of monkhood was missing. Small amounts of it rubbed on the skin is useful for helping with ailments like sore muscles and the gout, but you wouldn't want to eat it. It is highly poisonous. It's why we keep it locked up."

Master Reynolds frowned. "You should have reported this to me immediately." He examined the storage cupboard. "Care to explain, John?"

"It was the night of the so-called attack on Sir Robert, when the nun was going on about a ghost. In the chaos of it all, I found it open and bottles on the ground. I think whoever broke in just grabbed a medicine at random and hoped it would be lethal. I cleaned up the mess."

Bronwyn wondered: *Did he clean up his own mess?* What if *he* had delivered the bread? And if he was local, he would be able to know of anywhere else to go to buy bread.

Father Reynolds's bushy, grey eyebrows furrowed. "We'll have to tell the queen. This is very bad. Very bad, indeed."

"May I leave these with you?" Bronwyn asked.

"Yes."

"How is Sir Robert?"

"You may speak with him yourself."

Bronwyn looked over. Sir Robert was lying there, resting. He looked asleep, so Bronwyn didn't disturb him. She instead went to the kitchens, where Master Christopher was in an uproar.

The other cooks quieted as he paced and railed about the kitchen, throwing his arms in the air. He turned and laid eyes on her. "You."

He crossed the kitchen in a few strides and stood in her face. "What on earth did you do? I was woken up this morning by guards, who demanded to know why I'd let a man come in here and poison my bread, as if I'd *invited* the man in."

Before Bronwyn could take a breath, he continued. "They are blaming me for this. Some woman dies and somehow, it's all my fault. I tell you, I won't stand for it. Not in my kitchen. I don't stand for baseless accusations when it's not me, it's you. This is all because of you. Nothing like this ever happened until you came here."

"That's not my fault. Sister Joan—"

"Oh, so it was a nun, was it? Well, that's no great loss. One less woman to get on her knees and pray for her soul instead of working for a living like the rest of us. I tell you…"

He went on, growing red in the face. Bronwyn began to get bored. She knew that he was having a proper rant and just wanted to yell at someone, with her being his favorite target. But she needed to figure out this mystery.

"Is she going to blame me? Oh, God, I'm going to be hanged like a criminal. I might be beheaded at dawn. I might—"

Bronwyn sighed. "You'll want to post a guard at the entrances to make sure no one comes in who shouldn't."

"Yes, I know that. Of course we're doing that. It's obvious. Thom…" He shot a look at one of the cooks, who nodded.

"Sorry, I need to speak with Sister Rebecca. She should know."

"But—"

"Sorry." Bronwyn left.

His muttered curse grated on her ears, but she didn't care. Bronwyn might have ruined her chances of ever working in the kitchen again, but something compelled her to move on. She'd work in the kitchens if she could, and it gave her joy, but she wanted to figure this out. It was like a puzzle that niggled at her mind. Like strands of pastry that needed to be woven and plaited together.

She found Sister Rebecca outside in the courtyard, pacing. Bronwyn approached her as the clouds clustered above and rain began to lightly fall. "Sister?"

Sister Rebecca turned. "Oh, Bronwyn." Tears coursed down her cheeks. "You've heard. Sister Joan—" She clasped Bronwyn in a tight hug.

"I'm so sorry," Bronwyn said. Her shoulder was getting damp from the nun's tears, but she didn't mind. "It's my fault. I should've tried harder to convince them to let her go. If only she hadn't… If only I had—"

"I don't want to hear it." The older nun released her and looked her in the eyes. "It's not your fault she died. You didn't kill her. It was that horrible person, that ghost she was talking about."

"I know. Whoever it was—"

"It was a real person. Not a ghost. She was terrified of it. But you know what she was more afraid of?"

"What?"

"That the person might try to kill Sir Robert again. She knew when she found him that first time that he'd been up to no good, even though no one believed her." Seeing Bronwyn's face, she said, "You're not alone—I didn't believe her, either. No one did. But she was adamant that someone was trying to kill him. She didn't want to leave his side after that."

"But why? Why would someone want to kill Sir Robert?"

Sister Rebecca shot Bronwyn a look. "We would all be prisoners were it not for the grace and kindness of the queen. Sir Robert is the right hand of the empress, the queen's rival. Anyone would want to kill him and try to ingratiate themselves and get closer to the queen. I should think that's obvious."

"And now someone killed Sister Joan."

"That's no accident. I heard she died from some poisoned bread. Did anyone else get the bread?" Sister Rebecca asked.

"Theobold, a squire. And Peter, the brewer who was captured with us. No one else."

"Doesn't that seem odd to you?"

"Yes." Bronwyn looked at her. "Only certain people got the poisoned bread. The other prisoners didn't."

"To me, that suggests whoever did it wasn't just trying to kill Sister Joan, but also anyone associated with the empress. That nasty brewer man was despicable, but he is allied to the queen. And the squire…" She tapped her chin thoughtfully.

"But not everyone here knew that there were such prisoners here."

"So that narrows down your list of suspects. Who knew?" Sister Rebecca asked.

Bronwyn ticked off her fingers. "The ladies-in-waiting, the queen, Sir William of Ypres, the guards, some of the cooks, and the two doctors in the infirmary… Any number of people."

"You're forgetting someone."

"Who?"

"Sister Joan's ghost. I think they followed us here. Why else would they try to kill Sir Robert and those four people?"

Bronwyn had a funny suspicion that the nun was right.

"There is something you should know," the nun began. "I did not believe Sister Joan, and I hold no belief in her theories, but… Before we were found by you and the cook, back at the castle, she thought she heard someone talking to the brewer, laying out a plan. She didn't tell me who it was. And I didn't believe her, but my hearing is not so good as hers. And I don't have her imagination. I thought she was creating silly stories."

Bronwyn opened her mouth to speak, but the nun held up a hand. "This person, whoever they were, she saw them. She had taken to exploring the castle at night and was in the laundry when a person came in, stripped down, and threw their clothes in the laundry. But she didn't see his face. She hid because she felt it would be indecent to see a naked man. But she knew his clothes were covered in blood; otherwise, why would he be doing that at such a late hour?"

"How would she know they were bloody?"

"Sister Joan came to our nunnery from a simple family. She's used to butchering animals."

Bronwyn gasped. "You mean she saw the person who killed

the sheep."

"But she didn't say who it was. She only had her suspicions. I thought perhaps it was the brewer, or another squire, or maybe a cook. And then when she started talking about ghosts, I couldn't stand to hear of it. Such notions are not appropriate for the women of our order. But now it's too late." She sighed. "I'm sorry I never let her speak. I wish I could have been more helpful. But I thought you should know."

Bronwyn had just exited the privy when a page found her. She was summoned to the queen's chamber. She followed the page up the steps to the queen's solar, where the queen, now dressed properly to receive visitors, stood by with Sir William. Her pretty face was drawn, her eyebrows furrowed. There was no polite wait for ceremony here.

"Bronwyn, you should know. I want whoever is behind these attacks on Sir Robert and the sister to be found, and within the week."

Bronwyn's eyes widened.

"I had sent letters on to Gloucester, but Maud is proving… difficult."

Bronwyn frowned. "What did the letters say?"

"You are impertinent, girl," Sir William of Ypres growled and then said more gently, "That is none of your concern."

Queen Matilda held up a hand. "Peace, Sir William. Bronwyn, we are looking to make an exchange, of Sir Robert for my husband. It is the usual thing in situations like this. Maud agreed to take Sir Robert back in exchange for twelve earls and a large amount of gold, but that is an insult. She has ignored our other entreaties since then. I have sent more than one messenger since we took up residence here, so I assume she is simply not interested."

"And if she continues to ignore them?" Bronwyn asked.

The queen smiled. "I have a plan for just that occurrence."

Bronwyn met her eyes and repressed a shiver. The queen's smile was all-knowing and self-satisfied, as if she knew something

Bronwyn didn't, but also something that would surely rile the empress. Bronwyn wondered what it was.

"I expect to have my answer in a week. You have until then to catch this person. Understand?" the queen asked.

"Yes, Your Grace." She curtsied and left.

Bronwyn was met outside the room by Sir William. "Mistress Bronwyn," he started, a hand resting comfortably on his belt. "What have you found so far?" he asked.

She weighed whether to trust him and decided she had nothing to lose. "I have a ghost of a dead squire, and his body is missing, It's possible that he was moved or already buried, but people have seen him since his untimely death. It doesn't make sense. He might be alive, or he might not be. The situations lead me to believe that the culprit is one of Maud's people who are imprisoned here, but they're all either dead or in the cells. So maybe… This man is alive. I don't believe in ghosts."

"Quite right." He walked with her down the corridor. "I know what I would do. Lay a trap. No doubt the person has killed the nun and tried to kill some of the other people from Maud's camp, so he'll likely either try to kill them again, or aim for Sir Robert."

She stroked her chin. "There's no way we'll be able to know which he'll try for."

"Just as well you have me to help," he said with a smile.

That evening, Bronwyn hid in the infirmary. She'd taken a pallet nearby Sir Robert's and lain there, quiet as a mouse, with a scratchy, woolen blanket drawn up to her nose. A flea bit her knee, and she resisted the urge to scratch it irritably, in case someone was watching. She thought to herself, *Who could have possibly wanted to hurt Sir Robert, or the others?* Her list of suspects was so small, it was practically non-existent. Tristan was her most likely suspect, what with the brewer being in jail, but she'd seen his dead body itself, while it had still been warm. He'd just been attacked, she'd seen the blood.

But… what if it hadn't been a killing blow? What if it had just been meant to look like he'd gotten hurt, and he'd been faking his own death? But why? He was loyal to the empress, she had no doubt about that. So why would he be behind all these tricks to hurt his own mistress? And now that Sir Robert was due to be ransomed or traded off in exchange for King Stephen. Even though Maud was refusing to do this, perhaps she could be convinced. So either someone must have wanted Sir Robert dead to prevent King Stephen from regaining his position and armies, or they wanted him dead to destabilize the empress's regime. Either motive spoke of trouble. But then, the person who'd been behind these attacks might not have known that Maud was refusing to participate in the prisoner exchange. If they didn't, they still had a motive for wanting Sir Robert dead, which ruled out Sir William of Ypres. Not that she suspected him, anyway, but it was good to have someone to trust.

She wondered, had she been too quick to trust in the two physicians? Father Reynolds had seemed knowledgeable about the poisons in the cupboard, but the younger man, John, had also aroused her suspicion. Could he be trusted? John would have had easy access to their supply of medicines and could have stolen the monkshood himself, then blamed it on someone else. Or what if he and Tristan were working together? Perhaps Tristan had paid the younger man a bribe, or promised him wealth or fortune. And with his place being at the infirmary, John would have had easy access to the monkshood and no one would think anything amiss. Time would tell.

Bronwyn lay quietly, her body mostly covered by the thin blanket. She only hoped that whoever was behind this would show their face soon. But then she yawned and realized that the room was warm and comfortable. She had the luxury of sleeping on a raised pallet with a blanket, and for once, she was cozy. The hard boards of the wooden pallet were hard and stiff against her back, but it beat sleeping on the floor and worrying about mice or rats.

She pinched her arm. She needed to stay awake. She needed

to be ready in case this person came by again and tried to kill Sir Robert. She needed to... Her thoughts faded into sleep.

A noise.

A rustle. A shift of movement.

There were steps nearby. Someone had entered the infirmary and was moving closer.

She kept her eyes closed but suddenly was wide awake. Who was there? She waited and listened. She didn't move a muscle. Whoever it was was the culprit, perhaps.

The person came closer, despite the subtle snores and coughs of the people lying there. She waited as the steps grew louder. They had a heavy tread, unmistakably a man's. She wished she had a weapon or something. Anything.

She waited one minute, and two, then shot up out of her bed.

"Aah. Bronwyn, what are you doing here?"

"I might ask the same thing of you, Tristan." She stood. "I thought it was you. I couldn't believe there was really Sister Joan was seeing a ghost."

He snorted. "Is that what that nun was saying? I thought she'd lost her mind. But then that brewer started spouting nonsense about ghosts, too. Scared the wits out of him. Made it a damn sight easier to move about, too. Shame it didn't fool you, though."

He stood over near Sir Robert's bedside. She threw off the light blanket and got out of the bed.

"She interrupted you that night, didn't she? You were planning to kill him."

"You're not as dumb as you look."

She came closer. "But why? He was hurt in battle and is only just recovering from a fever. He still might die."

"I couldn't wait that long. He'll be exchanged for Stephen any day now."

"You're wrong. Maud is preventing the exchange."

His face contorted in anger, then stilled into a hard mask. "Doesn't matter. The plan will still go ahead."

Aha, Bronwyn thought. *So he didn't know about the obstacle to the prisoner exchange. But then, whose side was he really on?* "I don't understand."

"You wouldn't, would you? It's because you're just a servant. A nobody, even if the empress likes you." He smirked. "Sir Robert's time is done. Now back off and pretend you never saw anything, unless you want to meet this." He pulled out a familiar savage-looking knife. It reminded her of a sickle used to cut grass but with a longer blade.

Her eyes widened. "I know that blade."

"'Course you do. It's the one I stuck in the empress's pillow. Gave her a real fright, hopefully. And I used it to cut that sheep's head off. Not what the blade's meant for, though. It's a relic, taken off one of the Saracen fighters from the crusade. Nasty way to go."

"But why? You're loyal to the empress. Why harass her so?"

He grinned and played with the blade. "Because my master bade me to do it."

Bronwyn's mouth dropped open. "Your master. You mean… Sir Miles Fitzwalter?"

"The very same. How do you think he knew the empress's whereabouts so often? He's at her side at all times, and when he's not, his spies are. He made it easy for me to slip in and carry out his plans. He was the one who placed Mistress Agatha in her service. She's loyal to him. We all are."

Things clicked in Bronwyn's mind. "Your master wants to prevent Maud from winning the war. You're playing both sides."

"Now she understands." He mimicked a slow clap with the blade in his hands.

"And what of Lady Susanna?"

"She and Mistress Agatha were the perfect spies for us. If Mistress Agatha didn't play along, Lady Susanna would inform on her. She made sure Agatha did as she was told."

"But wait. Mistress Agatha I knew was playing a part in this, but why did you try to kill the others? Why the brewer and Sister

Joan?" Bronwyn asked.

"They'd seen me. They knew I was behind it. The brewer knew because we'd been working together. He didn't believe I'd died, even if you did." Tristan grinned. "There are spies loyal to Sir Miles, even here. One of them let me in. I hid in the brewery. Then whenever I'd go down to the cells, the brewer would shout out about seeing me. The nun was just a casualty of war. She saw me. I couldn't let her live. Same with Sir Robert."

"So that's it, is it? You already came in here once, I found a bit of hops grain on him from you. Now you thought you'd just cut him down in his sleep?"

"It seems easier." He wielded the blade.

"So that night when the empress wanted you to reveal who was behind these attacks on her, you faked your own death."

"Couldn't very well turn myself in, now could I? Could've turned in one of the others, but then they might have given me away, and I couldn't have people asking too many questions. So I spooked one of the horses and when I heard the stableboy come near, I groaned and ran at the wall. Actually knocked myself out there for a while. Came to when I heard you all coming and so I played dead. The rest you know."

"You won't get away with this." His mouth curved into a smirk. "You think you're so smart, but you're clueless. My master wants him dead, and I aim to please. I'll give you till the count of ten, and then you're next. Run, little Bronwyn. Run."

She threw the blanket at him. Tristan laughed and tossed it away, but not before she'd closed the distance between them and launched herself at him, tangling him and her up in the blanket, and the knife of his.

He cursed as they tumbled to the floor. "What do you think you're doing?"

"What's it look like?" She kicked at him and her knee met the blade. It tangled in the blanket but still cleaved through the cloth.

He punched her in the face and she snapped back, falling. Pain shot through her head like an arrow.

Tristan scrambled up and reached for the blade when she kicked with her long legs and got him in the gut. He lurched back and cursed. The squire reached for her as she scrambled, her feet tangling in the cloth. "Witch," he said.

She moved. She had to protect Sir Robert. "Help!" she cried.

Some of the snores stopped. Bronwyn and Tristan froze, looking. "Help!" she called again. "Somebody help me!"

The snores started again as the people slept. Bronwyn cursed. Tristan laughed.

"Stupid girl. No one's going to help you now." He disentangled himself from the blanket and pulled out the knife. "You get in my way, you'll die. You help me, maybe I'll let you live."

She stood in front of Sir Robert, who lay as if dead. She blinked hard. Was he dead already? Had Tristan succeeded? No, his chest rose and fell. She needed to stall for time. Anything to save Sir Robert's life.

"Why does Sir Miles want him dead?"

Tristan circled around her, waving the Saracen knife from side to side. "Because the empress relies on him too much, and he won't see reason. She was never supposed to be the Queen of the English, or rule. She should have stayed in France. Ruling is a man's job."

That raised Bronwyn's ire, and from the knowing grin on Tristan's face, that was his aim.

"But the empress is still alive."

"For now. People have met with accidents before. Perhaps she'll have a hunting accident. Or drink too much and die in her sleep. Or maybe she'll eat a bread roll, poisoned by the young cook whom she thought was so loyal to her. Your head would end up on a spike before dinner." He grinned at the prospect.

"So Sir Miles would rule. But he's just a constable," Bronwyn said.

"A royal constable. And an earl. And a better military commander than her."

She looked at him curiously.

Tristan tossed the blade from hand to hand. "You really don't know, do you? He made a deal with Matilda. Eliminate Sir Robert and then he'll take over. They'll reach peace negotiations in days and in no time at all this anarchy will be over."

"With Sir Miles at the head of her armies."

"*His* own armies. Stephen will place him highly in his court."

"So that's why Sir Miles is doing all this." She paused. "You were behind it all from the beginning. The notes. The knife in her bed. The sheep's head. The fire. That was all you."

"Well, not entirely me."

"No, you blackmailed her taster, Agatha, to help you. And the brewer. He'd been drawing the rude pictures of the empress."

He grinned and gave her a nod. "Well done. He was easy to convince. With any luck, he'll be dead soon."

Bronwyn realized then, "You're not working alone still. You've had help this entire time." She swallowed. "Lady Susanna. You took advantage of her affections and put them to good use. You made her think that you cared for her, as long as she helped you in your plan."

"We've known each other long before Winchester. We just kept it a secret. She's good at following orders."

"Like locking Rupert and Theobold in the room the night before the empress's coronation in London. That was on your order."

"Now you're getting it. She helps me. I give her a bit of what she wants. Win-win."

He feinted and she dodged. He laughed. "You almost found me in the brewery down there, you know. Thought that little bump on the head would have sent you a message to stay away." He lunged and she got in the way. His blade cut through the sleeve and bit into her skin. She felt the sting and hissed.

"Hurts, doesn't it?" Tristan said. "The game's up, Bronwyn. You tried to protect Sir Robert and failed. Now move aside. Otherwise, I'll kill you."

"What do you get out of all this?" She stepped back, bumping into Sir Robert's pallet. She grabbed fistfuls of his thin blanket in her hands.

He stepped closer. "I rise higher. Get made a knight. Get lands of my own and a pretty rich girl to marry. I'm thinking Lady Alice would do. I'm bored of Lady Susanna."

Bronwyn swallowed. The blade was almost at her throat. She threw the blanket at him, and he waved it aside with a cut of his blade.

"Lady Alice would never marry you."

"Wouldn't she? Especially when I say I caught you trying to kill Sir Robert and saved the day? People would do anything for a hero."

"She'd never believe you."

"Doesn't matter. I have ways of making fine ladies do what I want." He sneered.

Tristan lunged and Bronwyn did what she did best, according to most people around her. She got in the way.

His blade slipped past and grazed her side, but she kneed Tristan in the groin and shoved him back. Their legs tangled together as she cried out, and she rammed his forehead with hers. It hurt both parties, but she didn't care, and she punched him, getting him in the nose. Blood dripped freely from his nostrils, and he landed back on the floor.

Bronwyn leaned back against the bedframe and watched as Tristan slowly rose and wiped away blood on his chin. "Stupid brat. You'll pay for this." He spat out a mouthful of blood.

She started to kick back when a hand gripped her right shoulder.

"I've got this, girl," Sir Robert said, his voice weak. He held a small blade in his other hand and threw it at Tristan. He missed.

Tristan let out a triumphant laugh, when at that moment, the guards thundered into the room, led by Sir William of Ypres, shouting and aiming their spears. Tristan slowly raised his hands up in defeat.

Chapter Seventeen

BRONWYN STOOD, HER arm and side bandaged, before the queen. Also in attendance were Sir Robert, who was given a chair, Sir William, and a few of the queen's trusted men. Bronwyn swallowed. She almost felt as if she were in trouble, even though Tristan sat mutely in a jail below, under heavily armed guard.

"Tell us what happened," the queen said. "Start at the beginning."

Bronwyn took a deep breath. "For weeks now, someone has been plaguing the empress. Little tricks, that got worse. From an upturned chamber pot in her bed, little drawings of her dying in a fire, to a knife in her pillow, and a sheep's head placed in her bed when she was asleep. Horrible things. The empress was worried there was a spy, so she asked me to look into it. Me and Tristan Langforde, Sir Miles Fitzwalter's squire."

Queen Matilda's eyes widened slightly at this, and she murmured, "And here I thought military tactics were the way to frighten her off. Apparently, all I needed was a quill and a good servant." To Bronwyn, she motioned. "Go on."

"I figured out that it was one of the squires, who was either paying people close to her or blackmailing them, to write her rude notes and let him slip into her room unnoticed. This man was Tristan. But then I doubted myself. Because he died."

Sir William of Ypres shot her a look. "Don't be talking about ghosts now, girl."

"I'm not. But to the empress's court, he'd died. He could have been behind it, but it didn't matter at that point, if he was no longer a threat. And then when the queen's armies took over, we were captured. Peter the brewer seemed responsible—and Mistress Agatha made me think that I'd been wrong entirely about Tristan."

She paused to let that bit of information sink in. "I'd made a mistake, you see. I'd told Tristan before that Lady Susanna, one of the empress's ladies-in-waiting, fancied him. He laughed and acted like it was a great joke. I didn't know that they had been lovers for months already, and she was already helping him with his tricks."

"Such a disloyal young woman. Why would she do this, and go against her mistress?" Queen Matilda asked.

"Because she thought herself in love with him."

"Hmph. Her loyalty is misplaced. I deplore the use of schemes and intrigues at court, even if they are to my advantage. This all is most distasteful. It leaves a sour note on my tongue. I actually feel sorry for Maud, how she has surrounded herself with traitors and spies. How miserable she must be." The queen sat straighter. "Guards, arrest the Lady Susanna. Put her in a cell near the squire Tristan so they may shout at each other all they like. See how long their love lasts then."

Within minutes, Lady Susanna sat in a nearby jail cell.

Bronwyn continued, "With Lady Susanna helping him, disturbing the empress was easy. And once your armies attacked and the empress was on the run, Tristan could escape here. His plan had changed. His master had charged me with delivering a note to Sir Robert. I don't know what it said. But it got me out of the castle and put me in harm's way. I suspect they wanted me gone, for the next step in their plan."

"Which was?" Sir William asked.

"Once the empress was bothered and feared for her life, killing off her main military commander, Sir Robert, would be sure to ruin her plans in the war. She depends on him. That would be sure to end things quickly."

"Maybe, maybe not," Queen Matilda said. "That would still mean that my husband sits in Bristol Prison, and then we would have no leverage to use to bargain with for his release."

"True. But Tristan didn't know about Maud refusing to take part in the exchange of prisoners. He was following his master's orders and only wanted to get rid of Sir Robert. So he tried, first by attempting to find him in the infirmary, but Sister Joan found him and thought she'd seen a ghost. He'd been hiding in the brewery and the air around Sir Robert smelled like hops. He'd broken into the store cupboard and stolen some monkshood, a poison, and even shed a grain when Sister Joan had interrupted him. When I went looking down in the brewery later, I was attacked."

The people were unmoved. "Tristan, I suppose?"

"Yes. Only Lady Susanna and the doctors knew where I was headed. So no one else besides her, the doctors, or Tristan would have had the knowledge or opportunity to hit me. I'm just lucky that Rupert and Lady Alice found me. Then Tristan tried to poison anyone who could recognize him, see he was alive and well, and give him away, which meant Theobold, Sir Robert's squire, the brewer, and Sister Joan. He'd poisoned some bread and had walked right into the cells, convincing the guards that he was bringing some late-night food and drink for the prisoners. They had seen me and other servants before, so they probably didn't think anything out of the ordinary."

"How do we know what you're saying is the truth?" the queen asked.

"Ask Mistress Agatha Carre. Tristan caught her lying and blackmailed her to do his bidding. He was behind it all. She might deny that Tristan was blackmailing her, but I doubt it now that all has been exposed."

"Find her," the queen said, and a guard quit the room.

In moments, Agatha was brought in. She glared at the pair of guards and said, "I don't know what sort of court you're running here, but I don't care to be so rudely treated. I want these guards whipped for their impertinence. I want—"

"Mistress Agatha, please withhold your demands for the moment. There are some questions we'd like to ask you," the queen said.

Agatha turned and curtsied. "Your Grace."

The queen motioned Sir William close and whispered behind her hand.

As they talked, Agatha waited, then sniffed loudly. She clearly disliked being summoned, then ignored. She looked down her nose at Bronwyn. "Proud of yourself, aren't you? Think the empress will treat you better and give you some reward for finding out who was behind it all, eh? I could've told her that myself. Peter always had it in for the empress. He and Tristan were working together the whole time. I was just waiting for the right moment."

Bronwyn snorted. "And would that be before or after Tristan decided to blackmail you?"

Agatha's eyebrows narrowed. "You've got a sharp tongue, you little wretch. What makes you think you can talk to me that way?"

Bronwyn went on the offensive. "He knew just like I did that the night of the empress's so-called poisoning, you were faking. Why did you do that to her?"

She shrugged. "The woman was getting full of herself. She needed to be taught a lesson."

What a vengeful creature, Bronwyn thought. "So he threatened to tell the empress what you'd done unless you did what he asked. He'd slaughtered the sheep and with your help, hid it in the empress's bed."

Agatha gave a sharp nod.

"I'm guessing you helped slip the note in the empress's Book of Hours as well."

"Yes. But I didn't write it. The brewer did. He wanted to play a little trick on the empress too, but when Tristan caught him and saw his inky fingers, he knew who was behind it. He threatened us both unless we helped him."

"So Lady Alice had nothing to do with the tricks on the empress," Bronwyn said.

Agatha shook her head. "Lady Alice did nothing. Useless as usual. Lady Susanna had been helping from the start. But she was always watching, every move I made. It was unnerving. The stupid wench, she fancied they were in love. Tristan didn't have to blackmail her. She'd do anything he said, the silly woman."

The queen interrupted. "How disgusting. I actually feel sorry for Maud. She clearly struggles with whom to trust. What a pity she put her faith in you."

Agatha shot her a glare but wisely kept her mouth shut.

The queen turned to Bronwyn. "So, it's true, then, that this Tristan was behind these nasty pranks on Maud. But how did you know that Tristan was the same person who killed the nun?"

"Because she, the brewer, and the squire, Theobold, were the only people who could recognize him when he walked around the prison cells and raise the alarm. And with Sister Joan in jail, she could tell the other prisoners what she'd seen. Hiding in the brewery, Tristan wouldn't know if she had already raised the alarm or not. He'd only have to act and try to eliminate the problem."

"So she was his target," Sir William said.

"I think so. It's why the brewer started talking about ghosts when he saw him and likely knew what he was about. That didn't save Sister Joan, however." Bronwyn looked away. She'd liked the young nun.

"But they weren't the only ones who came from the empress's camp. There was yourself, Lady Alice, and the other nun, Sister Rebecca. Why weren't all of you targeted as well?"

"Honestly? I think it was only a matter of time before he did. Moving targets are a lot harder to take out than ones sitting in jail cells." Bronwyn repressed a shudder at the thought and imagined

Lady Alice drinking a poisoned cup of wine, or Sister Rebecca dying from a knife in the back at church, or…

"So that brings us to tonight. What can you tell me of this?" the queen asked.

"Simple. Sir William and I hatched a plan. We agreed with the physicians in the infirmary that I would pretend to be a patient and hide and pretend to be asleep, to surprise Tristan when he came in and catch him in the act. Sir William?"

Sir William spoke up. "We didn't know if the man would try to attack Sir Robert again, or if he'd try to kill the others down in prison again, so we had our men hiding in both areas. I was down in the cells hiding with some of the guards with the doors closed but unlocked. The guards manning the post were the same as usual, so no one would be the wiser."

"Let us see what Lady Susanna has to say about all this. Bring her to us," the queen commanded.

In minutes, the noblewoman was brought up from the cells, heavily guarded. "I tell you, it's all a mistake. You're wrong. It was an innocent mistake," Lady Susanna protested. She was held back by the arms by two guards, and her face was pale. "Your Grace, I don't know why I was sent to jail."

"Ha. A likely story. Your Grace, this young woman is either naive, stupid, or lying through her teeth. I cannot believe she didn't know what she was doing," Sir William said. "Lady Susanna, we know that you were helping the squire, Tristan Langforde, in his plans to kill members of the empress's camp, and that you were informing on others. What have you to say for yourself?"

"Why would I want to kill anyone?" Lady Susanna said. "I wouldn't want to harm anyone."

Sir William barked a laugh. Lady Susanna reddened. The other knights in the room exchanged dubious looks.

Sir William paused. "One of the prisoners died before we could save him."

Bronwyn's heart pounded in her chest. "Who?"

Theobold. Is he alive? She dreaded to think.

"The brewer," Sir William said. "He'd gone mad, kept raving about ghosts walking the halls. Then he clutched his chest and collapsed. Died within minutes. Nothing we could do. His was the only death."

Bronwyn's shoulders relaxed. Theobold was safe, for now.

Bronwyn said, "Lady Susanna, I recall the other ladies at Maud's court teased you, for having a secret lover. But you seemed to only start romancing Tristan recently. Was he your lover?" Bronwyn asked. She knew the answer, but if she could get the noblewoman to admit it here, in front of everyone, they might be able to get more information from her.

Lady Susanna glared at her. All thoughts of friendship had disappeared from her face, and she spat at her. "I'm not saying anything."

Spittle hit Bronwyn's chin, and she wiped it away.

"Young lady, this might be your one chance to escape the noose. Would you die for that young man?" Sir William asked.

She glared at him mutinously.

"It's true," Mistress Agatha said. "They were lovers, have been for months. She was always watching and she helped Tristan from the start. She was involved in every little plot to hurt the empress. And if you let her stay here at court, she'll try to destroy you too, Your Grace."

"Guards, take these two women away. I find their presence foul," the queen said.

Mistress Agatha and Lady Susanna were removed, the former hissing and cursing.

"So Bronwyn stopped the murderous squire, Tristan," Queen Matilda said.

"With a little help from Sir Robert and the guards," Bronwyn said.

"No need to be so humble, girl," Sir Robert said brusquely. To the queen he said, "I was just waking up when I heard the squire reveal it all. He confessed and was going to try and kill me.

I was as weak as a newborn kitten. Tried to throw a knife at the boy but missed. She saved my life."

"I am glad to hear it." Queen Matilda gave him a demure smile and looked at him kindly. "Sir Robert, are you sure we cannot tempt you to join us? We could use a man of your stature and gravity. Your skills on the battlefield are renowned."

Sir Robert looked at the queen for a minute. He paused, as if thinking. *Is he truly considering her offer?* Bronwyn wondered. Then he slowly smiled and shook his head. "Your Grace, I appreciate your offer, but I am loyal to the empress." He stood. "By your leave, I will return to my cell."

Queen Matilda nodded. "Guards, take him. See he comes to no harm."

Sir Robert was led away. Queen Matilda shook her head and *tsked*. "What a disappointment."

Epilogue

NOT LONG AFTER Tristan was captured, the orders came through. Sir Robert and the other prisoners were to be exchanged for Stephen and his other men who sat with him in Bristol prison, including Sir Baldwin of Clare, Rupert's master.

She felt happy for Rupert, that he would see his master again and regain his rightful place in Stephen's court, but she also felt a tug at her heart, for Theobold would be leaving. Now that he was soon to be out of jail, he would be leaving to aid with the prisoner exchange, she assumed.

Bronwyn still worked in the kitchens, but the other cooks mostly left her alone. When word got around that she had helped foil plans to kill Sir Robert, she wasn't treated poorly, but the other cooks kept a distance. Thanks to Master Christopher's spreading rumors about her, she had no friends amongst the other servants, nor anyone to talk to.

Lady Susanna eventually admitted that Tristan had asked her to do these things, but she maintained that she was not at fault, it was all his doing.

Bronwyn paid a visit to Sir Robert in the cells, along with Theobold, who attended to his every need. Sir Robert stood when she approached, and said, "Hello, Mistress Blakenhale."

That brought a slow smile to her face. He'd actually addressed her properly.

"Sir Robert." She nodded. "I wanted to ask... What did that

note that I was sent to deliver to you that day say?"

His face darkened. "It is none of your concern." Then he paused. "It held the news from the empress that their supplies were running low, due to Matilda burning the city, and she wanted to leave via a small escape that very night and make for Gloucester. Her earls and knights would lead, I would provide the rearguard."

He looked at her. "It also held an order to kill you. It said, 'The bearer of this message is untrustworthy and should be killed.'"

Bronwyn gasped. She'd unknowingly delivered her own death warrant. A shiver spiraled down her spine. "But you didn't kill me."

"I had no reason to. You'd only delivered a message. And I could see that the empress likes you. I knew the handwriting was from Sir Miles himself, but I didn't know why he would want you dead. So I decided to ignore that part of the message. Besides, Theobold hasn't stopped talking about you, and he is a good judge of character. Even if the characters are kitchen maids." He paused. "I think Sir Miles is mistaken. No doubt his mind was twisted by the devious young squire Tristan, and he doesn't know whom to trust. It wouldn't surprise me if Tristan revealed himself to Sir Miles after his pretend death, to work behind the scenes.

"Mistress Bronwyn, you must understand that we rely on our squires for everything. We need them. Closer than brothers or sons or nephews, they are like family, but more. They look after our animals, our bodies, our lives. We rely on them implicitly, and we have great trust in them. In turn, they trust that we will look after their futures and give them every opportunity. With us, they can see the world. It is an attractive concept, and not one people take lightly, but it changes lives."

She glanced at Theobold in the corner of the cell, his face unreadable in the darkness.

Sir Robert said quietly, "I will let Theobold make his own choices about whom he courts. I make no apology for disapproving of you, because of your different levels of station. He will be a knight. You are a maidservant. I see no chance of upward advancement for you." He looked at her. "But I have been wrong before."

She cocked her head at him.

"His choices may not be his own. And in love, they are not always what I would choose for him. But I will not stand in his way." Sir Robert scratched his chin. He needed a shave. "Thank you for saving my life. I do think Tristan would have killed me if you hadn't woken me with your fighting. A lesser woman would have screamed and ran, but you stayed and fought. If only you'd been born a boy, I would have taken you on as a squire or page." He smiled.

Bronwyn knew it was meant as a compliment, but it made her inwardly bristle at being deemed unworthy due to her sex.

He added, "You should be wary. Lady Susanna may escape the noose, but Tristan will likely hang or be offered the chance to join Stephen's ranks, as I was."

Her eyebrows rose. "Really?"

"It happens more often than you'd think. Men change allegiances in war all the time." He gave her an even look. "What will you do now? The queen likes you, as the empress does. Will you stay here, or join us to return to the empress?"

"I don't know. I haven't thought about it."

"You'll need to decide soon. We are to be exchanged very soon. From what I gather, the queen herself, and her son, Prince Eustace, will ride to Bristol to be tokens of good faith, and then Stephen will return here, by which time I will be exchanged. Theobold, however, will travel with you and the others to rejoin the empress." Sir Robert grunted and his grim expression returned.

She sensed rather than heard the low rumble of discontent from Theobold's corner of the cell. No doubt they had had disagreements about this, with Theobold not wanting to leave his master's side.

"What is it?" Bronwyn asked.

"From what the men tell me, this prisoner exchange was arranged without the empress's consent. With my return, she loses a valuable bargaining piece. Losing Stephen won't lose her the war, but it will cost her. Maud will have a fit of temper." Sir Robert shook his head. "Whatever your choice, I hope you make the right decision. God be with you."

Bronwyn let out a small sigh. She knew Theobold watched her, but she did not want to stay. She turned to go, when Theobold said, "Wait."

She turned around.

"Don't go."

She returned to the bars. Theobold had taken the place of Sir Robert. He smelled, and his dark curls hung around his head. He needed a shave, and a bath, considering the small fuzz of dark facial hair creeping along his chin. But she still fancied him terribly, and thought he looked rather roguish being a bit dirty. "What is it?"

"I can't promise I will always put you first. In fact, I cannot promise that at all."

She tossed her head. "Give me a reason why I shouldn't walk away from here right now."

"Because I'm asking you. Stay."

She looked at him.

"I've never felt this way about a young woman before. There have been other girls, some I've fancied, but never… Not like this. I am to go to the empress's court. Say you'll come with me. I don't want us to be separated."

Her heart fluttered and her blood raced in her veins.

"I may have to go on a mission soon to help with the exchange, but, Bronwyn… Will you wait for me?"

She met his eyes. They watched her, sharp and hawk-eyed. Something about him seemed dangerous, as he was only a hair's breath away from drawing a weapon. But at the same time, he looked so vulnerable, she ached to smooth away his greasy curls and comfort him.

"Please, Bronwyn. Wait for me, and I promise I won't dally with any other woman. I will be true to you, if you are to me." He reached for her, through the iron bars, and tugged on her fingers, taking her small fingers in his. "I promise you, my own will be true. I will not love another but you."

She emitted a soft gasp. He was spouting poetry. Here, as they stood face to face on opposite ends of a jail cell. Did she love him? She thought she just might. Her heart lifted. His eyes shone, and they were like black pools that threatened to draw her in. Part of her never wanted to leave, and if she were to drown in his affectionate gaze, then so be it.

A snort from the back of the cell brought her back to reality. "For God's sake, boy. Leave the girl in peace. And leave the poetry to the minstrels and jonglers. I'm hungry. See if there's any food to be had, will you?"

Theobold released her hand immediately.

She bowed and walked away, feeling slightly embarrassed that Sir Robert had overheard all of that, but there was also lightness in her heart. Theobold was so intense, it had made her shiver when he'd looked at her.

As she passed by Lady Susanna's cell, she stopped. "Are you well?"

Lady Susanna cursed and strode up to the bars, her face contorted with anger. "This is all your fault. If you hadn't started pointing fingers and sticking your nose into things, none of this would have happened."

Bronwyn faced her. "Your sweet mask is slipping, Lady Susanna. You knowingly tormented the empress and helped Tristan try to kill Sir Robert. Can you really blame *me* for your actions?"

Lady Susanna glared at her. "You're wrong. You don't have a clue. He will come for me. He will rescue me."

"Or he'll watch you hang if he stays that long." A part of her wanted to torment Lady Susanna, to hurt her feelings and lie, and tell her that Tristan was already flirting with other women. His words about wanting Lady Alice rang in her head. She was sure that given the opportunity, he surely would turn from Lady Susanna for the next-best option. But that wasn't the case, and she felt bad for Lady Susanna. The handsome young man she'd fallen for was a traitor, and he'd used her for his own ends. She left amidst the sound of Lady Susanna's hissing.

Tristan was in the cell farthest from the entrance, which had an armed guard outside it, watching. She had nothing to say to him, so she left the jail, and almost as soon as she had, she ran into Lady Alice.

"Oh, Bronwyn, just the girl I was looking for. I thought you'd be down here. What are we going to do?" Lady Alice wrung her hands. Her energy was like a bird, darting from place to place.

"What do you mean?"

"Matilda has given us ladies the option to stay with her, as ladies-in-waiting. It is not something she offers just anyone. She is trading Mistress Agatha back to the empress, but me, she offered a place here."

"Will you stay?"

"I don't know." Lady Alice led her down a corridor. "A part of me wants to so that I could be near Rupert. And I won't deny that being closer to him will make things easier for us to be together." She blushed.

Bronwyn grinned in spite of herself. She knew how Alice felt. To have a young man tilt her face up to his and kiss her, to feel his hands entangled in her hair and the touch of his lips trailing kisses down her neck—it was intoxicating.

"Sister Rebecca is staying, to supervise the reconstruction of her former nunnery. You could stay too if you wanted."

It was tempting. To be there with her friend, with a queen who liked her. But Bronwyn hadn't been asked, and if she was being honest with herself, the kitchens weren't a welcome place for her. She belonged in the kitchen and yet didn't feel part of the group. To stay and work somewhere where she wasn't welcome, it would make her living there not only awkward, but intolerable over time. She might as well try her luck returning to Lincoln.

It hit her. She could try returning home and seeing if her family were still alive. She could perhaps revive their bakery and work there. She blinked.

"I mean if I stay, then you would have us, Rupert and I, but of course, you wouldn't see Theobold. Are you in love with him?" Lady Alice asked. "I think I am in love with Rupert," she admitted.

Bronwyn smiled at her friend, then faltered. These walls had prying ears, and she didn't wish to say too much, in case anyone was listening. But it tore at her to take even one step away from Theobold. She loved him. She just didn't want to admit it out loud. She didn't want to be hurt. And something Sir Robert had said had bothered her. What did he mean when he'd said that Theobold's choices may not be his own? Surely, they were. Maybe if she stayed with the empress, they could be together. Maybe her return to Lincoln could wait just a little while longer. She said, "I should get back."

"First, the queen wants you. She sent me to find you. She'd sent a page to the kitchen, but you weren't there, so I offered to look. I thought you might be down here," Lady Alice said. "If the man I loved were down in the cells, wild horses couldn't drag me away. Come, I go to her now. We'll go together."

The women shared a smile.

Once she was standing before the queen, Bronwyn watched as Lady Alice, Lady Muriel, and just a pair of guards stood in attendance. They held spears and wore light shirts over hose but had the stances of men who knew their weapons.

The queen wore a slim-fitting blue dress and surveyed Bronwyn. "I will make no bones about it. You have done me a service and saved the life of Sir Robert. I will not deny that if he had been killed, it would have disrupted our plans, and my husband might still languish in prison." She nodded her thanks.

"I am glad I could help."

"Would you like to stay in my court? You would work in the

kitchens, of course. I have developed a fondness for your sweet white rolls with honey." Queen Matilda flashed her an impish smile.

Bronwyn hesitated.

"Isn't that what you want, Bronwyn?" Queen Matilda asked. "It is only us here. You may be as honest as you wish. Would you like to stay here and work for me? I would treat you well."

The queen might, but the fellow cooks would not, Bronwyn thought. Until Master Christopher was replaced, she would never have a moment's peace and would always have to keep one eye over her shoulder. And yet, she could not trust the king. He had imprisoned her father for a crime of which he'd been innocent, and her father had almost died in the process. Could she truly claim allegiance to such a man?

Bronwyn swallowed. But here was a queen, offering her a place in her kitchens. It was an offer that any servant would jump at. Not so long ago, she would have jumped at it. And yet...

"I'm sorry, Your Grace. But I will return to Maud's court."

A flash of surprise passed over the queen's face. Her lips pressed tightly together. She recovered quickly, however, and straightened in her chair. "Why, may I ask?"

"I—" Bronwyn wanted to offer her comfort and reassurance, that it was not her personally she was stepping away from. But she somehow doubted the queen would see it that way. How to save face?

"Oh, but of course, I forgot. Lady Alice told me of the romance you have with a young squire in that woman's court." She smiled lightly, but it was strained.

"Yes, Your Grace. Theobold Durville. He is squire to Sir Robert. He's down in the cells right now."

Queen Matilda's eyes widened. "Is he? My word." This time, her smile met her eyes. "You have no doubt heard that we plan to exchange Sir Robert and the other prisoners from her court for Stephen and his men."

"Yes, Your Grace."

"Then I suppose you will be going with them, to stay by your young man."

"Yes. If that is acceptable to you."

"Of course it is. I am not your mistress." Queen Matilda spoke archly, as if Bronwyn should have known better. "Very well. You may go. Safe travels."

Bronwyn turned to go when the queen bid her wait. "Yes, Your Grace?"

"I wish to pass on a message to her. Your mistress."

Bronwyn waited.

"Tell her that I have no spy in her court. She won't believe me, I'm sure. But the treacherous squire Tristan Langforde is not one of my men. I would never have had one go through such charades. I have no interest in underhand dealings."

Bronwyn looked at her. If what she'd heard was correct, that was exactly what Queen Matilda had done. The rumors were that the queen, being fed up with the empress's refusal to acknowledge her messages and requests for a prisoner exchange, had simply written to Sir Robert's wife, who was in Bristol, looking after the prisoners. All it had taken was a simple exchange of letters between wives and the matter had been settled, no messengers or armies needed. There would be a heavily armed exchange taking place somewhere between Winchester and Bristol, near Devizes, a place Bronwyn had never heard of. But that didn't surprise her.

The queen added, "Maud possesses a foul temper, especially when provoked. Are you sure you wish to return to such a woman?"

Bronwyn nodded. "Yes."

"Very well. Tell me, do you believe in fate? In preordained action?"

Bronwyn cocked her head. She didn't know all of those words. "'Preord...' Sorry?"

"The idea that some things are already written and meant to happen, as decided by God. Or do you believe we make our own fate?"

Bronwyn had never thought about such things. She'd always lived one day to the next, working. "I couldn't say, Your Grace."

"Fair enough. It is a funny feeling I have, this feeling in my gut, but believe me or not, I do think that we will meet again, Bronwyn. I have the feeling you will be in my court. I shall keep a place open for you in my kitchens."

Bronwyn smiled and curtsied. "Thank you, Your Grace."

The queen motioned her away and Bronwyn left. She wanted a place to think and wandered toward the depleted castle gardens, where she breathed in the final aromas of warm summer air. She hadn't meant to eavesdrop, but then she found herself near two raised voices, and it was rather hard not to overhear. She blushed when she realized that she was listening to Rupert and Lady Alice.

Bronwyn quickly pressed herself up against the stone wall of the castle and listened. Were she to walk any farther, she would come across them, and it was clear they were having a private conversation. They sat on a wooden bench, hidden by some trees and bushes. But their voices carried.

"I don't understand," Lady Alice was saying. "How could you do it at all? I was so worried about you. Why on earth would you defect? It's dangerous out there. You could have died."

"I didn't, Alice. I'm fine," Rupert said.

"And now, just when we are back together again and safe, now you say you won't stay." Her voice rose. "What have I done to you, to make you want to avoid me so?"

"I'm not avoiding you. I would never—" he started.

"Then why won't you come with me?" she demanded.

"My duty is to my master, Alice," Rupert said. "I would think that you of all people would understand that."

"How could you say that? Of course I do. But things are different. We have lived through a siege, Rupert. That must count for something. I have let you…" Lady Alice stopped.

"You have let me steal a few kisses from a pretty woman, but we are not engaged, Alice. And I can't tie myself down to anyone right now. I must return to my master, and escort the queen to Bristol. This prisoner exchange is due to be a major affair. I cannot miss it to follow you to Maud's court. My duty is to Sir Baldwin, and to the king and queen."

"I know, I—" Lady Alice was silent for a moment. She took a breath and let it out. "I understand your obligations to your master. I just thought—"

"My master holds the keys to my future, Alice. I'm twenty and should be made a knight next year. I can't do anything to prevent that from happening, and I cannot advance or do anything without him. I should have been at Bristol all this time, instead of wasting—"

"Is that what you think? That you're *wasting your time* with me?" Lady Alice demanded.

"No, I never meant that. I only meant—"

"It's fine. I understand you perfectly. I'm sorry to have wasted your time with such frivolities as giving you my heart. On second thought, Rupert, if anyone has wasted their time here, it has been me, dallying with you." Lady Alice huffed and walked off, stamping her feet.

Rupert cursed under his breath. "Alice, wait." He hurried after her.

Bronwyn let out a breath. Were Rupert and Lady Alice ending their relationship? She didn't know. It had sounded like a lover's quarrel. And yet, she felt sad for Alice, that Rupert was treating her this way. Alice was a lady. It seemed like at times Rupert forgot that, and just whom he was getting involved with.

"At least I know where Theobold's allegiance lies," Bronwyn said aloud to herself. "He always said that his master comes first. Without a doubt."

The knowledge of that fact made her sad. And yet… she loved him, even if she was second in his eyes.

The next day, Bronwyn joined the other released prisoners as they formed a small party to rejoin the empress's court. Under armed guard, they were to be escorted from the city and marched south, while the queen and her son, along with her lady-in-waiting Lady Muriel and a party of warriors, would travel west for the prisoner exchange, to a place that lay between Winchester and Bristol, Devizes.

Bronwyn had been one of those to collect food for the journey, and upon entering the castle kitchen, she received dark looks from the other cooks, especially Master Christopher.

He handed her a basket of food, but as she reached for it, he withheld it. "As far as I'm concerned, you're a traitor like the lot of them. You should've been in the cells this whole time," he said, showering her with spittle.

He knew he'd spat on her and the food but didn't care. That much was clear from his knowing grin.

She met his eyes and calmly used her apron to wipe her mouth and cheeks clean. She sighed. "Give me the food, Master Christopher, or you get to tell the queen why you're allowing her party to go hungry."

He shoved the basket at her—hard. She stumbled back but held it and straightened. A few of the other cooks snickered.

Christopher leaned toward her, his face inches from her own. His breath stank. "Mark my words, girl. If I ever see you in my kitchen again, it'll be the worse for you. Don't let me see your face here again, or I'll set the dogs on you."

She turned away when he grabbed her braid and pulled. She dropped the basket, whirled around, and smacked him in the face. The slap rang out in the silent kitchen, and he dropped her braid and stumbled back.

"Don't you ever touch me again. You hear?" she said, loud enough for the other cooks listening to hear. "Ever."

Christopher glared at her and opened his mouth when he stopped and looked behind her.

"So this is why we've had such a delay. I might've known. You bloody cooks," Sir William of Ypres said. He stood by, with a group of guards and Rupert by his side. "Mistress Bronwyn, this man is giving you trouble?"

Sir William walked forward, swarthy and girthy in his gait, wearing chainmail, a sword hanging at his belt. His accent was strong and he glared at Christopher. "You. Who are you?"

"I am Master Christopher, the head cook here." Christopher drew himself up importantly. He rather looked like a stork, with a long beak of a nose, but for his beady eyes that darted everywhere.

"You don't look fit to clean my boots," Sir William said. "I saw you spit on our food and pull her hair. You treat all your fellow cooks this way or only the pretty ones?"

Bronwyn started. Christopher turned red. "It's my kitchen. I'll do what I like."

"Not anymore, you won't. Clear off." He turned and pointed to another, senior cook. "You. You take over. Clean this food. And you're head cook from now on."

"W-Who do you think you are?" Christopher sputtered. "You can't do that."

"I'm Sir William of Ypres, and yes, I bloody well can. Clear off. I command Their Graces's armies, and we could always use a good man for the front, especially one full of hot air." He grinned.

Christopher stiffened. "I'm not a fighter. I'm a cook." His voice shook.

"Then I'm sure you'll find employment somewhere else. We don't want you. Clear off. And if I hear that you're still skulking around the castle like some miserable sod, I'll run you out of the city myself. Understand?" He rested a hand on his sword pommel.

Christopher nodded.

Sir William of Ypres said, "Now where's our bloody food? We need it for the journey. Come on." He looked at the new head cook. "Well? Are you going to make us new baskets for the journey or not?"

The cook clapped his hands and said, "Come on, lads."

Cooks started moving, filling crates and baskets full of bread, meat, cheese, and pitchers and jugs of ale.

"Get these out to the courtyard in the next quarter hour. If I don't see them, I'm coming back," Sir William said.

"Yes, sir." The new head cook bowed.

"Mistress Bronwyn, with me." William crooked his finger, and she followed him out, forming part of the group of armed men.

As they marched, Bronwyn felt waves of embarrassment, unease, surprise, and gratefulness. Part of her knew that Christopher would never have given her a moment's peace. And yet he'd only really listened when another man had stood up for her. It was the best possible outcome and yet she felt she needed a better response for standing up to bullies, for certainly, the world was full of them.

She followed the men out to the courtyard, where the armed party was waiting. It was a few days' journey, so she helped load a small wagon with blankets and foodstuffs, with the help of the other cooks, who quickly came out.

Sir William came to her and asked quietly, "You all right?"

She nodded. "Yes. Thank you."

"It's nothing. Can't stand to see a man torment a woman like that. He needed to be thrown out on his ear. Maybe he'll learn something out on the road." Sir William grinned.

"What will happen to Lady Susanna and Tristan, the squire?" she asked.

Sir William shrugged. "If what he says is right, he's proven himself a traitor to both our causes. No one will want him. The lady... I'm not sure. The queen is benevolent. For now, they'll sit in jail. Let the king decide once he returns. And that rude taster woman of hers is to travel with us too. Let's hope she gets indigestion and spends most of her time in the privy, eh?" He turned and bellowed orders to the grooms sorting the horses.

She spotted Lady Alice nearby on a dull, brown roan, sitting stiffly in the saddle and looking straight ahead.

A familiar figure came up to Bronwyn and sighed. "She's not talking to me," Rupert said at her shoulder.

"Oh?" Bronwyn realized she should play dumb.

"She can't forgive me for not abandoning my master."

"I thought you were coming with us," Bronwyn said.

"I'm not. This is where we part ways. I go with the queen and prince and to rejoin my master. Not to be with her. Once the exchange is done, I'll see what comes. Maybe I'll return here." He rubbed the side of his face. "I can't seem to get my words right around her. I always say the wrong thing." He paused. "Would you give this to her? To let her know I'm thinking about her, even if she's mad at me?"

Bronwyn looked. In his hand he held out a rose. It was pink and lovely. She could smell its sweetness from just a few feet away. Seeing it made a part of her wistful. *Would that gift were for me,* she thought. But then, Theobold had spoken poetry to her from the depths of his cell, and in that moment, it had seemed as those he'd spoken from the darkness of his soul. He'd laid his intentions bare to her, and she would take that honesty with open arms. How could she even think about Rupert when Theobold had promised his fidelity and loyalty to her? His heart was hers. She couldn't throw that away. But she knew, looking upon Rupert's face, that she wasn't entirely Theobold's either. She looked over her shoulder to see Theobold watching. "Sure."

"Thanks. You're a good friend." Rupert clapped her on the shoulder and went to help with the packing and loading of the horses as Bronwyn twisted the rose's stem in her hands. She went to Lady Alice and held it up. "This is from Rupert."

Lady Alice sniffed. "I'm not talking to him."

"Will you accept the rose?"

Lady Alice looked down and gave her a filthy look. "No. He will have to do better than that to prove his worth to me. Keep it for yourself if you like, I don't care." With a swift kick, she sent it flying out of Bronwyn's hand and onto the ground, where her horse soon trampled on it.

Bronwyn felt sorry for it. She would have loved to receive such a gift. She looked over at Theobold, who was fussing with his horse and trappings. He'd been so busy, he'd barely said two words to her, so focused he was on preparing for the journey. Maybe once they were on the road, Theobold might look upon her kindly again. Maybe.

As the groups exited the city of Winchester and set out on their separate paths, Bronwyn wondered what the next few days would bring. An ill wind blew, sending leaves spiraling around her feet, heralding the coming of a harsh winter.

Author's Note

This was really Empress Maud's last great battle during the period of English civil war known as "the Anarchy." Her and Stephen's forces still fought, but what became known as "the Rout of Winchester" has been described by historians as kind of her last hurrah.

I've read a few sources on the subject, and it seems as though the empress took up residence in Winchester Castle (of which only a part still remains), Sir Robert was stationed at St. Swithun's Cathedral (today known as Winchester Cathedral) and later defended Wolvesey Castle, during a six-week siege. Then during the empress's escape, he was covering the rearguard. Whilst her earls and knights safely got her to Gloucester, Sir Robert was captured at Stockbridge, about eight miles away, at the river Test. I've played a bit fast and loose with historical facts as the background and setting for this story, so do forgive the artistic license I've used here. I thought the idea of figuring out a murder during a siege would be fun to write. Do let me know what you think; I love to hear from my readers.

About the Author

E. L. Johnson writes historical mysteries. A Boston native, she gave up clam chowder and lobster rolls for tea and scones when she moved across the pond to London, where she studied medieval magic at UCL and medieval remedies at Birkbeck College. Now based in Hertfordshire, she is a member of the Hertford Writers' Circle and the founder of the London Seasonal Book Club.

When not writing, Erin spends her days working as a press officer for a royal charity and her evenings as the lead singer of the gothic progressive metal band, Orpheum. She is also an avid Jane Austen fan and has a growing collection of period drama films.

Connect with her on Twitter at twitter.com/ELJohnson888 or on Instagram at instagram.com/ejgoth.